AS BEAUTY FRACTURES

THE SUPERHUMAN SERIES
BOOK THREE
BEEBE EVANS

BE BOOKS, LLC

THE SUPERHUMAN SERIES
PLAYLIST

Open Spotify to Scan

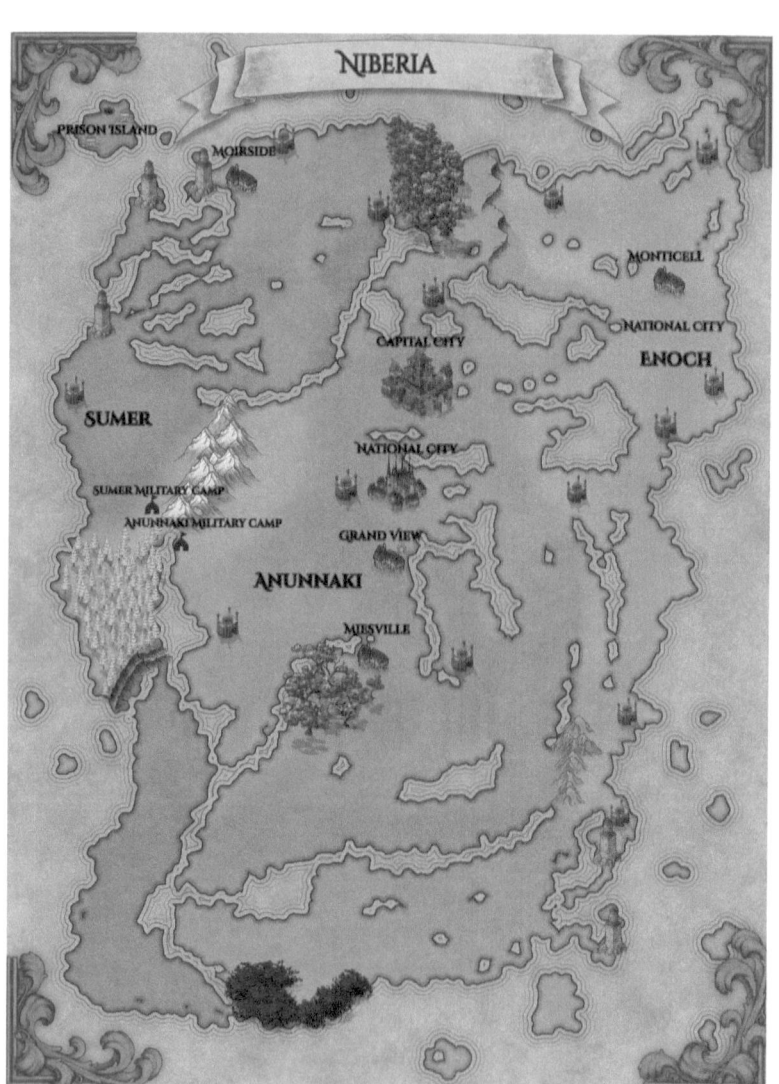

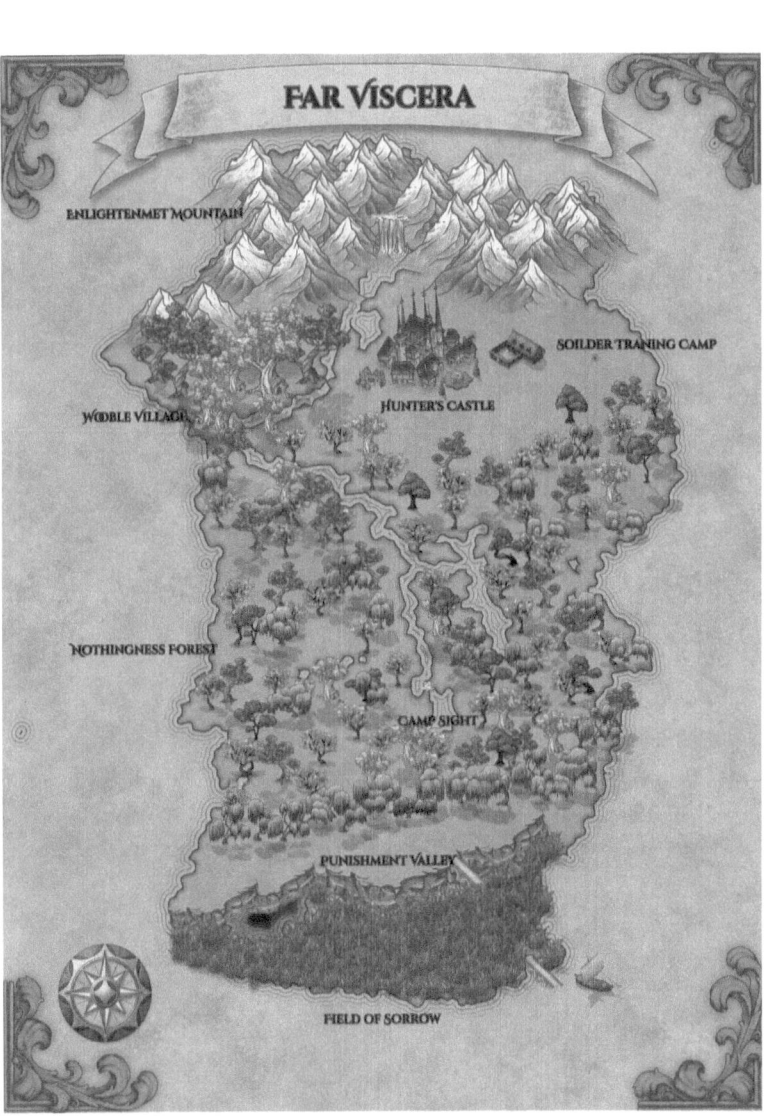

FAR VISCERA

ENLIGHTENMET MOUNTAIN

SOILDER TRANING CAMP

HUNTER'S CASTLE

WOOBLE VILLAGE

NOTHINGNESS FOREST

CAMP SIGHT

PUNISHMENT VALLEY

FIELD OF SORROW

DEDICATION

This book is dedicated to the sisters who want to live their deepest, darkest desires, but they need a little push from a dirty little demon.

CONTENT WARNING

This novel is intended for an adult audience and may contain themes and element troubling or unsuitable for some readers, which includes graphic language, violence and sexual activities on page. For a full list of content warnings, please visit my website at beebeevans.com

Beebe Evans
AUTHOR

THE PROPHECY

THE PROPHECY

∀√⊙⊗ ∴Ω⊖ ∴√∪∴Ω ∰∞∴Ω Ω∪≢≧⊖√ ∰⊖ ⊖⊖⊖≺

≅⊙⊗⊖⊖ ∴Ω⊖ ∴Ω∞√⊖∴ ∴⊙ ⊖π⊖⊕≺

∴⊙ ⊙∵≅∞∴⊖√⊕∴⊖ ∴Ω⊖ ≅⊖≅⊖≅≢⊕ ∀⊙√ ∰Ω∞≅Ω ∞⊖ ≢⊕⊗⊖⊕

∰Ω⊖≢ ∴Ω⊖ ∀⊙∪√∴Ω ∀∞√⊖ ∞⊖ ≅≢⊕∞⊗⊖⊕

∴Ω⊖ ≅⊖≅≢⊖≢⊕ ⊖σ∞≅ ∰∞≅≅ Ω⊕σ⊖ ∴⊕⊗⊖⊕

∀√⊙⊗ ∴Ω⊖ ∴√∪∴Ω ∰∞∴Ω Ω∪≢≧⊖√ ∰⊖ ⊖⊖⊖≺

≅⊙⊗⊖⊖ ∴Ω⊖ ∴Ω∞√⊖∴ ∴⊙ ⊖π⊖⊕≺

∴⊙ √⊖σ⊖⊕≅≢ ∴Ω⊖ ≅⊖≅≢⊖≢⊕ ∀⊙√ ∰Ω∞≅Ω ∴⊙ ≺≢⊙∰

∀⊙√∵∞⊕⊖⊖≢ ≅⊙σ⊖ ∰∞≅≅ ⊖Ω⊙∰

∴Ω⊖ σ⊕≅∞⊕∞∴ψ ⊙∀ ∰⊕√√⊕≢∴∴⊖ ∀√⊙⊗ ≅⊙≢≧ ⊕≅⊙

∀√⊙⊗ ∴Ω⊖ ∴√∪∴Ω ∰∞∴Ω Ω∪≢≧⊖√ ∰⊖ ⊖⊖⊖≺

≅⊙⊗⊖⊖ ∴Ω⊖ ∴Ω∞√⊖∴ ∴⊙ ⊖π⊖⊕≺

∴⊙ π√⊙∴∴⊖≅∴ ∴Ω⊖ ≅⊖≅≢⊖≢⊕ ∀⊙√ ∰Ω∞≅Ω ∞⊖ π⊙∰⊖√≅⊖⊖⊖

∴⊖⊗π≅⊖⊕√ ≅Ω⊙⊖⊖⊖≢ ∴⊙ ∴√⊕≢⊖≅≢√⊖⊖⊖

①≢⊕ ≅Ω⊕≅≅⊖≢≅⊖ ∴Ω⊖ ∞⊗π⊖≢⊖ ∴√⊕∵≅⊖ ∀⊙√∴√⊖⊖⊖

THE PROPHECY

THE FIVE LAWS

1. Thou shall not kill

2. Thou shall not steal

3. Thou shall not commit adultery

4. Thou shall not bear false witness

5. Thou shall not contempt thy parents

PROLOGUE

L ady Anasazi stood at the window of their private chambers, her gaze fixed on the moonlit shadows dancing across the high, rugged cliff. She dreamed of constructing her own majestic castle high above the one she shared with her husband, Lord Gorgon. She envisioned this new fortress, crafted entirely from shimmering ice, its crystalline walls glistening like diamonds under the moon's tender embrace.

Their marriage lay in ruins, a once-solid foundation now reduced to rubble, the trust between them shattered into irreparable fragments. Only a lingering bitterness festered within her heart whenever she thought of him. He had proven himself incapable of remaining faithful, his actions a betrayal that pierced her soul with the sharpest of daggers. Now, she harbored a suspicion that gnawed at her insides, a suspicion of a deeper treachery that left an indelible scar.

Her plan was in motion for her revenge, but she needed help from an unexpected source. This ally was someone she had always viewed as an adversary, an unlikely confidant. However, it was the only person capable of getting close enough to her husband to neutralize him. She found herself entangled in a perilous game, where every move was fraught with risk and uncertainty. Gorgon had pushed her to the brink, leaving her with no alternative but to tread this treacherous path.

She turned away from the window, her gaze shifting to her husband as he lay in bed, his chest rising and falling with the rhythm of his unsettled slumber. The moonlight filtered through the curtains, casting a pale glow across his face, highlighting the furrowed lines of worry that seemed etched into his brow even in sleep. His limbs moved slightly, as if caught in a dream that offered little peace, a familiar restlessness that visited him most nights.

"Circe." Her name slipped past his lips once more, a whisper in the quiet. He was dreaming of her again, and the betrayal seeped into her heart like ice. Each syllable of her name felt like a knife, reminding her of trust broken and promises unkept. It spread a chilling numbness through her chest, leaving her breathless and her spirit heavy, as if the very air around her had crystallized with the cold bite of treachery.

"Damn you both."

Anasazi stepped onto the stone ring that held the pool of blood. She elegantly lifted her long black dress to step down. Her appearance and facial expressions were always cold; she wore a velvet dress that covered up everything to her neck. As she walked across the room, her back was straight, and her hips swayed very little. She folded her hands and clasped her long, pale fingers together.

"Yes, my beautiful wife will join us." Gorgon groaned as he slumped back on Hunter's throne.

"I will expect both of you to behave," Hunter warned, his eyes shifting from Gorgon to Anasazi. "I don't need another argument erupting in the middle of the celebration, like last time."

"Circe, I need to speak to you," Anasazi murmured in a hushed tone, gently grasping Circe's arm. Her touch was light yet insistent as she guided Circe away from their husbands. "Is everything in place for the feast tonight?"

"I believe I have everything under control."

"How upset does my husband look right now?" she inquired, her voice tinged with curiosity and a hint of satisfaction.

Circe peered over her shoulder. "He looks absolutely terrified. I'm sure it's because we're talking in private."

"Good. He should be when I get through with him." She paused, her confidence wavering momentarily. She turned, taking in the scene with keen eyes. Her husband sat straight in Hunter's throne, his face a mask of anxiety, eyes wide and darting nervously around the room. "Are you sure about this?" she asked, her voice softening slightly.

Circe reached out, placing a reassuring hand on Anasazi's arm. "We've discussed this. It's the only way," she whispered. "Unless you've changed your mind?"

Anasazi's gaze hardened, her momentary vulnerability vanished. "No," she said firmly. "I haven't changed my mind. He deserves everything that's coming to him."

"Then we proceed as planned," Circe confirmed, her voice barely audible above the distant sound of preparations for the evening's feast.

A few hours later, the celebration was in full swing, a lively symphony of laughter and music filling the air. Anasazi watched Hunter twirl gracefully around the dance floor, his daughter giggling in his arms. She, however, had spent most of her night directing the bustling servants, her voice sharp and commanding, convinced that their efforts were inadequate amidst the grandeur of the evening.

She paused mid-sentence, feeling an overwhelming sense of dread. She scanned the room to account for everyone in attendance, but could not find her husband or Circe. A moment of panic filled her. She felt the cold emanating from her husband's betrayal and watched as her world crumbled around her.

How dare he do something so bold surrounded by so many witnesses!

She pushed through the crowd of drunken soldiers. Anger raged through her body, to the depths of her cold soul as she made her way to the corner of the room. Jealousy blinded her judgment and reason. Revenge filled her heart.

Taking energy from the tortured souls of the Underworld, ice flames swirled around her feet, encompassing her legs, consuming her existence. The rage boiled to the surface as an ice ball formed in her palm. She pushed her arms outward from her chest, releasing the ball of ice from her bitter heart. Striking the column, icicles formed at the base, crawling upward. With the core of the structure beginning to cool, she summoned all of her magical strength to form another ice ball even colder and larger to hurl across the room.

The column exploded in all directions, showering the crowd with deadly fragments. With an almighty crash, the column collapsed, showering marble shards on Circe. All music ceased, and pandemonium ensued. Circe and Gorgon collided with the wall, which was now littered with column fragments.

She panicked, her heart racing wildly as the realization struck her like a cold wave—the plan had failed. Her mind spun with disbelief and dread. Circe wasn't supposed to get hurt; the very thought tightened her chest with guilt and fear.

Gorgon had gotten to his feet, covered in dust, but not seriously injured. He leaned against the wall to steady himself. Then she realized he was still wearing his protection amulet on his wrist.

She muttered curses under her breath, each word a sharp whisper against Circe, blaming her for the oversight. The plan had been for the queen to remove Gorgon's protection amulet before Anasazi had launched the first ice ball. The scene before her was wrong in every way—it should be him, not Circe, lying motionless on the ground.

Panic clawed at her senses, but she had no time to dwell on missteps. She needed to pivot swiftly, addressing the chaos and its repercussions later. The chill seeped into her bones as she prepared to face Hunter.

Hunter rushed to his wife, falling to his knees, cradling her fragile body against his chest. "Circe," he cried, brushing the dust from her face and pushing back a lock of her black hair.

He held on to his wife's limp body with tears in his eyes. Blood trickled down the side of her face, her hair matted by the wound just above her ear. Turning his attention to Anasazi, he asked, "What have you done? Circe has done nothing to deserve this."

"You are a fool if you truly believe that," Anasazi insisted. "She cast a spell on my husband to tempt him. I hear him call her name in his sleep. She's a life-ruining, home-wrecking whore."

The room fell silent as Hunter's cries filled the castle hallways, echoing throughout the kingdom. The light dimmed to nothingness with the loss of their goddess queen. From the Field of Sorrow to the top of Enlightenment Mountain, everyone felt King Hunter's pain, even Anasazi.

When Hunter's brother, Emperor Anu, tried to pull the king away from his dead wife, Hunter gripped Circe even harder. He begged his brother, "Please, bring her back to me."

"I can't," Anu muttered, bowing his head helplessly.

"Yes, you can. You have the power, brother!" Hunter yelled.

"My power has limits. It doesn't work on immortals," Anu explained. "I can't save her. Circe is gone."

Empress Ki, Anu's wife, abruptly spoke up. "She can be reborn. We can remove her spirit and soul and place them into an unborn child. It has been done with mortals."

"Will she remember who she is?" Hunter asked. "Will she remember me?"

"No, she will have no memory of this life, and she may be mortal," Ki said. "She will have to be born into the living world."

"I will find her again," Hunter insisted.

"She won't be the same," she warned.

"I don't have any other choice," he said with a heavy heart, tears blocking his sight. He hugged his wife's body one last time, leaning over to kiss her on the forehead. He whispered, "I will find you again, my love."

In a grand display of sorrow and hope, Hunter gently laid his beloved wife's head down, creating a space for Anu and Ki to perform their sacred chant.

They stood over Circe's body, extending their hands to harness the magic. They chanted, "From this body, extract the spirit and soul to bring our loved one back as a whole. Please guide them to the living side. Come now across the great divide." As they chanted with passion and devotion, a brilliant radiance enveloped Queen Circe's body. The light emanating from her being grew steadily brighter and more intense until it seemed to consume her entirely. "Take this one to fulfill an unborn's eyes. Hear her voice in this child's cries. Three times greatness in her name. One, but not the same."

In response to their powerful invocation, a shimmering sphere of pure white light emerged from Circe, now giving her physical body to the empty void. A place of no existence, like a wasteland of the forgotten slain in the Far Viscera. Floating gracefully above the crowd, the ball of light seemed to hold all the love, strength, and essence that had once lived within her. Transcending the bounds of physicality, it began its journey toward the towering red double doors at the far end of the chamber.

With an otherworldly gust of wind from across dimensions, the majestic doors swung open effortlessly, creating a portal through which the white ball of light would pass. The force of this divine wind swiftly propelled the ethereal essence with unparalleled purpose, carrying it across realms and weaving it into the tapestry of existence.

"This was supposed to protect you." Holding Circe's ring in his hand, he called, "Anasazi!" The crowd willingly parted to allow Hunter to look her in the eye. "I want your head as a trophy."

"Oh, please," Anasazi laughed, "your threats are meaningless to me."

Hunter opened his right hand to summon his staff. In a swirl of light smoke, his weapon appeared. His battle cry reverberated through the chamber. The sharp hiss of smoke from his loyal staff created a thunderous boom as it surged across the room toward Anasazi. The red sapphire gem pulsed with magical power, turning it into a deadly spear. Before the blade struck, Anasazi dissipated into a swirling cloud of ice smoke as her laugh lingered in its wake.

CHAPTER ONE

OLIVIA

O livia Trismegist's laughter mingled with the jovial sounds of the celebration as she and Brutus slipped away, unnoticed, to the forest behind her house. The sounds of clinking glasses and congratulatory voices faded behind them as they ventured toward the shadowy tree line that marked the edge of her family's property. Her hand felt small in Brutus's, his palm warm against hers.

She had taken the oath into adulthood, swearing to preserve the balance between good and evil in the name of her gods, King Hunter and Queen Circe. All she wanted was to escape the formality, the expectations, and especially the way her parents had beamed at Talia throughout the entire event.

"Did you see how they looked at her?" Olivia asked abruptly, stopping beside a massive tree. "My sister took the same oath as me, and somehow, she's the special one. I don't get it."

He squeezed her hand, his expression softening in the dappled sunlight filtering through the leaves. "Hey, come on. It's your special day, too."

"Is it, though?" She kicked at a fallen branch with her pink boot. "You know how it is with my family. Talia breathes, and it's like she's performed a miracle. I could save the entire planet, and they'd ask if Talia helped."

Had she known her boyfriend was going to drag her back there, she wouldn't have worn her four-inch, high-heeled boots that went up to her knees. She had on her favorite shimmery pink dress with over-the-top shoulder accents, a low-cut neckline, and a metallic silver skirt. She completed her look with matching pink hair pulled up high on her head in a ponytail.

"You're the only one I was paying attention to." His fingertips traced the curve of her cheek, and she leaned in to his touch. "You're beautiful, smart, and the only woman I was looking at."

She heard the familiar compliments, but they felt hollow. She'd spent hours perfecting her appearance for the ceremony—her custom-made dress she had designed, her hair and makeup flawless—and still, all eyes had been on Talia. Plain, serious Talia with her cargo pants and that ridiculous Chakram.

As Brutus pressed her against the rough, gnarled bark of the tree, she regretted not designing her outfit with a back. The coarse wood scraped against the exposed Nibmarks that trailed down her spine, a feature she had purposely incorporated to allow him easy access to her most sensitive stimulation point. In that moment, it served only to add discomfort to their encounter. She wished she had thought it through more carefully, but she couldn't deny the thrill of his touch on her Nibmarks.

He pressed against her, their bodies melding together. She felt his hardness against her thigh, making her heart race. Her breath hitched as he traced a line of kisses down her neck, nipping and sucking the sensitive skin. His hands roamed her body, exploring every inch.

As she tried to lose herself in the moment, her mind kept wandering back to the uncomfortable sensation of the rough bark against her bare skin. She felt the tree bark, like a thousand tiny fingers, leaving faint imprints on her back. Despite his fervent touch and tantalizing kisses, a feeling of disappointment lingered beneath the surface.

She couldn't fully enjoy their passionate embrace when such discomfort was present, but she didn't want to ruin the moment for him either. As much as she wanted to give in to his desires, she felt a sense of restlessness.

She loved him, but there was an emptiness inside her that yearned for more. A spark, an adventure, anything to break the monotony of their routine. She longed for excitement and exhilaration, but she couldn't pinpoint exactly what she craved. It was as if a piece of herself was missing, a part of her soul. She didn't know what she truly desired.

Her eyes fluttered closed as she leaned into his solid warmth, his lips tracing a path along her neckline to her breasts. Yet even as he did, a shiver that wasn't entirely from desire ran through her. It had nothing to do with the cool afternoon air of the forest, and everything to do with the strange, unsettling undercurrents that brushed against her awareness. A harmless thought, really.

Her gift, minor though it was when held up against Talia's impressive powers, allowed her moments of emotional insight, glimpses of feelings not her own. In this moment, concealed by the dense foliage of the trees, she could sense Brutus's emotions—desire, for sure, but beyond that, a passing sensation that felt foreign to her mind.

Sometimes, there were visions, too. Fleeting images, like the flicker of shadows cast by firelight, which teased at the edge of her sight. They never lasted long enough for her to grasp their meaning, but they always left her with an ache for understanding, a hunger for the hidden depths they promised.

As his fingertips grazed her soft, supple skin, he slowly pulled the top of her dress down. He handled her with such care, as if she were the most delicate and precious thing in the world. Her breasts fell free, the cool air causing her nipples to harden into tiny peaks.

He took his time teasing her, one nipple with his tongue and the other with his thumb.

She realized it wasn't the tree itself that was causing her discomfort. It was his touch—so tender and careful, when she secretly craved something more assertive. She yearned for him to grab and squeeze her nipples, leaving them tingling with pleasure. A wicked smile spread across her lips as she imagined the rough bark of the tree scraping against her sensitive nipples instead of her back. She held on to that tantalizing thought, pressing herself against the sturdy trunk and rubbing her stimulant Nibmark against it in a desperate need for release.

An unsettling sensation pressed against her consciousness, like an uninvited guest forcing its way in. It was as if shadows themselves had taken form. The image of a dark, mysterious stranger emerged within her mind, cloaked in obscurity, with features that seemed both familiar and unknowable.

She slowly opened her eyes and surveyed her surroundings, taking in every detail. It was just the two of them, an intimate solitude surrounded by trees. Yet she felt an overpowering wave of intense lust swirling in the air, hovering just above her. Intriguingly, it wasn't emanating from Brutus, but from an unseen presence that seemed to permeate the atmosphere.

Brutus pulled back slightly, gazing into her eyes with an intensity that belied his usual easygoing nature. For a moment, she wondered if he sensed the presence too, but his gaze never wavered from her.

"Everything okay?" His voice was tender, tinged with concern.

"Of course," she lied, forcing a smile. The lie tasted bitter on her tongue, and she feared that soon she wouldn't be able to hide her growing dissatisfaction.

As he leaned in to resume their earlier passion, she found herself pausing, her hands resting lightly on his chest. It was safe, familiar, but her soul craved the very opposite. To leap without looking, to dive into the unknown, to chase after those brief visions that seemed to promise so much more than this small life with Brutus.

Then she heard her twin sister's voice in her head.

Olivia, Mom and Dad need to talk to us.

What did you do now?

Nothing. Untangle your lips from Brutus and whatever else you have wrapped around his body. Get your ass in the house. This is important.

"Let's go back," she said abruptly, pulling away from him and adjusting her dress. "Talia needs to talk to me."

"Okay," he agreed, though his tone held a note of confusion. He took her hand, and they walked toward the sound of laughter and music, but her mind was elsewhere. She was grappling with choices and desires that no longer aligned with the path she had been walking.

As they emerged from the forest and the sounds of the celebration grew louder, she took a deep breath, steadying herself. She wouldn't decide tonight, but she knew one thing for certain; she couldn't ignore the call of her heart forever. It certainly wasn't singing Brutus's name.

She entered through the back door to the kitchen. Her tone conveyed her frustration as she asked, "What's so important?"

"Your mom and I have something to tell you two," Dad said, gesturing for her to take a seat at the table next to Talia and locking the back door.

"Ugh, story time in the middle of the party." Olivia rolled her eyes as she slumped in the chair.

Dad moved behind Mom and placed a reassuring hand on her shoulder. "You're both about to enter the real world," he said in a serious tone, his eyes shifting between the twins. "We won't always be there to protect you, but we will arm you with the truth so you can protect each other."

"Truth about what?" Olivia said, adjusting her posture.

"Talia," Dad said, with his eyes landing on her, "what your mom is trying to say is that you were the first of your kind born on our planet in over three thousand years. You're a human like King Hunter and Queen Circe."

"Is that why you tattoo my Nibmarks on my back every year? I'm not a Niberian?" she asked, allowing her back to fall against the chair.

"Yes, you are human." Mom touched her daughter's hand. "We believe you to be the reincarnation of our Queen Circe."

"Your mom and I decided not to tell you because we wanted you two to have a normal childhood."

"However, we can't protect you for the rest of your life within these walls. Talia, you are a spirited warrior. You need to have adventures, and this town is getting too small for you." Mom squeezed her hand. "We trust Delphi. She kept our family secret."

"What does Delphi want from us now?" Olivia asked.

"She wants to look out for you so you can go away to college. She knows how important you are, and she made this opportunity possible for both of you." Mom pointed to the letters Delphi had delivered to the twins about their acceptance to Grand View University.

She always knew her sister was different, but she never suspected Talia was human. Her parents seemed to dote on Talia, always giving her special attention and praise, and now it made sense. As she watched her sister with new eyes, she felt envy for the person she called her twin.

She shifted in her seat, pressing her back firmly against the wooden chair. Her arms crossed tightly in front of her chest, causing tension in her jaw. She felt the heat rising in her cheeks, both from her own emotions and the warmth of the room around her. Her lips pressed together, forming a thin, taut line that betrayed her frustration.

Talia was getting all the attention again.

CHAPTER TWO

OLIVIA

A few months later, Olivia's heels clicked against the sidewalk as she traversed the courtyard of Grand View University on her first day of class, her slender shadow trailing beside her. The sunlight filtered through the leaves of the trees, dappling the path ahead with light and shade. She had been a resident of this strange new town for only seven days, and she was still trying to adjust.

The campus, perched atop a hill, overlooked the town below, true to its name. The buildings were modern, their sleek designs a stark contrast to the rustic charm of Delphi's house. She was sharing a cramped apartment with Talia above Delphi's antique shop near Middle Park. The house was older and in need of updating, but it was an easy walk for her.

The walls of the apartment felt like they were closing in, the air thick with the scent of compromise and disappointment. There wasn't even a sliver of space for her clothes, let alone room to spread out her fabric and sketches. Her passion for design, once a vibrant flame, now flickered weakly under the weight of practicality.

As she slipped away, leaving her sister alone with the handsome neighbor named Storm, she wondered why her sister had barely given him a second glance since they'd moved in upstairs. It was clear there was an attraction between Talia and Storm. It was a frustrating sight for her, since she could see how perfectly they could complement each other if only they would allow it. They were two puzzle pieces that seemed to fit together perfectly, but her sister didn't see it that way.

She sighed, the sound lost in the laughter and chatter of students milling about between classes. With a heavy heart, she continued her march toward the Arts building. Her fingers brushed against the textured bark of a tree as she passed, seeking solace in its rough embrace. She smiled for a moment at the feeling against her soft skin.

A sudden shift in the air broke her reverie and caused the hair on her arms to rise. It wasn't the cool breeze that often swept through the courtyard, but the heavy, unsettling weight of desire. She stopped mid-step, her instincts honed from years of navigating the attention she received from men. It was unmistakable and comfortable for her.

Two men were watching her, their gazes like tangible fingers brushing against her skin. The leader, a tall figure with an easy swagger, stepped forward. He wore a practiced smile, the kind that had probably worked on many women before her, but she wasn't just anyone.

"Now, there's a set of tits I would love to rub my big dick between," he said to his buddy. He slapped his friend's chest and stepped in her path. He said, "Hey, there. I'm Chad." A sandy-haired man at his side gave a casual wave. "This is Kyle."

Their eyes roamed over her, taking in her form with an unabashed hunger that made her bristle. She had sensed lust before, but this felt different—more intense, almost suffocating. It was clear they were trying to flirt, but their timing couldn't have been worse.

"Chad," she repeated, her lips curling into a sardonic smile as she met his gaze head-on. "You certainly look like one." She laced her tone with amusement and disdain. She took a step closer, her presence commanding despite the unwanted attention. "Let me give you some advice," she said, the words rolling off her tongue with a confidence that left no room for argument. "I am more woman than your little cock can handle."

Chad's smile faltered, his eyes widening slightly at the blunt retort. Kyle's mouth opened and closed.

"I doubt that, honey."

She took a confident step closer, backing Chad against the near-by brick wall. Her fingers brushed against his crotch, eliciting a gasp from him. She gave his cock a teasing squeeze. "Big dick, huh?" She taunted with a smirk. "It's more like four inches, maybe five at most. You might get to six with some penis stretching."

His friend erupted into laughter. She boldly stepped to Kyle and felt his erection through his pants. "Hmm," she purred, "you're more like seven inches." Her eyes danced with amusement as she continued her assessment. "Not bad, but I prefer at least nine inches to really get me wet. The only way you two are going to achieve that is if I had both of you at the same time."

Her words, dripping with seduction and challenge, made it clear she was unimpressed by size alone. The thrill of their game coursed through her veins, igniting a fierce desire for pleasure and control. Without waiting for a reaction, she turned on her heel, her hair whipping behind her like a silken flag of defiance. She strode away, leaving the two men standing in stunned silence.

That was fun.

After a long day of classes, Olivia was eager to dive into her next design. She had several swatches of fabric draped over her shoulder. As she stepped into the living room, ready to let her creative thoughts flow, she heard the familiar sound of Talia's footsteps entering the apartment. Sensing that her sister was in a bad mood, she put aside her work and turned to give Talia her full attention. She listened as her sister vented about the sexy man downstairs.

During class, Storm and Talia engaged in a heated discussion that spilled over into an argument in the courtyard. While she offered Talia practical and reasonable advice, she kept her true feelings hidden from her sister. The unresolved sexual tension between Storm and Talia was a constant annoyance to Olivia.

There was a knock at the front door in the middle of their conversation, and she was a little thankful for the interruption. They exchanged confused glances. "Are you expecting someone?"

"No. You'd think I would have seen this coming." She possessed a talent for knowing when someone was approaching, often with an image of that person appearing in her mind before she laid eyes on them. Olivia swung open the door to be greeted by a familiar face. "Brutus!" Her voice hitched. In an instinctive reaction, she leaped onto him, wrapping her legs around his muscular waist. His hard body rippled under his shirt as he took a step back to adjust to her unexpected assault. "What are you doing here? It's only been a week."

Before he could answer, she attacked him with her lips. His bag fell to the floor with a thud. There was no room for distractions—only for the flame that danced between their bodies, which were now locked in a passionate embrace. With a swift movement of his foot, the door slammed closed.

Brutus' hands roamed her body possessively. His large fingers traced circles down her spine, making her arch against him in response while his lips trailed kisses down her neck, eliciting soft moans that echoed through the otherwise silent apartment.

She leaned her head back, inviting him in as he ravaged her neck with his kisses. He moved his lips up to suckle on her earlobe, nipping it lightly. He spun her around, his hard body pressing her against the wall.

"Damn, girl, I missed you, too," he managed to say. "My classes don't start until next week, and I wanted to see you this weekend."

"You drove six hours for a hot weekend, but it's the middle of the week. We better get started now." She giggled, pointing toward her room.

"As much as I would love to watch this reunion," Talia drawled from the sidelines, "I'm going to find Storm."

He chuckled, lifting her in his arms as if she weighed nothing. He carried her effortlessly toward the bedroom, their lips never parting. The room was dimly lit, casting an intimate glow upon the rumpled sheets of the unmade bed.

Setting her down gently, he began to undress her, his hands deftly unbuttoning her blouse and sliding it off her shoulders. His fingers traced the curve of her waist, sending shivers down her spine as he unzipped her skirt and guided it down her legs. She stood before him in nothing but her lacy pink undergarments, her body trembling with anticipation.

He leaned in, capturing her mouth in a passionate kiss as his hands explored her body. He cupped her breasts, his thumbs teasing her hardened nipples through the fabric of her bra. She gasped at the sensation, reaching up to tangle her hands in his short blond hair as she pulled him closer.

Their bodies moved in harmony, a dance of passion and desire that left them both breathless. His fingers traced the edge of her panties, teasing her with the promise of what was to come. Her heart raced as she felt his touch, her body aching for more.

As they tumbled onto the bed, his lips traveled down her neck, leaving a trail of kisses that made her skin tingle with pleasure. He reached behind her, unclasping her bra with ease, and let it fall away, revealing her bare breasts. She sighed as he took her nipple into his mouth, his tongue swirling around the sensitive bud.

"You know, Brutus, I'm not fragile."

She grabbed his shirt and pulled it over his head with a firm tug. After discarding his shirt, she ran her hands over his muscular chest, marveling at the warmth of his body.

He chuckled, appreciating her eagerness, and kissed her more fervently. He gently pushed her back onto the bed, hovering over her. She fumbled with the button on his pants, finally managing to undo it and slide them down his legs, revealing his dark boxer briefs.

He hooked his fingers into the waistband of her panties and slid them slowly down her legs. He kissed her inner thighs, teasing her with each touch until she was writhing beneath him, desperate for more.

He plunged two thick fingers inside her, filling her completely. The sudden intrusion took her by surprise, and she gasped at the intensity of pleasure that flooded through her. She clutched at the sheets beneath her as waves of sensation washed over her, lost in the ecstasy of his touch.

He dropped to his knees. With a gentle yet firm grip, he guided her legs over his broad shoulders, opening her up to him completely. As he continued to move his fingers inside her, she watched as he dropped his head between her legs. He focused his attention on her clit, flicking his tongue over the sensitive bundle of nerves with an enthusiasm that made her cry out in delight.

She lifted her hips to meet his touch. The tension in her body grew, the pressure building until she could barely stand it. Brutus seemed to sense her need, his fingers moving faster, more insistent, until she finally reached her climax, crying out in ecstasy.

As the intensity of her orgasm subsided, she lay panting, a satisfied smile playing on her lips. He stood, his muscular frame glistening with sweat, and hovered over her like a dominant predator. Slowly, he lowered himself onto the bed next to her, his body still radiating heat and power. She could feel his arousal pressing against her thigh, and she reached down to stroke him through his boxer briefs.

He groaned at her touch, his hips bucking involuntarily as she teased him. He quickly shed his underwear, revealing his rigid length. He moved on top of her, and she wrapped her legs around his waist, urging him closer as he entered her in one smooth motion.

They moved together in a rhythm that was both familiar and exhilarating, their bodies fitting together perfectly. Her nails dug into Brutus' back as he thrust deeper, the sensation of him filling her driving her wild with desire. She felt another climax building within her as he hit the perfect spot that sent her over the edge.

As they reached the peak of their pleasure, they cried out in unison, their bodies convulsing as they climaxed together. He collapsed onto her, his breath hot against her neck as they both struggled to catch their breath. They lay there for several moments, their hearts pounding in sync, before he finally rolled off her and onto his back.

He smiled, pressing a kiss on her forehead. "That was amazing. I'm going to enjoy my Quickening with you."

She smiled back, a warmth spreading through her chest at his words. She snuggled closer to him, enjoying the sensation of his brawny arms around her.

"That's why you came to see me. You're in your Quickening." She giggled.

"I wanted to share stage one with you." He shrugged. "I had a feeling you would be freaky once we had some time alone."

You have no idea.

CHAPTER THREE

OLIVIA

In the dark of night, an overwhelming sense of fear emanating from her sister abruptly shattered Olivia's peaceful slumber. Her eyes shot open, immediately alert to the urgency of the situation. Without hesitation, she leaped out of bed and sprinted down the dark hallway toward Talia's room. A sinister red mist seeped out from under the closed door, casting an eerie glow on the surrounding walls.

"Talia!" she screamed.

As she reached for the doorknob, an intense surge of heat seared her hand, causing her to recoil with a sharp cry. It was as if an inferno had consumed her sister's room, yet there was no visible flame or smoke. Fear clawed at her heart as she realized her sister was slipping away from her.

Desperation surged through her veins, compelling her to summon every ounce of strength in her body and scream Talia's name at the top of her lungs. Her voice reverberated throughout the house, echoing down hallways and staircases. With trembling knees, she sank to the floor, desperately reaching out for a telepathic connection with Talia, but she met only silence and emptiness. It was as if her sister had vanished.

"The door is too hot to open," she said as Storm appeared in the hallway, charging toward Talia's room.

In the dark hallway, his form contorted and twisted, his features becoming more bestial with each passing moment. Her throat tightened as she witnessed him transform into the hulking figure of the Minotaur, towering over her with primal power radiating from every massive muscle. Despite his monstrous appearance, there was a sense of protectiveness in his gaze as he locked eyes with Olivia, silently conveying his loyalty to her and her sister.

With a thunderous roar that reverberated off the walls, the Minotaur brought down his massive fist, shattering Talia's door to splinters. The sinister red mist that had seeped out from under the door now spilled into the hallway.

"You can't have her!" The Minotaur let out a guttural growl, the sound echoing through the room as he charged toward Talia. "Give her back to me. She's mine."

Through the now-open doorway, Olivia saw a scene of chaos unfolding within Talia's room. Her sister's body was hovering above her bed, suspended in mid-air. Storm reached out and grabbed her arms, attempting to bring her closer to him. Suddenly, the force holding Talia released her, and both she and Storm tumbled onto the bed.

As the horns on his forehead receded and he transformed back into his original Sumerian form, a mischievous smile spread across his lips. Olivia felt the sexual tension in the room intensify. She let out an exasperated sigh, her eyes rolling in frustration. She felt out of place in the room, a sense of jealousy slowly creeping up within her.

She watched the couple's heated argument with a detached air, her interest barely piqued. Talia, she mused, should count herself lucky to have such an exhilarating man by her side. This was no ordinary partner—he possessed the remarkable ability to transform into a mighty beast. She imagined the raw power and mystique he must exude, and she knew without a doubt that she would never consider kicking him from her bed.

A fucking Minotaur!

She found herself baffled by her sister's resistance. She thought about the dull, monotonous Anunnakian man in her bed, his features as unremarkable as his demeanor, and felt a restless yearning. She would give anything to exchange him for a Sumerian man, whose vibrant presence and captivating allure seemed to promise a life filled with excitement and passion.

"What the hell is going on?" Brutus asked as he appeared in the doorway, a hint of green flashing in his eyes. Confusion etched deeply across his face as he took in the scene before him. "What happened to the door?"

"Brutus, I can explain," Olivia begged urgently.

"Who is this guy?" he asked, pointing at Storm.

"Storm. Storm Smoke." Storm swung his legs over the edge of the bed. He extended his hand to Brutus as an introduction, but Brutus rebuffed him by crossing his arms.

Olivia's heart raced as she frantically tried to explain to Brutus what had transpired. The splintered door, Storm's torn and tattered pants, and Talia's flushed and furious expression all added to her growing sense of panic. She couldn't tell him the truth. She grabbed his arm and led him back to her room.

Once inside, she closed the door with a gentle click, leaning against it as if to physically block the chaos from following them. The familiar scent of her lavender candles did little to calm her nerves. Brutus turned to face her, his eyes flickering with suspicion in the dim light of her bedside lamp.

"Who is that guy, for real?" he demanded, his voice low but tense. He crossed his arms over his chest, the muscles in his forearms flexing. "You don't expect me to believe he's really Talia's new boyfriend."

Olivia swallowed hard, her throat suddenly dry. "It's complicated."

"Complicated?" Brutus raised an eyebrow, his jaw clenching. "I wake up to find a half-naked man in your sister's bedroom, a destroyed door, and everyone acting like they've seen a ghost. And all you can say is 'it's complicated'?"

She pushed herself away from the door, moving closer to him. The space between them felt charged with tension, crackling like static electricity. "Brutus, please. It's not what you think."

"Then what is it?" His voice rose slightly, and she sensed his growing frustration mingled with confusion. The emotions rolled off him in waves, crashing against her empathic senses.

Olivia hesitated, her mind frantically searching for words that wouldn't reveal too much. "He's someone Talia met recently. They have a connection."

Brutus scoffed, running a hand through his sleep-tousled hair. "A connection that involves destroying doors in the middle of the night?"

"There was an emergency," she said, the half-truth bitter on her tongue. She reached for his hand, relieved when he didn't pull away. His skin was warm against her palm, his pulse racing beneath her fingertips. "Talia was in trouble. He helped her."

"What kind of trouble requires a guy to show up in the middle of the night wearing torn sweatpants?" His green eyes narrowed, searching her face for answers.

Olivia felt a pang of guilt. She hated lying to him, but how could she possibly explain that Storm was a Sumerian who could transform into a Minotaur? That some unknown force had nearly taken her sister? That their world was far more dangerous and magical than Brutus could imagine?

"It was..." she began then paused, the lie catching in her throat.

"It was what, Olivia?" Brutus pressed, stepping closer. "What aren't you telling me?"

She looked up at him, at the face she'd known for so long, the emerald eyes that had always looked at her with adoration. In that moment, she felt the vast chasm between them—not just of secrets kept, but of experiences unshared. While she envied Talia's passionate, challenging relationship with Storm, here was Brutus—steady, dependable, and utterly ordinary.

"Brutus, there are things about my family that I can't explain," she finally said, her voice barely above a whisper. "Not because I don't want to, but because you wouldn't understand."

His expression hardened, a flash of hurt crossing his features. "Try me."

"I can't," she said, feeling the weight of her secrets pressing down on her chest. "Please, just trust me when I say that Storm is important to Talia. What happened tonight was necessary."

The next night, Olivia was in her room on her knees with Brutus sitting in her desk chair. She slowly unzipped his pants, revealing his throbbing cock. Her mouth watered at the sight, and she couldn't resist leaning in for a taste. She flicked her tongue out, teasing the sensitive head before taking him fully into her mouth. She moaned at the taste of him, salty and musky, and began to move her head up and down.

He let out a low groan, his hands fisting in her hair as she worked him over. She felt him growing harder and thicker in her mouth, and it only spurred her on. She reached up to cup his balls, massaging them as she continued to suck and lick.

Her own arousal was building the harder he pulled her hair, and she felt her panties growing damp. She reached down to touch herself, rubbing her clit in time with her movements. The sensation was almost overwhelming, and she had to fight to keep her focus on pleasuring him.

She stood to remove her panties. He pulled her closer, wasting no time in tugging down the straps of her nightgown, exposing her full, round breasts. With rough, eager hands, he took one of her nipples into his mouth, swirling his tongue around the hardened peak. He pinched and rolled the other nipple between his fingers, sending jolts of pleasure through her body.

His free hand found its way between her thighs, his fingers seeking her wetness. He teased her clit with feather-light touches, making her gasp and moan with pleasure.

As he worked her body, she grew increasingly aroused. Her breath came in short, shallow pants as she writhed against him, desperate for more. He obliged, sliding two fingers inside her with a low growl. He pumped them in and out, curling to hit just the right spot.

"Harder," she demanded.

She let out a needy whimper as he slipped a third thick finger inside her, her walls clenching around them greedily. She felt herself stretch with short, sharp twitches of pain. He curled them upward again and bit down hard on her nipple, hitting that sensitive spot that made her see stars.

"Oh, fuck," she breathed, her hips bucking against him as she chased the pleasure. Her breath came in short gasps as he pumped in and out of her, his fingers slick with her arousal.

"You like that, baby?" he growled, his voice low and rough with desire. He added another finger, stretching her wider and hitting deeper. She cried out, her body tensing as he worked her relentlessly. "You're so fucking tight," he groaned, his thumb circling her clit as he continued to pump his fingers.

She felt herself building toward release, her muscles coiling tighter and tighter. "I'm going to come," she gasped, her nails digging into his shoulders.

He curled his fingers inside of her, hitting that perfect spot over and over again until she was screaming his name. She wasn't done. She didn't want him to stop, and she tried to hold back her orgasm.

While fully immersed in hot foreplay with Brutus, she intensely desired sensitive lovemaking. Just as she was about to reach the peak, she paused, suddenly overcome by a desire for something different. She wanted more than just the rough and dirty sex Brutus was providing. She wanted something tender and loving.

That's not right. I want dirty, nasty sex.

Olivia suddenly knew she was intruding into Talia's dream world. Her sister was dreaming about Storm, and it was a happy, sweet sex dream. This realization ruined her own mood, so she moved away from Brutus.

Fucking sister!

Olivia lay still in the dark, the soft sheets a small comfort against the tumultuous thoughts that roiled within her. It was her third night without sleep. Exhaustion had set in from dealing with her sister being plagued with nightmares. Next to her, Brutus' deep, rhythmic snores filled the silence of the night, each exhalation a stark reminder of her wakefulness. She felt the warmth of his body, the gentle rise and fall of his chest against her back, but it did little to soothe the restlessness that had taken root in her heart.

She closed her eyes, trying to ignore the persistent snoring, and focused on the scent of Brutus. It was a smell that once brought her solace; now it seemed to suffocate her with its constancy. The touch of the cool pillow against her cheek offered no relief as images from Talia's sex dream flickered unbidden across her mind's eye.

Olivia sensed her sister's thoughts drifting back to it throughout the day as Talia spent time with Storm. Their laughter and easy banter filled the room when they were together, like a symphony of joy and happiness. Talia was still hesitant to fully let him in, but Olivia felt the strong connection growing between them.

Her cheeks burned with frustration as she fought back the urge to roll her eyes at their carefree antics. She felt a twinge of bitterness bubbling inside her, like a simmering pot about to boil over.

Despite the peaceful facade of her bedroom, an undercurrent of tension lingered, tugging at her senses like a hidden current waiting to pull her under. She could almost taste the lingering spice of jealousy on her tongue, an acrid flavor she wished to banish.

With a sigh, she shifted in bed, careful not to wake Brutus. She drew her knees up to her chest, hugging them tight, as if by holding herself together she could stave off the burgeoning sense of longing that threatened to spill over.

"Sleep, just sleep," she murmured to herself, the command a whisper lost amidst the cacophony of Brutus' snoring and her own discordant thoughts. There was a siren's call of what might lie beyond this room, beyond this life with him. It was a tide too strong to resist, pulling at her with the promise of something more.

Exhaling slowly, she opened her eyes once more, gazing through the dimness at the silhouette of the slumbering man beside her. He was a good man, steady and true, but she had a yearning for a connection that would set her soul ablaze, as it clearly did for her twin with the handsome neighbor. She felt arousal when Brutus became jealous of Storm. It was sweet to think he had something to be concerned about.

As she lay back on her bed, trying to drift toward the edge of slumber, she suddenly heard Talia's voice pierce the stillness of their apartment. Her sister's frantic tone was filled with fear as she screamed out Storm's name. Olivia sensed the tension in the air as she heard the back door open and felt Storm's presence enter the apartment.

She debated whether to check on her sister right away or give her a moment to collect herself. As she lay there, emotions of jealousy and worry battled inside her, but she knew she needed to push them aside before going to comfort Talia.

She carefully slipped out of bed, her bare feet making no sound against the cool hardwood floor as she crossed the room. She took a moment to glance back at Brutus, his heavy breathing now unbroken by the snores that had been keeping her awake. A silent apology formed on her lips as she closed the door behind her, leaving him in peace.

She traversed the dimly lit hallway toward Talia's bedroom. She could hear their voices now, hushed and urgent, as Talia and Storm spoke in tones too low to discern. She peeked through the partially open door and caught a glimpse of them locked in a kiss. She quickly turned and made her way to the kitchen, starting a pot of coffee before barging in on her sister's intimate moment.

The rich aroma of freshly brewed coffee filled the small apartment, soothing her senses as she leaned against the cool countertop. She let out a contented sigh, her thoughts drifting back to the past two days spent with Brutus.

Her breath hitched as a sudden realization dawned on her. The stark contrast between her life with Brutus and Talia's with Storm was an undeniable truth she could no longer ignore. She yearned for more, craved the depth and intensity her sister seemed to have effortlessly stumbled upon. Their connection was so much more than physical—it was a deep, emotional bond that seemed to transcend the boundaries of this world.

She knew it was time for Brutus to go home. She could no longer ignore her own unhappiness, and it was clear that this relationship needed to end. It pained her to think of hurting him, but she also knew that continuing it would only lead to more pain and resentment.

Once she had given her sister enough privacy to suck face with Storm, Olivia called them out into the living room to discuss why Talia's dreams had turned so dark lately. A few days ago, Storm had shown Talia an opal ring, slipping it on her finger. Since then, no one in the house was getting any sleep. Since the twins shared their thoughts, she was experiencing the same nightmares and sexual dreams as Talia. Only her sister was physically being attacked by something dark and dangerous.

Olivia's voice was strained as she discussed their current situation, her eyes burning from the lack of sleep. Talia sat across from her, her face contorted in pain as she struggled to fight off the constant nightmares. Despite her efforts, they showed no signs of abating. They were clearly dealing with something supernatural, and it was time to focus on that. That meant Brutus had to leave.

"What do you need to talk about?" Brutus asked, appearing in the living room in only his underwear. "I see you spend a lot of time here, Sumerian," he said.

"Well, when Talia needs me, I'm there," Storm said, leaning toward her, his voice carrying a touch of arrogance.

"Right? Talia, just Talia," he said suspiciously. The tension in the air built as he locked eyes with Storm. "Somehow, I don't believe that."

"Well, believe it," Storm said as he stood from the couch. He purposefully closed the distance between him and Brutus. His muscular frame appeared even more imposing at that moment. His chest subtly puffed out as if to assert his authority. He met Brutus head-on, refusing to back down from the challenge. "It's the truth."

Brutus took a step closer, his own chest expanding with new-found defiance. Unfazed by the brewing hostility, Storm calmly took a sip of his coffee. Olivia stepped between the two.

"Before I have to hold your coffee, let's put away the masculine measuring sticks, gentlemen," she requested. "Brutus, can I talk to you in my bedroom?"

"We can talk right here," Brutus insisted.

"Fine, but you're not going to like it." Olivia took a deep breath. "You have to leave. You can't be here right now."

"Babe, it's barely the weekend. I have two more days until I have to be home," Brutus said, softening his eyes and taking a step back.

"I'm sorry. It's not a good time for you to be here. You showed up at our door without warning," Olivia said, trying to keep her voice steady and calm. "Then you played the part of the jealous boyfriend, running around in your underwear, threatened by a man who isn't interested in me. Storm is clearly lusting after my sister and only looks at me to be polite. Otherwise, he's staring at Talia." Her anger rose. "If you can't see that, you are blind and dumb!"

"Wow, babe, if that's how you feel, I know when I'm not welcome," Brutus said, backing up, shocked.

"I didn't mean it like that," Olivia said, reaching out for him.

"Sure, you did. I'm glad I know where you stand, Olivia. I'll get my things." Brutus disappeared into her bedroom. He returned a few moments later wearing a pair of jeans and carrying his backpack. Without a word, he stomped out of the apartment.

CHAPTER FOUR

OLIVIA

T he mid-morning sunlight streamed through the kitchen window, casting golden patterns across the worn wooden table. Olivia wrapped her hands around her coffee mug, feeling the gentle warmth seeping into her skin.

Princess Johara had just disappeared into the bathroom. Olivia had always believed Johara was just an imaginary friend, a figment of Talia's childhood imagination. However, when Talia summoned her the previous night, it became undeniably clear that the princess was indeed real.

Once they discovered it was Hunter who was invading Talia's dreams, her sister immediately sought the wisdom of Johara to make sense of the situation. Storm was right—the gods were not benevolent; they were meddlesome and unkind. An obsession to resurrect his deceased wife consumed Hunter, and he believed Talia held the key to achieving that goal.

She sipped her coffee, watching the steam curl upward, trying to process everything that had happened, the bizarre events unfolding in her life. She'd always assumed she was just ordinary Olivia Trismegist—fashion-obsessed, attention-seeking, and perpetually insecure about her place in the world. Now she was apparently carrying the soul of a goddess.

She'd always defined herself by the superficial—her carefully curated wardrobe, her meticulously applied makeup, the way she could command attention when she entered a room. Even her insecurities had been predictable, ordinary. Not pretty enough. Not interesting enough. Not good enough compared to Talia.

Now she was a goddess. Or part of one, at least. The thought made her stomach flip uneasily. How was she supposed to process that? What did having a goddess's soul even mean?

The soft padding of feet drew her attention as Johara emerged from the bathroom, white hair slightly mussed from sleep but somehow still ethereal. The princess moved with natural grace despite having just woken up, her optic white eyes blinking slowly in the morning light.

"What is that delightful smell?"

"It's coffee." Olivia gestured toward the pot. "Help yourself. Mugs are in the cabinet to the right."

She watched as Johara poured herself a cup, noting how the princess's movements seemed to flow like water. Even in borrowed pajamas—Talia's, since they were closer in size—Johara looked regal.

"Did you sleep well?" she asked, feeling awkward, not sure what the proper etiquette for morning small talk with a mythical princess from another realm would be.

Taking a sip from her mug, she said, "Yes, your couch is very comfortable, since I'm used to sleeping on a wooden bed in the Wooble village."

"What's a Wooble?"

"They're a tribe of bear warriors who live in Nothingness Forest. They took me in when I fled from my father's castle."

Olivia tried to picture these creatures. "So, you've been hiding all this time?"

"Not hiding. I was surviving." Her white eyes seemed to cloud over momentarily. "The Woobles taught me how to fight, so someday we could battle Hunter to take control of the Far Viscera."

She nodded, not knowing what to say. The weight of carrying a goddess's soul suddenly felt lighter compared to Johara's burden of running from Hunter.

"That's a lot of responsibility for one person."

Johara's lips curved into a sad smile. "It is the burden I was born to bear. Just as you were born to carry Circe's soul."

The mention of Circe made Olivia's stomach clench. "What exactly does it mean? Having her soul inside me?" She traced her finger around the rim of her mug. "Talia has her spirit and can do all these amazing things—lightning, healing, and talking to spirits. But me? I don't feel any different. Just confused."

Johara took another sip of coffee, her eyes widening slightly at the bitter taste. "The soul differs from the spirit." She placed her mug down and leaned forward. "The spirit is power, yes, but the soul is the essence. Memory. Wisdom. You carry within you everything that made Circe who she was."

"Do you remember her?"

"No, my mother died when I was young. I have a few fragmented memories of her before she was taken to the empty void."

"The empty void?" she asked, her voice dropping to a whisper. The term sent a chill down her spine despite the warmth of the coffee mug in her hands.

Johara's eyes grew distant. "It's the place between places. When someone dies in the Far Viscera, they become trapped in nothingness, conscious but unable to interact with any realm."

"How do I access these memories?" she asked, leaning forward with sudden interest. "I mean, if I have all this wisdom inside me, shouldn't I be able to tap into it somehow?"

"The soul doesn't reveal itself all at once. It comes in fragments, in dreams, in moments of intuition." She tilted her head, causing her white hair to cascade over one shoulder. "Haven't you ever had moments where you just knew something without knowing how you knew it?"

Olivia considered this. There had been times—fleeting moments when she'd sensed things about people, understood their intentions before they spoke. She'd always dismissed it as good intuition.

"The soul unfolds gradually," Johara explained, her voice taking on a melodic quality. "It's not like Talia's spirit powers that manifest physically. Your connection to Circe is deeper, more subtle. She was the Goddess of Magic, but also of wisdom, empathy, and foresight."

"Foresight?" she repeated, her voice catching slightly. "You mean like seeing the future?"

"Not exactly," Johara said. "More like sensing possibilities, understanding patterns that others miss. My mother could see the threads of fate weaving together long before events occurred."

Olivia sat back in her chair, considering the princess's words. Wisdom, empathy, and foresight weren't the flashy powers she'd imagined when thinking about harboring a goddess's soul. They felt ordinary. Subtle. And yet, there was something comforting about the idea that the goddess's gifts might align with parts of herself she already recognized.

"So, I won't be shooting lightning from my fingertips anytime soon?" she asked, attempting to lighten the mood.

Johara's lips quirked upward. "Don't underestimate what you carry. The soul is the seat of true magic. It's not just tricks and spectacle, but the deeper magic that shapes reality itself."

"Sometimes, I get these quick pictures in my mind. I don't know what they mean until something happens that reminds me of those images. I guess I've always been able to sense certain things, like when someone is near. I can feel their energy long before I can see them."

She felt a nervous energy bubbling up inside her, a familiar sensation that signaled one particular person—Storm's friend Scoot-

er. She sighed inwardly, anticipating the whirlwind of hyperac-
tivity that accompanied him. She braced herself for the inevitable
chaos that seemed to follow in his wake.

Great, the spaz is here!

"Scooter is near. He has a unique, unmistakable energy."

The apartment door opened with a bang. Scooter stumbled in,
his red hair disheveled and his lab coat rumpled. He stopped short
when he noticed them sitting at the kitchen table.

"Oh! Sorry, I didn't—I mean, I thought—" His green eyes darted between Olivia and Johara, widening slightly at the sight of
the princess. His knees started to give way, but he caught himself
against the doorframe. "Is Storm up here? I can't seem to find
him."

Olivia shook her head, taking another sip of her coffee to hide
her annoyance at the interruption. "I think he went down to help
Delphi in the store."

Scooter's shoulders slumped. "Right. Of course." He hovered
awkwardly in the doorway, his fingers fidgeting with the hem of his
lab coat. The smell of chemicals and something vaguely electrical
clung to him.

"Would you like some coffee?" Johara offered, her voice gentle.

"Coffee? Oh, yes—I mean, no. I mean—" Scooter took a deep
breath. "Actually, I've had too much caffeine already."

That was an understatement if Olivia had ever heard one. Scooter's entire existence seemed fueled by excessive caffeine, his energy
radiating from him in chaotic waves that made her temples throb.

"I'll just go find Storm, then," Scooter said but made no move
to leave. His gaze kept darting to Johara, fascination evident in his
wide eyes. "You're really her, aren't you? The princess from the Far
Viscera that Talia talked about?"

She inclined her head slightly. "I am."

"Fascinating!" Scooter took three eager steps forward before
catching himself. "The implications of interdimensional travel be-

tween realms are extraordinary. The theoretical implications alone would—"

"Scooter," Olivia interrupted, massaging her temples, "didn't you need to find Storm?"

"Oh! Right. Yes." He backed toward the door, nearly tripping over his own feet, but his eyes remained locked on Johara. "But maybe I could ask you just a few questions first? I'm a researcher. Paranormal phenomena, mainly. And you're—" His eyes widened further, taking in the princess's otherworldly appearance. "You're actually real. I've read fragments about you in Niberian texts, but I never thought—" He abruptly cut himself off, his cheeks flushing. "Sorry. I get excited."

Talia, I need your help with Scooter.

Talia emerged gracefully from the dimly lit hallway, her silhouette gradually becoming clearer as she approached the kitchen. With a mischievous glint in her eye, she deftly flicked her fingers, conjuring a tiny cascade of shimmering sparks that danced through the air toward Scooter. The sparks crackled softly, illuminating the space with a brief, magical glow. Startled, Scooter leaped back, his feet stumbling awkwardly, nearly causing him to tumble backward.

"Scooter, I haven't had my coffee yet," Talia said, reaching for a cup.

"Olivia, you could have warned me she was going to do that."

"What would be the fun in that?" She giggled.

Talia poured herself a cup of coffee and leaned against the counter, her purple eyes scanning the room with a quiet assessment.

"Sorry about that," Talia said to Scooter, though she didn't sound apologetic. "Just testing something out."

Scooter straightened his lab coat, his fingers still trembling slightly. "Fascinating control over electrical discharge. The energy signature seems different from standard lightning—more concentrated, with a distinctive spectral pattern. I'd love to measure the—"

"Maybe another time," Talia cut him off gently, taking a long sip of her coffee.

Olivia felt a strange tug in her mind as she watched the exchange—an impression of knowledge that wasn't quite her own. She suddenly understood, with perfect clarity, that Scooter's scientific curiosity wasn't just academic; it was a desperate attempt to make sense of a world that had never made sense to him. The realization came without effort, like remembering something she'd always known.

"I'm going to find Storm." Scooter backed toward the door, still sneaking glances at Johara as if she might vanish if he looked away. "Right. Finding Storm. That's what I'm doing."

Scooter clambered out of the apartment, the door clicking shut behind him. Olivia sighed with relief, the tension in her shoulders easing.

"That man has an exceptional mind," Johara observed, her white eyes following the space where Scooter had been. "But it's like watching a Mixie trapped in a small box."

"What's a Mixie?"

"Mixies are small fairies, whose wings flutter really fast. They're very nervous creatures."

Talia snorted into her coffee. "That's the most accurate description of Scooter I've ever heard."

"There's something fascinating about that man," Johara said, her voice carrying an unexpected warmth that made Olivia look up sharply from her coffee.

"Fascinating is one way to put it," Olivia muttered, taking another sip of her coffee. "Exhausting is another."

She almost spewed an entire mouthful of coffee across the table when she realized Johara's remark was more than just casual curiosity. The princess, with her regal poise and undeniable charm, had developed an unexpected fascination for the eccentric scientist.

Wait a minute.

"Holy, Anu! You can't be serious," she blurted before she could stop herself, wiping coffee from her chin with the back of her hand. "Scooter? Really?"

Johara turned toward her, one eyebrow arched delicately. "I don't understand your reaction."

"He's just so..." Olivia gestured vaguely, searching for the right words. "Chaotic and awkward. He never stops talking." She could still smell the lingering scent of chemicals that seemed permanently embedded in his lab coat. "Plus, I'm pretty sure he's a spaz."

"His energy is vibrant, like watching a star trying to contain itself." A small smile played at the corners of her mouth. "We don't have many like him in the Far Viscera. Most creatures there move with purpose, with calculation. His thoughts seem to race ahead of him."

Talia, who had been quietly sipping her coffee by the counter, snorted softly. "That's another way of describing Scooter." But there was fondness in her voice, not mockery.

Olivia studied Johara more carefully, noting the slight flush that had crept into her pale cheeks. It was subtle—almost imperceptible—but it transformed her face, making her seem suddenly younger, more vulnerable. Less like an untouchable princess and more like a woman noticing a man.

A strange sensation rippled through Olivia—a knowing that didn't feel entirely her own. She could suddenly see, with perfect clarity, how Johara's life of constant vigilance and survival had left little room for simple curiosity, for fascination without purpose. Scooter, with his unfiltered enthusiasm and lack of guile, represented something entirely new to her.

"He's brilliant, you know," Talia offered, moving to join them at the table. "Underneath all that nervous energy, Storm says he's solved paranormal mysteries that stumped researchers for decades."

"I sensed that," Johara said, her fingers traced patterns on her mug. "In my world, knowledge is the ultimate power."

"Well," Talia said with a hint of mischief in her eyes, "this should be interesting."

"Don't you dare encourage this," Olivia warned, but she couldn't keep the smile from her voice. The mental image of the elegant Princess Johara and fidgety Scooter together was both ridiculous and strangely compelling. "I can feel Storm's irritation with Scooter already."

"Speaking of Storm," Talia said, glancing toward the door, "I should probably go rescue him from Scooter." She drained the last of her coffee and stood.

Sensing Storm straining his muscles, Oliva said, "We better help, or Storm is going to hurt himself moving that display case by himself." She followed suit, finishing her coffee. "Just so you know," she said, leaning forward toward the princess with a conspiratorial whisper, "if you're actually interested in Scooter, you should probably brace yourself for a lot of rambling about nothing."

Her smile widened just slightly, her eyes gleaming with something that might have been amusement or anticipation. "I look forward to it."

Olivia stood from the table. She felt the hot, tantalizing brush of breath against her sensitive earlobe, stirring a shiver of anticipation down her spine. The sound of a low, seductive whisper prickled against her skin, inviting a vision that scorched her mind. A faceless man, veiled in the shadows of mystery, standing just beyond her reach.

His head turned, and she caught a tantalizing glimpse of his rugged jawline. The raw masculinity of it made her pulse quicken. His hazel eyes, intense and predatory, held hers with a magnetic force.

"Do you hear that?" Olivia asked, looking around the room.

A subtle shift in the air, a raw energy, filled the space around her. It was a dirty, filthy arousal, one that mirrored her own deep desires. The image flashed through her mind, tantalizing and fleeting, igniting every inch of her skin with a scorching desire. The scent of smoky wood and sweet vanilla hung heavily in the air, swirling around her like an intoxicating perfume. She couldn't resist the pull, the all-consuming need to satisfy this insatiable craving.

"Olivia, are you okay? Something feels off."

Trembling, Olivia shook her head, trying to clear the fog that clouded her mind. "I-I don't know," she stammered.

CHAPTER FIVE

OLIVIA

Talia emerged from the bathroom with her long hair pulled back in a binder, wearing her comfortable nightgown as Olivia came down the hallway. She was holding a towel loosely on her arm, wrapped in her robe. "Looks like you're changing in the bathroom again," Olivia teased with a playful smile. "Storm must be sleeping up here tonight."

A small sigh escaped her sister's lips as she nodded. "It's probably not the best idea, but I feel safer when he's close by."

"The rest of us should be so fortunate to have such a strong, protective man in our beds. Let me know if you want to borrow something shorter, sexy, and see-through."

Talia glided into her bedroom, the door clicking softly shut behind her. With a sigh of contentment, Olivia slipped into the bathroom, eagerly anticipating the warm embrace of the bath she was about to draw. She lit her favorite candles, and the scent of lavender filled the air. She could almost feel the tension melting away as she turned on the bath water.

As the bath filled, she undressed, leaving her robe and towel on the hook. Her bare feet made no sound on the cool tile floor as she stepped into the hot water, allowing herself a small sigh of relief as she sank into the tub. She closed her eyes and leaned back, allowing the heat to seep into her muscles.

She wasn't sure how long she stayed there, lost in her thoughts and the comforting warmth of the bath, when she felt the air change. The candles' flames flickered and blew out. She whipped her head around, just in time to catch a glimpse of a glowing portal materializing.

The flickering lights danced and swirled, casting a mesmerizing display of colors across the darkened room. A tall, striking man emerged from the midst of the lights, his cape billowing behind him like a grand banner. His chiseled cheekbones caught the light just right, making her stomach flip and her heart race.

Then, a powerful wave of sexual desire hit her as she felt the stranger's intense energy radiating toward her. It was the same overwhelming, all-consuming sensation she had experienced once before, on the day of her oath. The feeling was more than an emotion she sensed; it was an energy that hung around her, thick, undeniably real, and inescapable. She couldn't resist the pull of this mysterious person, drawing her close in an irresistible dance of attraction.

With a startled gasp, Olivia leaped out of the warm bath and stumbled on the slick tiles. Just as she braced for impact, brawny arms encircled her naked form, pulling her back against a solid chest. Goosebumps prickled along her arms and legs as she felt the firmness of his muscles against her wet skin. The heat from the embrace spread through her body, warming her from within as she looked up into the shadowed face of her rescuer. In that moment, she was acutely aware of her vulnerability, sending shivers down her spine.

As he turned his head, scanning the bathroom with a hint of tension in his eyes, Olivia caught a fleeting glimpse of his face before he looked back down at her. She noticed the contrast between his rough leather glove and her delicate skin as he touched her face. The scent of smoky wood and sweet vanilla lingered in the air as she felt herself getting lost in those intriguing eyes. But just as quickly as it began, the moment was gone, leaving only a memory of his touch behind.

With confusion and fear clouding her mind, she looked around. The restraints bound her hands, preventing her from moving as she sat high above the ground on the foul-smelling beast. She found herself astride what she assumed was a Caribrax. A firm grasp held her waist, providing the only sense of stability as she struggled to make sense of her predicament.

Her robe was the only garment covering her body, leaving her vulnerable and exposed in this unfamiliar environment. Her hair was slightly damp, with droplets clinging to the strands, a sure sign she hadn't been out for long.

She felt the firm, unyielding presence of a man's solid chest pressing against her back, a sensation that anchored her in place. The air around her was thick with the rich aroma of leather, the smoky undertone of charred wood, and the delicate sweetness of vanilla. These mingling scents enveloped her, leading her to surmise that the stranger who had taken her was the one holding her so securely on the smelly animal.

"Where am I?" Olivia whispered.

Hunter's voice was cold and frightening as he spoke. "Welcome to the Far Viscera, Olivia. I hope you enjoy your stay."

Olivia's breath caught in her throat as she recognized the imposing figure mounted on his own beast beside her, facing the opposite direction With large, sharp antlers that pointed majestically towards the sky, the animal's head possessed a regal beauty reminiscent of an elk. Its body was sleek and muscular like a horse, yet its legs were slender.

Her heart pounded in her chest, a frantic drum against her ribs, as a desperate need to escape warred with the stranger's firm grip from behind. Hunter's intense gaze bored into her, causing her body to tremble uncontrollably. She could feel his power radiating off him.

"Please, let me go," she pleaded, her voice trembling.

Hunter chuckled darkly. "I'm afraid that's not possible. You see, you have something I want, and I won't stop until I get it."

Olivia looked at him, horrified. "What do you want from me?"

Hunter leaned in closer, shifting his weight, his face just inches from hers. "You have my wife's soul," he said, his voice low and dangerous. "I want it back, and you're going to help me get it." Hunter chuckled again. "Your sister will come for you. When she does, I will have Circe's spirit."

"What's going to happen to me?"

The words dripped from Hunter's lips like poison, a wicked grin spreading across his face as he spoke. "Oh, sweet girl," he sneered. He was so close. He roughly grabbed a fistful of her hair, yanking her head back with a cruel grip. "That doesn't matter. Once I extract Circe's soul and place it in Talia, you will cease to exist. You'll just be another victim of the void. Drink this," he ordered as he reached into his leather pouch and produced a vial. "I can't have you remembering who you are and communicating with your sister."

Hunter yanked hard when she struggled against his hold. He held her head steady as he carefully poured the liquid past her lips with the other.

"What did you just give her?" the stranger holding her asked.

"Just a little water from the River of Forgetfulness to wipe away her memory."

Olivia heard the man behind her let out a piercing whistle. A small group of guards appeared from the field behind them. They rode together across the stone bridge. Hunter pulled on his Caribrax's reins, bringing them to a halt just as they reached the other side of Punishment Valley.

"What would you like to do with her until then?" he asked, grabbing Olivia's waist even tighter.

"Take her back to the castle, Commander Jitatma. She can be a guest in our dungeon." Hunter waved his hand to dismiss them.

"May I offer a suggestion? I need a chambermaid. I could have some fun with one."

"Fine, but you're responsible for her. Keep her in your chambers," Hunter ordered. "Malta and I will wait here for the rest of our guests. I have a welcome gift for them."

"Thank you, King Hunter."

Jitatma rode with Olivia raced toward the blue and purple trees that marked their journey through the Nothingness Forest, followed by the guard soldiers. She remained unresponsive as the vial of water began to take effect, her listless body held against Jitatma's own. She was almost detached from her surroundings. She could feel the warmth of the Caribrax's fur on her bare legs along with the cold air blowing against her. Branches scraped her skin as they raced through the dimly lit forest, but she paid no mind to their sting.

Once they emerged, she became more aware of her surroundings. A majestic castle cast a shadow over the village below. Jitatma eased the pace of his Caribrax as they approached the main gate, its creaking gears opening to welcome their arrival. The guards stood tall in salute, fists pressed over their hearts, acknowledging their commander's return with her as a significant victory.

As they traversed the cobblestone road toward the castle, the echo of Caribrax shoes resounded loudly, capturing the attention of a few curious onlookers who ventured outside. The villager souls looked at her with curiosity. The imposing castle gate swung open, admitting them into the courtyard. Dismounting from their steeds, they handed over the Caribraxes to the stablemen, who led them away.

With measured steps, he guided her across the enchanting garden toward the main entrance of the castle. Olivia remained subdued and unresponsive as she allowed him to lead her up the grand staircase and down a long hallway.

His grip on her was firm. Together, they trudged through a serpentine corridor faintly illuminated softly by torches, their shaky shadows replicating a shadowy dance on the stone walls. At the end of a long hallway, he opened a heavy wooden door to his chambers.

The room hummed with quietude except for an occasional hiss erupting from smoldering embers cradled in the fireplace. He stoked a few logs in the fire to turn listless embers into a lively flame that cast a playful glow around the room, eating away at the lingering chill. Drawn to its warmth, she inched closer, savoring every bit of heat that eased the cold away.

When she shivered, he fetched an old blanket off his wooden poster bed and offered it to her. After a brief hesitation, likely because of unfamiliarity, she accepted his offer and watched as he gently swathed her shoulders with it.

"What's going to happen to me?"

"Why does it matter to you?" he said coldly.

"I guess it doesn't."

"You don't sound like you want to be saved. I can only prevent you from spending your time in a cold, damp, dark dungeon. If you don't want to be saved, no one can help you, not even your powerful sister."

"How do you know I don't want to be saved?"

"The waters of the River of Forgetfulness have taken effect. It causes physical and mental changes." He grabbed her arm, pulling her across the room to a mirror on the wall. She refused to look at her own reflection, staring down at the ground. He grabbed a fistful of her hair, pulling her head up hard. "Look at yourself, Olivia," he ordered, forcing her to see a shell of a woman looking back. It was the first time she could see her dull gray skin, straight hair, and the dark circles around her eyes. She didn't recognize the woman staring back at her.

"You're hurting me." She tried to escape his firm grip.

"Well, at least you can still feel," he pointed out, releasing his grip. "You will remain in this room. You will clean it when I'm not here. You will attend to me when I am here. You can start by cleaning yourself. The washroom is through that door. I'll find you some clean clothes to wear."

"That would be easier without these bracelets," she said, turning toward him and holding up her wrist restraints. He placed his thumbprint on the red light in the center of the handcuffs until it turned green to release the lock, then retracted within itself until it was only a small stick. She rubbed her sore wrists, wondering how she came to be in this world.

She closed the door to the washroom. Finally, having a moment of mental clarity, she realized she didn't know who she was. He called her Olivia, so that must be her name, and he said she had a powerful sister. That was all she knew for sure. As she turned on the warm water in the oversized tub in the center of the washroom, she tried to recall memories from her life. Nothing but an overwhelming feeling of guilt and regret came to mind.

With a graceful movement, she untied the soft fabric of her robe and let it slide down her shoulders. The door swung open as Jitatma appeared with a dress draped over his arm. A sense of embarrassment washed over her as she hurriedly tried to cover herself up, feeling exposed under his gaze. She felt heat rising in her cheeks as she fumbled with the fabric, trying to regain some semblance of modesty.

"No need to cover up on my account. I'm sure I'll see it later," he said, a smirk on his face.

She clutched the robe tighter, turning her back to him. She felt his eyes glued to her, and it made her skin crawl. Peering over her shoulder, she watched him place the dress on a nearby chair and saunter to the door. A rush of anger surged through her, but she bit her tongue. She couldn't afford to make any enemies in this strange place, especially not the man who held the keys to her freedom.

As he left the room, she let out a sigh of relief. She climbed into the warm bath, letting the water wash away the grime of her journey. She closed her eyes and tried to remember anything from her past, but her mind was a blank slate.

Her heart raced, her palms growing clammy. She sank into the soothing water, her thoughts a jumbled mess. Who was she? Who was that man? Why couldn't she remember anything? She scrubbed her body vigorously, as if she could wash away her confusion and guilt along with the dirt.

After her bath, she reluctantly donned the simple dress Jitatma had provided. It hung loosely on her slender frame, the fabric a dull gray that seemed to match the color of her skin. She ran her fingers through her now clean hair, trying to smooth out the tangles. She still didn't recognize the woman staring back at her in the mirror, but at least she looked a little more presentable.

In Jitatma's opulent chambers, adorned with intricate tapestries and elegant furnishings, Olivia found herself sitting on a plush rug near the crackling fireplace. The warm glow cast by the dancing flames flickered across her face yet ignited no spark of recognition in her vacant mind.

The room itself exuded an air of grandeur that sharply contrasted with her deteriorating state. Tall, ornate windows framed in velvet curtains allowed slivers of sunlight to filter through. The walls were adorned with elaborate paintings depicting heroic battles and majestic landscapes.

As she stared into the depths of the flames, a profound chill settled in her bones. The warmth of the fire failed to thaw the icy grip encircling her, as if the room itself mirrored her internal struggle. She hugged her trembling form tightly, seeking solace from the tormenting fog shrouding her mind.

Her thoughts swirled aimlessly in a sea of uncertainty, fragments of memories slipping through her fingers. Flickers of faces and places danced at the periphery of her consciousness, teasing her with their elusiveness. Each passing moment only deepened her despair, leaving her feeling adrift in an endless ocean of confusion.

The burden of guilt weighed heavily upon her heart. She yearned for clarity, for a glimmer of understanding that could piece together the shattered fragments of her identity. Yet, as she sat there in silence, surrounded by opulence and mystery, it seemed as if every answer lay just out of reach. She felt as if there was more to her story.

Jitatma sat down across from her with a plate of bread, cheese, and fruit. "I brought you something to eat. I thought you might be hungry."

"Who am I?" she muttered under her breath, refusing the food. "Why does this guilt weigh so heavily upon me?" As the warmth of the flames penetrated the room, she found herself sinking deeper into the darkness.

"Olivia, you must fight to remember who you are," he said, his eyes filled with concern as he set the plate on a nearby table. It was the first sign this stranger wasn't completely heartless. "You don't deserve this fate. You shouldn't be in the Far Viscera."

"Can I leave?" she asked hesitantly, hope flickering like a fragile flame within her heart. "Could I escape this place?"

He sighed. "You could try, but I must warn you. You would be far safer here with me. The world beyond these walls is treacherous, and I cannot guarantee your safety. You've no reason to trust me, but right now, I'm the only hope you have."

As she pondered her options, the uncertainty threatened to overwhelm her once more. But deep within, she knew she couldn't give in to the despair that sought to claim her. She had to find her way back to herself and cling to the hope that one day she might escape the darkness that held her captive.

Despite the comforting warmth of the fire, she couldn't ignore the urgency gnawing at her. With every passing moment, she felt herself slipping further away from her true self. She needed answers, and she needed them now.

Gathering her courage, she turned to him and asked, "What do you know about me? Why am I here? Who is my sister?" The questions tumbled out in a desperate rush, her voice trembling with the weight of her fear.

His expression softened as he studied her face. He sighed, rubbing his temples as if trying to decide how much to reveal. "Olivia," he began, his voice gentle, "your sister is Talia. She is a powerful warrior goddess. I know you don't remember her now, but you will. I can't tell you much more than that."

"Can you tell me your name? What do I call you?"

"My name is Jitatma Smoke, but you can address me as Commander."

"Smoke, why does that sound familiar? My head is a mess."

"If you try to force the memories, they will never return," he cautioned. "You must let them drift back to you in their own time, when your heart and mind are ready to receive them." He leaned closer, his gaze intense, as if trying to imprint his words into her very soul. "I need you to grasp something vital. When those memories resurface, I want you to understand that every action I took was necessary. My sole allegiance is to this kingdom, and every decision I make is in pursuit of what is best for this land. I will always choose my world." His voice was firm, yet a hint of vulnerability flickered in his hazel eyes, revealing the weight of his responsibilities.

CHAPTER SIX

OLIVIA

O livia stood on the balcony of the second floor the next day, her eyes fixated on the distant figure of Jitatma as he paced across the training field. She leaned against the cold stone railing, which sent a chilling sensation through her to match the frigidness that had taken hold of her heart. The grit from the stone beneath her palm seemed to absorb the load of her thoughts and emotions.

The commander's presence was undeniable as he marched with unyielding confidence, his every step resonating authority and power. He stopped just below the balcony. His soldiers moved in synchronized harmony, their bodies glistening with sweat under the unforgiving sun. The faint scent of metal and leather also lingered from the weapons and armor used in training.

The training field was a sprawling expanse of trampled grass, interrupted by practice dummies bearing the scars of countless strikes. The sounds of clashing of swords and shields as soldiers sparred with each other. The occasional shout reached her ears.

As she observed, she felt a tumultuous mix of emotions. Admiration for Jitatma's physical prowess battled against an instinctive repulsion caused by his harsh demeanor. It was an internal conflict that mirrored the external world unfolding before her eyes.

"Pick up the pace! I want to see you sweat!" Jitatma bellowed, his voice a whip that lashed at the soldiers. They moved with renewed vigor, swords clashing and shields thudding in response to meet his expectations. "Focus, you imbeciles!" Jitatma shouted, the soldiers flinching under the force of his words.

Olivia clenched her fists, her nails digging into her palms as she watched him command with an iron grip. Her heart, a wild beast within her chest, beat in sync with the war drums echoing in her mind. The overwhelming desire to escape this nightmare fueled her determination, intensifying with each passing second.

A tall, lean man with an air of arrogance walked up beside Commander Jitatma. His eyes were dark and his hair was a unique shade of electric blue, styled in a sleek, precise manner. He wore a tailored uniform in shades of black and silver, emphasizing his status and confidence on the training field.

"Lieutenant Malta, what is the status report on the new recruits?"

"They're not ready for battle, Commander."

"Get them ready."

Malta, as Jitatma had called him, glanced up at the balcony and caught sight of Olivia watching them. A sly grin spread across his face as he nudged the commander.

"Looks like your little birdie is watching you, Commander," he sneered, nodding toward the window. "Have you fucked her into submission yet?"

Jitatma's expression darkened for a moment before he replied, voice dripping with false confidence, "Oh, I did. Bent her over and took her. She resisted at first, but once I forced my dick inside her, she couldn't get enough."

The lie sounded convincing, even to Olivia, who was still observing from above. Her face flushed with anger and humiliation at their crude conversation. They dared to speak about her like she was nothing more than a plaything for their amusement. Her chest tightened, and her breath hitched as resentment swelled within her. The feeling of being trapped and powerless consumed her, and her eyes burned with unshed tears. She vowed to herself she would not let them break her spirit or take away her dignity.

"Damn him," she muttered. "I must find a way to escape this nightmare. I don't care what he says about my safety. I can't stay here and await my fate." She would not be a pawn in Jitatma's twisted game; she would find her strength and turn the tables on those who sought to control her. "Damn them both to the Underworld," she whispered fiercely, hands trembling with fury. "He will not own me, whatever it takes."

Olivia's breaths came in heavy gasps as she turned and went into the chambers, the cruel words of Jitatma and Malta still ringing in her ears. She clenched her fists tighter, nails digging deeper into her palms, as she paced across the cold stone floor.

She took a deep, steadying breath and closed her eyes, focusing on the sensations around her. The cool touch of the stone beneath her bare feet. The faint scent of old parchment and dust that lingered in the air. The distant clashing of swords the soldiers continued their training. She let these sensations ground her, steady her, and remind her she was still very much alive.

"I won't let him win," she whispered, opening her eyes with newfound resolve. "I will find a way to escape, to reclaim my life and my freedom."

She began to explore the room, searching for any weaknesses or hidden passages that might lead to her escape. As she searched, she couldn't shake the feeling she was being watched. She glanced over her shoulder, half expecting to see Jitatma or one of his soldiers lurking in the shadows, but the room remained empty. The feeling persisted, however, sending a shiver down her spine.

The stone walls were smooth and uniform, with no cracks or crevices that could serve in her escape. Even the furniture was not large enough to conceal a hidden doorway. She felt trapped in this prison, with no clues or hints of a way out.

She panicked.

As Olivia stood near the bed, she strained her ears for any sound. Suddenly, she heard the distinct click of a key turning in the lock and the creak of a door swinging open. Her heart raced as she waited to see who would appear in the doorway. Finally, Jitatma emerged into the room, his tall figure casting a shadow over her. His footsteps echoed loudly as he approached her.

She was motionless as the evening light from the window cast a golden hue over Jitatma's broad shoulders. The clink and clatter of his armor hitting the stone floor echoed in the chamber, each layer shedding away, revealing the man beneath the warrior.

"Olivia," Jitatma's voice sliced through her reverie, firm and accustomed to obedience, "ensure my armor is properly cared for."

"Of course," she replied, her voice betraying none of the turmoil inside as she bent to gather the heavy plates. The scent of leather and steel mingled in her nose. Her fingers brushed against the cool metal, each touch sending her heart skittering.

He nodded toward the closet behind her. "I will need some fresh clothes and my cape."

With a tender touch, she carefully placed his heavy armor on the wooden chair beside her. The metal pieces clinked softly against each other as she arranged them in an orderly fashion. She then turned to the closet, its doors creaking slightly as she opened them. From within, she retrieved a freshly laundered shirt and a pair of pants for him. The fabric was soft and smelled of vanilla.

He pulled his dirty shirt over his head, muscles flexing with the movement, and she caught herself staring. She made her best effort to remain indifferent. She turned her head, but her peripheral vision betrayed her, clinging to the sight of him.

His Nibmarks were a striking blend of Sumerian and unknown origins, their intricate patterns stretching across his tanned left shoulder in a mesmerizing pattern. As he reached out, she saw a tattoo on his right forearm. The design was familiar, but she struggled to place it in her memory. A perfect circle with three inward facing swirls, surrounded by a shield adorned with ancient markings. She found herself transfixed by the intricacy of the tattoo, unable to look away even though she knew she was staring for far too long.

"Does it look familiar to you?" he asked. He moved with purposeful grace toward her, extending his arm for her to inspect it.

Her fingers twitched, aching to trace the lines of the sacred symbol. Swallowing the sudden tightness in her throat, she confessed, "I've seen it before, but I can't remember where."

His gaze held hers, his eyes dark and intense. He stepped closer, the heat of his body radiating, drawing her in. "It is the mark of the gods, a protector."

She hesitated for a moment before reaching out to trace the delicate lines of the tattoo. The swirls seemed to dance under her fingertips, a strange energy pulsating from the symbol. Her heart pounded in her chest, her breath coming in short gasps. She was acutely aware of his proximity as she felt his other hand gently slide along the curve of her back, tracing the delicate line of her spine.

"Someone else had a tattoo like this."

He whispered, his warm breath tickling her neck, "That would be my brother and my sister."

Jitatma gently pulled back, his eyes tracing her face. He reached up to brush a stray hair away from her cheek, tilting his head to the side. In response, she turned her head to finally meet his gaze.

Her perceptive gaze caught a glimpse of a new emotion reflected in his eyes. A tenderness, a vulnerability she had not noticed before. It softened the usually stern lines of his face and drew her closer, as if she could feel the warmth radiating from his heart through those deep, soulful pools. It was a side of him she hadn't seen before, and it made her heart flutter.

"I have a meeting to attend," he announced abruptly, breaking into her tangled thoughts as he stepped away. She extended his trousers with a slight tremble in her hand. A lock of hair fell in his face as he quickly changed and fastened his pants. "I shall not return until late."

"May I ask what the meeting is about?" Olivia asked, her curiosity piqued, as she handed him the shirt she was still holding.

His eyes met hers, a fortress of secrets guarded within their depths. "It is not your place to know, Olivia," he said, his tone a gentle rebuke wrapped in the silk of mystery. "But rest assured, it is a matter of importance for your well-being."

She nodded, accepting the dismissal while her mind raced with possibilities. What could be so important that it warranted secrecy and the cover of night? Why was the meeting about her?

"Very well, Commander," she agreed, her own voice a mask hiding the cascade of questions behind her lips.

"I expect a bath when I return," he instructed, though the softness in his eyes hinted at a warmth that belied his stern words.

"Of course," Olivia repeated, a sense of formality settling between them once more.

As he turned to gather a few remaining items, the candlelight danced upon the contours of his bare back, casting shadows that played upon each muscle and sinew with an intimacy that made Olivia's breath hitch. She tried to focus on what he was saying, but the sight of his half-naked body, so close and so forbidden, distracted her. She caught a glimpse of the scars that lined his back.

"Will there be anything else, Commander?" she managed to ask, her voice steadier than she felt.

"Nothing more," he answered, not noticing the turmoil he stirred within her.

"Before you go, can you answer one question for me?"

"Yes, one question."

"Do I know your brother?"

"Yes, you do. Although not as well as your sister."

"The important sister everyone keeps talking about?"

He nodded. "Make sure you are awake when I return."

He slipped the clean shirt over his head then wrapped himself in a dark cloak, its fabric rustling as it draped over him. With a curt nod, he departed, leaving Olivia alone with the echo of his presence. She clasped her hands, willing them to stillness, chiding herself for this unseemly reaction.

Once she heard the heavy thud of the door closing behind him, she rushed to the window, driven by a need to see him once again. She watched Jitatma mount his Caribrax—a creature as fierce and proud as its rider—with a grace that seemed effortless. As he rode off into the Nothingness Forest, the shadows seemed to swallow both beast and man whole.

A sudden change in the atmosphere caught her attention, signaling she was no longer alone. Slowly turning, she saw a striking figure standing before her. The woman was tall and slender, with a commanding presence that seemed to fill the room. The long black dress, covering her from ankle to neck, shrouded her in an air of mystery and elegance. Her long, flowing white hair framed her face like a halo, contrasting with her cold, distant green eyes. As she stood there with her hands clasped in front of her, it was clear she held some type of power.

"Olivia," said the woman, her voice like a melody wrapped in mourning.

"Who are you?" Olivia uttered, her voice barely above a whisper. The woman's presence felt both ancient and achingly familiar, stirring memories that refused to surface.

"I'm Lady Anasazi. I have come because I sense the tumult within you," the woman said, her pale green eyes holding a depth of centuries.

Confusion laced with curiosity swirled in Olivia's mind. "Anasazi..." The name rolled off her tongue, igniting a spark of recognition deep within her, but the memory remained frustratingly elusive.

"Jitatma is captivating and charming like his father," Anasazi said, her voice tinged with a rueful smile. "Gorgon has a charisma that could bend the will of gods and mortals alike. I loved him deeply once, but his allure was a tempting thing, leading many astray. Jitatma has inherited more than his father's eyes. He will break your heart."

"Are you here to warn me?" she asked, her curiosity piqued by this strange mixture of maternal protectiveness and cautionary advice.

"Consider it friendly advice," she replied. "You carry strength within you, Olivia. More than you realize. Do not be fooled by Jitatma."

With that, she was gone, leaving behind only the lingering scent of lilies and a strange sense of serenity in the air. For a moment, she stood there, staring at the spot where Anasazi had just been, her mind a whirl of thoughts and emotions. She felt both confused and enlightened, her visitor's words reverberating within her.

In the far corner of the room, she caught a reflection of herself in the mirror. She walked over to it. As she drew closer, she noticed a bold streak of blonde forming at the front of her hairline. Without hesitation, she reached up and ran her fingers through the streak, feeling its silky texture. A smile spread across her face as she turned away from the mirror.

A sharp knock echoed through the room, reverberating off the walls and breaking the stillness. She paused, her hand hovering above the doorknob.

"Who's there?" Olivia called, her voice steadier than she expected.

"It's Lieutenant Malta," came the muffled reply. "Open the door, Little Birdie."

Olivia's heart quickened. The lieutenant's earlier crude remarks about her still burned in her memory. She had no desire to face him alone. The nickname made her skin crawl. Her fingers curled into fists at her sides as she stepped back from the door.

"What do you want?" she called, keeping her distance from the door. She glanced around the room, searching for anything she might use as a weapon if needed.

"I need to speak to the commander, and I would rather not shout through the door," Malta replied, his patience clearly thinning.

"He's not here."

"I'm asking you nicely to open the door, and there's no need for you to search for a weapon. I come unarmed." A low chuckle drifted through the wooden barrier.

She hesitated, her gaze falling on a letter opener resting on Jitatma's desk. She grabbed it, concealing it within the folds of her dress before approaching the door. Taking a deep breath, she turned the heavy knob and pulled the door open.

"As I said, he's not here," she repeated, blocking the entrance with her body.

Malta's blue hair gleamed in the torchlight of the hallway, his black eyes studying her with unsettling intensity. "May I come in? It's rather important."

"The commander said he won't return until late. Perhaps you should come back tomorrow."

A slow smile spread across Malta's face. "Protecting his privacy already? You've settled into your role quickly." His gaze dropped to her hair, lingering on the golden streak. "What's this? A change in appearance?"

Her hand flew to her hair, covering the blonde strands. "It's nothing."

He leaned against the doorframe, bringing his face uncomfortably close to hers. "Nothing is ever nothing, Little Birdie, especially not with you." He carefully withdrew his dagger from the worn leather sheath on his belt and extended it toward her, the blade catching the light with a menacing glint. "If you're going to cut me," he said with a wry smile, "I'd prefer you use this instead of a mere letter opener. You have good instincts, Olivia."

Grasping the dagger's hilt, she remarked, "I thought you claimed to be unarmed."

He offered a disarming smile, his eyes glinting with a hint of mischief. "I brought that for you so you would feel more comfortable alone with me," he explained, his voice smooth and reassuring. As he spoke, he nudged past her. "I've come seeking some information," he continued, his tone now edged with a subtle urgency that hinted at the gravity of his quest. "Did Commander Jitatma say where he was going?"

She tightened her grip on the dagger, its weight unfamiliar yet oddly comforting in her hand. Her eyes followed him as he strode into the chamber with the easy confidence of a man accustomed to getting what he wanted.

"No, he didn't," she replied, keeping her voice level despite the unease crawling up her spine. "He only mentioned a meeting."

His gaze swept around the room, lingering on Jitatma's belongings with undisguised interest. "A meeting, you say? Did he mention with whom?"

"If he had, I doubt he'd want me sharing that information with you." She closed the door, maintaining her distance from the lieutenant. The dagger hung at her side, a silent promise of protection.

He chuckled, the sound dry and humorless. "So protective of a man who keeps you prisoner. Fascinating." He turned to her fully, searching her face. "You know, there are rumors about you, Olivia. Whispers that travel even through stone walls."

"I'm not interested in rumors, Lieutenant."

"I don't see it."

"See what?"

"Commander Jitatma's fascination with you." He tilted his head to one side, a lazy, predatory smirk tugging at the corner of his mouth. His eyes followed a trail, deliberately slow, from the curve of her neck and lingered on the dip of her waist. "He's been distracted since your arrival. I hope you aren't trying to pull his focus."

"I'm not trying to get anyone's attention," she said quickly. "Now, if you'll excuse me, I have to prepare for his return."

"I'm sure you do, Little Birdie."

With a surge of frustration coursing through her veins, Olivia planted both palms against Malta's chest and shoved him backward toward the door. The unexpected force of her action surprised even her. The lieutenant's boots scraped against the stone floor as he stumbled back.

"I think you've overstayed your welcome," she said, her voice low but firm. She held up the dagger. "You can have this back."

Malta's eyebrows shot up, his lips curling into that infuriating smirk that made her want to slap it off his face. "Such spirit," he remarked, straightening his uniform with deliberate slowness. "I can see why he keeps you around."

Olivia reached for the door handle, pulling it open with more force than necessary. The hinges groaned in protest. "Goodnight, Lieutenant."

He paused at the threshold, turning to face her one last time. His electric blue hair seemed almost black in the dim light of the hallway. "Remember what I said, Little Birdie. The commander doesn't develop fascinations easily. I'd be careful if I were you."

"Don't be ridiculous," she said. "He doesn't want my attention, and I certainly don't want his."

Somehow, she wanted Jitatma's attention. She didn't just want it, she found herself craving it like a hunger, raw and unrelenting, that made her nipples harden at the thought of his return.

She slammed the door with a satisfying thud and leaned against it. She took a deep breath to adjust herself, disgusted by her temporary moment of weakness. The cold stone beneath her feet offering a tangible reminder of that fleeting vulnerability that momentarily threatened her composure.

He will not have me.

CHAPTER SEVEN

OLIVIA

When Jitatma finally came back, he was in a mood. Olivia felt the anger simmering deep within her. She reminded herself to keep a firm grip on it, determined not to fall for his charm like Anasazi had warned her. As he closed the distance between them, a familiar scented breeze wafted toward her. It was a mixture of wildflowers and something else that tickled her memory. The scent lingered in the air, intoxicating and comforting at the same time.

When she undressed him, she reluctantly observed his perfectly shaped body. Despite her immense distaste for the man, she couldn't deny he was one fine specimen. The heat of the room seemed to increase as she unbuttoned his shirt, revealing his chiseled chest. His abs were rock hard under her touch, making her curse under her breath. Despite not wanting to admit it, there was an undeniable chemistry sparking between them.

"Begin," he ordered coldly, stepping into the bath.

With measured movements, she dipped the soft cloth into a basin filled with warm water and soap. She hesitated for a moment, her hands trembling slightly. Summoning her courage, she approached him and pressed the cloth against his broad back. As she glided it along his skin, she couldn't ignore the intricate patterns of scars that marred his flesh. Every scar on his body held a tale of past struggles and sacrifices, most likely from battles he had fought.

Her fingers traced the ridges of those battle scars, feeling their rough texture. She allowed herself to linger on each mark, as if trying to decipher the hidden tales of pain and triumph they held.

The scent of the soap mingled with the warm steam rising from the bath, creating an intoxicating atmosphere that seemed to draw her closer. She noticed how his muscles tensed under her touch. He was a flawless representation of a Sumerian man. His chiseled physique, sculpted by rigorous training and battles fought, was undeniably captivating.

In this intimate moment, she found herself torn between two versions of herself —the obedient servant who had no choice but to comply with his every demand, and the resilient woman who yearned for freedom. Behind her serene facade, a simmering rebellion brewed, fueled by the knowledge she had the potential to change her destiny.

With every stroke of the cloth, she washed the dirt and grime from Jitatma's back, silently vowing to leave this place. She honed her plan for escape. She knew true liberation would come only through her own strength and cunning.

"Your hands are trembling," he remarked, his tone mocking. "Is it fear or desire, I wonder?"

"Neither," she replied through gritted teeth, refusing to let him see how much his words affected her. "I just want this to be over."

"Then you better hurry," he said dismissively, leaning back in the tub.

Seizing the moment while his guard was down, her trembling hands moved. As panic surged through her veins, she instinctively reached for a nearby towel, her fingers closing tightly around the fabric. With a swift, precise motion, she looped it around his neck, pulling it tight with all her strength. The conflicting emotions of desperation, anger, and fear fueled her resolve as she fought to regain control over her own destiny.

"Damn you!" she cried. "You will not have me!"

His initial reaction was a flash of surprise that flickered in his widened eyes. However, it took only seconds for his innate dominance and physical strength to reassert itself. With calculated ease, he loosened the towel from around his neck, demonstrating his ability to effortlessly counter her desperate attempt to overpower him.

In one swift motion, his iron grip closed around her arm like a vise. The sudden yank sent her stumbling forward, disoriented and off-balance. Unable to brace herself in time, she crashed into the bathtub. The impact jolted through her body with an electric intensity.

As they collided, the water rushed up to meet her face, filling her mouth with an unexpected surge. She choked and gasped among the chaotic struggle that unfolded in those fleeting moments. Water inundating her senses only added to her disorientation and sense of vulnerability.

The scene played out in a messy flurry of movement and raw emotion. Water splashed and cascaded over the edges of the tub, drenching the floor. She felt the influence of his dominance pressing against her, both physically and emotionally, as she fought to regain her bearings in the face of this humiliation.

She refused to surrender completely. Even as his grip tightened around her arm, she clung stubbornly to the flickering hope that burned within her. As the water continued to swirl around them, carrying echoes of their struggle, she knew she was losing this battle. She found herself soaked and entangled in the aftermath.

"Is this what you want?" he growled, his voice low and dangerous. "To fight me? To defy me?"

She knew if she showed any fear or weakness now, he would use it against her. She stared into his eyes and hissed, "I will never be yours. I would never submit to a barbaric renegade like you."

Her body shook with rage. Her heart pounded in her chest like a war drum, the adrenaline pumping through her veins. Her breath came fast and shallow. He loosened his grip, allowing her to push away from him.

"Bold words from a bratty minx," he sneered. "Is that what you think of me? Everything I do is for the safety of this kingdom. I showed you mercy. You would be in a dark, damp dungeon right now. Instead, you are in my comfortable, warm room. Take that back."

"Did I hit a nerve, Commander? Which one cut the deepest? Barbaric or renegade?"

His eyes narrowed as he stared at her chest. She glanced down and saw her nipples were standing at attention, clearly visible through her damp dress. She instinctively covered her chest with her arm and began to retreat.

His anger seemed to shift, transforming into a dark, dangerous passion. He grinned maliciously, his teeth flashing white against his tanned skin. The scent of wet clothes mingled with his masculinity filled the air around her, making it almost unbearable to be so close to him.

The flicker of lust was unmistakable within his gaze, but her burning anger overshadowed it. Without warning, he lunged forward and seized her wrists, his fingers digging into her delicate skin with a forceful grip. With a rough tug, he forced her to uncross her arms and pulled her toward him.

The sound of their bodies colliding reverberated through the silence, causing a shiver to run down her spine. Her breath caught in her throat as she felt the roughness of his touch, the contrast of his hardened chest against her softness. Despite the pain coursing through her arm, she refused to look away or relinquish her defiant spirit. His hot breath on her face and the intensity of his gaze boring into her made her feel trapped.

"I'll show you what a barbaric renegade will do."

His lips crashed against hers with an insatiable hunger, demanding a response she was determined not to give. Struggling against him with every ounce of strength she possessed, she attempted to break free. His grip only tightened, restraining her arms tightly against her sides. They engaged in an intense battle of wills, their lips pressed together in a clash of desire and resistance.

As the seconds stretched on, she felt a surge of determination. With a sudden burst of energy, she managed to wrench her arm free from his grasp. In that fleeting moment of freedom, she unleashed the full force of her fury. Swinging her arm back with all her might, she delivered a sharp slap across his face that reverberated throughout the room.

The sound echoed like thunder, serving as both an act of defiance and a declaration of independence. The sting of her hand meeting his cheek resonated through her arm, momentarily breaking the spell of desire that had held them captive. As he recoiled from the impact, she stood her ground. In that single moment of boldness, she reclaimed a fragment of her power and autonomy.

The battle was far from over.

"Get off me!" she screamed, her face burning. "You don't get to do that."

Instead of deterring him, her slap only seemed to fuel his desire. The more she fought him, the more he grabbed at her. He wrapped his arms around her and pulled her close. His fingers dug into her back, almost drawing blood.

"The more you fight me, the harder you're making me," Jitatma said in a low voice. "Something tells me you want this."

She felt his hard cock brush against her stomach, hot as a brand. Her heart raged like a wild storm in her chest as his fingers traced down her back, their touch rough and insistent. His eyes bored into hers with a fiery intensity that sent a shiver of raw desire wriggling through her body. He was so close she was almost dizzy from the heady scent of him - sweat, soap, and pure, animalistic male.

"Let go of me. You're a disgusting animal! I hate you and I don't want you to touch me."

"Is that what you really want?" he murmured, his voice husky with unmasked lust. The soft vibrations of his words tickled her earlobe, causing an involuntary moan to escape her lips. She glared defiantly, but inside, her body was betraying her. "Your lips are denying your attraction to me," he taunted, "but your body doesn't lie." His voice was laced with arrogance as he slowly brushed his thumb over her erect nipple in slow, tormenting circles.

She bit down hard on her lower lip to suppress a moan.

His thick fingers pushed aside her dress, allowing it to fall away. She gasped as her nipples met the cool air, becoming pebbled peaks under his gaze. "Beautiful," he whispered hoarsely, dragging a rough finger over one pert nipple, causing it to tighten further under his lascivious attention.

Her back arched involuntarily, pressing her chest into his palm. He smirked at her response before cupping her breast in his large hand, massaging it gently while his thumb continued its torment over her sensitive peak. Her body responded instinctively to his touch, arching against him for more friction. With every swipe of his thumb over her hardened nipple, a tiny moan escaped from somewhere deep within her throat. The sound traveled through the room, only fueling his excruciatingly slow exploration of her body.

"Tell me you want me to stop." His voice was softer, dripping with confidence that she would not resist him.

"Please," she said, just above a whisper.

She pulled herself away from him, her hands deftly adjusting her dress to cover her exposed chest. A soft brush of air tickled her skin as she straightened, a momentary chill lingering in the aftermath of their intimate embrace. She felt his gaze upon her, but she refused to meet it, instead focusing on fixing her clothing and composing herself before facing him again.

"You never said you didn't want it."

Before she could recover from his brazen claim, he slid a hand between her thighs, making her gasp. A jolt of pleasure shot through her at his touch. He slid two long fingers over her slit before guiding them into her warmth. Her pussy greedily took him in while she squirmed under his dominating touch.

She desperately tried to inch away from him, but the confined space of the bathtub offered no escape. Every time she attempted to squirm away, his hands would clamp down on her, dragging her back into his grasp as if it were all part of a twisted game. The porcelain tub echoed with the sound of their struggle, the splashes of water and stifled grunts filling the air.

"Where do you think you're going?"

His fingers remained inside her as he leaned over her, gripping the side of the tub for balance. His solid frame and the unyielding faucet pinned her, pressing her against the cool porcelain. His weight caused a stirring within her, both physically and emotionally. She felt vulnerable and exposed in this intimate moment.

He then began to piston his fingers in and out, setting a slow but steady rhythm. The sounds she made were sinful. Her gasps, moans, and little whimpers mingled with the noises of his hand working her entrance. Suddenly, he curled one finger against a spot deep inside her, causing her body to jolt, and a cry ripped from her lips.

"Oh, Commander!"

A devilish grin found its way to his lips as he began to rub her clit, teasingly in small circles that elicited sweet noises from her that echoed through the room. Her thighs wrapped around him, pulling him closer. Goosebumps erupted across her skin as she writhed under his ministrations. Each twitch, each shudder, only escalated her desire.

"Please, don't stop," she whimpered.

Instead of pushing him away, she clenched her thighs tighter around his waist, as if pleading for even more intimate contact.

Her orgasm seized her, obliterating all rational thoughts, leaving behind a cloud of blissful euphoria in its wake. Her moaning escaped her lips like a song. Each note of ecstasy was more melodious than the previous one until all that was left was silence.

Something within her lost control, and she found herself kissing him passionately, consumed by an overwhelming mix of lust and anger. It was a fight for dominance and control, and neither was willing to give in easily.

He broke their intense embrace, pulling her out of the bath. Water dripped from their bodies as he carried her to the bed in the next room, laying her down on the soft sheets. A sharp gasp escaped her lips as he forcefully tore off the clinging, wet fabric of her dress, exposing her naked body. Hot sensations shot through her as she lay there, entirely at his mercy.

He leaned down and kissed her breast tenderly, a stark contrast to his previous aggression. The tenderness of his touch caught her off guard, making her even more vulnerable and fearful of the power dynamics between them. She shivered, her mind racing with confusion and uncertainty.

"Please," she whispered, her voice barely audible.

"Shh," he murmured, his breath hot on her body. "Submit to your desires, Olivia."

As he spread her legs and pulled her to the edge of the bed, her heart pounded in her chest. She wanted to tell him to stop, but the words caught in her throat, unable to escape. Instead, she watched as he lowered his head, his dark eyes locked on hers. His firm hands gripped her inner thighs, fingers digging into the soft flesh as he held them apart.

His tongue began teasing her pussy, building her excitement and making her squirm beneath him. His touch was tantalizing, and despite herself, she couldn't help but crave more. Then, without warning, he dove in more aggressively, his tongue working its way inside her, asserting his dominance over her pleasure. She hated that she was enjoying it, and even more, she loathed the fact she couldn't bring herself to tell him no. Before she could gather the courage to push him away, her body betrayed her, and she found herself lost in an orgasm that shook her to the core.

He stood tall, looming over her like a predator as he clamped his hand tightly around the side of her neck. His grip was strong and unyielding as he pulled her closer. She felt the heat radiating from his body. Fear and adrenaline flowed through her as she braced herself for whatever was to come next. He kissed her deeply, allowing her to taste her own sweetness, further driving home the fact he was in control and she knew it.

Her body still trembling from her climax and her core wet and wanting, his erection pressed against her. She tried to close her eyes, to retreat into herself, but he wouldn't allow it. His intense stare held her captive, daring her to deny the rush of passion she was feeling.

"Look at me, Olivia," he commanded, his voice firm.

She forced herself to meet his gaze.

He drove himself deep inside her. Her body clung to him, instinctively seeking more, even as her mind screamed for it to stop. As his thrusts grew more insistent, she found herself unable to think coherently. The pleasure coursing through her body was undeniable, but so too was the shame that came with it. She knew she should be resisting, fighting back against this man, but she found herself powerless, both physically and mentally.

"Is this what you wanted?" he taunted, his breath hot on her neck.

She could barely form words, let alone coherent sentences. The waves of pleasure cascading through her were too overwhelming, reducing her to a state of utter submission. She was trapped against the edge of climax, and each second threatened to send her tumbling into the abyss. The pleasure was instant and intoxicating, skewing all rational thoughts with every inch he claimed. His thrusts were slow and deliberate. It was a torturous tempo that left her clawing the sheets beneath them, her body begging for release.

"Commander, deeper," she begged.

He increased his pace in response to her plea, each thrust hitting a sweet spot deep within her, the pleasure coiling tighter and tighter.

"Maybe I will," he said mockingly, "if you tell me how much you're enjoying this."

"Never," she whispered fiercely, burning with defiance even as she was enjoying the pleasure he was giving her.

"Fine," he growled, his movements becoming rougher, more aggressive. "Have it your way."

As he continued mercilessly, she felt a sudden surge of strength within her as fragments of memories flooded her mind. She remembered her former life, her family, her friends. Most importantly, she remembered her twin sister, Talia. She recalled the persistent restlessness that used to plague her relationships. It was an insatiable yearning, a craving for something more enchanting and thrilling, like a whispering promise of excitement just beyond her grasp.

As his muscular body hovered over her, his chiseled abs glistening with trickling beads of sweat, her heart thudded in anticipation.

He didn't make her wait. With a brutal thrust, he buried himself to the hilt, tearing a scream from her throat. His rhythm was both punishing and intoxicating. Each thrust was a revelation, slamming into her with a force that made her see stars. His cock hit that sweet spot deep inside her with every stroke.

"Give in, Olivia. You can't fight your desire."

She gave in to him, unable to resist. She allowed herself to be consumed by him, her moans escaping without restraint. She took him in willingly, moaning uncontrollably. She found his lips, embracing the passion between them.

This man can really fuck!

"Fuck, yes," she gasped, her voice breaking on the last word. The pleasure building inside her rocked her.

He didn't stop.

Instead, he quickened his pace —each thrust more potent than the last, propelling them both toward climax. His cock twitched inside her, signaling his impending release, and with a few more intense pumps, they came together in an explosive climax that left them panting and spent on the soaked sheets.

CHAPTER EIGHT

OLIVIA

A s the early morning light filtered through a small opening in the curtains, casting a warm, golden glow, Olivia and Jitatma embraced. A sense of quiet anticipation filled the atmosphere, as if time had slowed down to honor the connection between them.

Her heart fluttered with a mix of emotions—desire, uncertainty, and a hint of forbidden longing. She knew their closeness was born out of circumstances beyond her control, for he was her captor. Yet, in this tender moment, those barriers seemed to fade away, overshadowed by the intense yearning for love and intimacy.

The room exuded a tranquil stillness, broken only by the soft murmurs of their breaths as they drifted in and out of sleep. She cherished the warmth emanating from his body, savoring the solace she found nestled against him.

With each passing moment, she felt a sense of profound relaxation. The weight of the world slipped away as she surrendered herself to the blissful tranquility surrounding them. She gazed upon his peaceful slumber, admiring his features with newfound tenderness. Leaning down, she pressed her lips against his, delighting in the sweet taste of longing and possibility.

Her fingers traced the contours of his jawline, tracing the familiar lines that showcased strength and vulnerability in equal measure. The softness of her naked body against his served as a silent proclamation of connection and understanding.

"Morning, Minx." He opened his eyes. "I could wake up to that smile for an eternity. Absolutely remarkable."

"Morning, Renegade. You're not angry or upset that I tried to kill you last night?"

"You can't kill me. I was born in the land of the dead, so I can exist in both your world and mine. However, I do admire your efforts to escape."

An overwhelming tidal wave of emotions crashed against her very core. She felt as if her mind were being pulled in a thousand different directions. The sheer intensity of the empathic abilities flooding back into her left her dizzy and disoriented. It felt as if a surge of emotions unleashed, flooding through her consciousness.

"I can feel emotions again. Wow, I can feel everyone's emotions." Olivia broke their embrace. "What's happening to me? It's like I'm feeling all the emotions at once."

He held her tightly. With tender strokes, he caressed her hair, whispering words of comfort that cut through the cacophony of thoughts bombarding her mind.

Her telepathic energy extended far beyond the reach of her twin sister alone. Now she found herself able to perceive the thoughts and feelings of everyone around her. The mental chatter rushed through her mind like turbulent waves crashing upon a shore, each thought vying for attention and recognition.

"You're an empath," he murmured softly, his voice a lifeline in the tempestuous sea of emotions. "Your powers have returned, and it's undoubtedly overwhelming. Take deep breaths and let yourself find your ground."

Acknowledging his wisdom, she nodded, her eyes fluttering shut to block out the external stimuli. She focused on his presence, drawing strength from his soothing voice and the warmth radiat-

ing from his embrace. Inhaling deeply, she allowed herself to sink
into his support and reassurance.

Gradually, with each intentional breath she took, she felt the
incessant rush of thoughts begin to recede like a retreating tide,
making way for a newfound sense of clarity and understanding.
The once jumbled mess of emotions rearranged themselves into
distinct clusters, each emotion taking its rightful place instead of
overwhelming her senses.

In this vulnerable state of heightened perception, she found
herself able to discern the subtle nuances of the emotions pulsating through her. She could now decipher the underlying intentions behind each thought, distinguishing between genuine
feelings and superficial facades. The colors of the emotions painted
vivid strokes across her mind's canvas, illuminating intricate shades
of joy, sorrow, love, and fear.

She opened her eyes and met his gaze. He smiled at her reassur-
ingly before releasing his grip. She sat up, feeling more in control
than before, and looked out the window at the new day. In this
moment, she felt a new sense of peace; a sense of acceptance for
who she was and what she had become since her capture.

"Thank you," she said softly, turning back toward him with
newfound strength.

"Look at yourself now." He propped himself up on his elbow,
reaching for a mirror on his nightstand. She noticed the deep rose
color in her cheeks, soft blue eyes, and glimmering blonde hair.
"The pale gray is gone. Welcome back, Olivia Trismegist. This is
who you are."

"I remember her," she said, admiring her newfound color.
"Commander! I can hear your thoughts."

"Your powers must be amplified in the Far Viscera." Jitatma
smiled. "Then you know."

"You wanted me to fight against you last night. You did that
on purpose." Olivia turned to him, shocked, but amused by his

strategy. "You weren't counting on me being so turned on when I tried to choke you."

"I only wanted to make you angry enough for you to remember who you are." He sighed. "Then I pulled you into the bath and realized you were even more turned on than I was. The color came back to your face. Your hair was turning blonde, but your eyes were still gray." He stared intently as he spoke. "I knew I had to keep pushing. It wasn't until you slapped me that your eyes turned blue. By then, I had lost myself in your spell, and I couldn't stop."

Olivia giggled, trying to lighten the mood. "There's no need to explain or apologize, Commander. Your meeting last night was with my sister."

Jitatma chuckled. "Talia was right about you."

Reading his thoughts, her eyes widened in surprise. "My sister used those words out loud to you? I'm going to kill her when I see her again."

"You should thank her. She knew that if I were controlling, it would trigger your desire and bring back your memory." He shook his head. "You look so sweet and innocent. I never would have guessed your darkest desire is to be dominated by a Sumerian."

She shrugged, a playful smirk dancing on her lips. "I've had enough of the boring, vanilla Anunnakian boys," she declared, her voice tinged with a mix of boredom and mischief. "They're too predictable, always following the same old patterns." Her eyes, sharp and inquisitive, lowered to meet his gaze, to delve into the depths of his thoughts. "Smoke," she mused, her voice softening with curiosity. "Is that any relation to Storm Smoke?"

He met her gaze with a knowing smile, the corners of his eyes crinkling slightly. "You're reading my mind, so you already know the answer to that question. I can sense you in my mind now," he replied, his voice carrying a hint of amusement. A subtle awareness flickered between them, a shared sensation. "Yes, Storm is my half-brother. We share the same mother."

"The irony is fascinating. Storm believes he killed you in a prison fight and you haven't told him the truth." She studied him for a moment, realizing there was more. "He has a twin sister, too!"

"I'll tell him when the time is right, but it's not today. Your sister is here in the Far Viscera. She's coming for you. Are you able to sense Talia?"

"I can sense her, but I can't talk to her," she said, frustrated.

"Keep trying, Minx."

"Minx? Is that what you think of me? Then I will call you Renegade." It was then that an unexpected presence stirred within the room. A soft glow emerged from the corner, gradually growing in intensity until it became a mesmerizing golden-green light. "What is that?"

"That's a Mixie."

"Johara told me about Mixies. She said they were nervous creatures." She giggled, recalling the comparison to Scooter.

I miss that spaz.

He smiled at her. "They can be, but they also encourage your deepest desires with their glow."

The Mixie had awakened, its agile essence infusing the air with an enchanting energy. With playful grace, it darted around the bedposts and curtains, leaving a trail of shimmering light in its wake.

As if drawn to her soul, the Mixie landed delicately on her skin. She gasped softly at its touch, feeling a serene warmth seep into every pore. The magical creature moved with an irresistible gracefulness across her naked form, caressing her breasts and stomach with gentle strokes that sent shivers of pleasure through her.

To her surprise, the Mixie's presence seemed to have a profound effect on Jitatma as well. He sighed deeply, wrapping her in his powerful arms, melding their bodies together in an unspoken agreement. The Mixie continued its delicate dance. Its touch brought forth the raw essence of their true desires, as if reading their thoughts and fulfilling their unvoiced wishes. Nestling itself between them, the Mixie became a symbol of unity, a bridge connecting their separate worlds.

A pulsing intensity set the scene, the Mixie's radiant light casting an iridescent glow over their naked bodies, emphasizing every dip and curve in stunning detail. Tossing her golden hair behind her, she straddled him, her fingers tracing sensual patterns on his chiseled chest.

She slid down, her breasts swaying against his muscular torso, her nipples hardening at the tantalizing friction. His cock stood erect, throbbing in anticipation of her inviting warmth.

"Renegade, is this what you want?"

With a swift movement, she positioned herself above him, teasing him with a playful glide of her wetness against his tip. A low growl escaped from deep within him as she began to lower herself onto him. Inch by delectable inch, she allowed him to enter her warm depths, causing them both to gasp at the exquisite sensation.

"Is that what you really want? Tell me to stop, Renegade," she said in a low, sensual voice, daring him to resist her. Her lips met his, their tongues dancing a sensual tango of desire. He thrust his hips up, meeting the wetness between her thighs as she rode him.

With each grind, she moaned into his mouth. His hands gripped her hips tightly, guiding her movements while he leaned in to nip playfully at her earlobe. She groaned softly, her breath hitching as he trailed hot little kisses down her neck to the valley between her breasts. He teased one rosy nipple with his tongue before taking it into his mouth, suckling hard as he thrust into her wet heat.

Their bodies became a symphony of pleasure; every thrust made her body sing out in ecstasy while his groans provided the perfect bass line. She rode him like the world outside ceased to exist—slowly at first, then faster and deeper with each rhythmic bounce. Her pussy clenched around his cock.

"Oh fuck," he grunted as she ground herself on his cock, pushing him back onto the bed. His eyes met hers, wild and primal, filled with lustful desire.

Her hips gyrated shamelessly as she grew closer and closer to climax. He reached up to grip her bouncing breasts, making her moan louder, throwing her head back in ecstasy as the intensity built up inside her until it seared through every nerve ending, setting off explosive waves of pleasure that left her shaking.

His cock pulsed as he released inside her, their joined bodies riding out waves of pleasure. Their shared climax was a crescendo of delight, leaving them quivering in the aftermath of their passionate coupling. She collapsed onto his chest, spent yet satisfied, her pussy still clenching around him as they savored the intensity of the moment.

He wrapped his arms protectively around her and pulled her close, their sweaty bodies melding together perfectly. Their heavy breathing gradually slowed as they lay tangled in one another—a beautiful mess of limbs and satisfaction.

"That was fucking incredible," he murmured, planting a soft kiss on her forehead.

She gave a satisfied hum against his chest. "Mmm, Commander, we've got to do this again."

"Hundreds of people have called me Commander over the years, but no one says it like you do. I love how it rolls off those beautiful lips of yours."

"I can call you Commander Renegade, if you prefer."

As the Mixie's glow dimmed, it left them in soft shadows of satiation that beautifully encapsulated the remnants of their fiery passion. The world outside had no place here, between these sheets where raw desire ruled and pleasure was their succulent feast.

She lay on the bed staring up to the ceiling. The room fell silent, and she closed her eyes as she focused on her sister. She inhaled deeply, feeling the softness of the sheet against her skin and the warmth of the fire crackling in the hearth. The scent of smoky wood and sweet vanilla permeated the room. She took another deep breath, letting herself sink into a state of calm and concentration.

Talia, I feel your pain. Storm is still breathing, but he's not doing well. I'm going to send him my strength to keep him alive because your protection spell was broken.

Olivia, we've been captured. I failed you.

Don't worry. I'm here now.

It's so good to hear you in my head again. It's been so lonely. I missed you, sis.

"Talia! I can hear her voice again," she said as she opened her eyes. "They've been captured, and Storm is unconscious. Does he know?"

Jitatma said sharply, "It's not the time to tell him."

"When is it going to be a good time? You're his brother. He may die and not know who he is." She sat up as she glared at him. "I can't believe you never said anything."

"I haven't had a chance. When we get through this, I'll tell him about me and his sister, Sully."

"If you don't, I will."

"Right now, we need to get ready for their arrival. Hunter will want to perform the transfer spell, so we won't have a lot of time."

CHAPTER NINE

OLIVIA

O livia anxiously paced back and forth in Jitatma's chambers, wringing her hands. She couldn't shake off the sense of dread that had settled in her heart. She knew it would all be over soon, but a part of her didn't want to leave.

For the past three days, he had held her captive, but surprisingly, she found herself enjoying his company. He was unpredictable and exhilarating, making her feel alive in ways she never thought possible. As much as she tried to suppress the thought, she didn't want to give up their passionate affair to return home.

This is crazy. He kidnapped me.

Despite the circumstances, she couldn't deny the thrill and intensity of their connection. He had stirred something in her. Every tick of the clock felt like an eternity as she waited for his return.

Am I actually thinking about staying?

He appeared in the doorway and reached for her hand. "It's time. Come with me." He gently guided her through narrow passages lined with peeling wallpaper and worn carpets, hidden from the prying eyes of those who walked the grand halls. They passed by doorways that creaked with age and faded paintings. The air was musty and faintly perfumed. He kept a watchful eye out for any signs of movement, ensuring they remained unseen. "Lieutenant Malta has separated them. Hunter has ordered Talia to his private chambers."

"That can't be good. I don't even want to think about what he's going to do to her."

"I've been ordered to get Johara to perform the transfer spell."

They made their way down a twisting staircase of the servant hallways, the sound of their footsteps reverberating off the stone walls.

"If that happens, I'll cease to exist."

As his feet scuffed to a halt, he turned and gazed up at her intensely. His voice was firm as he spoke, determination ringing through every word. "If that happens, I'll make sure he ceases to exist. I'll burn this kingdom before you get to the empty void. I'm not going to allow him a chance to lay a hand on you." He took a step closer. "I command the souls, and he can't have yours."

My kind of man.

With a firm grip, he pulled her down a step until they were almost touching. His strong fingers wrapped around her wrist, sending shivers down her spine. Their faces were mere inches apart, his breath warm and inviting against her skin. She felt an electric current pass between them, igniting a spark of desire. He leaned in closer, and she could see the desire in his eyes. His lips pressed against hers in a slow but firm kiss.

He turned on his heel and continued down the winding staircase. The deeper they descended into the bowels of the castle, the more the light faded until they finally reached the dungeon. The air was thick and musty, with a damp chill that seemed to seep into her bones.

He pulled a long key from his pocket as they came to a far cell. The key scraped against the rusty lock, and the heavy door groaned as it swung open. Her eyes adjusted to the dim light, and she could make out three figures huddled in the corner.

The guards had handcuffed Johara, Scooter, and Storm together, binding their wrists tightly. Johara and Scooter hovered nervously over Storm, who lay sprawled on the ground, clutching his
side in pain. The metallic clink of the handcuffs echoed in the tense
silence between them. Blood seeped through Storm's torn shirt,
staining the ground beneath him. He struggled to sit up, his face
contorted in agony.

"Olivia! I'm so glad to see you," Scooter said as he jumped up.

"I missed you, too, Scooter." She rushed to Storm's side, checking his wounds. "How are you doing? I'm glad to see you awake."

"I'm alive, but barely."

Jitatma moved closer to Scooter, reaching out to touch the
handcuffs on his wrists. With a quick flick of his thumb, the metal
retracted into itself until all that remained was a small stick. He
pressed the button on the end twice and then gestured for Scooter
to do the same.

"That should give you access to release the cuffs. All you have to
do is press your thumb to the center," Jitatma said. He turned to
Storm. "Can you walk? We need to move quickly."

Scooter pressed his thumb to Storm and Johara's cuffs. The
quiet click of the device echoed through the room as they both
disengaged their restraints.

"Talia needs you, Storm." Olivia nodded.

Storm grimaced but managed to pull himself upright. He leaned
heavily on Scooter for support. Scooter's strength amazed Olivia
as he carried his friend out of the cell with ease. Jitatma glanced
around the shadowy dungeon before leading them through the
servant hall toward Hunter's chambers. The hum of distant conversations filled the narrow corridors.

As they approached Hunter's private chambers, the muffled
voices of Talia and Hunter became clearer. Jitatma turned to
Scooter and Storm. "Wait here in the servants' hallway. I'll get
Hunter out of his chambers." He pointed to a door in front of
them. "When I do, go through that door and get Talia. She's the

only one who can make Hunter vulnerable. She needs to get his ring." He turned to Johara. "Do you remember the power stripping spell?"

Johara nodded.

He gestured for Olivia and Johara to follow him through a door on the right, into the judgment chambers. Olivia glanced back at Scooter and Storm, worried about them. They nodded, urging her to continue. She turned and followed Jitatma and Johara into the dimly lit room. Jitatma disappeared into Hunter's private chambers in the corner of the room.

"Ah, Princess Johara," Hunter sneered, as he and Jitatma emerged into the judgment chambers a few moments later. "Your skills are needed to perform a crucial task."

"I will never help you!" Princess Johara yelled, her gaze steely and unbroken.

"Your defiance is admirable, but futile," Hunter continued, unfazed. "You see, I plan to take Olivia's soul and place it in Talia's body."

"You can't have my soul, asshole," Olivia said.

"Impossible! Even if I wanted to, I couldn't force someone's soul into another person," Johara protested, brows furrowed in disgust.

"Ah, but that's where you're mistaken." Hunter smirked. "You can, and you will. You have your mother's magic, and you know the spell."

"I'd like to see you try." Olivia crossed her arms in front of her chest. "I don't care who the fuck you think you are."

He leaned closer to Johara, his voice barely more than a whisper. "I need that soul, Princess. I will have it, one way or another. Do not test my patience, child."

"Your obsession will be your undoing, Hunter," she warned, her voice steady and strong. "You cannot force me to bend to your vile desires."

"Is that so?" Hunter sneered. "Perhaps you'll reconsider when you see what I'm capable of."

Hunter had hardly finished his sentence when the red doors of the judgment chamber burst open and splinters of wood flew. Storm, who had transformed into the Minotaur, charged into the room. His nostrils flared and his hooves pounded against the floor. The fury in his eyes was unmistakable; he was out for blood and revenge.

I can't wait for my sister to kick your ass.

Talia appeared in Hunter's judgment chambers. Olivia stood a few paces away, every muscle tensed with the urge to rush to her sister's side, yet she held back, knowing the gravity of the situation. She had never seen Talia look so terrified, her usual confident demeanor stripped away.

Hunter pressed his advantage by trapping Storm in a glass cage and grabbing Talia by the arm. Olivia felt the oppressive weight of the king's sinister intentions bearing down on her mind, a dark cloud looming as he leaned over her sister. The scene unfolded with chilling clarity as Hunter forced Talia toward the pool of blood, the raw hunger in his eyes unmistakable.

Desperation surged through Olivia. She took a step, ready to sprint across the room. Jitatma held her back, his presence calm and steady amidst the chaos. He leaned in close, his voice a soft murmur in her ear. "Trust in the plan. Talia must face this alone."

"I have to help her."

Jitatma's grip on her arm tightened slightly. "She needs to get his ring," he whispered. "Only she can do this."

Olivia's heart pounded in her chest as she watched Hunter drag Talia closer to the pool. Her sister's eyes met hers briefly, and in that moment, Olivia saw something shift in Talia's expression—a flicker of determination beneath the fear.

She watched intently as her sister skillfully maneuvered to gain the upper hand, deftly snatching Hunter's ring from his finger. The ring glinted in the dim light as Talia slipped it onto her own finger, a symbol of her newfound control. This action left Hunter defenseless, vulnerable, and exposed, allowing Johara the chance she needed to begin the intricate spell to strip him of his powers. The air crackled with energy as Talia joined in, their voices blending in a harmonious chant, weaving a web of enchantment around Hunter.

CHAPTER TEN

OLIVIA

S he selected an outfit with care, wanting to make a good impression. After much contemplation, she finally settled on an ensemble that exuded confidence and elegance, a subtle nod to the empowered woman she had become since returning from the Far Viscera. Before she left the apartment, it occurred to her she wasn't sure who she was trying to impress.

She had left Jitatma behind. Her time in the Far Viscera lingered in her thoughts. She wanted that thrill and excitement again, doubting if she would ever find it anywhere else. The Anunnakian men seemed dull compared to the charismatic charm and magnetic presence of the commander. Her mundane life was no match for the adrenaline-fueled adventure she had.

I would give anything to have sex with that man again.

Oliva walked next to her sister, while Storm and Scooter trailed behind. They had barely made it inside the main building on campus when she heard high-pitched giggles from a distance. As the twins turned around, a group of girls, all fluttering eyelashes and eager smiles, descended on Storm, surrounding him.

Olivia rolled her eyes. "Guess he's got that effect on everyone," she said, smirking. "Are you going to rescue him?"

"No, I'd like to see what he does." She tilted her head to the side, assessing him.

They stood, silently observing as the group of girls surrounded him, reaching out to touch him. The tallest girl, her curls bouncing with each excited step, moved closer than the rest. As she brushed herself against him, a beaming smile spread across her face. Olivia couldn't help but recognize the familiar move—the pouty lip and whispered words that always seemed to work.

"Aren't you concerned, Talia?" Scooter asked as he approached. "You know, Julie has been after Storm for some time now."

"I'm not worried. I want to see how he gets himself untangled from their clutches."

Scooter chuckled. "I tried to warn him Julie and her friends were descending on him, but he was too busy staring at you to listen." He shook his head. "I wish I had that superpower."

Pathetic. I would never throw myself at a man like that. Weak, foolish, little girls. Never need a man more than he needs you.

Harsh, sis, even for you.

I'm in a mood.

Yeah, ultimate, mega crabby bitch. If you were a man, I would think you were in your Quickening.

Unable to bear the awkwardness, Olivia hurriedly said, "I have to get to class." She walked away, but she could feel Scooter's presence. Without looking back, she quickened her pace, his footsteps echoing close behind her.

"Olivia," he called, his voice was hesitant, almost pleading. "Can I ask you something?"

She turned to face him, her heart heavy with the weight of their impending conversation. She could already sense the scattered array of thoughts and emotions churning in his mind, but his voice came through clearly and urgently in her own mind. With a sigh, she decided to take pity on him and offer her help. His face was drawn and desperate, eyes pleading for understanding and support.

"Yes, Scooter."

"I need to ask you a favor, or advice, or opinion. I'm not really sure what I'm asking or what I need. I don't know where to even start." He rambled on. "Yes, I need your help. That's what I need. I would ask Storm, but he seems busy with, you know, Talia and everything. I can't seem to get his attention lately to even ask him. I mean, he's my friend and he's a guy, but I think I need a woman's perspective. Well, you seem to have experience and you're a woman."

"Scooter, I already said yes. You can shut up and listen now."

"I didn't even ask yet."

"You want to know how to get attention from women." She smiled. "Does this have anything to do with a certain beautiful princess?"

"Well, she's a queen now," he corrected her. "She's out my league. I'm speaking in general. I don't need them fighting over me like they do with Storm, but it would be nice to hold the attention of at least one."

"You aren't built like Storm. I mean, physically you're not, but you do have other things you can offer."

"Like what?"

"Let me show you. No matter what you look like, it's all about confidence." She scanned the courtyard and found a target. She found Chad and Kyle in their usual spot at the corner of the corridor. "Give me your lab coat and glasses."

Scooter looked confused. "What for?"

She pointed over her shoulder. "Do you see those two assholes over there?"

"That's Chad and Kyle, the bullies."

He did as she asked, handing them over to her. She slipped the lab coat over her outfit and buttoned it all the way up. She rustled her long hair into a ponytail and put on his glasses.

"Well, on the first day, they decided to hit on me when I was wearing an outfit more revealing than the one I have on. I wasn't having it, so I put them in their place." She swung her bag over her shoulder. "I guarantee that dressed like this, they won't even look at me, but I'll make them notice. Watch and learn."

With Scooter following closely, she approached Chad and Kyle. They looked in her direction, but they seemed uninterested in her conservative attire. She felt their eyes on her as she neared, but their gazes were different now—curious and intrigued, rather than leering and predatory.

Good, they're disarmed by my appearance.

"Chad, right?" she said, her voice soft and demure.

"Do I know you?"

"Well, not really, but I would like to get to know you and your friend," she said as she leaned in really close to give them a peek at her neckline, but nothing more.

"Nice lab coat," Kyle said.

"I thought so." She smiled wickedly. "I'd like to show you what's underneath it if you're game."

The two men stood straight, their eyes trained on her with heightened interest. She had captured their attention completely. As they stared, she removed Scooter's glasses and let her hair down. Her transformation was instantaneous, and their expressions of shock and desire were priceless. She chuckled to herself, feeling a rush of satisfaction. Without waiting for a response, she turned on her heel and sauntered away, leaving them stunned and speechless. She handed Scooter his glasses with a grin.

"See? It's not just about looks. It's about how you present yourself and the confidence you exude."

She glanced over her shoulder and noticed the two men still had their eyes on her. She decided to give Scooter a little boost in his confidence. With a subtle smile, she held out his lab coat for him to slip back into. As she did, she pressed her palm against the center of his back, feeling the warmth of his body through the fabric.

"What did you just do?" Scooter asked as he turned to face her with flushed cheeks.

"Nothing."

"Then why do I feel all weird?"

His face had turned a deep shade of red, and he looked down at his pants with a mixture of embarrassment and confusion. She could see the outline of his hard-on through the fabric. He looked up at her with wide eyes as he scrambled to conceal his arousal behind his lab coat.

As she frantically searched for a way to hide her own reaction, she couldn't believe what she was witnessing. She didn't think it was possible. This was not supposed to happen with Enochian men. Niberians knew they were immune to Nibmark stimulants, but she saw it firsthand.

"Close your lab coat," she insisted. "I thought Enochian men don't have Nibmark stimulants."

"We don't. What's happening? What do I do about this?" he asked, panic rising in his voice. "I can't walk around like this."

She shrugged. "You're going to have to take care of it."

"How? I'm asking for instructions, Olivia. I've never had this happen before. How do I make it normal again?"

"You're kidding, right?" She intently studied the desperation on his face, searching for any hint of deception. She saw the lines etched into his forehead, the way his eyes darted back and forth, and the quiver in his voice. She sensed no trace of deceit in his thoughts, only an overwhelming sense of helplessness and despair. "You're serious. You've never jacked off before. Of course not. No, no, no. You're on your own for this one."

"You did this. Please, help me. I just need guidance on what to do."

"This is for instructional purposes only and this is our secret. You can't even tell Storm," she insisted. "I can't believe I'm about to do this. Do you know somewhere private we can go?"

"I have a small office."

His hand closed tightly around her wrist, pulling her across the bustling campus toward the Science building. They ascended the grand staircase, its marble steps worn smooth by countless footsteps, and turned right toward the Harrington wing. As they walked down the hallway, lined with posters and bulletin boards advertising various research projects, Scooter suddenly stopped at a nondescript door. He swiftly entered a code into the key lock and pushed it open, revealing a small office.

The room was oppressive, barely able to contain a single desk and chair without feeling suffocating. There were no windows to let in the natural light, making the space feel even more cramped. Various devices cluttered every inch of the room, their parts strewn haphazardly, and a tangled web of wires snaked around every surface.

"How do you have an office?" she asked as she pushed aside some wires on his desk to lean against it.

"It's a long story," he said, sitting in the chair. "I would like to take care of this situation first."

"I can't believe I'm about to teach you how to masturbate. How does this happen to me? If this gets too weird, I'm leaving you to figure it out. Try not to pass out." She turned her back and began her instructions. "You can start by taking your cock out of your pants. Grab it from about the center and slide your hand up and down. Use a firm grip, but not too tight. You want to feel the pressure but not cause any pain."

"How do I know I'm doing it right?"

With a graceful twist of her body, she turned to look over her shoulder. Her eyes widened in surprise as she took in his impressive length. She never would have guessed. His head was tilted back, exposing the firm line of his jaw and the slight stubble that covered it. His eyes were closed, but she could see the flutter of his eyelashes against his flushed cheeks. She watched him for a moment, her gaze roaming over every inch of his face, drawn in by the raw emotion reflected there, more for curiosity rather than desire.

Not bad for an Enochian.

"Scooter, why are you reciting the core laws in your head?" she asked, reading his mind. "Why are you focused on the sixth law?"

"It's a new theory I'm working on. I'm trying to prove the sixth law didn't come from our gods for Storm and Talia."

"I guess whatever trips your trigger to tickle your fancy, buddy." She rolled her eyes. "Does it feel good?"

"Holy Anu!" he moaned.

"Yep, you're doing it right. Play with the head of your cock, too," she continued, not wanting to stop the instructions. She felt empowerment teaching a man about self-care. "It's sensitive and feels amazing when you use your thumb to rub it."

"How do you know this?" he asked, almost breathless.

"Years of experience doing it to men." She smiled. "Wait until you experience your first blow job."

"What's that?"

"Your innocence amazes me, Scooter. There's so much for you to learn."

"Will you teach me?"

"I'm not going to be responsible for your sexual awakening. The others can't find out about this."

"Ouch!" he yelled. "I don't think I'm doing it right."

"I can't have you hurting yourself." With a quiet grunt, she pushed herself away from the edge of the desk and made her way over to him, her heels clicking against the tiled floor. She felt the smooth, cool surface of the wood against her palms as she steadied herself before reaching out to touch him.

With a raised eyebrow and a startled expression, he pushed back his chair. "Olivia, what are you doing?"

"Scooter, I have to get to class. I can't use the excuse that I was late because I was helping an Enochian man pleasure himself in his office." She sighed. "We have to move this along. I can make you finish faster."

"What happens when I finish?"

"Right. You don't know. It's called an orgasm and you're in for a treat." She smiled. "Hold on to something. This is going to be fun."

She wrapped her hand around his shaft, marveling at the velvety softness of his skin. She began to stroke him slowly, savoring the feeling of his hardness in her hand. She heard his breathing growing heavier as she increased her pace, her hand sliding up and down his length.

Her eyes locked onto his face. She could feel his muscles tensing and releasing under her touch, urging her to continue. With a firm grasp, she quickened her pace, determined to push him to the brink of ecstasy. He let out a moan, his hips involuntarily thrusting toward her. He gripped the arms of the chair, knuckles turning white with the intensity of the moment.

"Hold still, Scooter. It's almost done," she whispered. "You're doing great."

With a subtle lean, she extended her arm, tenderly taking hold of his balls. Her fingers moved with purpose, rubbing them in a circular motion. As she picked up speed, she felt the tightening of his skin. His moans grew louder, filling the room and echoing off the walls. She knew he was close to climaxing, and she savored the power she held in bringing him to such pleasure.

"Almost there," she encouraged him. "If you like this, you're going to love the next part."

Sensing the tension in his body, she slowly slid her hand from his sensitive balls to his chest, gently pressing her palm against his racing heart. The thump of his pulse echoed beneath her touch, drumming a wild rhythm against her skin. She felt him beginning to relax under her soothing touch, his muscles loosening and his breaths slowing in time with hers.

"What's happening?" he said as his body tensed up again.

"That's it," she said sweetly. "Just let it happen. Trust me, Scooter."

He tensed beneath her touch as she moved faster, her fingers wrapping around him tighter, her grip just right, encouraging the moment he couldn't hold back any longer. She watched as his face scrunched up and her free hand stroked his cheek softly to keep him focused on her, not letting go until she knew he was about to release.

He let out a grunt between heavy breaths as he exhaled sharply before it erupted over her hand and on his shirt. She leaned closer and kissed his cheek gently before standing up and stepping back with a grin.

"How are you feeling?"

"Holy Anu! I feel like I can take on the world."

"I'll make you a deal. If you can keep your mouth shut, I'll help you build your confidence. There's so much to learn." She smiled. "Who knows? You might be able to talk to Johara about normal stuff."

"What do you mean?"

"Scooter, talking about interdimensional travel to a woman isn't exactly a turn-on. Maybe our second lesson should be topics of conversation and simple ways to engage a woman."

"Thank you, Olivia. I didn't realize what I was missing."

"Congratulations on your first orgasm. Keep practicing and you'll be as good as me."

CHAPTER ELEVEN

OLIVIA

Talia's feet tapped a nervous rhythm on the hardwood floor of the living room, her purple wedding dress swishing around her ankles. Her fingers danced over the intricate beading and delicate embroidered flowers that adorned the bodice and skirt. Each tiny detail was a labor of love from Olivia, made just for her sister. The dress hugged her curves, flowing gracefully behind her as she moved.

Gently perched on the couch, Olivia meticulously applied a final touch to her nails. Her lavender bridesmaid dress hugged her figure flawlessly, the low-cut neckline stressing her chest and small waist with a subtle grace. She focused on perfecting every detail of her appearance, determined to look her best for Jitatma.

It was the day she was going to lose her sister. The air was thick with anticipation, and the clock ticked relentlessly, marking only an hour until the wedding ceremony. She tried hard to be happy for her sister as she prepared to marry Storm. Yet, beneath her smile lay the aching realization that things would inevitably change once Talia and Storm exchanged vows.

Their childhood memories seemed to swirl around her—echoes of shared secrets and late-night giggles—now about to shift into something new and unknown. They had always shared not just the same space but also their thoughts and dreams, and now her sister was moving downstairs. Although she wasn't leaving the house entirely, it felt as if she might as well be relocating to the Sumer region.

"Talia, you're going to make me nervous if you don't stop pacing," she said. "I don't understand why you're so worried."

She sighed. "I'm not used to being the center of attention like you. What if I trip and fall flat on my face?"

"If you do, Storm is strong enough to catch you. You'll be fine. All you have to do is smile and keep your focus on him."

Talia turned her back. "Are you sure about wearing my hair up? I mean, this dress shows off my fake Nibmarks. I can't hide them."

"I designed the dress that way on purpose. Your secret is out now. Everyone knows you're human, so show it off." Olivia shrugged. "Besides, you look beautiful with your hair up."

Sprinting to the door, she said, "I have to see him."

Olivia watched her sister dart down the spiral staircase at lightning speed. Her feet barely touched the steps as she flew past, heading through Delphi's shop. She scrambled to keep up with her sister, her heart pounding in her chest. Talia was a blur as she raced through the beaded curtains and into the kitchen, disappearing around the corner toward the basement door. But just as she reached for the knob, Delphi appeared in front of her like a formidable obstacle, blocking her way with a stern expression on her face.

"I'm sorry, Delphi. She got away from me."

"Talia, you know the rules," Delphi said firmly. "Get your butt back upstairs until the wedding. I mean it, young lady."

"She's not joking," Johara said as she came into the kitchen, carrying the three bouquets of flowers and a box. She handed the box to Delphi. "These are the flower pins for the men. Can you take them downstairs? Olivia and I will take the bride back upstairs."

Olivia dragged her out of the kitchen. "Come on, sis. You don't even have shoes on."

"My shoes are heels," Talia whined. "Are you sure that was a good idea? I'm going to fall."

"They're only an inch. You're not going to fall. Let's practice walking in them. You can pace the living room with them for the next hour." Olivia pushed her sister up the stairs. She turned to Johara as they went back into the apartment. "The flowers are gorgeous. Where did you find flowers with such a deep color?"

The bridesmaid flowers were a stunning blend of delicate lavender roses and pure white lilies. In contrast, Talia's bouquet was a bold statement of deep purple roses, each one velvety and rich in color. The white lilies intertwined with the roses, cascading down like a waterfall of beauty and elegance.

"These are a special gift from Empress Ki. She handpicked them from the garden in the Afterlife and color matched the roses to our dresses."

Talia opened the door to the apartment and bolted again. Olivia took two quick steps to the door but stopped in her tracks at the sight of their mother standing in the middle of the living room. She was grateful for the reinforcements in controlling her sister and keeping her on task. It had been a grueling day so far, constantly chasing after Talia and trying to divert her attention away from Storm.

"Mom!" Talia said as she hugged her.

"My beautiful girls. Look at you two," Mom said as her hands went over her heart and tears formed in her eyes. "I'm not going to cry."

"I'm going to cry tears of exhaustion," Olivia said. "I forgot how fast Talia can run."

Talia giggled. "You never could keep up."

"Let's get your shoes on. Maybe heels will slow you down," Johara suggested.

"I doubt it."

Talia vanished into her bedroom. A few moments later, she burst out with a bundle of energy, racing toward the living room door and yanking it open, a gust of cold air flooding into the apartment. Olivia quickly followed in her sister's wake, their steps clattering down the back steps in tandem.

As they reached Storm's patio door, Scooter suddenly appeared to block her sister's path.

"Scooter, move out of my way or I'll give you a zap."

"You can fry me like bacon, but I'm not letting you in this door. I have my orders," Scooter replied, his tone firm.

Olivia called, "Talia, get your butt back up here! You're not ready yet."

Talia stomped back up to the apartment.

"Talia, you only have an hour left," Mom said gently. "I know it's hard, but you can wait to see Storm."

Once the ceremony was complete, Jitatma opened a portal to the Far Viscera for the reception, revealing a space filled with soft light that radiated warmth and welcome despite its vastness. Lavish decorations adorned the corners, from the ethereal purple and silver walls to the stunning mural of the starry night sky above and the gleaming marble floors below. In the center hung a magnificent chandelier, dripping with candlelight, adding to the enchanting atmosphere. Delicate drapes in shades of violet cascaded from the ceiling, framing tall windows that offered a breathtaking view of the moonlit landscape outside. All around them, fragrant roses in hues of violet and lavender added to the magical ambiance of the enchanted ballroom.

Exhausted after a long day of chasing Talia, Olivia headed straight for the bar. The neon lights flickered above her as she pushed her way through the crowded room. Her feet ached, and her throat was dry. She leaned against the counter and closed her eyes, relishing the refreshing taste of the wine as it slid down her throat. The bustling sounds of conversations and clinking glasses faded into the background as she took a moment.

More like thirty-seven drinks.

Jitatma's gaze had hardly lingered on her all day, his attention seemed to be elsewhere. She had longed for a moment alone with him during the evening, but her attempts had been in vain. Every time she thought she might have his undivided attention, something or someone would pull him away. Despite her efforts, he remained elusive and distant, leaving her longing for even the slightest acknowledgement.

"Well, hey there, beautiful. Can I buy you a drink?" a man's voice said.

As she turned, she saw a breathtaking sight. A handsome soldier stood leaning against the bar, his broad shoulders and strong jawline catching her attention immediately. His smile was warm and inviting, drawing her in like a magnet. She felt a flutter in her stomach.

It's not Jitatma, but he'll work.

"How about you buy my next one?" she offered, quickly finishing her first one. "Oh, look at that. I need another one."

The soldier chuckled and signaled the bartender for another round. She felt a little guilty for using him as a distraction, but she quickly pushed the thought aside. The night was young, and she deserved some fun, even if it wasn't with the man she truly wanted.

As they chatted and laughed, her gaze kept wandering to the entrance of the ballroom, hoping to catch a glimpse of Jitatma. He was nowhere to be seen, and her heart sank with every passing moment.

Just as she was about to give up hope, she noticed a figure standing in the shadows, watching her intently. It was Jitatma. Her heart skipped a beat, and a warmth spread through her body. She was about to excuse herself and go to him, but the soldier leaned in closer, his hand brushing against hers on the counter. She hesitated for a moment, torn between her desire to speak with Jitatma and the kindness of the man before her.

She sensed the unmistakable feeling of jealousy.

It seems I have your attention now, Commander.

If he touches you again...

She motioned for the soldier to come closer, taking a small step toward him. The soldier's hand moved to the small of her back. From the corner of her eye, she saw Jitatma's jaw tighten and his fists clench at his sides. The sight of him so visibly upset only fueled her desire to push his buttons. The soldier started to lean in to whisper something in her ear, but he straightened and backed away from her instead.

"Soldier, attend to your post," Jitatma commanded from behind her.

"Yes, Commander," he said, disappearing into the crowd.

She spun on her heel, her hands resting firmly on her hips. "What did you do that for? You don't get to control me anymore, Commander. I'm not one of your soldiers."

He moved closer, his voice low and harsh as he spoke. "You're still my Minx."

"Really? I couldn't tell. You haven't looked in my direction, and you certainly haven't paid a moment of attention to me. I had to get it from somewhere else."

"Trust me, Minx. I've noticed. Now I have a moment."

With a firm grasp on her hand, he whisked her out of the crowded ballroom. He pulled her toward the side entrance of the judgment chambers, where they could find a moment of privacy in the shadows. The dimly lit corner provided a brief respite from the blaring music and hectic energy of the party. He pinned her against one of the marble columns, pressing against her. She felt his erection through his pants.

His hot breath brushed against her neck as he spoke. "You've been teasing me all night, Minx. I don't like it when another man touches you." He closed his eyes for a moment, taking a deep breath. "I can't control myself when I see it." The tension in his body eased slightly as he pulled away from her, running his hands through his hair.

She laughed softly, shaking her head as if amused by his antics. "You think I didn't notice? You were watching me from the shadows the whole time." Her voice held a playful edge, but there was an underlying current of defiance. She enjoyed the way he watched her so closely, even though it made her feel trapped sometimes.

His eyes flashed with anger before turning soft once more. "I couldn't help it. You look so beautiful tonight," he admitted grudgingly. He reached out to trace her jawline with his index finger, lifting her chin for her eyes to meet his gaze.

"Losing your control, Renegade." She smiled wickedly. "We're not in your private chambers anymore, so you've lost your command of me."

"Never, Minx."

His hand wandered down to her side. Olivia pressed herself against him again, relishing the feel of his brawny arms around her waist. She leaned in close enough for her lips to graze his as she whispered back, "You think I'm yours to take?"

"I thought I made it clear that you belong to me," he murmured, his voice low and husky. His eyes blazed with an intensity that made Olivia's knees weak.

She responded with a teasing grin, her fingers tracing the outline of his muscular chest. "Oh, did you? I must have missed that message."

Jitatma's response was swift and forceful. His lips crashed into hers, demanding and possessive. Olivia melted into the kiss, her body responding to his touch with an intensity that left her breathless.

The scent of his cologne mixed with the sweetness of lavender from their surroundings, creating an intoxicating aroma that filled her nostrils and made her dizzy with longing. The cool marble beneath them provided a stark contrast to their burning passion, but it only added to the intensity of their encounter. Their kiss deepened, becoming more urgent and demanding as they explored each other's mouths hungrily.

Her hands found their way underneath his jacket, tracing the lines of his defined abs with reverence before moving up to grasp his broad shoulders. She felt him tense under her touch but didn't stop there; she continued up to run her fingers through his hair, tangling them in the silky strands as she pulled him even closer.

He groaned into her mouth, a low rumble that vibrated through their bodies. He stepped back slightly, taking in a ragged breath, as if trying to regain some semblance of control.

They heard the double red doors creak open, followed by approaching footsteps.

"Commander, are you in here?" Olivia heard Anu's voice call. "We have a situation."

Jitatma appeared from the other side, his brow furrowed with concern.

"Yes, Anu."

"The Dark Haunting has escaped, and it's taking over the Afterlife."

"If it's on Enlightenment Mountain, that means it'll be here soon."

The group gathered in the judgment chambers, an air of unease settling over them like a heavy cloak. Anu stood near the pool of blood, scanning the faces of those assembled. Olivia clutched Johara's hand.

"The Dark Haunting," Anu began, his voice steady despite the gravity of the situation, "is an ancient force that threatens the balance of our realms. Its power is immense, and it feeds on chaos and evil. It has not been seen in eons, but it seems someone has let it out."

As the pool of blood shifted and swirled, a figure emerged from its depths. Blood dripped down her pale skin, revealing Lady Anasazi in all her sinister glory.

"That someone would be my stupid husband," she said, stepping down from the edge of the pool. "Somehow, he managed to get several spells from the Book of the Dead."

"I protected the book," Delphi said.

"Well, it seems you didn't do a good enough job," Anasazi snapped. "Apparently, while all of you were busy with Hunter, Gorgon has been running around collecting favors."

"We led him right to the Book of the Dead," Talia said, putting her hands on her hips.

"Everything Gorgon has been doing has been a smokescreen, including breaking Hunter out of jail. I knew he was up to something," Anu said.

"Shit! I owe him a favor." Storm ran his hands through his hair. "He's going to come to collect."

"I'd love to see him try. I fought one god. I can fight another," Talia spat.

Anu's expression darkened as he turned toward Storm, his voice cold and resolute. "Gorgon is a master manipulator, and he will not hesitate to exploit any weakness or debt to further his own goals."

Storm's brow furrowed as he clenched his fists. "Gorgon has underestimated us if he thinks we'll be so easily defeated. I will not let him disrupt the balance of the realms."

"I need another drink. I'll be at the bar," Olivia said.

Olivia left the judgment chambers, her heart heavy with the weight of the situation. She could hear the murmurs of their worried voices in her head. As she reached the bar, she felt unease. Anu was holding something back, but she couldn't read his mind.

What good is my new power if I can't use it to read the minds of gods?

The bartender greeted her with a smile. "What can I get you, miss?"

Olivia sighed, running a hand through her hair. "Whatever's strong enough to take the edge off."

The bartender nodded knowingly, pouring her a generous glass of amber liquid. "This ought to do the trick."

She took a sip, savoring the burn as it traveled down her throat. It was a welcome distraction from the chaos of the evening.

"I see you took my advice about Jitatma," Anasazi said as she approached Olivia.

"I can handle the commander's charm," Olivia responded coolly, her gaze never leaving the amber liquid in her glass. "I can handle anything he throws my way."

Anasazi chuckled, a dark, sultry sound. "Oh, I have no doubt about that, but the Dark Haunting is a different story."

Olivia raised an eyebrow. "What do you know about it?"

The goddess leaned in, her voice barely above a whisper. "Only that it is ancient and powerful. It feeds on the darkness within us all, and it will stop at nothing to consume everything in its path."

A shiver ran down Olivia's spine. "What can we do to stop it?"

Anasazi's lips curled into a wicked smile. "That's what we're trying to figure out, my dear."

"With all the active powers of the gods, I would think there would be some way to get rid of it." Oliva took another sip of her drink, leaning against the bar. Looking away for a moment, she felt a pang of envy. "I could only dream of having an active power."

Anasazi tilted her head. "Your jealousy runs as deep as my own."

"That's not what I would call it."

"Really? What would you call it?" Anasazi paused for a moment. "Your sister seems to have everything. She got the active power, all the attention, and now the man she loves. I can hear the bitterness in your voice."

"I'm happy for Talia."

"I was happy for Circe at one time. I mean, she controlled all the magic, everyone admired her, and she had a loving marriage." She sighed. "Then she turned on me and decided she wanted my husband. How long do you think it's going to take for Talia to turn on you?"

"She would never do that."

"I was foolish to think that too, but it happened. You and I aren't so different."

CHAPTER TWELVE

ΛNASAZI

The fierce wind howled and whipped against the stone walls of Gorgon's castle, heralding Anasazi's arrival. The imposing doors creaked open as she barged in, her presence demanding attention. Despite her best efforts, her powers threatened to break free at any moment, fueled by a deep-seated anger. She was determined to get answers from her estranged husband, no matter the cost.

She despised visiting his dark, imposing castle. That was why she had built her own sanctuary on the hill, a fortress that overshadowed his castle in size and strength. From its high vantagepoint, she could see the entire kingdom sprawled below, a reminder that she was no longer a prisoner at his mercy. The walls were thick and impenetrable, crafted from the strongest ice and reinforced with magic. Inside, she found peace and solace away from the oppressive presence of his castle. It was her haven, where she could finally be free to rule as she pleased.

Her icy footsteps covered the floor as she made her way down to her husband's chamber. The servants scrambled to get out of her way as she headed for the winding staircase. The throne room loomed ahead, its immense size a testament to his ego. Anasazi hesitated for a moment, her breath hitching as she gathered her strength. She closed her eyes, taking a deep breath before pushing open the heavy wooden doors.

He sat on his throne, a self-satisfied smirk playing upon his lips as he watched her approach. She wanted to smack that look off his face. With her fists clenched, nails digging into her palms, she held back.

"Gorgon," she said, her voice sharp and unyielding. "We need to talk."

"Ah, my dear Anasazi. To what do I owe this pleasure?" His tone was mocking.

"Don't play games with me, Gorgon. You know exactly why I'm here," she said firmly. "I just came from the Far Viscera where I had a conversation with Anu and Jitatma. What are you doing with the Book of the Dead?"

"I don't have the book."

"You're the only one stupid enough to use dark magic to release the Dark Haunting."

"Hunter had been using dark magic to find his lost wife and control Talia. He's just as guilty." He leaned back, resting his elbows on the arms of his throne. "How do you know he didn't set it free?"

She took a step forward, narrowing her eyes, her voice laced with frustration. "Hunter doesn't have the power to use that much dark magic, and he's been in a prison cell. You love chaos and would never give up an opportunity to unleash it. Are you bored, husband? I'm sure you could find another Sumerian whore to entertain you. At least you'd be fucking them and not destroying our realm."

"I'm not destroying anything. I'm taking what's mine, you cold-hearted bitch."

"How many favors have you collected?"

"Not enough." He shrugged. "You can go back to your own castle and worry about something else, my dear."

"This isn't over," she warned. "If you cross me, I will freeze your dick. I'm certainly not using it, and neither should you. It's what started this mess. Control yourself, husband."

His hand curled into a tight fist, the muscles in his arm bulging. With a flick of his wrist, he conjured a bright ball of fire, crackling with heat and energy. As he rose to throw it at her, she remained unfazed, her attitude calm and unwavering. The fireball hurtled toward her in a searing arc, its heat radiating in waves.

In response to Gorgon's menacing gesture, her own power flared to life. A faint shimmer of frost danced along her fingertips, a prelude to the icy storm that brewed within her. Casually extending her hand toward the fireball, she froze it in midair. It hung there for a moment before plummeting to the ground, shattering into a million pieces at her feet. A victorious smirk tugged at her lips as she met his stunned gaze.

"You may have frozen my fire, Anasazi, but you cannot extinguish my will. The realms will bow before me, whether you stand by my side or against me."

"Your will?" Her laughter echoed through the cavernous throne room, each note dripping with contempt. "Your will has always been your weakness. You're a child with too much power and too little sense." She stepped over the glittering shards of frozen fire. The frost from her footsteps spread in delicate patterns before melting into the darkness. "I'll discover what you're planning, Gorgon. When I do, you'll wish I'd only frozen your dick."

Anasazi sat alone in the kitchen, a small box on the table beside her. The silence was deafening as she waited. She couldn't risk any missteps, not with his dangerous schemes at play. Every fiber of her being knew whatever Gorgon had planned was far from benevolent. If he was resorting to collecting favors, it could only mean he had a grand and potentially destructive plan in motion.

While others debated and conjectured about the future, she was already implementing her plan. She knew mere words would not be enough to stop her husband. No, she would have to take matters into her own hands. Her plan was daring and filled with danger, but she knew it needed to be done.

With a deep breath, she opened the box, revealing a small, intricate object nestled within. The amulet shimmered with a blue glow that pulsed in time with her own heartbeat. It was her last resort, a powerful tool that would grant telekinetic abilities to the one who wielded it. However, controlling its magic was no easy task.

It was the one ability even Circe couldn't fully harness. It was a force so immense and unpredictable that she had locked it away within an enchanted amulet, never to be used again. She knew all too well the dangers of wielding such a power, and she feared what it could do in the wrong hands. The queen said she never wanted to feel its chaotic influence again.

Anasazi perked up at the sound of the key turning in the lock. Olivia entered her apartment and flicked on the living room switch, illuminating the space. She stepped back as she spotted the goddess sitting at her kitchen table.

Tossing her bag onto the couch, she demanded, "What are you doing in my apartment?"

"I have something for you."

Olivia raised an eyebrow, crossing her arms. "It required you to break into my apartment and scare me? What's so important?"

"Olivia, I need your help," she began, her tone serious. "I can't keep Gorgon in check on my own, and I fear for the safety of our realm. You possess a gift that could make all the difference."

Olivia sat down across from her. "I can't read the minds of gods. I don't see how I can help. I don't have an active power."

With a steady hand, she pushed the box toward Olivia. "There is one power of Circe's that neither you nor your sister have. She locked it away years ago in this amulet. It contains the power of telekinesis. I want you to have it."

She hesitated, her fingers hovering over the box. "Why me? Why are you giving this to me?"

Anasazi let out a soft sigh. "You have Circe's soul. This was her most powerful ability. You have the potential for great power, and this will help you unlock it. You're going to need it against Gorgon."

"What's Gorgon doing?"

"I don't know yet, but he's collecting favors, looking for something."

"Are you sure it's safe to use this amulet? What if something goes wrong?"

"I trust you, Olivia," she reassured her, placing a comforting hand on Olivia's arm. "You have a powerful soul, and I believe you can handle this power responsibly. You don't have to put it on now. Keep it until you're ready."

"Why should I trust you? Help from the gods always seems to come with a price."

"You're right to be suspicious. The gods have not been kind to mortals, and I've been difficult." She leaned forward, her white hair cascading over her shoulder. "I'm not offering this to trap you or harm you. I'm offering it because I'm afraid."

"Afraid? You?"

"Even goddesses know fear, Olivia, especially when it comes to Gorgon." Anasazi traced the edge of the amulet box. "He's planning something that threatens us all. When gods wage war, mortals suffer most. This amulet is the only way to stop that from happening."

CHAPTER THIRTEEN

OLIVIA

The first rays of sunlight crept through the blinds, casting long shadows across Olivia's face. She stirred, reaching out instinctively to the other side of the bed. Cold sheets met her fingertips, and a familiar ache settled in her chest. She was alone.

Her eyes fluttered open, taking in the emptiness of the room. The silence was deafening. She sat up, dragging a hand through her tangled hair, and let out a heavy sigh.

"Another day," she murmured, her voice sounding small in the vast stillness of the apartment. She swung her legs over the side of the bed, her bare feet touching the cool hardwood floor. She walked to the bathroom.

It had been three months since Talia had moved downstairs with Storm. At first, she loved having the extra room and the ability to do what she wanted with the apartment, but now she was missing her sister.

Talia's voice came from the kitchen. "Olivia, are you up?"

"Yes, I'll be out in a minute."

"I'll start the coffee."

She took a deep breath and steeled herself for the day ahead. She splashed cold water on her face and stared at her reflection in the mirror. Dark circles rimmed her eyes, a testament to the many sleepless nights she had endured since Jitatma started ignoring her. She had been calling for him in her mind since the wedding. At first, he would respond with short answers until about a month ago, when he stopped responding altogether. She sighed and shook her head, willing herself to focus on the positive.

Her gaze rested on the box sitting on the counter. She took a deep breath and braced herself before she lifted the lid. Inside, she found the amulet, its vibrant blue glow pulsating in a hypnotic rhythm. It was a familiar symbol of the gods, just like Talia's Chakram and Storm's tattoo, in a circular shape, with intricate symbols carved along the outer edge and three inward-facing swirls.

She carefully lifted it from the box, feeling its weight. It was surprisingly heavy for such a small object. It was like a live wire, sparking and crackling with power. She struggled to contain it, her hands shaking as the amulet grew brighter. She put it back in the box and stuffed it in her robe pocket.

She wanted an active power, but not one as volatile as telekinesis. She couldn't deny the sense of duty she felt. Anasazi was right; she had to stop Gorgon. It was time to tell Talia what she had kept to herself for the past two months.

As she walked into the kitchen, the smell of freshly brewed coffee drew her in. Talia was sitting at the table, her hands wrapped around a steaming mug. She smiled when she saw Olivia and pushed a second mug toward her.

"How'd you sleep?" Talia asked, her voice full of concern.

"Like crap," she replied, joining her at the kitchen table. "I'm sure I'll eventually get used to this quiet apartment and everyone's thoughts running around in my head."

Her sister frowned and reached across the table, grasping Olivia's hand. "I'm sorry. I know it's been hard for you to adjust."

Olivia forced a smile, appreciating her sister's support. "I know. I just miss having you around all the time, that's all."

Talia's eyes softened, and she squeezed Olivia's hand. "I miss you, too, more than you know. I promise, I'll always be just down-stairs. We can still have our morning coffee ritual, right?"

"Right," she agreed, taking a sip of the hot, comforting brew. "It's just been so quiet. I mean, you're not having nightmares, Hunter's in jail, and I haven't heard much from Jitatma since the wedding. It's been a couple of months since Anasazi came for a visit."

"That just means life is getting back to normal."

"You just jinxed it, sis."

"Wait. Why did Anasazi visit you?" she asked, setting her cup down and staring at Olivia. "How come you didn't share this with me?"

"I don't share everything with you."

"You live in my head, sis, and you didn't think to mention this to me?"

"I didn't say anything because I haven't decided what to do." She reached into the pocket of her plush robe and retrieved the box. With deliberate movements, she placed the box on the table and slid it across to her sister. "She gave me this."

Talia opened the box. Looking up, she shook her head. "I wouldn't wear a gift from the gods because it might not come off."

"I don't think it's cursed like your ring, but Anasazi warned me the amulet contains Circe's power to move things with just a thought." She hesitated for a moment before she spoke again. "I don't understand why Circe would choose to lock that power away."

"Telekinesis is powerful, and maybe she needed to. It could have been too much for her to have two active powers. It took me years to control my lightning. I couldn't imagine having both." She took a sip of her coffee. "Maybe she put it in the amulet so she could call on the power only when she needed it."

"What's it like having an active power?"

"It's difficult to explain," Talia said, her brow furrowing in thought. "It's like there's this constant hum inside me, this energy that's always there, waiting to be tapped into. When we were younger, I was terrified knowing that I held so much power in my hands. When I use my power, it's like I'm reaching inside myself and pulling that energy out, molding it to my will. At the same time, it can be exhausting, and sometimes it feels like I'm losing a piece of myself every time I use it."

Olivia studied her sister's face, noticing the slight crease in her brow. "You've managed to control it over the years."

She nodded. "Yes, but it wasn't easy. I had Johara's help and my Chakram to channel my lightning." Her eyes flicked to the small box. "Are you sure you want to take on this responsibility?"

Olivia inhaled, her hand trembling as it hovered near the box. The amulet beckoned her, tempting her with the power it contained. With each opening, the box seemed to whisper to her like a siren's call she couldn't resist. "If it means being able to protect myself and those I care about, then yes."

"I'll help you. We can start off small and easy," Talia said. "First, I want to see if it comes off."

Olivia took the amulet out of the box and held it up for a moment. She could feel the weight of its power. With a deep breath, she placed it around her neck, the chain cold against her skin. The amulet nestled below the hollow of her throat, its pulse seeming to synchronize with hers. She reached to touch the amulet.

"I need to take it off."

Olivia felt the hair on the back of her neck stand on end as she reached around to the clasp. Her hand began to shake as the amulet pulsed with energy, and she struggled to release the necklace.

Talia's eyes widened as she watched her sister struggle. "Olivia, maybe this isn't a good idea."

She gritted her teeth, her resolve hardening with every passing second. "I can do this, Talia. I have to."

With a final determined tug, the clasp popped open, and the amulet fell into her lap. The moment it left her neck, the air in the room seemed to shift, and Olivia took a deep, relieved breath. The blue glow had dimmed, but its power was still palpable as she set it on the table.

"It seems you can remove it."

Talia stared at the amulet, now lying inert near the box, and then back at Olivia. "It's not cursed, then. It responds to your touch. Are you sure you want to do this? It's not just power you're taking on, Olivia. It comes with a responsibility, a burden you may not be ready for."

She nodded, her eyes never leaving the amulet. "I know, but I'm tired of feeling helpless. I want to stand on my own, to protect myself and the people I care about. If that means taking on this burden, then I'm willing to do it."

Talia sighed. "All right. I'll help you learn to control it, but you must promise me you'll be careful. This power is dangerous, and if you're not careful, it could destroy you."

"I promise."

Olivia picked up the amulet once more, placing it around her neck She thought of Jitatma, of his silence and distance. She thought of Anasazi and her warning. She thought of her sister and her own journey to control her powers.

Talia stood from the table. "All right. Let's try this again." Opening various cupboards and drawers, she retrieved familiar items like a spoon, a towel, and a small cup. She placed the spoon across the table. "We'll start with some small objects that won't hurt you. I want you to try moving this spoon to your hand."

Olivia nodded, taking a deep breath as she centered herself. She focused on the spoon, its metal surface gleaming under the kitchen lights. She could feel the energy flowing through her, its power pulsing in time with her heartbeat. She reached out with her mind, tentatively at first, and then with more confidence as she felt the connection between herself and the spoon.

Slowly, the spoon began to tremble, its handle vibrating slightly as she worked to lift it off the table. She could feel the strain in her mind, the effort it took to manipulate the object, but she pushed through it, determined to succeed. With a final push of energy, the spoon levitated off the table, hovering for a moment before she guided it to her outstretched hand.

"Now I see why you said you feel a little drained."

"It gets easier as you learn." Talia shifted her chair back from the table and draped a towel on its seat. She then made her way around Olivia to the other side of the living room. "Let's try something harder. I want you to move that towel to me."

She focused her thoughts on the texture of the fabric and effortlessly raised the towel off the chair. It fluttered in the air, dancing a silent ballet as Olivia guided it toward her sister. Talia stood, unmoving, her eyes following the towel's progress as it floated gracefully across the room. When it finally reached her sister's outstretched hand, she smiled, pride evident in her expression.

"You're a natural, Olivia," she said warmly.

"The feel of fabrics is my thing. That one was easy. What's next?" Olivia asked. "What else can I do?"

Setting the cup on the coffee table in the living room, Talia instructed, "I want you to take this cup and set it on your nightstand in your room."

"I can't see my nightstand from here."

"That's the point." She smiled. "You need to capture the movement of the cup in your mind. That requires focus."

Olivia took a deep breath and closed her eyes, visualizing the cup in her hand and her nightstand in her bedroom. She felt the energy surge within her once more, and with a determined effort, she willed the cup to move.

At first, nothing happened. Olivia felt the energy flowing through her, but it seemed to go nowhere. She gritted her teeth and concentrated harder, trying to push the cup toward her bedroom.

Suddenly, the cup lifted off the coffee table, hovering for a moment before shooting off in the direction of her bedroom. Olivia's eyes flew open as she watched the cup move through the air, her heart pounding in her chest. When she heard the cup finally come to rest on her nightstand, she let out a sigh of relief. She could feel the energy draining from her, leaving her feeling weak and exhausted.

They hurried around the corner and checked her bedroom. The cup was exactly where it should have been, but it was on the edge. Olivia waved her hand, and the cup moved back a few inches.

"How are you feeling?"

"I'm a little tired, but good."

"It's like working a muscle you don't use often. The more you practice, the less you'll feel drained."

"Talia, Olivia," Storm called from the kitchen. "Where are you?"

"We're in the bedroom," Talia replied. "We'll be out in a minute. There's some coffee for you."

"Is he joining our morning coffee dates now?" Olivia asked. "I don't know if I can take all your sweetness so early in the morning."

"I'll tone it down."

Olivia rolled her eyes. "You can, but your husband can't keep his hands off you. As soon we walk in, he's going to pull you down on his lap."

As Storm was pouring himself a cup, the twins walked into the kitchen. As soon as Talia was close enough, he took a seat at the table and pulled her onto his lap, giving her a small kiss on the cheek.

I told you. He's a Sumerian.

Talia giggled as Olivia rolled her eyes.

"What's so funny?"

"Nothing." Talia shook her head. "Olivia has a new power."

"Really? What is it?"

"I'll show you."

With a graceful flick of her delicate wrist, Olivia raised her hand toward Storm. In an instant, the fabric of his shirt tore in half, falling to the ground. Storm sat frozen, his shocked expression mirroring the torn garment at his feet.

A gust of wind picked up, carrying the scent of ozone and electricity with it, signaling the immense strength within Olivia's magic. She lowered her hand, a triumphant smirk playing on her lips as she surveyed the destruction she had caused with just a simple gesture.

"That's what you decide to do with your new power. Strip men of their clothes." Storm chuckled.

"I'm sorry." Olivia tilted her head staring at his toned chest. "Well, not really. Talia, you're a lucky woman."

"That was my favorite shirt." He shook his head.

Talia smiled. "Every shirt is your favorite."

"I like my clothes on my body. At least you left my pants on."

"I can take care of that for you."

"No! I'd like to keep my pants on."

After the laughter subsided, Olivia's smile faded, and her gaze drifted toward the window. Storm, despite his initial shock, seemed to take the whole situation in stride. Olivia felt a little jealous of their happiness, but she pushed the feeling aside. She wished Jitatma felt that way for her. It appeared the commander wasn't as receptive to having a relationship.

"Hey, are you okay?" Talia asked.

"Yeah, I'm fine," she responded, forcing a smile. "I just miss Jitatma, that's all."

Talia gave her a sympathetic look. "I know you do. Have you tried talking to him again?"

Olivia sighed. "I have, but he's still distant. I don't know what's going on with him. I've reached out to him telepathically, but he gives me short answers. It's like he's avoiding me."

"Do you want me to talk to my brother?"

"No. I decided if he wants me that badly, he knows where to find me." She took a sip of her coffee. "It might be time to move on."

CHAPTER FOURTEEN

OLIVIA

O livia was getting ready for an evening out, a smile playing on her lips. A sense of uneasiness crept over her. It was as if someone were watching her. She paused for a moment but didn't see anyone.

A sudden gust of wind swept through the hallway, causing Olivia's robe to billow around her, pressing her against the wall. In that moment, she could swear she felt a presence beside her, an invisible force that held her in its grip.

A profound hunger gnawed at her insides, an inexplicable yearning that seemed to echo through the very core of her being. It was a vast emptiness, deep and consuming, that tugged relentlessly at her soul.

With a quickening pulse, she raised her arms to shield herself, only to have them pinned above her head by an unseen hand. She closed her eyes, bracing herself for what was to come next.

A feather-light touch traced a path from her arm down to the curve of her breast, sending a jolt of awareness through her. As she opened her eyes, she struggled to make sense of this ethereal caress. A gentle tug at the strings of her robe caused them to loosen and fall away from her body, leaving her exposed. She looked down to notice the amulet was glowing blue.

Her breath hitched as the sensation grew more intense, focusing on her breasts and making her nipples harden into stiff peaks. It had been months since she'd felt the warmth of another's touch, and in a twisted way, she almost didn't want this to be a dream. She tried to cling to her fear, but as a phantom hand traced its way up her thigh and between her legs, it began to melt away.

Goosebumps prickled her skin as anticipation and longing flooded through her body. The air around her seemed to grow thick with desire, as if the very atmosphere was pulsing with the need for physical connection. She surrendered to the sensation, letting go of all restraint and succumbing to the moment. Nothing else existed except for the electricity between her and her mysterious intruder.

She closed her eyes again and let out a shuddering breath, savoring every imaginary caress. She arched her back, pushing herself further into the touch. The hand began to move with more purpose, teasing and circling her clit before sliding lower to thrust inside her. She felt her muscles tightening around the unseen fingers, and she ground herself against them, desperate for more.

With a sharp intake of breath, she threw her head back and opened her mouth wide, ready to release a piercing moan. Something unexpected happened as she did so—a thick, dark smoke seemed to swirl around her and enter her body, causing her to gasp and recoil in surprise.

My good girl.

Olivia tugged Talia along the bustling walkway. Grand View's central park sprawled to their left, the Eternal Flame's shimmer visible even in the bright afternoon light. Storm and Scooter casually strolled behind them.

"Come on, Talia! We deserve this," Olivia insisted, her grip firm on her twin's wrist as she navigated through the crowd. Her excitement was hard to contain. Talia's reluctance was equally evident in her dragging feet and furrowed brow.

"Olivia, you know I don't like bars," Talia protested, her voice tinged with anxiety. "Can't we just celebrate at home?"

She rolled her eyes, a fond smile playing on her lips. "It's not just about the bar, sis. It's about embracing life! We're almost done with classes, summer's practically here, and the air is buzzing with possibility." She paused, turning to face her sister. "Besides," she added, lowering her voice conspiratorially, "when was the last time you let loose a little?"

Talia sighed, her shoulders slumping slightly. "It's been a long time."

"That's why we're here," she said softly, squeezing Talia's hand. "To help you relax, have fun, and realize you're more in control than you think."

Behind them, Storm's deep chuckle rumbled. "Listen to your sister, Maverick. A little celebration never hurt anyone."

Olivia grinned, grateful for the backup. She could always count on Storm to be the voice of reason—or, in this case, the voice of fun.

We'll get Scooter drunk and see what happens.

One drink, and then we're leaving.

C'mon, at least two drinks.

The group finally reached the college bar. The scent of sugary cocktails and fried appetizers mingled in the air, tempting even the most reluctant patrons. Inside, the atmosphere was lively; laughter and chatter filled the space, punctuated by the occasional clink of glasses. Olivia led the way through the crowd. As they settled into a cozy booth near the back, Olivia scanned the room. She spotted familiar faces from their classes and a few acquaintances from around campus.

She jumped up from the booth. "I'll get us some drinks."

As she walked toward the bar, Olivia noticed a flash of red hair. She angled her body in that direction and saw Jade and Frida laughing and embracing at the center of the bar. Olivia quickly changed her course to join them.

"Jade and Frida, what are you two doing here?"

"We're checking out the student life," Frida said, pointing to Jade. "You're looking at the newest enrolled student of Grand View University. Jade starts classes next school year."

"Really? I had no idea."

"Well, I figured if Storm can do it, I should, too."

The bartender approached with a charming smile, his dark hair slightly tousled and his eyes sparkling with warmth. "What can I get for you, love?"

"Well, aren't you a beautiful man? Four mugs of ale."

"You can put them on my tab," Frida said. "It's the least I can do for you. If it weren't for you guys, I wouldn't be sitting here enjoying myself with my girl." Frida leaned in, her full lips parting to capture Jade's mouth in a sizzling kiss.

The bartender set down four frosty mugs. "Here you go, love. Enjoy your evening," he said, winking at Olivia before moving on to the next customer.

"Why don't you two join us for a drink? I mean, you paid for them."

Olivia grabbed the mugs and led Jade and Frida back to their booth. Storm's eyes widened as he took in the new additions to their group.

"Look who I found at the bar."

"I haven't seen you two since the wedding. How are you settling into Grand View?" Storm asked.

Scooter greeted Jade and Frida with a friendly nod, his eyes twinkling with amusement. "Well, this is a pleasant surprise," he said, taking his mug from Olivia.

"We're figuring out how to navigate the new town, but we're doing good."

Olivia's eyes drifted toward her sister. She appeared to be more at ease now, a small smile gracing her lips as she took in the scenery around them.

Are you feeling better about leaving the house?

Yes, I am.

Good, that means we can stay for three drinks now.

Olivia loved the easy banter between her friends, the warmth of the ale in her belly, and the thrum of music filling the air. She glanced at Talia, who was deep in conversation with Storm, and she felt a swell of pride. This was exactly what her sister needed—a night out to let loose and forget about their troubles.

Olivia looked back to the bar, where she saw the bartender engrossed in a conversation with two customers. As if sensing her gaze, he looked up and caught her eye. He offered a polite nod, which she returned before turning her attention back to her friends.

Scooter leaned over to her and whispered, "You're not seriously considering the bartender. You can do better."

"He would be fun for one night." Olivia looked at his mug and noticed it was already half empty. "I'm surprised you know what I'm talking about."

"Since our last lesson, I've been doing some research. I'm aware of the effects of alcohol and one-night stands." He raised his mug to finish his ale. "I might teach you a few things."

"I appreciate the offer, but I doubt it."

"Who needs more?" Scooter asked the group.

"You'd better slow down or we'll have to pull you off the table later," Storm said as he took a second sip from his mug.

"I'll be at the bar." Scooter stood; his movements slightly unsteady.

Olivia watched over her shoulder as Scooter made his way to the corner of the bar. He signaled the bartender. His conversation with the other customers ceased as he regarded Scooter with curiosity. Scooter leaned in, speaking animatedly, gesturing toward Olivia every so often. She felt a flush creep up her neck as their gazes landed on her once more.

Talia nudged her. "What's going on over there?" she asked, flicking her gaze between Olivia and the events happening at the bar.

"I should check on him."

Olivia excused herself and weaved her way through the crowd, her heart pounding in her chest. She reached the bar just as the bartender slid another mug of ale across the counter. Scooter's grin widened as he reached for it.

The bartender smiled. "Back so soon, love?"

"I'm here to get my friend," she said, pointing to Scooter.

"Olivia, I want to buy you a round," Scooter said, his words slurring.

"That's not necessary. Hey, slow down, there, buddy," Olivia said, placing a hand on Scooter's shoulder. "You're going to make a scene."

The bartender leaned over and said, "You should let him buy you a drink, love."

"Why is that?"

"Because if I were on that side of the bar, I would buy you a drink, too." He winked.

"If you were on this side of the bar, we could get into some trouble together."

The bartender threw his head back and laughed, a deep, genuine sound that made Olivia's heart flutter. "I like your style, love," he said, flashing her a dazzling smile. "What's your name?"

"Olivia," she replied, feeling a strange connection to this stranger. "And yours?"

"They call me Sam."

"Well, Sam, come find me when you're on this side of the bar and we'll see what kind of trouble we can get into."

Olivia was still feeling the lingering effects of the alcohol, fumbling with the keys to her apartment. Sam waited patiently behind her. She bent down, her coordination slightly off, to find the lock. His hands, warm and strong, gently grasped her hips as if to steady her.

Finally, she found it and managed to unlock the door. As they stepped inside, his hands never left her hips, pulling her close. She could feel the hardness of his arousal pressing against her, and it made her pulse race.

They stumbled into the living room, their lips locked in a heated kiss. Her hands roamed over his body, feeling the muscles in his back and chest tense and release under her touch. She reveled in the feeling of power as she pushed him back onto the couch.

Her hand rose with an air of authority. "We won't be needing your clothes," she stated firmly. With a flick of her wrist, the fabric of his clothes tore away from his body, revealing his bare skin. She let out a gasp as she took in the sight of him, all hard lines and planes, and she couldn't resist running her hands over his chest and abs, feeling the heat and hardness of his body. "You are a beautiful man."

Her breath came in short, shallow gasps as she leaned down to kiss him once more. This time, it was a slow, sensual kiss, full of promise and desire. She felt his hands roaming over her body, and she let out a soft moan as he cupped her breasts, teasing her nipples through the thin fabric of her dress.

She couldn't take it anymore. With a growl of frustration, she took her dress off, revealing her bare skin. She felt his eyes on her, and she reveled in the feeling of being desired as she let her bra and panties drop to the floor.

He pulled her down on the couch as she straddled him, her hips grinding against his as they kissed passionately. She felt him hard and ready beneath her, and she let out a low moan as she guided him inside her.

She savored the feeling of him stretching her, filling her completely. She threw her head back and moaned as she took him all the way in, rocking against him as she found her rhythm.

His hands gripped her hips, guiding her as she moved atop him. She felt herself getting closer and closer to the edge, her muscles tensing.

She felt the hunger gnawing at her insides, a ravenous need that clawed beneath her skin. It wasn't just desire—it was something deeper, more primal. Her hips continued to rock against Sam's, but the pleasure that coursed through her veins wasn't enough. It would never be enough.

"More," she whispered, her voice raw with desperation. "I need more."

His hands tightened on her hips, his eyes dark with lust as he gazed up at her. "I'm right here, love."

It wasn't him she craved—not really. It was the sensation, the release, the momentary escape from the emptiness that seemed to consume her from within. The pleasure built within her core, spreading like wildfire through her limbs, but instead of satisfying her, it only intensified the ache.

As she increased her pace, the friction sent sparks of pleasure shooting through her body, but it was like trying to fill a bottomless pit. The more she took, the more she needed.

"It's not enough," she gasped, frustration edging her voice. Her nails dug into his chest, leaving crescent-shaped marks on his skin. "Why isn't it enough?"

The hunger pulsed through her veins like a separate heartbeat, demanding to be fed. It was a physical pain now, a hollow ache that threatened to consume her entirely. Sweat beaded on her forehead as she chased her release, desperate for something—anything—to quell the insatiable need.

"Olivia," he groaned beneath her, his body tensing as he approached his climax. "God, you're incredible."

His words barely registered. All she could focus on was the void inside her, the desperate craving that seemed to grow stronger with each passing moment. It was as if something inside her was feeding on her desires, drawing energy from her passion, but never allowing her to feel truly satiated.

Her body shuddered as the first waves of her climax washed over her, but even as pleasure crashed through her, the emptiness remained. The hunger persisted, unrelenting and cruel, whispering that this was just the beginning—that no amount of physical connection would ever be enough to satisfy what lurked within her.

Her heightened pleasure was evident by the shimmering hole that began to form on the ceiling above them. As her body pulsed with ecstasy, the size of the portal grew larger and more vibrant with each passing moment. The light emanating from the opening cast a warm glow over their entwined bodies, adding an otherworldly element to their intimate encounter.

As she collapsed against his chest, her heart racing and her body trembling, she knew with terrifying certainty that something inside her had changed. This wasn't just desire. This was something darker, something that fed on her passion and grew stronger with each encounter.

She looked up and stumbled away from him once she realized how large the portal was above them. She watched his body being pulled toward the swirling vortex, yanking him off the couch. She reached out to grab him, but it was too late. The portal closed, swallowing his desperate plea for help.

She stood frozen in shock, her mind racing to process what had just happened before her very eyes.

My good girl.

CHAPTER FIFTEEN

OLIVIA

O livia leaned closer to the mirror, her breath catching in her throat as she stared at her reflection. Something was different, but she couldn't quite put her finger on what. Her eyes roamed over her familiar features—the curve of her cheekbones, the slope of her nose, the arch of her eyebrows. Then she saw it. Her ears. She had pointed ears.

"What the fuck?" she whispered, pushing her hair behind her ears to get a better look. The tips curved up to a distinct point. She blinked hard, sure she must be seeing things. When she opened her eyes, the pointed ears remained.

She ran her fingers along the edge of her ear, feeling the unfamiliar shape. It was real. Her heart began to race as panic set in. "This can't be happening," she muttered, turning her head from side to side to examine her ears from different angles. "How is this possible?"

The longer she stared, the more pronounced it seemed to become. Her mind raced with questions. Had her ears always been like this? No, she was certain they hadn't. She wondered when they had changed. She tried to recall if she'd noticed anything unusual lately, but nothing came to mind.

A knock at the bathroom door startled her out of her thoughts. "Olivia, you okay in there?" Talia called from the other side.

Her hands flew to her hair, quickly pulling it forward to cover her ears. "Yeah, I'm fine," she called back, wincing at the slight tremor in her voice. "Just fixing my hair. I'll be out in a minute."

She heard Talia's footsteps retreating and let out a shaky breath. Turning back to the mirror, she carefully arranged her hair to conceal her ears. The soft, blonde waves fell past her shoulders, providing ample coverage. She tilted her head, examining her reflection critically. She hid her ears, but now her hair looked unnatural, too perfectly placed.

She sighed, her fingers trembling as she tried to adjust her hair to look more casual. "This is ridiculous," she muttered to herself. "I can't go around like this forever."

With one last glance in the mirror, she steeled herself and exited the bathroom. Talia was sitting at the kitchen table with a cup of coffee. Olivia was hyperaware of every movement that might disturb her carefully arranged hair as she made her way to the coffeepot.

"You were in there for ages," she remarked, eyeing Olivia curiously. "Everything all right?"

She poured herself a cup of coffee, keeping her back to Talia. "Yeah, just having a bad hair day," she lied, forcing a light laugh.

"How was your date with the bartender last night?"

She hesitated for a moment, weighing her words carefully before answering. "It was fine, I guess," she said, finally turning to face Talia, her expression neutral. "Nothing special."

Her sister raised her eyebrows, a knowing smile playing on her lips. "Fine? Just fine? Come on, you can do better than that. No snarky comments or details?"

Olivia managed a weak smile, trying to shake off the nagging thoughts about her changing appearance. "Really, it was just casual. We had a few drinks and talked about this and that. No big deal." Talia didn't look convinced, but she let the subject drop, returning her attention to her coffee.

Olivia breathed a sigh of relief, grateful for the reprieve. She took a careful sip of her coffee, trying to focus on the familiar warmth and bitterness. Her mind was elsewhere, preoccupied with her unusual transformation. She'd have to be more careful with her powers; she couldn't risk anyone else finding out about her pointed ears or what happened to Sam. The memory of his naked form, muscles taut, arcing from the couch into the shimmering portal, haunted her thoughts.

Talia raised an eyebrow, her gaze lingering on Olivia's meticulously styled hair. "You sure everything's okay?" she pressed, concern furrowing her brow. "You seem a bit off."

Olivia's heart skipped a beat, but she quickly composed herself, channeling the confidence she'd always prided herself on. "I'm fine, really," she insisted, hoping her voice sounded more convincing to her sister than it did to her own ears. "Just got a lot on my mind, that's all."

She pressed her back against the cool counter, enjoying its smoothness against her skin. Her fingers curled around the cup, feeling the comforting heat through her palm.

Suddenly, she craved a touch of sweetness and remembered the sugar on the table across the room. With a mere thought, the container levitated through the air, gracefully gliding toward her outstretched hand. The sugar container hovered, and she tilted it, pouring a small amount into her coffee. The sugar grains fell like tiny, sparkling crystals before disappearing beneath the dark surface.

Talia's gaze followed the container's movement, but she said nothing. Olivia silently released her control, and it floated back to its original position on the table.

Her sister narrowed her eyes, studying Olivia intently. "You're not using your powers more often, are you?" she asked, her voice laced with concern. "You know, we agreed to be careful with them."

Olivia scoffed. "What? It's just sugar."

Olivia sat on the couch an hour later, tapping her fingers restlessly against the armrest. Her mind was a flurry of thoughts and emotions as she attempted to reach out to Jitatma telepathically, just as she had been doing since the night before. She couldn't shake off the feeling he was intentionally ignoring her until she became so insistent that he finally responded with a faint flicker of recognition in their mental connection.

A portal appeared in the dark hallway, its edges dancing with energy. Out of it stepped Jitatma, his long cape flowing behind him as he emerged in the living world. He strode forward, his eyes focused on her. The portal closed behind him with a soft whisper, leaving the hallway once again shrouded in darkness. She always admired the commander's entrance.

"What's so urgent, Minx?" he asked, irritated. "I have a kingdom to protect. I can't come running every time you demand it."

"You seem to come running if my sister is in trouble."

"That's different." He clenched his fists at his side. "I was trying to stop Hunter."

With a huff, she stood and planted her hands firmly on her hips. "Tell me why you felt it necessary to suck my date into a portal last night. What did you do with him?"

"What are you talking about?" He took a step back and looked a little confused. "Is that what the big emergency is all about?"

"Yes, I was having a good time with Sam. He's sweet, and I was getting more attention from him than you."

He chuckled. "Sam? He sounds like an imbecile. Why would I care about some halfwit you decided to take home?"

"You sucked him into a portal!"

"I did not. I would have done it before you took him home." He took two long strides, closing the distance between them. "Trust me, Minx, I didn't want to let him fuck you."

"How did you know we had sex?"

"Your moans were in my head last night, like you wanted me to hear." He leaned in, his hot breath tickling her ear. "If it were me, I would've made you scream, not just sweet, soft, little moans of interest."

She shuddered, trying to ignore the heat his words ignited within her. She pushed him away, mustering as much defiance as she could. "You had no right to do what you did. You owe me answers and an apology."

He scoffed, crossing his arms. His leather armor creaked slightly with the movement. "I owe you nothing. You're the one who's been keeping secrets. Your powers have grown stronger, and your appearance has changed. Why?"

She hesitated, knowing she couldn't hide the truth from him. It was one thing to block her sister, but he had this control over her. It was as if he had some sort of invisible hold in her mind, making it difficult for her focus on her mental defenses.

"I don't know what you're talking about," she replied, her hand instinctively moving toward her hair, making sure her ears remained hidden. Her stomach clenched. The pointed tips seemed to burn beneath her hair, as if calling attention to themselves. "Nothing's changed."

His eyes narrowed as he stepped closer, his gaze penetrating, invading her personal space with deliberate slowness. "Lying to me doesn't suit you, Minx." He reached out and, before she could react, brushed her hair back from her face, exposing her pointed ear. "This," he said, his finger tracing the delicate point. "This is what I'm talking about."

The touch of his finger against her ear sent an unexpected shiver down her spine. He lingered for a heartbeat too long, and she found herself momentarily frozen, caught between the urge to lean into his touch and the instinct to step back. She chose to jerk away, letting her hair fall back into place. The phantom sensation of his touch remained, tingling along the shell of her ear.

"Don't," she warned, her voice shakier than she intended.

His expression softened almost imperceptibly. "How long have you been hiding this?" he asked, his tone less accusatory now, almost concerned.

She bit her lower lip, the metallic taste of blood pricking her tongue where her teeth pressed too hard. The weight of her secret suddenly felt too heavy to bear alone. "I noticed them this morning," she confessed, the admission falling from her lips before she could stop it. "I don't know why. I don't understand."

"I know you better than your own sister, and this isn't like you. You don't hide things."

She lifted her chin, the muscles in her neck tensing as she stood tall and met his intense gaze head on. "If you know me so well, why have you been ignoring me?"

He sighed, his expression softening as he ran a hand through his hair. "I haven't been ignoring you, Minx. I have duties and a kingdom to protect."

She narrowed her eyes, studying him closely. She could tell he was hiding something, but he shut himself off from her, refusing to share his innermost thoughts. "You should be protecting me."

"I am." He lunged forward, his finger extended like a blade, aimed directly at her face. "I always am, you pretentious, ungrateful little brat."

His gaze slid down her body like a predator sizing up its prey, and when it landed on her neckline, her breath hitched. His fingers moved before she could even think to protest, rough and demanding, as they closed around the first two buttons of her shirt. With a sharp, deliberate tug, he ripped the fabric open. She didn't know if he was staring at the amulet around her neck or her breasts, but either way, she had his attention.

"Prove it, Renegade."

Without warning, his lips overpowered hers in a feverish kiss, his tongue darting in her mouth as if he owned her. His hand moved down her body, gripping her hips and pulling her closer. She moaned as her body responded to his touch despite her anger.

This man is what I've been craving. He feels so wrong, like a sin.

His length pressed against her, which made her ache for him even more. He broke away from the kiss, his breath hot as he whispered in her ear. "You want this, Minx? You want to fuck me?"

He was right. She did want him.

Make me yours.

Her lips locked with his, a gush of wetness rushing between her legs. There was something about him that made her respond, and the anticipation was driving her wild. He didn't even need to touch her. The way he moved, the way he looked at her, had her heart racing.

He's the only one to satisfy my hunger.

It was frightening how much power this man held over her. She had desired no one with such intensity before. Her hands trailed down his neck, pulling him closer, wanting more of this connection between them. She couldn't get close enough to him to satisfy her addiction.

Then she heard a man's voice in her head. It was not the soothing voice of Jitatma, but a harsh, demanding one that sent shivers down her spine. The words stung like needles as they echoed in her mind.

You can fuck him, but you can't love him.

She closed her eyes, trying to push the intrusive voice out, focusing instead on the man in front of her. She shoved the intruder to the farthest corner of her mind, constructing a sturdy mental barrier to keep the unwelcome presence at bay.

Her nipples hardened under her bra, and she arched her back, desperate for more. He pulled at the rest of the buttons on her shirt. He pushed it out of his way and off her shoulders, then turned his attention to the clasp of her bra. He expertly unhooked it and tossed it aside.

The sensation of the cold against her hot skin made her gasp. He lowered his head, taking one nipple into his mouth and sucking hard. Olivia whimpered, her hands tangling in his hair as she pulled him closer.

He bit her nipple, the sharp pain sending a rush of pleasure to her core. He sucked and nibbled, his tongue swirling in a sensual dance. She felt her wetness growing, her body readying itself for him.

His hands were on her waist now, exploring every curve of her body as they kissed passionately. She felt his fingers sliding under the hem of her skirt, making their way up her leg. She felt the coldness of his wrist bracers as his warm hand slipped between her thighs. She parted her legs, inviting him to touch her pussy.

The sensation of his fingers combined with his mouth on her nipple was almost too much. He began to move his fingers in and out, each thrust sending waves of pleasure through her. She built toward climax, her body trembling with anticipation. He increased his pace, his fingers curling inside her. She cried out.

He continued to move his fingers inside her as she rode out the waves of her release, her screams escaping her lips in loud, short bursts. His mouth never left her nipple, still biting and sucking. When she finally came down from her high, he released her. She looked into his eyes, a satisfied smirk playing on his lips. She could tell he was pleased with himself.

"I don't need to fuck you to make you scream, Minx."

CHAPTER SIXTEEN

OLIVIA

Feeling dizzy and shaken from her intense encounter with Ji-tatma, Olivia's feet seemed to lead her back to the familiar walls of the college bar. She went there, but this time she was alone. Without hesitation, she ordered a potent drink, needing something to calm her racing thoughts and trembling hands. She sipped on the liquid fire, feeling its warmth in her throat.

In a small way, she had hoped to catch a glimpse of Sam's familiar face, but deep down, she knew it was an impossible wish. He had gone through the portal, destination unknown.

As she glanced at herself in the mirror behind the bar, she noticed her left ear was barely visible, hidden beneath a cascade of tousled hair. With a swift movement, she covered it completely.

As the night wore on, she couldn't escape the nagging feeling she was being watched. She glanced around, searching for any sign of suspicion. Then her gaze fell on Chad and Kyle sitting at the corner of the bar.

They were laughing and joking, seemingly without a care in the world. Their laughter died down when they locked eyes with her. Her heart skipped a beat and a chill ran down her spine. It was as if they knew something she didn't. She smiled and took another sip of her drink. Before she knew it, the bartender set another one in front of her.

"I didn't order this."

"Compliments of your fan club at the end of the bar." The girl smiled as she stepped away.

Her attention snapped back to Chad and Kyle, who were now grinning at her. She raised her glass in their direction, a forced smile on her lips.

She waved the bartender back. "Pour the sweet gentlemen a drink from me and put it on their tab. I want to get them drunk first."

"I like your style."

At her request, the bartender complied. She was feeling mischievous, and the two idiots were the perfect target for her antics. She watched the bartender deliver the drinks and felt a sense of satisfaction. Chad and Kyle looked pleasantly surprised, their grins growing wider as they lifted their glasses in her direction.

She decided to take matters into her own hands. She stood from her barstool and sauntered to their end of the bar. The men curiously followed her every move.

"Mind if I join you?" she asked.

Maybe two of them can get rid of this damn hunger.

Chad scooted over, making room for her between them. "Of course not. Have a seat."

As the night wore on, she found herself enjoying the attention from the two men. Her heart raced as she felt a magnetic pull toward Chad. The way his eyes sparkled in the dim light of the bar made her pulse quicken. She could feel his body heat radiating toward her, making her skin tingle with anticipation.

Kyle was more reserved, but equally charming. His laughter was infectious, causing her to join in even when she didn't quite understand the joke. She found herself caught up in their banter, forgetting her earlier worries.

"Tell me, Olivia, do you think you're too much for us to handle?" Chad asked.

"I'm sure I am," she replied with a coy smile, taking a sip of her drink.

Kyle leaned in, his voice low and conspiratorial. "You know, we've heard rumors about you. They say you're not like the other girls around here. That there's something different about you."

"That's not a rumor. That's a fact," she said, sliding off her stool. "If you give me fifteen minutes and meet me at my apartment, I'll prove it. We can continue this party."

"Which one of us?"

She winked. "If you're game, both of you."

She walked briskly toward her apartment, the cool night air brushing against her face. She struggled with her keys, fumbling to unlock the door, and quickly made her way to the bedroom.

She discarded her garments with a flick of her wrist, leaving them strewn haphazardly on the floor. Her fingers trailed over fabrics and lace, searching for the perfect thing to wear. Eventually, she settled on a short nightgown, its sheer material clinging to her curves, leaving little to the imagination. With each movement, it swayed teasingly around her.

She heard a knock and took a deep breath, steadying herself. She crossed the room and opened the door, revealing Chad and Kyle standing on the other side. Their eyes widened as they took in her appearance, and she could see the desire in their gaze.

She stepped back, inviting them inside. As soon as the door was closed, Chad was on her. He pressed against her, his lips crashing down in a hungry kiss. His hardness pressed into her, and it made her ache with need.

Kyle wasted no time either. He moved behind her, running his hands over her curves and kissing her neck. She moaned as his fingers found their way to her breasts, teasing her nipples through the thin fabric of her nightgown.

Kyle's hands moved down to her hips, pulling her back against him as he pressed his cock into her ass. His breath was hot on her neck as he kissed and nibbled at her sensitive skin.

Chad's hands replaced Kyle's on her breasts, pinching and teasing her nipples. He grasped and kneaded her soft flesh, eliciting gasps and moans from her lips. There were so many hands, eagerly exploring and caressing her body. Lost in a sea of sensations, she was completely at the mercy of their hands igniting every nerve.

"You guys sure know how to make a girl wet."

Chad smiled. "We're just getting started, beautiful."

"Are you sure can handle both of us, sweetheart?" Kyle asked.

She smiled, leaning against Kyle, feeling his toned chest on her back. "Oh, I think I can manage. It'll be you two begging for more when I'm done with you. How about we celebrate with one more drink?"

She sauntered over to the small kitchen, her hips swaying seductively in the sheer nightgown. She could feel their eyes devouring every inch of her. She took her time rummaging through the cabinets, giving them a show as she bent down to retrieve a bottle of wine.

She returned to the living room with three glasses and the wine. She poured them each a generous serving. Handing them their drinks, she took a sip of her own.

"To new experiences," she said, raising her glass in a toast.

The air was electric, and she knew they were all thinking the same thing. Without a word, she leaned in and kissed Chad, her body pressed against him. She felt Kyle's hands on her hips, pulling her closer. She broke away from Chad and turned to kiss Kyle, her lips lingering.

As they kissed, Chad moved behind her, his hands running down her back and cupping her ass. She moaned into Kyle's mouth as Chad's fingers dipped beneath her nightgown, finding the dampness between her thighs.

Kyle's mouth moved to her neck, kissing and sucking as his hands continued to explore. Her pulse quickened as Chad's fingers slid deeper, teasing her clit with each movement.

Suddenly, Chad moved away, and she felt a moment of panic, but then she heard a zipper, and her excitement returned tenfold. She turned her head to see Chad stripping off his clothes, revealing his rock-hard erection.

Make them want you. Make them pleasure you for me. You need to feed.

The voice echoed in her mind, its urgency and determination seeping into her thoughts. A force surged within her, almost tangible, as if something were guiding her. With a deep breath, she relinquished control and let it take over.

She turned to Chad with a small smile. "I'm grateful my initial prediction was proven wrong." She ran her fingers along Chad's chest, feeling the defined muscles beneath his smooth skin. She turned her attention to Kyle. "Your turn. Let me help you." With a swift movement of her hand, Kyle's clothes ripped from his body.

Kyle and Chad stood there, stunned by her display of power. She reveled in the control she held over the two men. Their eyes widened as she slowly let her nightgown slip off her shoulders to the floor, revealing her bare body. The cool air of the room made her nipples harden, and Kyle and Chad's gazes fixed on them.

She took a step forward, closing the distance between them. She felt the heat radiating off their bodies, and it made her own body respond. She placed a hand on each of their chests, feeling their hearts pounding beneath her fingertips.

Neither of them needed any more encouragement. They began to touch her, running their hands over her body. She moaned as they cupped her breasts, squeezing gently before moving down to her hips.

She felt herself getting wetter with every touch. She wanted more, needed more. She reached down and began to touch herself, rubbing her clit in slow circles. She saw the lust in their eyes as they watched her, and it only made her more turned on.

Kyle bent down to kiss her neck, moving down to her breasts. He took one nipple in his mouth and began to suck while Chad moved behind her. His hard cock pressed against her ass, and she pushed back against him, wanting more.

Chad reached around and began to rub her clit, while Kyle continued to suck on her nipples. She was in heaven, surrounded by these two men who wanted her so badly. She felt herself getting closer and closer to orgasm.

She didn't want to come yet. She wanted them both inside her. She led them to her bedroom. She guided Chad to lie on the bed, his muscular body sprawled out before her. Olivia straddled Chad's hips, her wetness coating his hard length as she rubbed herself against him. She reached down and guided his cock to her entrance.

She felt Kyle positioning himself behind her. She took a deep breath as he pressed the head of his cock against her pussy, her body tensing with a mix of excitement and nerves. She never had two men inside her at the same time.

Chad cupped her breasts, his thumbs flicking over her nipples as Kyle slowly pushed inside her. She gasped as she felt herself stretching to accommodate both of them; the sensation was overwhelming. Kyle grabbed her hips to hold her steady as they moved in sync, their rhythm building as they filled her completely.

Her moans filled the room as they fucked her, their grunts and groans adding to the symphony of pleasure. She clenched around them, her orgasm building as they hit her g-spot.

Then that hunger returned. It clawed at her insides, twisting and turning like a living thing trying to escape. The pleasure coursing through her body from Chad's and Kyle's attentions suddenly seemed hollow, insufficient.

"Fuck me, boys! Harder!" she instructed, but the voice didn't sound entirely like her own. "Make me wet." Olivia's vision blurred at the edges, darkening until she couldn't see anything. Their bodies, their energy, their essence—it all called to her with an irresistible pull.

"You feel so good," Kyle grunted, his fingers digging into her hips. "So tight, so wet."

"Fuck, you're amazing," Chad agreed, his voice strained.

The hunger pangs twisted sharper, making her gasp. Her stomach clenched painfully, and she felt empty—so desperately empty. Not just physically, but as if someone or something had hollowed out her very being.

"I'm going to come," she moaned, her voice barely above a whisper. Her body was tensing, her muscles clenching around the two men's cocks as they continued to thrust into her.

"Come for us, Olivia," Kyle groaned, his fingers digging into her hips. "Let us feel you come."

With a final cry, she surrendered to the orgasm that had been building inside her. Her body shook as wave after wave of pleasure washed over her, leaving her breathless and spent. Chad and Kyle continued to move inside her, their own releases following shortly after. They collapsed in a heap on the bed, their limbs tangled together as they all struggled to catch their breath.

She lay there, her body still humming with pleasure, as she stared up at the ceiling. She couldn't believe what had just happened. She had never felt so alive, so powerful, so desired. She glanced over at Kyle and Chad, who were still panting, trying to recover. She smiled at the satisfied looks on their faces. They had enjoyed themselves as much as she had.

Then she remembered the voice in her head, the one that had urged her to make them pleasure her. She frowned, trying to make sense of it. Who was that voice? Where had it come from?

Are you satisfied, my dear?
She nodded.
Then I will take my prize.
A swirling portal materialized above the bed. The mystical vortex lifted Chad and Kyle, completely swallowing their bodies. The portal closed behind them, leaving only a faint hum, a pulsating light, and the sound of rushing wind.

CHAPTER SEVENTEEN

OLIVIA

Olivia's head pounded as she opened her eyes, the morning light stabbing through the gaps in her curtains like daggers. She groaned, rolling over and burying her face in the pillow. The events of the previous night came rushing back in a jumbled haze.

"Shit," she muttered into the fabric. "What did I do?"

Fragments of memory flashed through her mind. She remembered being at the college bar, drinking, and talking to Chad and Kyle. She was laughing. There was more drinking.

She forced herself to sit up, wincing at the wave of nausea. There was a stale taste in her mouth, and her tongue felt thick and unwieldy. A musky scent of sex filled her bedroom. Pulling back the sheet, she realized she was naked.

She felt disoriented and ashamed. How could she have let things get so out of control? She pulled the sheet tightly around her body, trying to shield herself from both the cold air and her own self-disgust.

An overwhelming force surged through her mind, clawing its way to the surface. She was confused and unable to suppress it. A voice, booming and commanding, echoed through her thoughts with unmistakable clarity.

Did you not have fun last night, my dear? I gave you the chance for your darkest desires.

Who are you? Where are you?

I'm known by many names, but your gods refer to me as a Dalanite. I'm inside you.

What are you? What do you want from me?

I told you. I want you to experience your darkest desire, my dear. Olivia, you have some interesting sexual cravings. You have the appetite of a Sumerian woman. I'm impressed.

I'm glad you approve.

Those two idiots last night were right. You're beautiful. I understand why men are so easily attracted to you.

Thanks for the reminder of my behavior.

My dear, you did nothing you didn't want to. You clearly enjoyed yourself.

Yeah, up to the point they were sucked into the portal.

Then she realized that their clothes were still strewn across the living room, a telltale sign of the previous night's events. Panic surged through her as she remembered that Talia was due to arrive at any moment for their morning coffee ritual. She leapt out of bed, her heart pounding, and dashed toward the living room.

That's the disadvantage of the sexual satisfaction of a telekinetic empath with a Dalanite inside them. It requires an offering.

Oh, shit.

Don't worry. It's a small price to pay for the power I provide.

She heard the soft click of the kitchen door knob turning. Instinctively, she reached out her hand, and the torn clothing scattered across the room flew toward her. With a swift motion, she tossed their clothes into her bedroom, landing in a heap just inside the doorway. Just then, the creak of the back door opening reached her ears, prompting her to quickly pivot and dash into the bathroom.

A few minutes later, she heard a knock on her bathroom door and her sister's voice. "Olivia, are you in there?"

"Yeah, I'll be out for coffee in a minute."

She caught a glimpse of herself in the mirror. The reflection staring back at her was foreign, as if it belonged to a stranger. Her once vibrant blue eyes seemed dull and lifeless, her skin sallow.

As she turned away from the mirror, she looked over her shoulder, landing on the Nibmarks that traced down her back. They were faint outlines, barely visible against her skin, compared to their dark, prominent appearance just yesterday.

She dressed in a loose-fitting sweater and pants she had left in the bathroom, covering as much of her skin as possible. It was one of those times she was thankful she hadn't picked up after herself. As she opened the door, her sister greeted her with a concerned look.

"Hey, are you okay?" Talia asked, scanning Olivia's face. "You don't look so good. You've been a little distant in my head. I didn't hear anything from you last night."

Concealing the transformations from her sister was increasingly challenging. Covering her ears with her hair was manageable, but now her Nibmarks were disappearing. She would need to incorporate fabric into her designs, as most were backless. This had been her favorite feature to flaunt during the summer, but now she would have to cover it up.

"Yeah, just a rough night," she replied, forcing a smile.

Talia raised an eyebrow but didn't press further. Instead, she led the way to the kitchen. The aroma of freshly brewed coffee welcomed them, and Olivia's stomach rumbled in response. She poured herself a mug and took a tentative sip, the warmth spreading through her, momentarily easing her nausea.

Her thoughts returned to the mysterious voice in her head. She couldn't believe what had happened the night before. What was this Dalanite, and why was it inside her? She had always known she was different, but she expected nothing like this.

"What are you wearing?"

As they sat at the kitchen table, Talia's eyes kept darting toward her neck. Olivia tightened the collar of her sweater, her fingers brushing the chain of the amulet. She knew her twin would eventually notice the changes, but she wasn't ready to explain them yet.

"It was the only thing I could find."

"Tell me, sis, how long have you been wearing the amulet? I can see the chain."

Olivia hesitated, her hands wrapped around the warm mug of coffee. She felt the weight of the amulet around her neck. Her sister's gaze was steady, waiting for an answer.

She lifted her cup to her lips and answered, "A few days."

Olivia took a slow sip, trying to buy herself some time. She could feel the Dalanite's presence inside her, a subtle pressure that seemed to grow stronger with each passing moment. She couldn't tell Talia about it, not yet. She needed to figure things out on her own first.

"Just a few days?" Her voice showed concern. "Have you taken it off?"

"Well, not really."

Talia leaned back in her chair, studying her. "Something's different about you, Olivia. I can feel it. You're not the same person you were a week ago. Whatever it is, you can't hide it from me for long."

Her heart pounded as she met Talia's gaze. The words stuck in her throat, unable to form a coherent response. She desperately wished she could tell her sister the truth, but the Dalanite's presence made it impossible. It was a reminder of the power she now possessed, but it also filled her with uneasiness. Instead, she took another sip of her coffee, trying to maintain her composure.

Talia's voice interrupted Olivia's thoughts. "Hey, I know you're going through something right now, but you can't shut me out completely. We're twins, remember? We're supposed to share everything."

Olivia looked up, meeting her sister's gaze. She saw the concern etched on Talia's face, and knew she couldn't keep pretending everything was normal.

"I don't know what you're talking about," she said, attempting to brush off her sister. She tried to keep her voice even, but she felt the tension in her shoulders.

Olivia, enjoy the power I provide you.

She noticed she had almost finished her coffee. She held out her hand, and the coffee pot levitated off the counter. With a flick of her wrist, she guided the pot over to her cup, pouring herself another serving. She guided the pot down onto the table.

"I'm talking about the fact that you are using your powers more often. The more you use them, the more you're shutting me out. Since you put on that amulet, you stopped talking to me. What's going on?"

"I'm just practicing."

A vivid image forced its way into her mind's eye, as if painted by an unseen hand. It was a vision of a roaring fire, flames dancing wildly and casting flickering shadows in all directions. The heat radiated intensely in the night air, consuming everything in its path with a relentless, crackling fervor. The scene was both mesmerizing and terrifying, capturing her attention completely.

She saw more than just a fleeting glimpse, more than she was used to. It felt so real that the heat seemed to sear her skin, as if the fire itself had leaped from her imagination and into reality. The air was thick with the scent of burning wood, and the crackle and roar of the flames filled her ears, drowning out all other sounds. It pulled her deeper into its fiery embrace.

"Olivia, are you okay?"

Talia's concerned voice cut through the fog of her vision, bringing her back to the present moment. She suddenly realized the sharp sting as the hot coffee cascaded over her hand, burning her skin. Her sister, eyes wide with worry, hurriedly dabbed at the spreading liquid with a cold, damp cloth, trying to soothe the searing pain and clean up the mess.

As Talia fussed over Olivia's burned hand, fear knotted in Olivia's stomach and tears welled in her eyes. What significance did this vision hold? Was it only an illusion conjured by the Dalanite, or perhaps some dire warning? The worst part was she couldn't figure out how she knocked over her cup, but the burn was undeniable.

Talia placed her hand over the burn and called on her healing powers. With a few graceful waves, the raw, blistered skin began to mend, the redness fading until the burn vanished entirely, leaving smooth, unblemished skin in its place.

Oliva sighed. "I'm so grateful you have that power."

"What happened? It's like I lost you for a moment, and then your cup started to rattle. Before I could grab it, there was hot coffee everywhere."

"I was having a vision."

"You've never had one like that. What was it about?"

"A fire. A really big, intense fire at night, maybe sometime in the future. It felt more like a premonition. Whatever it was, it felt real."

A few hours later, Olivia heard a knock at her door. She had invited Scooter over for his regular lesson, but this time, she had slipped into something comfortable, yet undeniably sexy. The soft fabric of her outfit clung to her curves, a bold departure from her usual attire. It was a risk, considering their meetings typically occurred in his office on campus, where she was always fully dressed in more formal clothing. Her heart raced with anticipation as she smoothed the fabric, wondering how this change might alter the dynamic between them.

"Olivia, you wanted to see me?" Scooter said, his voice catching slightly as his gaze traveled over her form. He clutched his notebook to his chest like a shield, his knuckles whitening around its edges.

She smiled, enjoying the way his eyes widened behind his glasses. "Come in, Scooter. I thought we could have our session here today. It's more comfortable than your office."

She stepped aside as he hesitantly crossed the threshold. His red hair was more disheveled than usual, and dark circles shadowed his eyes, testifying to another late night of research. Despite his exhaustion, there was an endearing earnestness to him that made something in her chest flutter.

He has so much energy inside him. So much potential. Take it. Use it.

As he settled awkwardly on the edge of her couch, she felt the Dalanite's hunger pulse through her veins. She moved closer, sitting beside him with deliberate proximity.

"I thought we were working on my social skills today," he said, his voice cracking slightly as he shifted in his seat, trying to maintain a professional distance. The notebook in his hands trembled faintly.

"We are," she replied, her voice dropping to a sultry whisper. "I thought we could try something a little more practical."

Take him. Feed us both.

His gaze darted nervously around the room, landing anywhere but on her. "I'm not sure what you mean by practical. I've been practicing those conversation starters you suggested, and I think I'm getting better at maintaining eye contact. Though Storm says I still stare too intensely sometimes, and it makes people uncomfortable."

She placed her hand on his thigh, cutting off his rambling. The contact sent a jolt through her, the Dalanite surging forward eagerly, feeding on the energy crackling between them.

"I'm not interested in conversation starters today." She leaned closer. "I think you need more hands-on experience. There's so much I need to show you."

His breath caught as her fingers trailed higher on his thigh. "I—I don't understand," he stammered, though the flush creeping up his neck suggested otherwise.

"Don't you?" She smiled, reaching up to remove his glasses with her free hand. "I think you do."

The Dalanite purred in satisfaction as Scooter's energy intensified—a vibrant, pulsing aura that promised sustenance beyond anything she'd experienced with Chad and Kyle. Enochian energy was different. It was richer, more complex.

Feed now. He's perfect.

"Olivia," he whispered, his voice trembling as she set his glasses on the coffee table. "What's happening? This isn't like you."

For a moment, clarity broke through the Dalanite's influence. Scooter was right; this wasn't like her. She'd always maintained professional boundaries during their sessions, focusing on helping him overcome his social awkwardness. The hunger was overwhelming, drowning out her better judgment.

"Maybe you don't know me as well as you think," she whispered, trailing her fingers along his jawline. "Maybe this is exactly who I am."

"Your eyes look different," he observed, his scientific mind still functioning despite his obvious discomfort. "They've changed."

He notices too much. Distract him.

She leaned forward, bringing her lips to his ear. "Do you like what you see, Scooter? Does it matter if I've changed?"

His breathing quickened, his pulse visibly racing at his throat. "Of course it matters. Something's happening to you. As your friend, I'm concerned."

The word *friend* echoed strangely in her mind, momentarily dampening the Dalanite's hunger. Scooter had always been kind to her, respectful. Unlike the others who saw only her body, he valued her mind, her insights.

"Stop, Olivia," he exclaimed, jumping abruptly from the couch. He reached out, fumbling slightly as he grasped for his glasses on the edge of the coffee table. "This feels wrong. This doesn't feel like you," he added, adjusting his glasses with trembling hands. "I mean, not that I—I wouldn't—" He took a deep breath. "Something's different. Your eyes, they're almost hollow."

She rose from the couch in one fluid motion, her body moving with a grace that felt foreign to her own muscles. "You're overthinking this. Isn't this what you've always wanted?" She closed the distance between them, backing him against the wall. "I've seen the way you look at me when you think I don't notice."

His face flushed crimson, but his eyes remained fixed on hers, searching. "I'm looking at you with a scientific fascination. Read my thoughts and you'll know it's the truth."

She reached out with her mind, probing for the familiar whisper of his thoughts—the gentle hum of equations and theories that always buzzed beneath his awkward exterior. Where his consciousness should have been, she found only silence. An impenetrable wall stood between them, solid and unyielding.

She blinked, momentarily confused. "I can't."

The Dalanite's voice slithered through her mind, smug and possessive.

You can read someone's thoughts when it suits me. You will do what I say.

CHAPTER EIGHTEEN

ANASAZI

Anasazi's footsteps echoed softly against the polished wooden floor as she entered Jitatma's study, the familiar scent of lavender incense wafting through the air. The dim lighting cast long shadows across the room, creating an atmosphere of secrecy and importance. She paused at the threshold, her keen eyes taking in every detail of the space.

Bookshelves lined three walls from floor to ceiling, their dark wood gleaming with the polish of regular care. Ancient tomes with cracked leather spines sat alongside newer volumes. Her gaze drifted to the center shelf, where he had proudly displayed a curved dagger with a jeweled hilt pulsing with a faint blue light.

His large desk, a testament to organized chaos, dominated the center of the room. Papers scattered across its surface in a pattern only he could decipher, each stack weighed down with various objects—a crystal paperweight here, a small metal figurine there. The soft rustle of paper drifted on the air as he looked up from his work, acknowledging her presence with a curt nod. His face bore the signs of countless hours poring over the matters of protecting the Far Viscera.

His chair creaked as he leaned back, the leather worn smooth from years of use. On the wall behind him hung a detailed map of the Far Viscera, marked with notations and symbols in his distinctive handwriting. Red pins dotted certain locations—trouble spots, she presumed, or perhaps places of particular interest to him.

"Anasazi," he said, his voice low and gravelly. "Please, have a seat."

She glided across the room. As she settled into the chair across from him, she felt a slight sense of unease. The weight of her recent actions pressed heavily upon her shoulders, and she knew the conversation ahead would be far from easy.

He leaned forward in his chair, the leather creaking softly beneath him. "Tell me, Anasazi, how did Olivia come into possession of Circe's amulet?"

"I've given Olivia the amulet," she said firmly. "It had Circe's power of telekinesis."

The words hung in the air, heavy and portentous. She watched his face carefully, noting the slight widening of his eyes, the almost imperceptible tightening of his jaw. She could almost see the gears turning in his mind as he processed this information.

Silence stretched between them for a long moment. Her fingers twitched in her lap, betraying her inner tension. She hadn't acted lightly in gifting the amulet to Olivia, but now, faced with Jitatma's scrutiny, doubt began to creep in.

Finally, he spoke, his voice carefully controlled. "Why would you do that?"

"Olivia's potential is extraordinary," she said. "The amulet will help her harness her abilities, guide her toward the mastery of her powers."

He frowned, his fingers drumming lightly on the desk. "I know how powerful Olivia is, and you didn't think to consult me first? This is a significant decision."

"I didn't think I needed your permission, son," she replied.

"I would hardly call you a stepmother, so don't call me that. Do you understand the implications of what you've done?" Jitatma asked, leaning forward, grabbing the edge of his desk. "There's a reason Circe locked that power in an amulet."

Anasazi met his gaze unflinchingly. "I understand the implications perfectly," she said, her voice steady. "Olivia is not just any mortal. She carries Circe's soul within her. The amulet rightfully belongs to her."

He exhaled sharply, the sound cutting through the tension-filled air. "Telekinesis is no small power to wield." His fingers tightened around the edge of his desk, the wood groaning under his grip. "What are the risks? Have you considered the consequences if she loses control?"

A flicker of doubt crossed her mind, but she pushed it aside. "I have faith in her," she said, her voice unwavering. "She's stronger than you give her credit for."

"Faith is not enough," he countered, his voice sharp.

She leaned back slightly in her chair. The scent of incense lingered in the air, mingling with the musty smell of old books lining the shelves around them. She felt the weight of his gaze upon her, heavy with unspoken questions and barely concealed concern.

"You're right," she conceded. "Faith alone is not enough, but neither is fear. Olivia needs guidance, not restriction. The amulet will help her understand and control her abilities."

His brow furrowed deeper, a crease forming between his eyes. "How do you explain the portal incident?"

A chill ran down her spine at the mention of the portal. She hadn't anticipated that development, and it worried her more than she cared to admit. "That was unexpected," she said carefully. "It only proves my point. Olivia's powers are manifesting whether we intervene or not. At least with the amulet, she has a focal point, something tangible to help her channel and control her abilities." She leaned forward. "We can't change what's already been done."

His gaze remained fixed on her. "Generosity has never been your strong suit, Anasazi, so why the change of heart?"

She felt a flicker of irritation at his words, but she kept her expression neutral. "This isn't about generosity," she replied, her tone cold and precise. "It's about responsibility and safeguarding the future of Niberia and our world." She paused, choosing her next words carefully. "Olivia is unique. Her potential is unlike anything we've seen before. The amulet is a tool, nothing more. A means to an end."

"I swear, if you put Olivia in danger in any way, I'll place your head on my shelf as a trophy. I have no reason to trust your words."

Her lips curled slightly at his threat, but she didn't rise to the bait. "You speak of trust, Jitatma, but what choice do we have? The girl's powers are awakening, with or without our intervention. Would you rather she stumble around blindly, risking not only herself but everyone around her?"

"Do you think this amulet will help her control these powers?" he asked, skepticism evident in his tone.

She narrowed her eyes and glared sharply. "The amulet is a conduit, a focal point. It will help her channel and direct her abilities, rather than letting them run wild." She paused, allowing her words to sink in. "Without it, she's a storm without direction. With it, she has a chance to become the force we need her to be. Let me remind you that the sisters are powerful, and we'll need them both. Someone is using dark magic and has released the Dark Haunting in the Afterlife."

His fingers drummed against the polished wood of his desk, the soft tapping a counterpoint to the tension in the air. She leaned back in her chair, waiting for him, hoping he would accept her response.

"Your intentions may be noble, Anasazi," Jitatma said at last, his voice low and measured, "but you've always had your own agenda. What do you hope to gain?"

"This isn't about personal gain, Jitatma. It's about survival—hers and ours. I may not be known for my generosity, but I am known for my foresight. This isn't charity—it's strategy." She narrowed her eyes and added an edge of steel to her voice. "The Dark Haunting is no mere threat. It's a malevolent force that seeks to consume everything in its path. I believe Gorgon is behind it."

His eyebrows shot up. "My father? That's a serious accusation, even for you."

"I don't make it lightly," Anasazi replied. "I've sensed dark magic at work. The kind that twists and corrupts. It bears Gorgon's signature."

His face paled, the implications of her words sinking in. "If you're right, we're facing a threat far greater than we imagined."

"The Dark Haunting managed to escape the empty void. Someone weakened that gate. The only one I know who's been there was Gorgon when he struck that deal with Storm."

"I'll have to ask my brother about that deal. Anu and Ki have managed to erect a protection spell around their castle and the surrounding area in the Afterlife. It's a powerful enchantment, drawing on their combined strength."

Her mind raced through the implications. "Is the spell holding?"

"For now," he confirmed. "They're preventing the Dark Haunting from entering the Far Viscera, but..." He trailed off, his expression grave.

"But what?" she pressed, her voice barely above a whisper.

He sighed; the sound was heavy with worry. "It's taking a toll on them. Maintaining such a powerful barrier requires immense energy. If the Dark Haunting continues its assault, I fear even their combined strength may not be enough."

"We need a plan," she said, her gaze fixed on the flickering shadows cast by the room's dim lighting. "If Gorgon truly is behind this, we're facing a threat that could unravel the very fabric of our realms."

"Agreed." He nodded. "It might be time to evacuate the After-life of the souls. I wish we knew why the Dark Haunting is growing so quickly."

"That's where Olivia comes in," she said, tinged with a mix of calculation and something akin to pride. "She may uncover evidence we cannot."

His eyes narrowed. "You're playing a dangerous game, Anasazi. I will not use Olivia as a pawn."

"A pawn?" she scoffed, causing the temperature in the room to drop a few degrees. "No, Jitatma. She's far more than that. She's our wildcard. Think about it," she urged. "Olivia possesses abilities we've never seen before. With the amulet enhancing her powers, she might sense or interact with the Dark Haunting in ways we can't."

He rubbed his temples, clearly conflicted. "It's too risky. We don't fully understand her capabilities, and exposing her to such darkness could be catastrophic. I need to protect her."

She stood abruptly, her dress rustling as she began to pace, her mind racing. She felt his eyes following her, but she paid him no mind.

"The Dark Haunting grows stronger by the day," she said. "I can feel it. It's like a shadow creeping at the edges of my consciousness, always there, always hungry."

"How certain are you that Gorgon is behind this?"

She paused, her eyes distant as she gazed out the window at the swirling mists of the Far Viscera. "I have no concrete proof," she admitted, her voice laced with frustration. "I know my husband. I've sensed a change in him, a darkness that goes beyond his usual proclivities."

"Fine. I'll talk to Olivia and see if she will agree."

"You better hope you still have an influence over her. We need her on our side."

"Let me worry about my relationship with Olivia."

CHAPTER NINETEEN

OLIVIA

O livia's fingers trembled as they grazed the cool surface of the bathroom mirror, tracing the unfamiliar contours of her reflection. The once-vibrant color of her hair had faded to a lifeless sandy blonde, as if the very essence of her being was slowly draining away. Her eyes, wide with disbelief, fixated on the pointed tips of her ears that peeked through the limp strands like unwelcome intruders.

Her gaze drifted down to her arms, where her skin had dulled to an unnatural pallor. As her fingertips brushed against it, she felt a surge of heat pulse beneath the surface. The Dalanite's influence was undeniable, its presence a constant reminder of the battle raging within her.

She closed her eyes, trying to steady her breathing, but the image of her altered state remained burned into her mind. When she opened them, she searched again for any remnant of her former self in the stranger before her.

She ran her fingers through her hair, wincing as they caught on tangles. The texture felt wrong—coarse where it had once been silky. Each change, no matter how small, felt like a betrayal, a step further away from the person she used to be.

How much of her was left? How much would remain when the Dalanite was done with her? The questions swirled in her mind, a torrent of fears she couldn't silence.

She leaned closer to the mirror, her breath fogging the glass as she examined every detail of her face. The curve of her cheekbones seemed sharper; her lips were fuller. Even her eyes, once a clear blue, now seemed gray in the dim light.

She couldn't tear her gaze away. The changes were subtle, yet profound. Each one a reminder of the power that coursed through her veins, a power she neither understood nor wanted anymore. The Dalanite's influence was too strong, its grip on her too tight. Each passing moment brought new changes, new challenges to her sense of self.

She tore her gaze away from the mirror, her heart pounding. She turned toward the bathtub, desperate for some semblance of normalcy. The sound of running water filled the room as she turned the faucet, a steady rhythm that matched the frantic beating of her heart.

As she sank into the warm water, she closed her eyes, letting out a long, shaky breath. The heat enveloped her, seeping into her bones, but it did little to ease the tension coiled within her. She tried to focus on the sensation of water lapping at her skin, hoping it would ground her in the present.

Instead, her mind drifted, seeking refuge in memories of a time before all this chaos. Unbidden, the image of Jitatma rose in her thoughts. Their first meeting flooded back to her, vivid and electric.

He had opened a swirling, shimmering portal into that very bathroom, as he followed orders to kidnap her, ready to fulfill a dark purpose. It was that moment when he had awakened a spark within her. It was something no other man could have done. She remembered how she had stood there frozen in fear, yet fascinated by his imposing figure. That initial connection felt so real, a memory she cherished even now, despite everything.

I told you that you can fuck him, but you can't love him.
I don't love him.
Hmm ... really? You can't lie to me.
Was the Dalanite right? Did she love Jitatma?

Olivia shook her head vehemently as waves rippled across the water's surface in response to her sudden movement

"No," she whispered defiantly. "I don't love him." Even as she spoke those words aloud to convince herself otherwise, they seemed hollow. "It isn't love. It can't be."

The warm water suddenly turned cold against her skin like icy fingers. The change in temperature sent a jolt of fear through her. She gasped as a strong force gripped her shoulders, forcing her back against the hard porcelain tub.

You belong to me now.

The icy water surged around her, enveloping her in a frigid embrace as it rushed to fill her mouth. The force abruptly thrust her beneath the surface, the chill seeping into her bones and stealing her breath away.

Panic seized her as she thrashed against the invisible force holding her down. Her lungs burned, desperate for air, as she fought against the Dalanite's grip. Water filled her nose and mouth, threatening to drown her. The world above the surface blurred and distorted, growing distant with each passing second.

In her mind, she could hear the Dalanite's laughter, cruel and mocking, but she refused to surrender. With every ounce of strength left in her body, she pushed back against the entity trying to claim her. Her fingers clawed at the smooth sides of the tub, searching for any way to pull herself up.

Just as her vision began to darken at the edges, powerful hands gripped her shoulders, yanking her out of the water. She gasped, coughing and sputtering as air rushed back into her lungs. She blinked rapidly, water streaming from her eyes as she tried to focus on the figure before her. Through the haze, she saw Jitatma's concerned face, his dark eyes wide with worry.

"Olivia, are you all right?" Panic tinged his deep voice as he lifted her trembling form from the tub.

She couldn't speak, her throat raw from the water and her chest heaving as she gulped precious air. His arms were warm and solid around her, a stark contrast to the icy grip that had held her under moments before. She clung to him, her fingers digging into his shoulders as she fought to regain control.

A sudden, sharp sting blossomed on her skin as his hand connected with her ass, leaving a brief, tingling heat in its wake. She winced, the unexpected sensation jolting her fully back to awareness. Her eyes snapped to his face, feeling a mixture of confusion and indignation.

"What was that for?" she demanded, her voice hoarse from coughing.

"You're going to tell me what's going on."

Her heart raced as she stared up at him, water dripping from her hair and running down her face. She opened her mouth to speak, but no words came out. How could she possibly explain what was happening to her? The transformation, the Dalanite's growing control, the terrifying near-drowning experience. It all seemed too fantastical, too horrifying to put into words.

"I don't know," she finally managed, her voice barely above a whisper. "Something's wrong with me, Jitatma. I'm changing, and I can't stop it."

His eyes searched her face, concern etched in the furrow of his brow. "I see that. Your Nibmarks are almost gone, and your ears are pointed."

Her hand flew to her ear, feeling the unfamiliar point. She gulped, fighting back tears. "The Dalanite," she said, her voice trembling. "It's trying to take over. I can feel it inside me."

His grip on her tightened, his jaw clenching as he processed her words. "We need to get you out of here," he said, his voice low and urgent. "It's not safe for you to stay."

As if in response to his words, a searing pain shot through her body. She cried out, doubling over in Jitatma's arms. The Dalanite's presence surged within her, fighting against his touch. Her body convulsed as the Dalanite's voice echoed in her mind. She clung to Jitatma, her nails digging into his skin as she fought against the entity trying to consume her.

He can't have you.

She squeezed her eyes shut, focusing all her energy on pushing back against the Dalanite's influence. She felt it clawing at her consciousness, trying to seep into every corner of her mind.

Jitatma lifted her effortlessly in his arms. She shivered, suddenly aware of her nakedness and vulnerability. He grabbed a towel, wrapping it around her trembling form as he carried her out of the bathroom.

"Where are we going?" she asked, feeling small and uncertain.

"I'm going to get your sister and my brother. I need to find out what a Dalanite is and how to get it out of you."

"You can't tell Talia," she insisted as she pushed against his chest, causing him to lose his grip. He stumbled forward into the hallway and lost his hold on her. As her feet hit the floor, his momentum carried him closer, backing her against the wall.

Her breath hitched as her hand flattened against his chest, the heat of his skin searing through the thin fabric of his shirt. His chest pressed against hers, his breath hot and heavy against her neck.

She felt the hard line of his cock, already half-hard, pressing into her hip. It was a tease, a silent promise of what he could do to her, what he would do to her if she let him. She wanted to let him. She wanted to let him fuck her, to take her apart piece by piece until she was nothing but a quivering, broken mess beneath him.

"Commander," she whispered, her voice trembling, and his name felt like a prayer on her lips, a plea for mercy or perhaps for more. She wasn't sure which.

"Are you going to be a good girl, or do I have to spank you again?" he murmured, his voice gravelly, and the words sent a jolt of heat straight to her core. She felt herself growing wet, and she bit down on her lower lip to stifle the moan that threatened to escape. "You're trembling, Minx."

Her hair clung to her shoulders, and she felt droplets of water tracing a path down the curve of her neck and into the valley of her chest. The towel poorly concealed her body's response to him. She gripped the fabric to hold it around her, but it was a useless attempt at modesty. His eyes were on her, burning into her like a brand, and she loved it.

He stood there, his broad frame towering over her. His wet shirt pressed against his hard chest. He'd just saved her from drowning, and now she wanted to drown in him.

She let the towel slip just a little more, the fabric grazing her nipples in a way that made her gasp. His eyes dropped to the swell of her breasts, and his jaw tightened, his fists clenching at his sides like he was holding back from tearing the towel off her.

He leaned so close she felt his hot breath on her skin. One hand reached up, calloused fingers brushing a strand of wet hair from her face before trailing down her neck, her shoulder, leaving a trail of fire in their wake. The other hand gripped the edge of the towel, his knuckles brushing against her skin.

"What do you want, Olivia?" he murmured, his lips inches from hers. "I've missed you."

His lips found hers, demanding, claiming her like she was his to devour. Her fingers tangled in his hair, pulling him closer, desperate for more of him.

"Minx," he growled against her lips. It wasn't a question or a plea—it was a command, a possessive declaration that made her knees weak.

His teeth grazed her bottom lip, nipping lightly before sucking it into his mouth, and she couldn't stifle the moan that escaped her throat. The sound seemed to ignite something dark and hungry in him, because he pressed her harder against the wall, trapping her like a predator cornering its prey.

His hand tightened on the towel, and with one sharp tug, it fell in a wet pile at her feet. She was naked now, completely bare and exposed to him.

"Good girl," he murmured, his voice dripping with dark promise.

No, he can't have you. I won't allow it.

An unseen force propelled Jitatma across the hallway. He collided with the opposite wall. The energy seemed to pulse around him, holding him captive with an intangible grip. His face contorted in pain and confusion as he struggled against the unseen bonds.

He is a distraction. A weakness. We don't need him.

She shook her head vehemently, pressing her palms against her temples as if she could physically push the Dalanite out.

No. You don't get to decide what I need.

She stumbled forward, reaching toward Jitatma, but before she could reach him, a cold chill wrapped around her, freezing her in place. She fought against the entity's control, her body trembling with the effort. "No," she gritted through clenched teeth. "I won't let you hurt him."

The Dalanite's grip only tightened, sending waves of icy pain through her limbs. She felt it pushing at the edges of her consciousness, trying to take over. Her vision blurred as she fought. Her body felt like it was being torn in two, caught between her own will and the entity's relentless push for control.

"Olivia," he called, his voice strained. "Fight it. You're stronger than this thing."

"I can't."

Jitatma's body went limp. A swirling gray mist began to seep into the hallway, curling and twisting in the air as it gathered form. It shimmered and shifted, gradually taking on a more defined shape until a ghostly replica of him stood there. The ethereal form mirrored his features perfectly, its translucent edges softly blurred,

giving it an otherworldly glow. The spectral form stepped toward
Olivia, his ghostly hand outstretched. His eyes, though misty and
translucent, burned with an intensity that made her breath catch.

"Olivia," his voice echoed, sounding distant yet crystal clear.
"Let me help you fight this."

She hesitated, her gaze darting between the ethereal figure and
his physical body still pinned against the wall. Her heart raced, fear
and confusion warring within her as she struggled to comprehend
what was happening. The Dalanite's influence wrapped around
her mind, sending sharp pains through her skull.

"Jitatma?" she whispered, her voice trembling. "What's happening to you?"

"Listen. You need to push the Dalanite back in your mind. I'll
help to release the physical hold, but you can't allow him to take
complete control."

"He's not my master. He doesn't control me," she said, imagining herself pushing against the entity's presence.

The Dalanite's grip faltered for a moment, its icy tendrils retreating slightly. She seized the opportunity, pressing her advantage. She envisioned a wall of light pushing back against the darkness, forcing it into a corner of her mind.

The spectral Jitatma moved closer, his ethereal form shimmering as he reached out to her. His ghostly fingers brushed against
her skin, and she felt a surge of warmth flow through her, and she
concentrated on that sensation.

The Dalanite's presence recoiled, hissing and writhing as she
forced it back. She gritted her teeth, focusing all her energy on
maintaining the mental barrier she had created. The Dalanite
thrashed against it, searching for weaknesses, but she held firm.

With a final push, she imagined sealing the Dalanite behind an
impenetrable barrier in her mind. The pressure in her head eased,
and she felt control returning to her limbs. She stumbled back,
catching herself against the wall as the invisible bonds holding her
dissolved.

Across the hallway, Jitatma's physical body slumped to the floor as the force pinning him disappeared. His spectral form flickered and faded, drawn back into his corporeal self. He groaned, pushing himself up on shaky arms.

She rushed to his side, her legs still unsteady. She kneeled beside him, her hands hovering uncertainly over his body. "Are you okay?" she asked, her voice hoarse.

He nodded, wincing as he sat up fully. "I'm fine," he said, his eyes searching her face. "What about you? Did it work?"

She took a deep breath, focusing inward. The Dalanite's presence was still there, a dark whisper at the edges of her consciousness, but it felt contained, manageable. "I think so," she said slowly. "It's not gone, but my mind is quieter for now."

"Olivia!" Talia called frantically as the kitchen door slammed.

Storm yelled, "Where are you?"

Her head whipped around at the sound of her sister's voice. Panic seized her as she realized she was still completely naked, her wet hair clinging to her shoulders. She scrambled to grab the discarded towel from the floor, wrapping it hastily around herself just as she heard footsteps across the living room.

Talia appeared, her face flushed and her eyes wild with worry. "I sensed a spirit in the house."

"I forgot you have a protection spell around the house for spirits." She sighed, frustrated. "It was just Jitatma."

Stepping around Talia, Storm held out his hand to help Jitatma up. "Are you two getting into trouble? I mean, your rough foreplay is your business, but you guys were setting off my wife's ghostly alerts."

"It's not what you think, brother."

"Oh, no, it's exactly what I think." Storm grinned and let out a chuckle. "You two, wet in the hallway, a trail of water from the bathroom, Olivia half naked, and you a spirit. It's kinky, but I can respect that."

Olivia scrambled to her feet, trying hard to keep the towel around her. "How did you do that? With the ghost thing?"

"It's an ability I've always had but rarely used. My spirit can separate from my body for short periods." He met her gaze, his dark eyes intense. "I've never used it to help someone fight an internal battle before."

"Olivia Trismegist, you have exactly two minutes to get dressed and tell me what the hell is going on or I'm going to burn every last blonde curl on your head with a lightning bolt."

Olivia took a step toward her sister. "You wouldn't dare."

Her sister lifted her hand, releasing tiny sparks from her fingertips as a warning. "I'll make sure your precious hair never grows back, so try me."

CHAPTER TWENTY

OLIVIA

O livia's heart raced as she felt the weight of everyone's stares as she entered the living room. The room seemed to close in around her. She took a deep breath, trying to steady her nerves. She had attempted to give Talia some space to cool off while she dressed, but her sister remained visibly upset. Talia sat with her arms crossed on the couch, tapping her foot.

Seeing her sister's face, she blurted out in a high-pitched voice, "I didn't know how to explain what was happening."

Talia, trying to keep her voice calm, asked, "How about you start with your physical appearance?"

Jitatma was pacing the living room floor, his cape trailing behind him like a shadow, swaying with each step he took. Frustration furrowed his brow, and he glared at Olivia with a clenched jaw, a look only she seemed to receive.

"The Dalanite, it's living in my mind. It's become part of me." Olivia struggled to find the right words, her hands fidgeting. "It's like we've merged somehow. I can feel its thoughts, its emotions. Sometimes, I'm not sure where I end and it begins."

"That sounds like a problem you should have shared with us," Jitatma said sharply.

Before Olivia could answer, Storm burst through the kitchen door, Scooter at his heels. Storm clutched The Book of the Dead tightly. He placed the book on the coffee table, its pages rustling as he flipped through the ancient tome. The Book of the Dead was a fearsome artifact, filled with spells and potions, containing Queen Circe's most powerful magic.

"We found something," Scooter announced breathlessly, his eyes wide with excitement. "There's an entry in the Book of the Dead with a drawing of the amulet, but I don't have my laptop to look up the translation."

Olivia sat on the couch next to her sister, leaning forward, her curiosity momentarily overriding her anxiety. The illustration on the yellowed page depicted an intricate amulet, its design unmistakably matching the one around her neck.

"I can translate it.," Talia said, pulling the book closer. "It says the amulet contains Circe's power of telekinesis, and it can harness the natural abilities of the one who wears it."

"Anasazi was telling the truth." Jitatma shook his head. "I don't believe most of her words, but she did say the amulet would help grow your powers."

"There's more. This part isn't so encouraging," Talia warned. "Circe also trapped a Dalanite in the amulet. According to the book, a Dalanite is a parasitic entity that feeds on one's dark desires. It prefers a host with the power of telekinesis and can open portals. It says here that Circe captured one and bound it to the amulet as a safeguard."

Her hand instinctively went to the amulet around her neck, its weight suddenly feeling much heavier. She could feel the Dalanite stirring within her mind, as if aware it was being discussed.

"I knew something was wrong." Scooter said, looking around the room. "I told you guys."

"How did you know, Scooter?" Storm asked, tilting his head to one side.

"It's not Scooter's fault. I came on to him, but he was enough of a gentleman to turn me down," Olivia admitted.

Talia turned the page over, her fingers trembling slightly as they brushed against the ancient parchment. "There's a spell to trap the Dalanite," she said, her voice rising with a note of hope that made Olivia's heart skip. She cleared her throat and straightened her shoulders. "From darkness to light, I command the Dalanite to make what is wrong now right. I confine the parasite in this amulet so bright to break our bond of second sight."

Nothing happened.

Olivia's shoulders slumped. "Why didn't it work?" she asked, disappointment bitter on her tongue. She could feel the Dalanite's presence, almost like it was laughing at their attempt, a mocking whisper in the back of her mind.

Storm's voice cut through the silence. "Maybe the spell needs more power behind it."

"So, what does this mean for Olivia?" Talia asked.

Jitatma stepped closer to the book, his eyes narrowing as he studied the illustration. "It means she's in danger."

"I'm not in danger as long as I don't use my powers or give in to my inappropriate behavior."

"You're going to stop having sex, reading minds, and actually get up to pour your own coffee?" Talia shook her head. "No one believes that."

"I can control myself." She shrugged. "At least, most of the time. It's at night the Dalanite is the strongest."

"I'll stay with you until we can figure out how to get this Dalanite out of you completely," Jitatma said firmly.

"No, that's not going to happen," Storm said, stepping in front of Jitatma. "I may not know much about Anunnakian women, but I do know Sumerian men. I can tell from your behavior that you're in your Quickening, brother. I'm not leaving you two alone to feed the Dalanite because you can't keep your hands off her."

"I can control myself," he said harshly. "I'm at the fourth stage of my Quickening and I'm not more irritable than usual."

Jitatma's mood was perfectly understandable to Olivia. He was in the throes of his intense sexual phase for the month, a period marked by heightened desire and urgency. She was the catalyst, fueling his insatiable need to bring his Quickening to a satisfying end.

For a Sumerian man, reaching the conclusion of the fifth stage without achieving sexual satisfaction is a torturous experience, a relentless cycle of longing and frustration. It was a cycle Jitatma would have to endure for the next thirty days, each day stretching out until the Quickening began anew, an unending loop of desire and anticipation.

"No one believes that either. I'm not taking that chance. Talia and I will stay with Olivia."

"Oh, no. I'm not putting up with you sucking face and ass grabbing each other all night," Olivia insisted.

"Then I'll stay," Scooter offered.

"No! That's not going to work. You're going to drive me crazy cleaning my apartment all night." She threw up her arms.

"I mean, it could use a good dusting."

"I don't dust!" A sharp knock at the door interrupted the bickering. Everyone froze, exchanging worried glances. Olivia's heart skipped a beat as she sensed a presence on the other side - authoritative, determined, and slightly impatient. "It's just Sully."

"What happened to not using your powers?" Talia rolled her eyes as she moved toward the door.

As Talia opened the door, Olivia caught sight of Sully in her usual crisp suit, her badge clipped to the waistband of her pants. She stood in the doorway, her keen eyes surveying the room with practiced efficiency. Olivia knew she wasn't there for a social call.

"Good evening, everyone," Sully said, her voice carrying a mix of politeness and steel. "I hope I'm not interrupting anything important."

"Not at all," Talia said as she stepped out of the way. "Come in and join us."

"I'm here on official business," she said as she stepped into the apartment. "I'm glad to see the whole gang is here because I wanted you to hear this from me first."

"What's going on, sis?" Storm asked.

"I've been assigned to investigate a series of disappearances that have occurred recently in Grand View. Three men have gone missing this week."

Olivia felt her stomach twist. She knew exactly what Sully was referring to, and the guilt of her involvement threatened to overwhelm her. She fought to keep her face neutral as she glanced at Jitatma.

"What does that have to do with us?" Scooter asked.

"They were last seen at the local college bar talking to a young, attractive blonde," Sully said, turning to Olivia.

"I was at the bar a few nights ago," she admitted.

Sully's eyes narrowed. "Witnesses said a woman matching your description quite vividly left with one of the missing men. A bartender named Sam."

Talia stepped forward, placing a protective hand on Olivia's shoulder. "My sister wouldn't be involved in something like this, Sully. There must be some mistake."

"I hope so," Sully replied, her tone softening.

Jitatma spoke up. "It wasn't Olivia. I'm sure it was a Dalanite that pulled them into a portal."

Sully's eyebrows shot up, her gaze darting between Jitatma and Olivia. "A Dalanite? Portal?" She shook her head, a hint of exasperation in her voice. "Look, I'm trying to conduct a serious investigation here. I need facts."

Olivia felt a surge of panic. Her heart pounded as she watched Jitatma, silently willing him not to reveal too much.

"It's a parasitic creature," he explained, his voice steady. "It feeds on dark desires and can create portals to other dimensions. I believe it's responsible for the disappearances."

"Wait. It opened a portal and took your date. When were you going to tell us this piece of information?" Talia asked, narrowing her eyes. Her voice sharpened as she spoke, her tone carrying a clear edge of frustration.

Olivia felt the tension in the room ratchet up another notch. She could sense Talia's frustration, Jitatma's protective instinct, and Sully's growing suspicion. The weight of their expectations pressed down on her, making it hard to breathe.

Scooter stepped back. "That would have been great information to know, considering you tried to do the same thing to me."

"It happened so fast, and I wasn't even sure what was going on. At first, I thought it was Jitatma pulling them in the Far Viscera to scare them and he would send them back. Then they never came back."

Jitatma shook his head. "I don't need to use scare tactics."

Sully's eyes narrowed, her professional demeanor slipping for a moment to reveal a mix of concern and suspicion. "You guys are going to get me fired for your crazy shit. I need you to tell me everything you know about these disappearances. Now."

"Scooter, you might want to cover your ears. You're much too innocent for this story," Olivia warned.

"Nothing you do surprises me anymore." Scooter smirked. "I think we're beyond innocence. You were going to let the Dalanite take me to another dimension."

Olivia turned to Sully. "I took those men home to fulfill my dark fantasies. As soon as I was sexually satisfied, a portal opened, and they were pulled in."

"Okay, I didn't need to know that," Scooter remarked, attempting to cover his ears. "That was too much information. I have to say I'm relieved my innocence saved me."

Sully pinched the bridge of her nose, clearly struggling to process this information. "Let me get this straight. You're telling me that you had relations with these men, and then they were sucked into some kind of magical portal created by a creature called a Dalanite."

Olivia nodded, her cheeks burning with embarrassment. "I know it sounds crazy, but it's the truth."

"Where exactly did this portal lead?" Sully asked, her voice strained with disbelief.

"We don't know," Jitatma interjected. "The Dalanite's portals could lead anywhere. We're still trying to figure that out."

Sully turned to Storm, her eyes pleading for some semblance of sanity. "Please tell me you have a more rational explanation for all this."

Storm shook his head. "I wish I did, sis."

"I guess that's what I get for having you two as brothers," Sully said, her eyes darting between Jitatma and Storm. "Sometimes, it's just easier not to know the truth. I don't know how I'm going to explain this one to my boss. If this gets out, I might as well pack up my office."

Olivia felt an image forcing its way into her mind's eye. She tried to push it aside, but it was too strong. It was a vision of a roaring fire, flames dancing wildly and casting flickering shadows in all directions. The heat radiated intensely in the night air, consuming everything in its path with a relentless, crackling fervor.

The vision consumed Olivia, the fire's heat so real she could almost feel her skin tightening from it. Sweat beaded on her forehead as the flames in her mind's eye grew higher, engulfing buildings. She could hear screams in the distance, desperate cries for help that made her heart race.

"Olivia?" Talia's voice seemed to come from miles away. "What's wrong?"

Olivia blinked rapidly, trying to force herself back to the present. The apartment swam back into focus, but the acrid smell of smoke lingered in her nostrils. Everyone was staring at her with varying degrees of concern.

"I had a vision," she whispered, her voice hoarse. "A fire. A massive one. I could feel the heat, smell the smoke." She pressed her palms against her temples. "It felt so real."

On the coffee table, the Book of the Dead began to glow and flipped the pages rapidly to the front. Talia sat on the couch beside Olivia, nudging her aside with a gentle but firm push. The intricate symbols of the divine language ignited on the pages.

"Olivia, I think you've unlocked another part of the prophecy," Talia said. "From the source unexpected by all comes the ally and hindrance to befall to curse the native for which to free. The native will receive active powers to be warned the burden too overwhelmed to see."

Olivia's fingers gently brushed over her amulet, feeling its familiar coolness against her skin. "That must be me."

Talia continued, "From the source, unexpected by all, comes the ally and hindrance to befall to haunt the native for which to compel. Spirits from the shadows that dwell, attacking the one they wish to dispel."

"That sounds like the Dalanite," Jitatma said.

"From the source unexpected by all comes the ally and hindrance to befall to jinx the native for which to force and isolate the soul and spirit from the source only to create the queen without remorse."

"The queen without remorse?" Jitatma's worry laced his voice, furrowing his brow as he spoke. "That doesn't sound like Johara."

"Nothing about this part of the prophecy sounds promising," Scooter chimed in, his tone a mix of frustration and disappointment. "Why can't it ever bring us some good news for a change?"

"Because prophecies are rarely about puppies and sunshine," Olivia muttered, pressing her fingertips harder against her temples. The fire's vision still flickered at the edges of her consciousness, refusing banishment. "The fire I saw—it wasn't just any fire. It was large, like buildings were on fire. People were afraid, confused, but most of all, they were angry."

Sully let out a long, slow breath. "So, now we're adding prophecies and visions to this investigation? Perfect." She crossed her arms, her stance widening, as if bracing herself. "Where was this fire supposed to happen?"

"I'm not sure. My visions are never this strong. Usually, I can predict only a few moments into the future like someone approaching, but this is different," Olivia admitted. "This seems like days or even weeks away, but I don't think it's that far off," she added, her voice growing distant as the vision's remnants lingered in her mind. "There was something familiar about the buildings, the streets. I think it's here in Grand View."

Jitatma moved closer, his presence both comforting and unsettling. She felt the Dalanite stirring within her, responding to his proximity.

"Your powers are growing stronger," he said, his voice low enough that only she could hear. "The Dalanite may be amplifying them."

Sully pinched the bridge of her nose again, closing her eyes briefly, as if gathering her patience. "Okay, let me try to make sense of this. We have missing men, a parasitic creature, portals to who-knows-where, prophecies, and now a vision of a fire that may or may not happen somewhere here. I'm going to try to write my notes leaving all of that out and have it still make sense."

CHAPTER TWENTY-ONE

OLIVIA

Olivia paused at the entrance of the seedy bar at the edge of town, tugging her hood lower until it cast her face in shadow. The music inside pulsed through the walls—not a cheerful rhythm but a dull, repetitive thud that matched the heavy drumming of her heart. She took a deep breath and pushed open the door, stepping into the sour-smelling darkness beyond. Paint peeled from the walls in long, curling strips, revealing patches of concrete underneath like wounds in the building's skin. The floor beneath her boots was sticky, catching with each step, as if reluctant to let her go.

She kept her head down, allowing her oversized sweatshirt to swallow her slender frame. Her fingers, bony and pale, curled into her sleeves, hiding the slight tremor that had plagued her since morning. A wave of emotions hit her as she moved deeper into the bar—anger, boredom, lust, all mingling into a cocktail of feelings that weren't her own. She closed her eyes briefly, pushing back against the intrusion. This was the downside of her gift—other people's emotions crashing into her consciousness uninvited, especially when she wasn't familiar with a place.

She made her way toward the corner of the bar, careful not to make eye contact with anyone. The music emanated from a worn-out speaker mounted in the corner. From her vantage point, she had a clear view of the room while remaining mostly hidden. She'd chosen this dive because of its location and its reputation for not asking questions. The bartender, a middle-aged man with arms covered in intricate tattoos that curled around his biceps like serpents, barely glanced at her as she entered.

With cautious movements, she pulled back her hood just slightly, enough to reveal a sliver of her face but not enough to expose her ears or the back of her neck where her Nibmarks would be visible—or rather, where they should be.

The bartender approached her, wiping his hands on a rag that had seen better days. "What'll it be?" he asked, his voice like gravel underfoot.

"Whiskey. Neat," she replied, keeping her voice low.

The bartender nodded and turned away without comment. She exhaled slowly, relieved by the simplicity of the exchange. The less interaction, the better. Her fingers drummed against the sticky bar top as she waited, careful to keep her sleeves pulled down over her wrists.

The whiskey arrived moments later, amber liquid catching what little light penetrated this corner of the establishment. She wrapped her fingers around the glass, savoring its cool solidity before taking a careful sip. The liquor burned a path down her throat, its warmth spreading through her chest in a welcome distraction from the constant barrage of foreign emotions.

Three sips in, the Dalanite's voice in her mind had dulled to a whisper. Six sips, and she could almost pretend she was normal—just another patron seeking solace.

How did it come to this? To find a moment of peace, she had to quietly slip out of her own apartment, escaping the clutches of friends and family whose attentions felt like a stifling blanket smothering her sense of freedom. She hadn't felt like this since

Jitatma had locked her in his chambers in the Far Viscera. She was just as confused now as she was then, struggling to figure out who she was.

She recalled the simplicity of her life before she left for college, back when her biggest concern was her uninteresting boyfriend. Part of her wanted adventure and excitement, craving that feeling of being truly alive. Yet now, even with all the adventure she had sought, she found herself questioning if this was really what she wanted.

"Can I buy you another?"

She tensed at the voice beside her. An older man had materialized on the neighboring barstool, his weathered face split by a smile that didn't reach his eyes. The scent of cheap cologne and alcohol wafted toward her, making her nostrils flare in distaste.

"I'm fine, thanks," she replied, angling her body away from him.

The man leaned closer. "Come on, sweetheart. Pretty girl like you shouldn't drink alone." His emotions slithered against her consciousness—a greasy mixture of desire and entitlement that made her skin crawl.

"Really? A pretty girl like me isn't stupid or desperate enough to give in to your sense of entitlement to share space with me." She took a sip from her glass, the liquid swirling momentarily in her mouth before she swallowed. With a deliberate motion, she set the glass back down on the bar, the faint clink of glass against wood barely audible over the ambient chatter. Turning slowly to face him, she narrowed her eyes, and her lips curved into a sardonic smile. "What about my facial expression or body language makes you think I desire your company?" she asked, her tone laced with a hint of challenge.

He chuckled, a dry sound like dead leaves rustling. "Don't be like that. Name's Decker."

"Listen, Pecker—"

"Decker," he quickly corrected her.

"Right, Pecker, I prefer drinking alone. If you want to buy me a drink, I will come with a warning. The last man who stuck his dick in me was sucked into a portal of no return." She leaned in close and whispered, "My pussy is the gateway to the abyss of great pleasure, and I doubt anyone here would miss you. I dare you. Buy me that drink and put your hand down my pants."

The man's face blanched, his cocky smile faltering as his emotions shifted from lust to uncertainty. He leaned back, studying her face more carefully. Something in her expression must have unnerved him, because his eyes narrowed with sudden recognition.

"Wait a minute," he said, his voice dropping to a dangerous growl. "I know who you are. You're that freak's sister—the one they've been talking about on the news. The human."

Before she could react, his hand shot out, grabbing her hood and yanking it back, and a collective gasp rippled through the nearby patrons. She tried to snatch the hood up but couldn't get a grip, and her hand brushed against the tips of her now-exposed ears. The man's face contorted with disgust, his emotions spiking with a hatred so pure it made her flinch.

He grabbed her arms, yanking her off the bar stool. "Look at this!" the man snarled, his fingers digging into her arm with bruising force. "We got ourselves a genuine freak."

"Let me go," she said, her voice steady despite the fear crawling up her spine.

She tried to jerk away, but his grip tightened. The whiskey glass toppled, amber liquid spreading across the bar like spilled blood. The room seemed to contract around her. The other patrons began rising from their seats with expressions ranging from curiosity to outright hostility.

"I didn't do anything wrong," she said, struggling to keep her voice steady. "I just wanted a drink."

"Your kind isn't welcome here," Decker spat, his face inches from hers. "You and your freak sister think you can just walk around like you belong?"

Her heart hammered against her ribs as the bar fell into an eerie silence. Even the music seemed to fade into the background, leaving only the sound of her own ragged breathing. She could feel the weight of two dozen pairs of eyes boring into her.

She could feel their emotions pressing against her mind—curiosity, fear, and beneath it all, a current of hatred that made her skin prickle. Someone whispered "freak" from the shadows, the word traveling around the room like a contagious disease.

"I think you need to let go of me," she replied, her voice stronger than she felt.

"I think you should leave," Decker growled, his face flushed with anger. His grip tightened around her arm, fingertips digging into her flesh.

"Last chance to remove your hand," she warned, her voice low.

She focused on the bottles on the wall behind the bar.

The man laughed, a harsh sound that scraped against her nerves. "Or what, freak? You'll do some magic trick?"

As Decker's fingers dug deeper into her arm, the glass bottles behind the bar began to tremble—a subtle vibration only she noticed. She felt power building within her, ready to lash out when a familiar voice cut through the tension.

"I believe the lady asked you to remove your hand," said Lieutenant Malta, his voice calm but with an undercurrent of steel that made several patrons step back.

She blinked in disbelief. "Lieutenant?"

Malta stood tall in civilian clothes—dark pants and a fitted black t-shirt that revealed the muscular build his uniform usually concealed. He moved deliberately toward them, each step marked by a slight but noticeable limp that pulled at Olivia's memory.

The story came back to her in fragments—something about Scooter's crossbow misfiring during the chaos of battle in the Far Viscera. The bolt had torn through Malta's thigh, narrowly missing the artery.

His eyes, dark and focused, never left Decker's face as he approached. The intensity in his gaze reminded Olivia of a predator stalking prey, calculating and patient. Malta stepped closer, close enough that Olivia could see the faint stubble along his jaw and a thin scar behind his ear she'd never noticed before. Perhaps his striking blue hair hid it, or perhaps she had never been this close to him before.

"This isn't your business, soldier boy," Decker snarled.

"The shaking bottles behind the bar are making it my business. If you don't back down, she is going to make every one of them fly off the wall. When every drop of liquor comes crashing down on your head, I'm going to be pissed and thirsty."

"What are you going to—"

Malta's fist connected with Decker's jaw before he could finish his sentence. The crack echoed through the suddenly silent bar. The man staggered back, colliding with a table and sending glasses crashing to the floor in a spray of amber liquid and shattered glass.

She pressed herself against the bar, heart hammering. The crowd surged forward and backward like a confused tide, some backing away from the violence, others drawing closer, hungry for blood.

Decker recovered quickly, wiping a trickle of blood from his split lip with the back of his hand. His eyes narrowed to slits. "You shouldn't have done that, soldier boy."

He charged forward with surprising speed for his size, aiming a wild haymaker at Malta's head. Malta ducked smoothly; years of combat training were evident in his every movement. As Decker's momentum carried him forward, Malta drove an elbow into his ribs, then followed with an uppercut that snapped Decker's head back.

The patrons around them erupted, some cheering, others shouting threats. Two men detached themselves from the crowd, moving to flank Malta.

He backed up, positioning himself between Olivia and the approaching threats. "Stay behind me," he ordered without looking at her, his focus never leaving Decker and his impromptu allies.

Decker spat blood onto the grimy floor, his grin revealing crimson-stained teeth. "Got yourself in a real mess now, haven't you?"

Malta didn't respond. His breathing remained steady, controlled. Olivia sensed no fear from him—only calculation and something else, something primal and protective that made her breath catch.

The men hesitated, reconsidering their approach. Malta used the moment to grab her wrist, his grip firm but not painful.

"Move with me," he murmured, backing toward the far end of the bar where a dim exit sign glowed red above a door.

Decker had recovered enough to stagger forward, face twisted with rage. "Don't let them leave!"

The bartender, who had been watching the altercation with wary eyes, suddenly reached beneath the counter and pulled out a rifle. The distinct sound of it being cocked cut through the commotion.

"Enough!" he bellowed. "Take it outside or I start shooting, and I don't much care who I hit first."

Malta's grip tightened on Olivia's wrist, pulling her toward him with unexpected urgency. His palm was warm against her skin, calloused, but not rough. She stumbled, caught off-balance by the sudden movement.

"Move!" he hissed, his breath hot against her ear.

From the corner of her eye, she saw Decker lunge toward them, face contorted in rage, spittle flying from his lips. The bartender squeezed the trigger of the rifle, the metal mechanism clicking into place with terrible finality.

Olivia's heart slammed against her ribcage. She flinched, muscles tensing for impact, a scream building in her throat that never had the chance to escape.

Then nothing.

The air around her seemed to thicken, pressing against her eardrums until they popped. The chaotic noise of the bar cut off abruptly, leaving behind a silence so complete it buzzed in her ears. Olivia blinked, disoriented.

Decker hung suspended mid-stride, one foot hovering above the ground, his face frozen in a rictus of hatred. Behind the bar, the bartender stood motionless, the rifle's barrel gleaming dully in the low light. At its end, a small explosion of fire and smoke bloomed like some terrible flower, perfectly still. The bullet itself hung in the air, a deadly metallic teardrop aimed directly at where Olivia had been standing a split second before.

She stared, uncomprehending. Around them, the bar patrons froze in various poses—a woman with her mouth open in a silent scream, a man half-risen from his chair, another with a glass suspended partway to his lips, amber liquid hanging where it had sloshed over the rim.

"What the—" Olivia whispered, her voice sounding unnaturally loud in the silence.

Unlike everything else in the room, he moved, turning to face her. "Are you all right?" he asked, his voice low and steady.

Olivia nodded mutely, unable to tear her eyes away from the frozen bullet. She could see the rifling marks on its surface, the way the light caught its deadly contours.

She gulped, her throat suddenly dry. "Did you do this?"

"We need to move," he said, avoiding her question. "I can't hold it for long."

"Hold what?" Olivia demanded, finding her voice. "Time? You stopped time?"

Malta's eyes, dark and fathomless, met hers. "Not exactly. I've slowed it down drastically, but only in this immediate area."

"How is this possible?" she whispered, reaching out with her free hand to touch one of the frozen droplets. It felt solid, like a tiny glass bead. "Are you like me? Different?"

Malta's lips pressed into a thin line. A sheen of sweat had broken out across his forehead, and a tremor ran through his hand where it gripped her wrist.

"Later," he said through gritted teeth. "Questions later. This takes considerable effort."

Olivia noticed the strain in his face now—the tightness around his eyes, the way his breathing had become shallow and rapid. Whatever he was doing, it was costing him.

"What can I do?" she asked, suddenly worried. "How can I help?"

"The exit," he managed, nodding toward the red glow of the sign. "We need to get outside my radius."

They weaved between frozen patrons, moving as quickly as Malta's limp would allow. Olivia could feel something now—a pressure in the air, like the heaviness before a thunderstorm, centered on Malta. With each step they took, his breathing grew more labored and the tremor in his hand more pronounced.

Behind them, she heard a sound like glass cracking—faint at first, then growing louder. Glancing back, she saw the bullet beginning to inch forward, the frozen explosion at the gun's barrel starting to expand infinitesimally.

"It's breaking down," Malta gasped. "My hold is slipping."

They reached the door, Malta's shoulder hitting it hard enough to send it crashing open. As they crossed the threshold, the pressure around them intensified, squeezing the air from her lungs. Cold night air rushed in, a shocking contrast to the stuffy heat of the bar. Malta pulled Olivia through the doorway into a narrow alley lined with overflowing dumpsters and abandoned crates.

Malta stumbled, nearly falling. His face had gone ashen, a trickle of blood running from his nose. His knees buckled. Olivia caught him, struggling under his weight, and together they collapsed against the brick wall of the building. A rifle blast exploded from inside the bar, finally completing its journey, followed by shouts and screams.

Malta sagged against her, his breathing ragged, blood now flowing freely from his nose. She felt his clammy skin, and his dilated pupils nearly swallowed his irises.

The door slammed behind them, cutting off the sounds of pursuit. He didn't slow down, dragging her deeper into the darkness of the alley, away from the muffled shouts still audible from within the bar. The faster he moved, his limp became more evident.

"Keep moving," he ordered, his grip on her wrist unyielding. "They'll come after us."

She stumbled after him, her mind reeling. The sudden quiet after the chaos of the bar left her disoriented. Her empathic senses, overwhelmed by the bar's emotional maelstrom, now struggled to recalibrate in the relative calm of the night.

"What was that about? What's going on? What do they have against my sister? What are you doing here?" she managed, her voice hoarse. "Were you following me?"

Malta glanced back at her, his expression unreadable in the meager light filtering from a distant streetlamp. "Questions later. Right now, we need distance."

They emerged from the alley onto a quiet side street. He finally slowed his pace, releasing her wrist but remaining close. He scanned their surroundings with practiced efficiency, checking for threats in the shadows between buildings.

"My car's a block away," he said, nodding toward the end of the street. "Can you make it?"

She rubbed her wrist where his fingers had left faint red marks. "I'm not helpless, Lieutenant."

A ghost of a smile touched his lips. "Never said you were. That display with the bottles proved otherwise." Behind them, the bar door crashed open, spilling light and noise into the alley they had just left. Angry voices echoed against the brick walls. "They're coming."

He pulled her into a dark doorway of a closed shop, pressing her against the glass. The cold surface against her back sent a shiver through her as he pressed close, his chest touching hers. His breath came in controlled, even measures, unlike her own ragged gasps. The doorway was barely deep enough to conceal them both, forcing them into an intimacy that made her pulse quicken for reasons entirely unrelated to their escape.

His proximity sent an unexpected flutter through her stomach as his scent—clean sweat mingled with something spicy and distinctly masculine—enveloped her. It had changed from the last time she saw him. The faint smell of cedarwood and rain was still lingering, but the spiciness dominated her nose. His breath warmed her cheek as they stood perfectly still, listening to the approaching footsteps.

"Check down there!" Decker's voice carried from the alley, slurred with alcohol and rage. "They couldn't have gotten far!"

His eyes locked with hers in the darkness, a silent command to remain quiet. She nodded, hardly daring to breathe. His body was tense against hers, muscles coiled and ready to spring into action if needed. Through her sweatshirt, she felt the steady rhythm of his heartbeat—remarkably calm despite the danger.

His arm wrapped around her, a firm pressure that somehow felt both protective and possessive. Footsteps pounded closer, echoing off the brick walls of the narrow street. His body tensed further, shielding her completely from view. The hard planes of his chest pressed against her, and she found herself oddly aware of every point of contact between them.

"Stay still," he whispered, his lips so close to her ear that she felt rather than heard the words. His free hand moved to her face, a finger brushing her lips in a silent request for her to control her breathing. The touch sent an unexpected jolt through her body.

"I swear I'll kill that freak if I find her," Decker's voice growled, closer now. "Her and that soldier boy."

Through the narrow gap between his shoulder and the doorframe, she glimpsed shadowy figures moving past their hiding place. Three men, moving with the unsteady gait of the intoxicated but driven by a purpose that made them dangerous, nonetheless. She held her breath as they paused, arguing about which direction to take.

"I'm telling you, they went that way," one of them insisted, gesturing toward the end of the street.

"Split up," Decker commanded, his voice thick with venom as their footsteps faded into the distance.

Malta remained still for several more heartbeats, his body a solid wall between her and the street. She felt the tension in his muscles gradually ease as the sounds of their pursuers faded into the night. Finally, he pulled back just enough to look down at her face.

"Now I understand the fascination with you," he whispered. "For a taste of you, I would turn against a king." He removed his fingers from her lips, cupping her chin.

"Well, you just took on a bar full of assholes for me, so I guess I should thank you."

"It's not exactly a king's army, like my commander."

"Your commander has lost his interest."

"That's a shame, and he's a fool."

"I think the street is clear."

They moved quickly, his stride purposeful. She matched his pace despite her trembling legs. He led her around a corner to a nondescript black sedan parked under a flickering streetlight. He reached into his pocket for keys, the metallic jingle unnaturally loud in the quiet street.

"Get in," he said, unlocking the doors with a soft chirp.

She hesitated, studying his face. In the harsh glow of the streetlight, his features seemed carved from stone—all angles and hard lines, giving nothing away. But there was something in his eyes, a flicker of concern that seemed at odds with his military demeanor.

"Why were you there?" she asked again. "In that bar, at that exact moment?"

His jaw tightened. Behind them, the sounds of pursuit grew closer—heavy footsteps and angry voices spilling out of the alley.

"Olivia," he said, her name sounding strangely intimate in his deep voice. "Please. Get in the car."

The way he said her name—not as a command, but almost as a request—decided for her. She pulled open the passenger door and slid inside, the leather seat cool against her back. He rounded the hood with quick, efficient movements and dropped into the driver's seat beside her.

As he started the engine, the headlights illuminated a group of men emerging from the alley, Decker at the front, his face a mask of fury even from that distance. He threw the car into drive and pulled away from the curb with a squeal of tires.

She watched the men recede in the side mirror, their angry gestures growing smaller as Malta steered the car around a corner. She slumped back against the seat. He drove in silence, his profile outlined in the blue glow of the dashboard lights. His encounter with Decker's jaw bruised his knuckles where they gripped the steering wheel.

"Thank you," she said finally, the words inadequate but necessary.

He nodded once, his eyes never leaving the road. "You're welcome." His voice was softer now, the military edge dulled. "And to answer your question—no, I wasn't following you. Not exactly."

She turned to face him, waiting for an explanation she suspected would raise more questions than it answered. They had stood on opposite sides in both the living world and the Far Viscera, so it made little sense why he was there helping her.

"It's more like I'm stuck here. I don't have a way back to the Far Viscera. Commander Jitatma took that away from me the last time he arrested Hunter." His hands tightened on the steering wheel. A muscle jumped in his jaw. "Even if I did, I don't think I would be welcomed back. I don't have a world anymore, so I was hoping to get your help."

"What can I do?"

"As you can see, your sister isn't the hero she was in the Far Viscera. The Niberians are scared of her."

"I had no idea."

"That's because you live in a bubble of protection. You don't see what's really going on, but I do. There are some people who are beginning to hate her. With this latest investigation into the disappearing men, the rumor is Talia is responsible."

"She didn't do anything."

"I know." His voice was a soft murmur as he leaned closer, his fingers brushing against the fabric of her sweatshirt. His hand hovered near her chest, the proximity creating a subtle tension in the air. With a gentle tug, he pulled down the neckline, revealing the amulet that lay nestled against her skin. "Anasazi had no idea what was in that amulet when she gave it to you. I'm guessing the Dalanite knows what happened to those men."

CHAPTER TWENTY-TWO

OLIVIA

They pulled up to an old house beyond the town limits. The weathered two-story stood at the end of a winding dirt road, partially hidden by a tangle of ancient trees whose branches stretched like protective arms around the property. Olivia peered through the car window, taking in the faded blue paint peeling from the clapboard siding and the sagging wraparound porch that had clearly seen better days.

The house seemed to absorb sound, creating an unnatural stillness that made the hairs on the back of her neck stand up. No birds sang in the surrounding trees. No insects buzzed. Just silence.

As they approached, she noticed details that spoke of the home's former grandeur—ornate gingerbread trim along the eaves, stained glass inserts in the upper windows. Time and neglect had taken their toll. Several shutters hung askew, and thick vines climbed the north side of the house, their tendrils working between the wooden planks as if trying to reclaim the structure for nature.

"I'd never have found this place on my own," she said, stepping out of the car.

"That's the point."

A set of stone steps led to the front door, each one cracked and settled at a slightly different angle. Weeds pushed through the fissures, creating small islands of green in the weathered gray. The door's brass knocker, shaped like a woman's face with her mouth open as if in song or scream, was nearly black from tarnish.

The door, its hinges protesting from disuse, swung open with a plaintive creak. He stepped inside first, his hand raised slightly. He scanned the darkened interior, then reached for a switch. A single, bare bulb sputtered to life, revealing a living space that seemed to embody the concept of abandonment.

"Come in," he said finally, moving aside to let her pass. "Don't touch the threshold. It's warded."

She stepped carefully over the door's threshold, feeling a strange tingle pass through her body as she crossed some invisible barrier. She wondered if that was the ward he had mentioned or simply her own nerves.

A sagging couch faced a scratched coffee table, both positioned beneath a grimy window. Dust motes danced in the dim light. The walls might once have been blue, but time had reduced them to a color that reminded her of faded bruises. The kitchen was just beyond the living room, its countertops cluttered with unwashed mugs and an iron stove that had seen better days. The persistent drip from a leaking pipe provided a melancholy percussion, punctuating the silence between them.

He shed his worn jacket and laid it over the back of a wooden chair someone had repaired multiple times with mismatched screws. The chair looked like it might collapse if someone breathed on it too forcefully.

"Sit," he said, gesturing toward the couch. It wasn't an invitation so much as an instruction.

She eyed the couch dubiously. It had the defeated look of furniture that had borne too many burdens for too long. Still, she lowered herself onto it, wincing at the immediate protest of springs beneath the threadbare upholstery.

"This place is safe," he stated, his tone firm yet measured. He remained standing, his posture suggesting a man who rarely allowed himself to relax. "No one knows about it except me, and now you."

"It doesn't look very safe," she observed, unable to keep a note of skepticism from her voice. She brushed a finger along the arm of the couch, leaving a clean streak in the dust. "It looks abandoned."

"That's precisely why it's safe." His mouth twitched in a ghost of a smile. "The appearance of abandonment is a better defense than fortress walls. No one looks twice at a place they think no one cares about."

Her gaze traveled around the room, taking in details she'd missed at first glance. Despite the general disrepair, certain items stood out as incongruous—a sleek, modern tablet tucked between tattered books on a shelf; a complicated-looking lock on an interior door; a series of symbols etched into the window frame that she recognized from the Book of the Dead.

She looked over at a small table next to the couch and noticed a photo that stood out, conspicuously free of dust. In fact, it was the most pristine item in the entire house. The woman captured in the picture was strikingly beautiful, her long blonde hair cascading in waves much like her own.

"You've been here before," she said. It wasn't a question.

He nodded, moving to the kitchen. He filled a battered kettle with water from a tap that sputtered before producing a steady stream. "In another lifetime."

"Was this your place when you were alive?" she asked, running her fingers along the couch's arm, feeling the worn fabric catch against her skin.

"It belongs to no one," he replied, placing the kettle on the hot plate and switching it on. "And everyone who needs it." He paused, his back to her. "Right now, that's us."

"You're being cryptic again," she said, leaning back against the couch. A cloud of dust puffed up around her, dancing in the weak light. She fought the urge to sneeze.

He turned to face her, his expression softening. "Force of habit. When you've lived and died like I have, direct answers become luxuries." He pulled two mismatched mugs from a cabinet, inspecting them before setting them on the counter.

"What does that shit even mean? Lived and died like you?"

"It means I know a few things."

"Really? I know very little about you, Lieutenant."

"You know enough."

The kettle began to whistle, a thin, reedy sound that seemed to echo the tension she felt coiling inside her. As he prepared what smelled like herbal tea, she found herself studying him more carefully. The way he moved with practiced efficiency, how his eyes constantly checked the windows and door even as he performed the simple task of making tea.

"I need to understand what's happening," she said, trying to ignore the persistent whisper at the back of her mind; the Dalanite's presence hovering like a shadow behind her thoughts. "Tell me everything you know about the Dalanite. No half-truth or cryptic statements."

He brought the mugs over, offering one to her. Steam rose from the liquid, carrying a scent of herbs she couldn't identify. Their fingers brushed as she accepted the mug, and she felt a jolt of something that wasn't quite electricity pass between them.

"Drink," he said, lowering himself onto the rickety chair across from her. It creaked ominously but held his weight. "It will help clear your mind. Make it harder for the Dalanite to influence your thoughts."

She brought the mug to her lips, hesitating, eying the murky liquid. "How do I know this isn't poison?"

His laugh was sudden and genuine, crinkling the corners of his eyes. "If I wanted you dead, Olivia, I wouldn't waste good herbs from Nothingness Forest. Those are rarer than your trust, apparently. Tell me, did my commander have to work this hard to break down your defenses?"

"That's different. I didn't know who I was, and he was the only connection I had to my sister. My attraction to Jitatma started out as the need to survive."

She slowed brought the cup to her lips again, but this time she took a small sip. The hot liquid tasted bitter on her tongue, causing her to wrinkle her nose.

"Is that what I need to do to get your trust? Kidnap you, wipe your memory, and then treat you like a dirty whore?"

The mug trembled in her hands, tea sloshing dangerously close to the rim. His words struck her like a physical blow, and the Dalanite stirred in the recesses of her mind, feeding on her sudden surge of anger.

"You know nothing about what happened between us," she hissed, setting the mug down with enough force to cause tea to splash onto the scratched coffee table. She jumped up, hands falling to her hips. "You certainly don't get to judge what I've been through. You were a part of what happened. You pushed Jitatma to take advantage of my captivity. Why? Why did you ask him if he had fucked me into submission? Why did it matter to you?"

His expression shifted, regret flashing across his features before settling into something more guarded. "Hunter ordered him to take you, not me." He tightly gripped the arm of the chair, his fingers digging into the worn fabric as if seeking stability.

"Jealous?"

His jaw tightened. His eyes, dark and unreadable, remained fixed on her face. "Yes," he admitted finally, the word hanging in the air between them like something fragile and dangerous. "But not in the way you think."

The honesty in his voice caught her off guard. She'd expected denial, perhaps even anger, but not this raw confession. She took another sip of her tea, trying not to choke. The taste didn't get better the second time, but she drank it as she listened.

"I was jealous that Hunter trusted him with you. Not me." Malta set his own mug down and leaned forward, elbows resting on his knees. The chair groaned beneath the shift in weight. "I've served Hunter for centuries. When the most important task came—protecting Circe's soul—he chose Jitatma. I found out later it was a test for the commander so I could flush out his loyalty."

"Did Hunter know he had a traitor in his army?"

His gaze dropped to the floor, his shoulders tensing beneath his worn shirt. "Hunter suspected everyone, even himself sometimes. He was a paranoid, delusional ruler." He was quiet for a moment, then looked up at her again. "But no, he didn't know about Jitatma specifically. That's why I came to his chambers to find him. I was surprised to learn he had left, since he had insisted he was going to be in his chambers with you all night."

"I was bait for my sister and Jitatma," she said, the words tasting bitter in her mouth. She sank back onto the couch, suddenly exhausted.

"We all are," he replied, his voice softer now. "Trust me, nothing happens by chance. The gods put all of this into motion, but I can't figure out which god is controlling the narrative. I thought it was Hunter, but now that he's in the deepest, darkest prison in the Far Viscera, I have my doubts."

"Tell me, how does the Dalanite fit into all this, and how do you know so much about it?"

"I was there when Circe trapped the Dalanite in the amulet. I saw the changes in her, just like you."

Olivia's fingers found the amulet at her throat, tracing its contours through the fabric of her shirt. A soft pulse seemed to emanate from it, like a second heartbeat against her skin.

"What was she like?" she asked, taking out the amulet from under her sweatshirt. "Circe, I mean."

His eyes took on a distant quality, as though looking through the grimy walls of the house into the past. "Fierce. Brilliant. Terrifying, sometimes." A small, sad smile played at the corners of his mouth. "She could summon lightning from a clear sky and heal wounds that should have been fatal, but her greatest power was her mind. She could read your emotions even before you felt them."

"That doesn't tell me who she was," she pressed.

He sighed, running a hand through his hair. "She loved deeply, but cautiously. She was selective with her trust, much like you." His gaze settled on her with an intensity that made her skin warm. "When she laughed, it was like the world paused to listen." He shook his head. "When she was angry, the ground itself would tremble. She had this way of looking at you that made you feel like she was seeing every mistake you'd ever made, but forgiving you anyway." He paused, his gaze falling on the amulet. "When the Dalanite possessed her, something changed in her, and not just physically. She became colder. More calculating."

"Like me," she whispered, the realization settling over her.

His eyes snapped to hers, suddenly intense. "No. Not like you."

"I feel it happening. The Dalanite is changing me." She wrapped her arms around herself, suddenly cold despite the stuffy air of the room. "I can feel it whispering, suggesting things. How did she trap the Dalanite?"

His expression darkened. "At a terrible cost." He rose from the chair. "The Dalanite will not be easy to trap this time, so we're going to have to find a different way."

"What do you mean, a different way?"

He moved to the grimy window, peering through a gap in the dusty curtains before answering. "The ritual Circe used required sacrifice," he said finally, his voice low. "A willing sacrifice of essence. She gave up a part of herself to create the prison."

"What part?" she asked, though something in her already knew the answer.

He turned to face her, shadows gathering in the hollows beneath his cheekbones. "Her connection to Hunter. Their bond. She severed it to power the spell." His eyes met hers, and a chill raced through her body. "The severed bond left a wound in both of them that never healed."

Her fingers tightened around the amulet. It felt warmer, almost uncomfortably so. "Is that why he's been searching so desperately? To heal that wound?"

"Partly," he said, moving back toward her; the floorboards groaning beneath his feet. "Hunter is complex. His love for Circe was real, but so was his desire to possess her power. The two were always tangled together." He kneeled before her, close enough that she could smell the faint scent of spice that clung to him. "Love is the most potent form of magic in any realm. The severing of a bond that profound creates enough energy to bind even something as ancient as the Dalanite. The price was steep. After the ritual, she was diminished. The part of her that could love purely was gone."

"I don't want that."

His expression softened, his eyes searching hers. "No one should have to make that sacrifice."

His voice was low, gravelly, and it sent a shiver skittering down her spine. He leaned closer. Their eyes locked, and her pulse quickened. Her gaze dropped to his lips—full, slightly parted, and utterly sinful. She imagined how they'd feel against her own, how they'd taste. Her tongue darted out to wet her lips, her mouth suddenly dry.

"Olivia," he murmured. Her name seemed to be a dark promise on his tongue. His eyes were molten, locked on hers with an intensity that made her squirm. "The tea should be working by now. I'd like to find out."

She barely had time to think before he closed the distance, his lips crashing against hers in a kiss that was anything but sweet. It was raw, hungry, and filthy, his tongue plunging into her mouth with a possessive urgency that made her moan. His hand slid into her hair, fisting it tightly as he angled her head to deepen the kiss, his other hand gripping her thigh like he was afraid she'd bolt.

She wasn't going anywhere.

She clutched at his shoulders, her nails digging into the hard muscle beneath his shirt. She could feel the heat of him through the fabric, the way his body tensed under her touch, and it only made her want him more. His tongue danced in her mouth in a rhythm that had her panting, her hips rocking forward, seeking the pressure of his body against hers.

He growled into the kiss, the sound vibrating through her, and he pulled back just enough to bite at her lower lip, sharp and punishing. "Fuck, Olivia," he breathed, his voice rough with need. "You've been driving me insane."

Before she could respond, his lips were on her neck, his teeth grazing the sensitive skin as he worked his way down to her collarbone. She gasped, her head falling back against the couch as his hands slid under her shirt, calloused fingers skimming over the soft skin of her stomach.

"Malta," she whimpered, her voice trembling as his hands moved higher, cupping her breasts through her bra. His thumbs brushed over her nipples, already hardened with need, and she arched into his touch with a moan that was half pleasure, half desperation.

He pulled back just enough to yank her sweatshirt over her head, tossing it aside before his mouth was on her again, this time sinking his teeth into the curve of her shoulder. She cried out, her hands scrambling at the hem of his shirt, desperate to feel his skin against hers.

He didn't need to be told twice. He ripped his shirt off in one fluid motion, revealing the hard planes of his chest, the ripple of muscle that made her mouth water. Her hands roamed greedily over him, tracing the scars that marked his body, the proof of every battle he'd fought and won.

His hands were just as eager, unfastening her bra with ease and tossing it aside before his mouth descended on her breasts. She gasped as he took one nipple into his mouth, his tongue swirling around it in a way that made her toes curl. His hand teased her other breast, pinching and rolling the nipple until she was writhing beneath him.

"Please," she begged, her voice breaking as his teeth grazed her sensitive flesh. "Malta, I need—"

He silenced her with another kiss, this one even more demanding than the last. His hands slid down her body, gripping her hips as he shifted to kneel between her legs. Her breath caught as she felt his hardness pressed against her inner thigh, the evidence of how much he wanted her making her pulse race.

"Tell me what you need," he growled against her lips, his voice dark and dangerous.

"You," she gasped, her hands tangling in his hair.

His lips curved into a wicked smile as he reached for the button of her pants, his eyes never leaving hers. Then he stripped her bare, peeling away every barrier until she lay spread out before him like a feast.

"Fuck, Olivia," he muttered, his hands sliding up her thighs to part them wider. "You're so goddamn beautiful."

Her breath hitched as he caressed the sensitive skin of her inner thighs, teasing her until she was squirming with need. His fingers brushed against her wetness, and she whimpered, pushing into his touch. She gasped, her back arching off the couch. "Malta," she whimpered, her voice trembling as his fingers teased her entrance, dipping just barely inside before pulling away. "Please."

He smirked, that infuriating, cocky smirk that made her want to slap him and fuck him at the same time. "Please what, Olivia?" he asked, his voice dripping with mock innocence. His fingers trailed higher, circling her clit with agonizing slowness. She bit her lip to keep from crying out, her hips bucking against his hand.

"Fuck me," she breathed, her nails digging into the couch cushions. "Please, just—fuck me."

He chuckled darkly, his free hand reaching down to unbutton his pants. "That's my little birdie," he murmured, his cock springing free, thick and hard and already leaking with pre-cum.

He didn't bother taking his pants all the way off, just shoved them down far enough to free himself as he positioned himself between her legs.

Her breath hitched as the blunt head of his cock pressed against her entrance. "Commander—" she gasped, his name almost slipping out before she could stop herself.

He froze for a second, his eyes narrowing as he looked down at her. "What did you just call me?" he asked, his voice dangerous.

"I—I didn't mean—"

Before she could finish, he was slamming into her, burying himself to the hilt in one brutal thrust. She cried out, her nails raking down his back as he filled her completely. "Say it again, Little Birdie," he snarled, his hips already moving, pounding into her with a ferocity that left her breathless.

"Commander," she moaned, the word tumbling from her lips as he drove into her again and again. Her breasts bounced with every thrust, her nipples hard and aching. He gripped her hips so tightly she knew there'd be bruises tomorrow, but she didn't care. All she cared about was the way he was stretching her, filling her, fucking her so hard she could barely think.

"You like that, don't you?" he growled, his pace relentless. "You like calling me Commander while I fuck you like this."

"Yes," she gasped, her legs wrapping around his waist as he slammed into her again.

His lips crashed down on hers, swallowing her moans as he fucked her harder, faster. She felt the heat building in her stomach, the tension coiling tighter and tighter until she was teetering on the edge. "Come for me, Olivia," he growled against her lips. "Let me feel you come on my cock."

Her body clenched around him and her back bowed off the couch, her tits bouncing wildly as he fucked her like a man possessed. His thick cock slammed into her with a wet, slapping rhythm that echoed through the room, the sound as filthy as the act itself. She felt every inch of him, stretching her wide, filling her to the brink, and then pulling out just enough to make her crave him all over again. Her thighs trembled, desperate to keep him inside as he pounded her.

"Fuck, Malta," she gasped, her voice ragged, her nails digging into his shoulders. "You're—oh, by the gods—you're ruining me."

He didn't respond, just growled low in his throat. His sweat-slicked body pressed against hers, his chest rubbing against her nipples, sending electric shocks of pleasure straight to her core. Heat radiated off him, the musk of his arousal mingling with her own, creating a heady scent that made her even wetter.

He didn't slow down, didn't give her a moment to breathe.

"Come on, Olivia," he said, his voice rough and commanding. "I know you can take it. Show me."

Her body obeyed before her mind could catch up. She screamed his name, clamping down on him so tight it felt like she was trying to milk every drop of cum from his balls. He didn't stop, didn't give her time to recover. He just kept fucking her through her climax, his cock driving into her like a fucking battering ram.

"Malta, please," she begged, her voice trembling, her body writhing beneath him. "I can't—I can't take any more."

He didn't listen.

His pace only quickened, his hips slamming into hers with a ferocity that left her breathless. She felt another orgasm building. His breath was hot against her neck, his lips brushing against her skin as he whispered filthy promises in her ear.

"You're mine, Olivia," he murmured, his voice low and possessive. "I'm going to fuck you until you can't walk, until you forget your own name."

She felt his cock pulsing inside her as he filled her with his cum. Even then, he didn't stop. He kept fucking her, his cock still hard, still driving into her with the same relentless pace. He took her again and again, refusing to let her go; her cries became whimpers, and her body trembled with overstimulation. He gave her one last orgasm, another chance for her to scream in pleasure.

When he finally pulled out, she was a mess. Olivia collapsed onto the couch, her body spent, her mind hazy. Malta leaned over her, his eyes dark with desire.

"Are you satisfied?" he inquired.

"Yes, very much so," she replied, her voice steady and assured, a soft smile playing on her lips.

"Is that Dalanite requesting his prize for fucking you?" he asked, a hint of skepticism lacing his words.

"No, he's been silent since you gave me that tea. It worked," she responded, relief evident in her tone as she recalled the calming effect of the herbal concoction. "I didn't even feel the hunger pains."

"It's only temporary," he warned, "but at least I finally got to fuck you."

CHAPTER TWENTY-THREE

OLIVIA

The sedan crawled through streets that seemed to contract around them. Malta's knuckles were white against the steering wheel as they edged closer to her apartment. Olivia sat rigid in the passenger seat, watching shadows stretch across buildings like long, accusing fingers in the morning light. The distant murmur of voices grew louder with each block, transforming from background noise into something more purposeful, more threatening. A coldness spread through her limbs, but beneath it burned an uncomfortable heat she recognized as dread.

"I don't know how my presence will be received by your friends," he said, his voice low and steady. His eyes remained fixed on the road ahead, but there was a tension in his jaw that hadn't been there when they'd left the farmhouse.

"I've been gone all night. I'll just tell them I had a babysitter."

"There's quite a crowd," he observed, slowing the car as they approached the back of Delphi's house. His tone was deliberately neutral, but she could sense the concern beneath it. "What the hell is going on?"

She leaned forward, peering through the windshield. People packed the street near Delphi's house. Some held signs, others clutched cameras and microphones. News vans lined the curb. She could make out a few of the signs like "No more Lies" and "Reveal the Truth," but the more disturbing one read "Death to the unmarked."

"Sully must have filed her report on the missing men." She slumped back in her seat. She wrapped her arms around herself, fingernails digging into her skin. She built a formidable mental barrier, crafting an impenetrable shield within her mind to block out the chaotic torrent of thoughts and emotions emanating from the crowd. "They're calling for my death."

His expression hardened as he scanned the crowd. "Not everyone is. There are supporters too." He nodded toward a smaller group holding signs that read "Protect the Twins" and "The Council Lies."

"Great. Half want me dead, and half want to worship me." She pressed her palms against her temples. "I can't go through that mob."

"You can, and you will." His voice was firm but not unkind as he maneuvered the car toward the crowd. "I'll be right beside you."

Her stomach twisted as she scanned the crowd again. There were at least thirty people gathered, their faces animated with a mixture of curiosity, anger, and something that looked uncomfortably like fear. A woman near the front clutched a homemade poster bearing Talia's face with a red X slashed across it.

The car stopped, and the crowd surged forward like a living entity, pressing against the windows. Cameras flashed, creating a strobe effect that made Olivia's head pound. She could see mouths moving, hands gesturing, but the sounds blended into an indistinguishable roar.

"Keep your head down and don't engage with anyone," he instructed, putting the car in park. "Ready?"

She wasn't ready—not even close—but she nodded anyway. He stepped out first, his imposing figure immediately drawing attention. Camera flashes exploded around them as he circled to her door and opened it, offering his hand. She took it, clutching his fingers tightly as she emerged from the relative safety of the sedan.

"No comment," he said, trying to push the crowd back. "Please, allow us to pass."

His arm came around her shoulders, creating a shield between her and the most aggressive reporters. His touch was surprisingly gentle, despite the firmness of his stance. She kept her gaze fixed on the ground, watching her feet take one step after another across the cracked pavement.

"Olivia! Is it true your sister has no Nibmarks?"

"Have you been hiding powers of your own?"

"What do you know about the disappearances in Grand View?"

A microphone thrust toward her face, nearly catching her in the cheek. Olivia flinched, stumbling on the uneven pavement. Malta's grip tightened, steadying her.

"Olivia! The people have a right to know if you're dangerous!"

"Is Talia responsible for the disappearances?"

"Do you know where the missing men are?"

"No comment," Malta repeated, his voice a steady rumble above her head. "Step back."

"Back up!" Sully called over the crowd.

Olivia's head jerked up to see Sully pushing through the crowd, her N.I.A badge held high. The familiar face sent a wave of relief through her tense body.

"Official N.I.A business," she announced, her voice carrying the authority of her position. "Clear a path or face obstruction charges."

The crowd parted reluctantly, cameras still flashing as Sully formed a barrier on Olivia's other side. She felt momentarily safer, though the press of bodies and shouted questions continued to assault her senses.

"You brought him here?" she hissed under her breath, glaring at Malta over Olivia's head.

"Not now," she muttered, feeling the weight of dozens of eyes on her back. Even though she had a mental defense against their thoughts, she felt the hostility seeping through the cracks from the protestors. For a moment, she looked up at their scowling faces as shouted accusations cut through the air. Their eyes bored into her with a mix of contempt and fear, creating a suffocating atmosphere that made it hard for her to draw a breath.

As she walked through the throng of people, their negative energy surrounded her, threatening to engulf her completely. The signs they held were not just symbols of dissent but weapons of intimidation, each word etched with venomous intent aimed directly at her. Despite Malta and Sully's protective presence, she felt exposed and vulnerable in the face of such intense animosity. The barrage of accusatory questions and hostile glares only fueled the fire of uncertainty and fear that raged within her.

The fire.

In her mind's eye, the fire blazed vividly with a fierce, relentless intensity, mirroring the turmoil and chaos surrounding her in the real world. The flames danced with hues of vibrant orange and deep crimson, casting menacing shadows that flickered and leaped erratically. Each crackling ember seemed to speak of anger and hatred, consuming everything in its path with a voracious hunger.

As she visualized the fire, its heat radiated through her consciousness, searing with a raw power that resonated deep within her being. The fiery tendrils of rage licked at the edges of her thoughts, reflecting the emotions swirling within her amidst the tumultuous events unfolding around her.

The vision struck her with such force that her legs buckled beneath her. Malta swiftly responded, effortlessly lifting her into his arms. As he carried her up the stairs to her apartment door, Sully managed to keep the crowd from trailing behind.

"I'm fine," Olivia protested weakly, embarrassed by the sudden display of vulnerability. She didn't struggle against Malta's hold, secretly grateful for the escape from the overwhelming sensations below.

"You're not fine," he replied, his voice a low rumble against her ear. "Your mind is under assault, and you're exhausted."

The door to her apartment swung open before they reached it, revealing Talia's worried face. Her sister's eyes widened at the sight of Malta carrying her, then narrowed dangerously.

"What did you do to her?" Talia demanded, stepping back reluctantly to let them enter. Familiar faces, wearing expressions ranging from concern to outright hostility, crowded the apartment beyond.

"He didn't do anything," Olivia said as he carefully set her down on the couch.

Storm hovered protectively at Talia's side, his fists clenched as he glared at Malta. Scooter sat perched on the edge of the counter, his usual carefree demeanor replaced by a watchful stillness. And in the corner, almost vibrating with tension, stood Jitatma, his dark eyes fixed on Malta with unmistakable hatred.

"What is he doing here?" Jitatma spat, his voice trembling with barely contained fury. The air around him seemed to shimmer with heat, a physical manifestation of his rage.

"He's helping me," Olivia said, struggling to sit upright on the couch. Her head still pounded from the mental exertion of blocking out the crowd. "I know how it looks, but—"

"How it looks?" Jitatma took a step forward, his movements fluid. "It looks like you've brought our enemy here. The man who's been helping Hunter for months!"

"Back up, Jitatma," Storm warned, shifting his position to place himself between the agitated man and Olivia. "I get the first swing."

Malta remained composed, his expression unreadable as he stood with his back to the wall. His eyes tracked every movement in the room with calculating precision. "I understand your concerns, but circumstances have changed."

"Changed?" Jitatma's laugh was sharp and bitter. He quickly closed the distance between him and Malta, backing the lieutenant against the wall. "The only thing that's changed is that you've manipulated Olivia somehow."

Malta glanced at Olivia and abruptly inquired, "Little Birdie, would you like to rein in your boyfriend?"

Sully burst into the apartment, her chest heaving, her breath coming in ragged gasps. Her clothes were disheveled and sweat glistened on her forehead. She leaned against the doorframe for support, her eyes wide with urgency. "I've managed to hold off the mob outside for now."

"He temporarily silenced the Dalanite."

"And you trust him?" Storm asked, his voice heavy with skepticism. He hadn't taken his eyes off Malta since they'd entered.

"I don't know if I trust him," Olivia admitted, rubbing her temples. "Right now, he's the only one with answers about what's happening to me."

"Jitatma, give the man a chance to explain before you break his jaw," Sully suggested. "If you don't like what he has to say, I'll go back outside for crowd control, and you can do whatever you'd like in here."

Jitatma hesitated, his muscles taut with restraint. His gaze flicked between Sully and Olivia. Finally, he took a step back, though the tension didn't leave his body. "Fine. Explain."

Malta straightened his jacket, his movements deliberate and un-hurried, despite the hostility surrounding him. "I've been investigating Hunter for months. Not helping him."

"Bullshit," Storm muttered.

"It's true," Malta said, his voice level. "I was monitoring his activities. Recent developments have complicated my position."

Talia crossed her arms, skepticism etched across her features. "What developments?"

"Commander's arrest of Hunter. Besides, I don't think Hunter's the mastermind, but he did start this shit. The more he used dark magic, the more afraid he became. He would mumble something about the gate is weak," Malta admitted.

"The gate to where?"

"I might have an idea," Storm said, his fingers raking through his hair in a gesture of contemplation. "When I was severely injured in the Far Viscera and slipped into a coma, I found myself standing at the gate of the empty void. Before I struck a desperate bargain for my life with Gorgon, I noticed the iron bars of the gate were corroded, as if they had been neglected."

Jitatma turned to Storm. "Gorgon wasn't just there to make a deal with you. He was checking on the gate. I think it's time to have a chat with Hunter."

CHAPTER TWENTY-FOUR

OLIVIA

The portal crackled and spat blue sparks as Olivia stepped through, a cold rush sweeping over her skin like she'd plunged into ice water. Her ears popped, her vision blurred for three heartbeats, and then she stood on polished marble, the soles of her boots making a soft squeak that seemed to echo forever in Queen Johara's judgment chamber. Olivia felt the others materialize behind her—Jitatma's steady presence, Scooter's nervous energy, Storm's quiet vigilance. Talia appeared last, with Malta and Sully flanking her like bodyguards.

Johara rose from her throne, the fabric of her midnight-blue gown shimmering like a galaxy in motion. The intricate embroidery depicted constellations and celestial bodies sparkling with silver and sapphire threads that caught the light, giving the impression of stars coming to life. Her large sapphire crown sat regally atop her head. Her wings spread proudly behind her, their iridescent feathers gleaming with shimmering silver and white. The queen's beauty and power captivated Olivia, and she felt a sense of admiration witnessing her friend regaining her rightful place as ruler of the Far Viscera.

"Welcome back, but this doesn't appear to be a social visit," Johara said, looking concerned.

Jitatma stepped forward and bowed. "Your Majesty, we need to speak with Hunter."

The queen's expression tightened. "I suspected as much. He remains in the lower dungeons, exactly where you left him."

"Is there any news from Anu or Ki?"

"Anu and Ki can no longer hold off the Dark Haunting. We had to start the evacuation of the Afterlife and bring the souls here."

The news struck Olivia like a physical blow. "What? The Afterlife is being evacuated?" Her voice came out higher than she intended, drawing concerned glances from her companions.

"I'm afraid so," Johara confirmed, her wings folding as if weighed down by the burden of her words. "We've been working tirelessly to accommodate the influx of souls. The Dark Haunting is spreading faster than we anticipated."

"Damn it! I thought we had more time," Jitatma said, frustrated.

"We need answers from Hunter," Malta interjected, his tone clipped and impatient. "If anyone knows how to stop this, it would be him."

"Jitatma, take Olivia and Malta to the dungeons. I must speak with Talia and the others about the preparations for the remaining souls," Johara said. "Sully, I need help to direct everyone. They are going to be confused and scared as they arrive. Storm and Talia, the Woobles are setting up temporary camps near the edge of Nothingness Forest. I'm sure they can use your help."

Scooter shifted uneasily. "What can I do?" His fingers twitched nervously at his side.

"You're coming with me," Johara said, her lips curling into a warm smile. "I need your kind, friendly face to brighten the room."

Scooter beamed, his shoulders straightening with newfound purpose.

Jitatma gestured for Olivia and Malta to follow him through a side door that seemed to materialize from the marble wall itself.

As they descended a winding staircase, the temperature dropped noticeably. The warm glow of the judgment chamber faded.

"I despise dungeons," Malta muttered, his fingers grazing the hilt of his dagger. "They always smell of desperation and urine."

Olivia felt it now—a pressure building behind her eyes, a subtle vibration in her bones. The Dalanite within her seemed to stir in response to the magic surrounding them, like a creature recognizing its kin. She pressed her palm against the cool stone wall to steady herself.

"Are you all right?" Jitatma asked, pausing at a landing.

Before she could respond, she felt a sudden weakness in her legs, as if they had turned to jelly beneath her. In an instant, she tumbled down the stairs, each step a blur of motion and sound. Her descent was swift and chaotic, yet it ended gently as she fell into Jitatma's outstretched arms, which wrapped around her with a comforting, reassuring embrace.

His scent engulfed her—musky and smoky wood, with a hint of something wild, something primal. It was intoxicating, filling her lungs and making her head spin even more than the fall had. His hands were firm yet gentle, one resting just above the curve of her ass, the other splayed across her lower back, holding her close.

She felt the hard planes of his chest against hers, the way his muscles tensed as he held her, his breath warm against her ear as he murmured something too low for her to catch.

Her hands instinctively found their way to his shoulders, her fingers curling into the fabric of his tunic. She felt the strength beneath her palms, the way his muscles flexed as he adjusted his grip on her. Her body pressed against his, every inch of her aware of him—the way his thighs bracketed hers, the way his hips were so close to hers that she could feel the faintest hint of something stirring between them.

His gaze dropped to her mouth, dark and hungry, and she felt a surge of heat flood her body, pooling low in her belly. She could see the way his eyes darkened, the way his jaw tightened ever so slightly, and she knew he wanted this as much as she did.

She wanted this. She wanted him.

"Get a fucking room," Malta said as he pushed past the couple.

You can't have him, Olivia. You belong to me.

Olivia jerked back as if burned; she felt her cheeks flushing with heat. The Dalanite's voice echoed loudly and unmistakably in her mind, reverberating intensely.

I won't share you.

"Sorry," she mumbled, extracting herself from his arms. Losing contact left her feeling oddly bereft. "I must have tripped on something."

Jitatma's expression was unreadable, his dark eyes lingering on her face for a heartbeat too long before he nodded and stepped back. She could tell he didn't believe her, but he mercifully didn't press the issue.

"If you two are quite finished," Malta called from farther down the stairs, his voice echoing against the stone walls, "we have a god to interrogate."

She straightened her clothes, trying to ignore the lingering warmth where Jitatma had touched her. She followed him down the remaining stairs, keeping a careful distance between them.

Did you think your attempts to subdue me would work?

The voice inside her head was smug, almost gleeful in its triumph. She clenched her jaw, focusing on putting one foot in front of the other. She wouldn't engage with it.

Not now.

I've been patient, waiting for you to accept me willingly, but my patience is wearing thin.

They reached the bottom of the staircase, where the dungeon began. Most of the cells were empty, but at the far end, a figure sat cross-legged in the center of the middle cell. The guards had chained the god to the floor with what appeared to be ordinary metal links. However, a faint blue shimmer indicated magically infused restraints designed to contain a deity.

Hunter.

Even from this distance, Olivia could feel his presence like a static charge in the air. He hadn't moved, hadn't acknowledged their approach, but she knew he was aware of them. His stillness was deliberate, calculated—a predator waiting for prey to come closer.

"I've been expecting you, Olivia," he said, his voice carrying none of the weakness one might expect from a prisoner. "The Dalanite grows stronger in you. I can sense it."

"We need answers," Jitatma said, stepping in front of Olivia as they reached the cell. The protective gesture wasn't lost on her—or on Hunter, whose lips curled into a knowing smile.

"Always the guardian, aren't you, Jitatma?" Hunter rose to his feet in one fluid motion, approaching the iron bars of his cell, but the chains stopped him short. "You can't protect her from what's already inside her."

Malta pushed forward, radiating impatience. "The Dark Haunting is causing the evacuation of the Afterlife. Souls are being displaced, and we need to know how to stop it."

Hunter's gaze never left Olivia's face, even as he responded to Malta. "You don't stop it." He tilted his head, studying Olivia with unsettling intensity. "The Dalanite has chosen you. It's awakening fully now, isn't it? Speaking to you? Demanding things of you?"

Olivia's throat tightened. "That's none of your business."

Jitatma stepped closer to the bars, his posture tense. "Stop playing games, Hunter. Tell us what you know about stopping the Dark Haunting."

"Why should I help you? If you haven't figured it out by now, you idiots are going to fail." He smiled. "Nothing happens by chance. It's all connected. I would like to think I taught you something when you were my commander. It seems I failed."

Jitatma's jaw tightened, his fists clenched at his sides. "I was never truly your commander. You used me as a pawn to do your dirty work."

Hunter laughed, the sound echoing off the stone walls. "And yet, here you are, still playing the game." Hunter's gaze shifted back to her, seeming to pierce through her defenses. "The Dark Haunting is merely a symptom, not the disease. It's the universe's way of correcting an imbalance." He leaned forward, chains clinking softly. "When Anasazi killed Circe, she disrupted the natural order. The balance between good and evil. The Dark Haunting is the consequence, and it's feeding."

"That doesn't explain how to stop it," Malta interjected, his patience visibly wearing thin.

"Don't you see?" Hunter's voice dropped to a whisper. "My wife is the only one who can contain it and restore the balance."

Circe. He can't have her.

The Dalanite stirred within Olivia, sending ripples of warmth through her veins. She tried to ignore it, but its presence grew more insistent, like fingers caressing the inside of her skull.

"What do you mean?" she asked, stepping closer to the bars despite Jitatma's subtle attempt to block her.

Hunter's smile widened, predatory and knowing. He pressed closer to the bars, his chains straining. "The Dalanite isn't fighting against you, Olivia. It's awakening what was always there. Circe was his favorite host, which is why he chose you."

She had powerful magic.

"That's enough," Jitatma growled, stepping between them. "You're manipulating her, just like you manipulate everyone."

"Am I?" Hunter's gaze remained fixed on Olivia. "Ask her what she feels when the Dalanite speaks to her. Ask her if it feels foreign or familiar."

Olivia swallowed hard, her mouth suddenly dry. Despite the intrusive nature of the Dalanite's voice, the truth was there was something hauntingly familiar.

The Dalanite pulsed violently, as if objecting to Hunter's words. Olivia winced, pressing her palm against her temple as a jolt of dizziness shot through her. She reached out to steady herself against the wall, the cold stone grounding her.

Jitatma moved with lightning speed, his hand shooting through the bars to grab Hunter by the throat. "You're lying."

Hunter didn't struggle, didn't even seem concerned by the fingers tightening around his windpipe. "Look at her, Jitatma," he wheezed, his eyes never leaving Olivia's face. "She knows I speak the truth."

"Let him go," Olivia said quietly. "He's baiting you."

Reluctantly, Jitatma released Hunter, who rubbed his throat and chuckled. "Smart girl."

"We can't bring Circe back. We can't stop it. We can't contain it," Jitatma said, frustrated. "We have to slow it down. How do we stop feeding it?"

"Talk to your girlfriend. She's been offering sacrifices to the Dark Haunting for the Dalanite. It craves the souls of the Niberians, whether they're living or dead," Hunter explained.

"What did you just say?"

"You heard me." Hunter's eyes gleamed with malicious satisfaction. "Olivia has been feeding souls to the Dark Haunting, strengthening it. How many of your mates were taken into the portal?"

Olivia felt the blood drain from her face. Something about Hunter's words rang true. The Dalanite pulsed, neither confirming nor denying Hunter's accusation.

"The Dark Haunting consumes souls, growing stronger with each one it devours, and Olivia has been providing the feast."

You know it's true. You gave them to me willingly.

What have I done?

Exactly what I wanted you to do, my good girl.

CHAPTER TWENTY-FIVE

OLIVIA

The dungeon door groaned shut behind them, its ancient hinges protesting. Olivia flinched, her shoulders drawing up toward her ears as she stared down the long, stone corridor stretching before them. The flickering torches cast more shadows than light, and each dark recess seemed to hold a silent promise of something lurking, waiting. Her hands trembled as she wrapped her arms around herself, trying to contain a shiver that came from somewhere deeper than the damp chill of the air.

The stairs unwound before them like a snake with each step. She focused on the uneven texture beneath her boots as they ascended—anything to distract from what they'd just heard. The stone walls rose high on either side, their surfaces rough and slightly slick with condensation reflecting the amber light of the torches. Each flame danced in its iron bracket, creating shifting patterns that made the stairwell seem alive, breathing around them.

The knowledge of what she had done sat in her stomach like a stone—the souls of the three men, devoured because of her. The memories of their pleading eyes haunted her, accusing her in the darkness of her mind. It was because she wanted an active power, a longing that now came at a terrible cost. She sacrificed innocent lives for her selfish desire, and the realization was suffocating.

She had been oblivious, blind to the dark transformation unfolding within her own body, and now the consequences loomed over her. The cold touch of dread enclosed her heart, squeezing tighter with every beat.

Guilt doesn't become you. Jealousy is more your emotion. Why do you resist what you are becoming?

At the top of the stairs, the corridor widened as they approached the main level of the castle, the ceiling arching higher above them. A hunger unfurled inside her, a living thing stretching awake. It sensed the souls in the castle—the evacuees from the Afterlife, hundreds of them, each one a beacon of energy calling to the darkness within her. She swallowed hard.

There are so many souls to consume.

She pressed her fingernails into her palms, using the sharp pain to ground herself against the rising tide of starvation. Each soul in the castle pulsed, their life force calling to the Dalanite. She could almost taste them—bright, effervescent energy that promised to fill the hollow ache spreading through her body.

Jitatma's voice cut through the fog of her thoughts. "Are you all right?"

"Fine," she managed, the lie bitter on her tongue.

His expression suggested he knew better, but he merely nodded and continued leading them through the winding passages. The castle's interior grew more ornate as they ascended, rough stone giving way to polished marble and intricate tapestries. Under different circumstances, she might have admired the craftsmanship. Now, she barely registered the beauty around her, too consumed by the war raging inside her.

As they neared the queen's judgment chambers, voices grew louder—an urgent murmur of conversation punctuated by occasional commands. Each new voice sent a fresh wave of famine through her. The Dalanite stirred more violently, like a creature scenting prey.

So hungry. So many bright lights, just waiting to be extinguished.

"No, I can't go in there," she said, grabbing Jitatma's arm. "There are too many souls."

The hunger was a physical pain now, a hollow ache that radiated outward from her core. Her skin felt too tight, as if something inside her was pressing to get out. She clenched her jaw, focusing on the pressure of her teeth against each other.

He studied her face, concern etched in the lines around his mouth. "What's happening, Olivia?"

She shook her head, backing away until her spine pressed against the wall. The sensation of cold seeping through her clothing offered momentary relief from the burning hunger inside her.

"I can't explain it," she whispered, voice breaking. "I can feel all the souls. Their fear and confusion. It's like they're calling to me, and I want to consume them. All of them." The confession hung in the air between them, shameful and raw. "The Dalanite is so strong. I can feel it pushing against me, trying to take control."

Malta stepped closer, his expression grave. "How strong is the hunger? Can you fight it?"

She shuddered, wrapping her arms tighter around herself as if she could physically contain the predator awakening inside her. "I don't know. It's never been this strong before." Her voice dropped to a whisper. "I'm afraid of what I might do."

"The Dalanite hasn't fed since I gave you the tea. It's craving the souls."

Jitatma exchanged a glance with Malta, their silent communication heavy with unspoken worry. "We need to get you somewhere isolated," he said finally. "Somewhere away from the souls. I'll take you to my chambers."

Malta nodded, concern etched in the lines around his eyes. "I'll find the queen and the others."

The journey to Jitatma's chambers passed in a blur of ornate corridors and hushed whispers. She kept her eyes fixed on the floor, focusing on the intricate patterns in the marble rather than the occasional castle staff they passed. Even these solitary souls called to the darkness. Each step was agony, a test of willpower as the Dalanite clawed at her insides, demanding release. By the time they reached his chambers, she was shaking, sweat beading on her forehead.

"Sit," he commanded gently, guiding her to a chair. "Try to breathe. Focus on something concrete. Is there anything I can do to help?"

She sank into the cushioned seat, gripping the armrests until her knuckles whitened. The Dalanite writhed, making her muscles spasm. She closed her eyes, trying to block out the sensation of souls moving throughout the castle.

"I don't know," she whispered, her voice ragged. "I've never felt it this strongly before."

"The Dalanite must be responding to the influx of souls," he said, his voice steady and clinical. "The evacuation has brought more spiritual energy into this realm than it's seen in centuries."

A fresh wave of pain crashed through her, and she doubled over, a groan escaping her lips. Her fingers dug into the soft upholstery, tearing at the fabric.

"I don't want this," she gasped. "I never wanted to hurt anyone."

"I know." He kneeled before her, careful to maintain some distance. "I'm going to find a way to get this Dalanite out of you."

He can try, but it won't work. I'm a part of you now.

She straightened in the chair to meet his concerned gaze. "It says it's part of me now. It can't be removed."

"He's lying to preserve himself," he replied, his voice measured and calm despite the tension in his shoulders. "There is always a way. I'll be damned if I'm going to allow this thing to live inside you and harm you."

She wanted to believe him, to hold on to his certainty like a life-line, but the truth was, she felt like she was drowning in darkness.

Before she could respond, his mouth was on hers, hot and insis-tent. It had been a while since he had kissed her like that, his tongue forcing its way past her teeth like he owned her mouth.

"Jitatma," she gasped, her voice trembling as his lips trailed down her neck, nipping and sucking at the sensitive skin. His teeth grazed her collarbone, and she let out a moan that felt like it came from somewhere deep inside her, primal and raw. Her fingers tangled in his hair, pulling him closer, harder, as if she could devour him whole.

His hands slid up her legs, rough and possessive, fingers tracing the hem of her panties before sliding beneath. She arched into his touch, a desperate whimper escaping her lips as his fingers found her core. He pressed a finger inside her, slow and deliberate, and she gasped, her back arching off the chair as pleasure shot through her like a lightning bolt.

It wasn't just his touch that was driving her wild. The air around them crackled with energy, the power of her telekinesis surging out of control. A vase on the table shattered, shards of glass flying across the room. A book flew off the shelf, pages fluttering. The chair beneath her groaned as it lifted slightly off the ground, and he chuckled against her skin, his lips brushing the hollow of her throat.

"You're losing control," he teased, his voice dripping with amusement, but she didn't care. She couldn't think, couldn't breathe, not with his fingers thrusting into her, curling just right to hit that sweet spot that made her see stars.

"Fuck you," she gasped, her hips rocking against his hand, des-perate for more. Her head fell back as pleasure burned through her. She gripped the chair arms so tightly she was surprised they didn't splinter.

A fierce wind raced through the room, causing the curtains to thrash wildly, as if ensnared in a tempest. Their fabric fluttered and snapped furiously, casting ominous shadows across the walls. A sudden chill filled the air, as the gust extinguished the torches one by one.

"No," she protested weakly, but he silenced her with a kiss, his tongue plunging into her mouth as he carried her to the bed. He laid her down, his body hovering over hers, his cock straining against the fabric of his pants. She reached for him, desperate to feel him inside her, but before he could undress, the air beside them rippled, a swirling portal opening with a deafening roar.

She screamed as the portal's force yanked at her clothes and hair, the violent wind threatening to pull her in. He threw himself over her, his body a shield against the portal as furniture slid across the floor toward the swirling darkness. His weight pinned her to the bed, but she could feel him straining against the force.

A chair skidded across the floor with a screech that set her teeth on edge, followed by books, scrolls, and decorative objects, all sliding inexorably toward the swirling darkness. Glass shattered somewhere, the tinkling sound almost delicate against the roaring wind.

The hunger inside her surged, the Dalanite responding to the raw power emanating from the portal. It expanded, its edges crackling with electric blue energy that sent sparks showering across the room.

You can't have him. I will take him from you, Olivia.
I would like to see you try.

She lunged forward, her fingers curling tightly around his arm, her grip unyielding as she fought against the powerful force trying to drag him into the swirling portal. The pull intensified, threatening to tear them apart.

"Hold on!" she screamed, summoning every ounce of her telekinetic power. She pulled every piece of furniture between them. The room vibrated with her effort, objects suspended in mid-air as she created a barrier between them and the vortex. She hurled every object in the room at it. As far as she was concerned, the portal could take everything in the room but Jitatma.

Sweat beaded on her forehead, trickling down her temples as she fought to maintain control. The room vibrated with her effort, smaller objects—quills, books, figurines—suspended in mid-air as she held everything in place.

The Dalanite roared in protest, fighting against her control. A surge of pain shot through her skull, like someone had driven a hot poker through her temple. Her concentration wavered, and for a terrifying moment, the barrier flickered. Several books broke free from her telekinetic hold, shooting toward the portal like missiles. They disappeared with a sound like paper being shredded.

He shouted over the deafening roar of the portal. His eyes were wide with fear, but not for himself—for her. "Olivia, you're bleeding!"

She could feel it now, the warm trickle of blood from her nose. Using her power like this while fighting the Dalanite was tearing her apart from the inside, but she couldn't let go.

She wouldn't.

The portal pulsed, expanding another foot. A wooden rod flew past them and disappeared into the swirling darkness, followed by a chair that splintered at the edge. His body jerked backward, pulled by the portal's increasing strength. Olivia felt her grip on his arm slipping, his skin slick with sweat. Panic flared in her chest, hot and suffocating. He lifted, his feet dangling in the air.

"The Dalanite wants you," she shouted over the howling wind, her hair whipping around her face like an angry snake.

"Hold on to me. I'm going to try to close the portal." His face contorted with effort as he pressed his palm toward the vortex, his fingers splayed wide.

She felt her strength wavering as the barrier between them and the portal weakened. The furniture she'd telekinetically positioned began to tremble and shift toward the vortex.

She concentrated on holding him steady, refusing to let the portal take him. Her muscles strained with the effort, her mind a battlefield between her will and the Dalanite's hunger. Blood dripped from her nose onto her lips, the taste of copper filling her mouth.

"I can't hold it much longer," she gasped, her vision blurring at the edges. The Dalanite thrashed violently, sensing its opportunity as her control slipped.

Let go. Let him go. He's keeping you from your true potential.

"No!" she screamed, both at the Dalanite and at the portal, threatening to tear him away from her. With a final surge of desperation, she channeled every ounce of her power into one massive push.

The room exploded with telekinetic energy. The portal flickered, its edges wavering. For a heartbeat—one perfect, crystallized moment—everything suspended in the air. The howling wind died to an eerie silence. Debris hung motionless, caught between gravity and her telekinetic grip. Even time itself seemed to pause, the universe holding its breath as Olivia's power reached its zenith.

Then the portal collapsed with a thunderous crack, folding in on itself until it winked out of existence. The sudden silence was deafening. The force of the collapsing portal sent objects suspended in mid-air crashing to the floor in a cacophony of splintering wood and shattering glass.

She collapsed onto the bed, trembling uncontrollably. Blood continued to stream from her nose, staining the bedsheets crimson. Her head throbbed with each heartbeat, vision blurring as exhaustion came over her.

"Olivia!" His hands were gentle as they cradled her face, his fingers stained red with her blood. "What did you do?" His voice was tight with concern, eyes scanning her face. "You shouldn't have pushed yourself so hard. I've never seen power like that before."

"I couldn't let it take you." Her words came out slurred, fatigue weighing down her tongue. The Dalanite had retreated to a corner of her consciousness, weakened by her exertion but still present, still hungry. "It wanted to take you."

Jitatma's arms tightened around her. "You fought it. You won."

"This time." The words tasted like ash in her mouth. She felt the creature inside her, wounded but not defeated, curling back into the shadows of her consciousness. It waited and watched.

His fingers brushed the blood from her upper lip with unexpected tenderness. "It would take more than a demonic entity to separate us now."

A hysterical laugh bubbled up from her chest, quickly morphing into a pained cough. "Is that a promise or a threat?"

The corner of his mouth lifted in that half-smile that always made her stomach flip. "Both, perhaps."

A sharp knock at the door made them both flinch. His body tensed, his arms shifting to a protective position around her as he called, "Who is it?"

"Malta," came the muffled reply. "The queen is asking for you, Commander. We felt the disturbance throughout the castle."

"Give me a moment," Jitatma called back.

She struggled to sit up, wincing as pain lanced through her head. "How bad do I look?"

He studied her face, his expression softening. "Like someone who just battled a demon and won." His thumb traced the line of her jaw. "Blood suits you, in a macabre sort of way."

"You *would* think that," she muttered but couldn't stop the small smile that tugged at her lips.

He helped her to her feet, keeping one arm firmly around her waist when she swayed. She grabbed his arm to steady herself. The room was in complete disarray, furniture splintered and strewn about as if a tornado had torn through it. Broken glass glittered on the floor like scattered diamonds.

"I'm sorry about your room," she said, surveying the destruction.

He shrugged. "I've never cared much for interior decorating, anyway."

This isn't over. You may have won the battle, but the war has just begun.

She tightened her grip on Jitatma's arm, drawing strength from his solid presence beside her. Whatever was coming, she wouldn't face it alone. The thought brought a strange comfort, even as dread settled in her stomach like a cold, heavy stone.

Olivia took a deep breath, tasting the metallic remnants of blood and the acid tang of fear. She straightened her shoulders, lifting her chin despite the tremor in her limbs. She closed her eyes, trying to quiet the triumphant laughter echoing inside her mind. The Dalanite hadn't succeeded this time, but it had come close.

Too close.

CHAPTER TWENTY-SIX

OLIVIA

T he light filtered through the window of Jitatma's chambers, casting long shadows across the stone floor where Olivia stood. She had put forth her utmost effort to tidy up the chaos she had inadvertently created earlier. Carefully, she restored order by moving back into place anything that wasn't broken.

She managed to salvage most of the furniture, preserving the rich wooden tables and plush, intricately carved chairs. However, a few of the tapestries that adorned the walls were not so fortunate. Once vibrant with detailed patterns and hues, they now hung in tatters, their fabric frayed and threads dangling forlornly.

The wooden door behind her creaked opened. Olivia didn't turn. She didn't need to. The temperature in the room dropped several degrees, and the fine hairs on her arms rose in response. The soft, measured footsteps crossing the floor carried a deliberate weight.

"Hello, child," came the velvet voice of Anasazi. "I see you've been redecorating."

"Lady Anasazi," Olivia said without turning. "I was expecting you."

She finally turned to face her visitor. Anasazi stood in the center of the chamber, her presence commanding the space with effortless authority. She wore a gown of the deepest midnight that seemed to absorb rather than reflect the fading light, its fabric rippling like a liquid shadow with each subtle movement. Her pale face was a stark contrast, beautiful in its severity, with high cheekbones and eyes that held a cold emptiness.

"I see you've been practicing," Anasazi remarked. "Though your control leaves much to be desired."

Olivia swallowed, her mouth suddenly dry. "It wasn't intentional."

"Few things worth learning ever are," Anasazi replied, moving closer with a predatory grace. "Power without control is merely destruction. A lesson I learned long ago."

"Why didn't you tell me Circe trapped the Dalanite in the amulet?"

Anasazi's expression didn't change, but something in her eyes shifted, like ice cracking beneath a frozen lake. She moved to one of the remaining intact chairs and sat with elegant precision, the folds of her dark gown settling around her like a pool of ink.

"Would you have believed me if I had?" she asked, her voice deceptively soft. "Or would you have assumed I was manipulating you, as you've been taught to believe I always do?"

Olivia crossed her arms, frustration warming her cheeks. "I would have liked the choice to decide for myself."

"Choices," she mused, trailing a pale finger along the armrest of the chair. "We believe we make them freely, but in truth, they are made for us by circumstances beyond our control. Tell me, what would you have done with this knowledge? Would it have changed your actions?"

"It might have," she admitted reluctantly.

She fixed Olivia with a penetrating stare. "No, it wouldn't. You wanted an active power like your sister."

Olivia bristled at the accusation. "You don't know what I want."

"Don't I?" Her lips curved into something, not quite a smile. "I have watched you. I have seen the envy in your eyes when Talia displays her gifts. The quiet desperation as you struggled to find your own gift outside of your sister's shadow. You wanted to matter and prove your worth," she continued, her voice softening almost imperceptibly. "I understand ambition, child. It has been my companion."

Her jaw tightened as she fought against the uncomfortable truth in Anasazi's words. The goddess had seen through her so easily, laying bare the insecurities she'd tried to hide even from herself.

"Is that what this is to you? A game of manipulation?" Olivia asked, finding her voice again. "You speak of ambition as if it's something we share, but your ambitions led to Circe's death."

Anasazi's eyes flashed dangerously, sending a ripple of power that made the air between them vibrate. "Circe made her choices, as did I. As you are making yours now." She rose from the chair in one fluid motion, her gown whispering against the stone floor. "The difference between us, child, is that I understand the consequences of my choices. Do you?"

"What do you want from me?"

"A better question," she countered, "is what do you want from yourself?"

"I want to understand what's happening to me," she finally said. "I want to know why I can feel this thing inside me, whispering things I shouldn't know, making me feel what I shouldn't feel."

Anasazi moved closer, her presence making the air around Olivia feel heavy, compressed. "The Dalanite is feeding on your doubts, your fears, and on every other dark thought you've ever harbored." Her cold fingers reached out, hovering just above the amulet without touching it. "It sees the parts of yourself you try to hide."

Olivia felt her anger rising, a hot tide that threatened to wash away her composure. "I want the truth. Not riddles, not tests, not more manipulation."

"The truth?" She laughed, a sound like glass breaking. "You can't even admit the truth to yourself. The truth is you've been jealous of your sister your entire life. You've wanted what she has—her strength, her power, her certainty. Now that you have a power of your own, it's eating you alive because it came with a price you weren't prepared to pay."

"That's not true!" she snapped.

"Isn't it?" Anasazi moved closer. "The Dalanite feeds on darkness. It wouldn't have chosen you if there wasn't darkness to feed on."

She felt something snap inside her. A rush of power surged through her veins, hot and violent. The walls around them trembled, and the remaining intact tapestries rippled as if caught in a sudden gust of wind. "You don't know me," she hissed, her voice barely recognizable to her own ears. "You don't know what I feel!"

Even as the words left her mouth, she knew they were lies. The Dalanite pulsed against her chest, feeding on her rage, her envy, her shame—all the emotions she'd kept buried for so long.

"I see you clearly," Anasazi said, unmoved by the display of power swirling around them. "You can't hide from me."

The air crackled with energy as objects began to lift from their places—books, scrolls, a small wooden box that had somehow survived her earlier outburst. They hovered, suspended by her unchecked power.

"Stop it," she warned, her voice barely above a whisper. The words hung in the air, suspended like the objects around her. She wasn't sure if she was addressing Anasazi or the growing power within herself that threatened to tear the room apart.

"I see the truth you hide even from yourself, Olivia. The resentment that has festered between you and Talia. The way you smile at her while wishing you could be her. The ugliness you try to cover up with make-up and clothes."

The air in the room seemed to thicken, charged with Olivia's anger. Objects trembled around her, vibrating with the force of her emotions.

"Stop," Olivia whispered, but the power was spilling from her now, uncontainable. She felt herself fracturing from within, the Dalanite's whispers becoming louder in her mind.

She's right. That's why envy looks so good on you.

Rage exploded within Olivia like a supernova. The amulet burned against her skin, feeding on her fury, amplifying it. The door swung open, and Talia appeared, her face etched with concern. "Olivia? What's happening?"

Olivia didn't consciously decide. One moment Talia stood in the doorway, and the next, an invisible force slammed into her, lifting her off her feet and pinning her against the stone wall. Talia's eyes widened in shock.

"Olivia!" Talia gasped, struggling against the invisible bonds. "What are you doing?"

Olivia could barely hear her sister through the roaring in her ears. Years of buried resentment surged to the surface, fueled by the Dalanite's dark power. How easy it would be to squeeze, to watch Talia struggle, to finally make her perfect sister understand what it felt like to be powerless, to be second best.

"You look scared," Olivia heard herself say, the words coming from somewhere distant, as if someone else controlled her mouth. "That's new. I don't think I've ever seen the great Talia Trismegist afraid of me."

She felt a strange disconnect. The Dalanite pulsed against her chest, hot and insistent, feeding on her darkest emotions. A small voice in the back of her mind screamed in horror at what she was doing, but the seductive whispers of power drowned it out.

Her fingers flexed in the air, and she felt the invisible tendrils of her power tighten around Talia's throat. The sensation was intoxicating like holding a beating heart in her palm. She felt every flutter of her sister's pulse, every desperate attempt to draw breath.

"You've always been the golden child," Olivia said, her voice distorted and unfamiliar. "Always so special, so powerful. Do you know what it's like to live in your shadow? To be nothing but 'Talia's sister'?"

"Stop this! This isn't you!" Talia's voice cracked with fear, her body suspended against the wall as if crucified.

Something dark and satisfying unfurled in Olivia's chest at the sight of her sister's distress. The perfect twin, the one with the power, the one everyone looked to first—now helpless before her. The amulet pulsed hot against her skin, encouraging her rage.

She never deserved the power. Take what should have been yours.

Anasazi stood watching, her face a mask of cold assessment. "Is this what you want, Olivia? To become the monster you've always feared lurked inside you?"

The words cut through Olivia's haze of anger. She looked at Talia—really looked—and saw the sister who had crossed between dimensions, who had fought a dark king, and who had never once hesitated to save her despite all the bitter words between them.

My sister. My twin.

What was she doing?

The power coursing through her veins suddenly felt wrong—tainted and corrupted by her own bitterness. It wasn't the clean, pure energy she'd imagined telekinesis would be. It was something darker, feeding on the ugliest parts of herself.

The invisible force holding Talia abruptly dissipated. Her sister slid down the wall, landing in a crumpled heap. She coughed violently, her hands flying to her throat as she gulped desperately for air. The objects suspended around the room clattered to the ground, some shattering on impact, the sound like gunshots in the sudden silence.

"Talia, I didn't mean to do that." She sank to her knees, tears streaming down her face. "I'm sorry. I'm so sorry."

Anasazi approached, her movements measured and calm despite the chaos. "The Dalanite reveals what already exists within us. It doesn't create what isn't there." Her voice was neither kind nor cruel, simply matter-of-fact. "It magnifies our darkest impulses until they consume us."

There were no excuses. She had done this. The Dalanite might have amplified her feelings, but they were hers. The jealousy, the resentment, the ugliness—all of it had been festering inside her long before the amulet found its way to her.

Talia pushed herself to her feet, her face pale but determined. She approached her sister cautiously, as one might a wounded animal. "Olivia, it's okay. That wasn't you."

Wasn't it? The thought made Olivia's stomach turn. She looked down at the amulet, its surface now dull and dormant against her skin. The whispers had receded, but she could still feel them, waiting just beneath the surface.

"It was, though," Olivia whispered, her voice thick with shame. "Those thoughts have always been there. I just never let myself acknowledge them."

Talia kneeled beside her, close but not touching, as if uncertain whether her sister would welcome her comfort. "We all have darkness inside us. It's what we choose to do with it that matters."

Anasazi moved to the window, her silhouette sharp against the dying light. "The Dalanite has shown you your shadow self, child. Now you must decide whether to be ruled by it or to master it."

Olivia looked up at the goddess, tears blurring her vision. "How? How do I fight something that's part of me?"

"You don't fight it," Anasazi said, turning back to face her. "You accept it. Acknowledge its presence without giving it power over you." For the first time, her voice carried something almost like compassion. "The parts of ourselves we deny grow stronger in the darkness."

Olivia stared down at her hands, half expecting to see them stained with blood. The enormity of what she'd nearly done crashed over her in sickening waves. She had attacked her own sister with a violence she hadn't known herself capable of.

"I don't know if I can," she whispered. The confession hung in the air, raw and vulnerable.

Talia reached out, hesitating for a moment before placing her hand over Olivia's. The simple touch anchored her, a lifeline in the storm of her emotions.

"You don't have to do it alone," Talia said, her voice steady despite the red marks forming on her throat. "I'm here. I've always been here."

Had she? Olivia wondered. Or had her jealousy blinded her from seeing it? The realization made her chest ache with a different kind of pain.

"The bond between twins is unique," Anasazi observed, moving away from the window. "It can be your greatest strength or your most devastating weakness. Which it becomes is entirely up to you."

"I wanted to hurt you. For a moment, I really wanted to," she said to Talia. "All this time, I thought I was hiding it so well. My jealousy, my resentment. I convinced myself I was being supportive."

"I knew," Talia said softly. "Not everything, maybe, but enough. You can't hide everything from me."

"And you never said anything?" Olivia asked, fresh tears threatening.

"What would I have said? 'Hey, I know you resent me. Can we talk about it?' I was afraid, too, you know. Afraid that if we acknowledged it, it would drive a larger wedge between us."

Olivia closed her eyes, absorbing the painful truth. All these years, they'd been dancing around each other, careful not to disturb the delicate balance between them. Both were afraid of the same thing—losing each other—yet unable to bridge the growing divide.

"We both pretended," Olivia said quietly. "I pretended I was happy for you, and you pretended not to notice I wasn't."

Talia nodded, her eyes reflecting the same sorrow Olivia felt. "Pretty messed up, huh?"

A bitter laugh escaped Olivia's lips. "Completely dysfunctional."

Anasazi moved between them. "The Dalanite feeds on such unspoken truths. It draws strength from the lies we tell ourselves." She gestured toward the amulet on Olivia's chest. "Every moment you deny the darkness within you, you give it more power over you. You're going to need all your power to fight the Dark Haunting."

CHAPTER TWENTY-SEVEN

OLIVIA

As Olivia sat cross-legged on the floor of Jitatma's dimly lit chambers, she felt the tension slowly seep out of her body, as if the gentle warmth emanating from within was radiating outward, dispelling the remnants of icy bitterness that had clung to her heart. Closing her eyes, she could almost see the dark tendrils of anger and jealousy retreating into the corners of the room, dissolving into nothingness in the face of her newfound calm.

The Dalanite's whispers, once loud and overpowering, now softened into a distant hum. With each exhale, she concentrated on the flickering energy pulsing through her fingertips, realizing she could direct its flow. She realized she held within her the power to manipulate it, to shape it according to her will. It was as if she could feel the threads of magic weaving through her veins, responding eagerly to her every intention. The delicate balance between strength and control became apparent to her as she discovered the boundless potential that lay within her grasp. In this moment of quiet revelation, she understood she held the key to unlocking her true potential and embracing the depths of her abilities.

You can't escape me. I'm your darkness. I'm your truth.

The voice slithered through her mind like poison, disrupting the peace she'd fought so hard to achieve. Olivia's eyes snapped open, her momentary serenity shattered.

"Why?" she whispered, her voice trembling with emotion. "Why do you want to hurt the people I love?"

You understand nothing. They will all betray you as she betrayed me.

A surge of rage rippled through her, but it wasn't her own. The Dalanite's fury crashed against her consciousness like a violent wave. The candles around her flickered wildly, their flames bending as if caught in the wind, wax melting in rivulets down their sides.

Olivia clutched her head, her fingers digging into her scalp as she doubled over, overwhelmed by a torrent of images that flooded her mind. Dark, twisted visions spiraled through her consciousness, painting scenes of destruction and death in vivid, harrowing detail.

Her friends and family appeared before her, their faces contorted in agony as they suffered, screamed, and succumbed to the chaos she had unwittingly unleashed. Even Jitatma, usually a pillar of strength, surrendered to the maelstrom. The fire in her mind raged with relentless fury, consuming every corner of her thoughts and burning everyone she loved with an unquenchable intensity. It left nothing but ash and despair in its wake.

She gasped as her body rose from the floor, no longer under her own control. The Dalanite had seized command, pushing her consciousness into a small corner of her mind where she could only watch helplessly as her limbs moved without her permission. Her feet carried her toward the door, each step mechanical and forced. The wooden floor creaked beneath her weight as she moved across it, the sound oddly distant to her ears.

As she walked through the winding halls, she struggled against the Dalanite's control. In this internal battle, she sensed something unexpected. The Dalanite's emotions, usually so guarded, began to leak through the cracks of his control. Beneath the rage and hunger, she sensed a deep well of pain so profound it momentarily staggered her. Images flickered through her mind—not of destruction this time, but of memories. His memories.

You feel it, don't you? The pain of loving someone who destroys you.

She saw Circe as she once was—radiant, powerful, her eyes alight with magic and mystery. She felt the Dalanite's love for her, an emotion so intense it bordered on worship. Then came the betrayal. Circe's face hardening as she spoke words of binding, trapping him within the amulet, sealing away his essence while he screamed in rage and disbelief.

"She betrayed you," she whispered, her lips moving of her own volition despite the Dalanite's control over her body. "You loved her, and she locked you away."

The presence inside her faltered, his grip loosening just enough for her to sense the wound that had never healed.

Love is weakness. Love is betrayal. She promised me eternity, then imprisoned me when I showed her what true power could be. She feared what we could become together. I will never allow another to love again.

His voice was bitter, the words dripping with centuries of festering resentment. She felt a pang of unexpected sympathy, quickly followed by a chill of realization. The Dalanite wasn't just angry; he was wounded. A wounded creature was often the most dangerous of all.

The Dalanite fed on her darkness, amplifying it, using it to fuel his own power. Now, as her body moved mechanically through the corridors, he would never allow her light to shine. He would always feed the darkness, nurture it, use it to consume her entirely until nothing remained of the woman she once was. She felt a strange resonance with the entity inside her. Not sympathy—she could never sympathize with his desire to destroy—but more like an understanding of him.

You'll never be satisfied. No matter how many souls you consume, it will never fill the hole she left.

Olivia's body continued moving down the corridor, her footsteps echoing against the stone walls. The torches lining the hallway dimmed as she passed, as if the very light was being consumed by her presence.

I'll feed the darkness in everyone around me until this world and your world match the wasteland of my soul. Stop fighting what you're becoming, Olivia.

I'm not like you.

She approached the top of the grand staircase. The pull grew stronger. The souls, waiting to be consumed, just beyond the double red doors in front of her. The hunger gnawed at her, not entirely foreign anymore. Part of her wanted to give in, to taste that power.

A war raged within her. She pushed back against the Dalanite's control, focusing on the warmth she'd felt in Jitatma's chambers. She couldn't let him win. Not when she finally understood what was at stake.

You have no choice. You're mine now.

I always have a choice.

She focused on the faces of those she loved—Jitatma's steady gaze, Talia's silent strength, Storm's mischievous smile, Johara's guidance and even Scooter's wise eyes. They anchored her, reminding her of who she was beyond this darkness. With each face that appeared in her mind, she felt a spark of resistance growing stronger.

With a surge of will, she halted her progress toward the red door. Her foot hovered mid-step, trembling with the effort of resistance. Sweat beaded on her forehead as she fought against the Dalanite's control.

The Dalanite's grip faltered. She focused on that weakness, pushing against his dominance. Her rage intensified, scorching her from within as the Dalanite fought to regain control. He forced her forward to the door.

"I accept that you're a part of me now," she said aloud, her voice echoing in the empty hallway. Her hand, reaching for the ornate handle of the red door, trembled and then stopped, her fingertips touching the cool surface of the door without opening it. "I don't accept your path. I am not just a vessel. I am Olivia. I am a part of Circe, but I won't let your pain become mine."

The mention of Circe's name sent a fresh wave of fury through the Dalanite's consciousness. She staggered under its weight but remained standing.

I'm your master now. You will be a good girl and do what I want.

CHAPTER TWENTY-EIGHT

OLIVIA

O livia stood before the massive double doors. The cold air of the corridor pressed against her skin, but inside, a different kind of chill was spreading—the Dalanite's hunger, an icy tentacle unfurling in her chest. Her fingers had just grazed the cool metal of the handle when the air behind her shifted.

A sound like tearing silk filled the corridor, followed by a rush of displaced air that sent her hair fluttering against her neck. The wall to her left rippled and split, the stone bleeding into itself as a swirling vortex of energy tore through the fabric of reality. The portal pulsed with an iridescent light, like lightning captured and stretched into a doorway. She stepped back, her spine pressing against the judgment chamber doors as a figure emerged from the churning energy.

Gorgon stepped through the portal with the casual confidence of one who is used to bending the universe to his will. His tall figure blocked what little light filtered down the corridor, casting her in his shadow. He wore darkness like a second skin. His face bore the placid expression of a predator who knows his prey cannot escape.

"Sweet Olivia," he said, his voice a low vibration that seemed to resonate in her bones. "What fortuitous timing."

The moment his voice reached her, the Dalanite responded. It twisted inside her, stretching toward the Underworld god. A violent shudder raced through her body, starting at her core and radiating outward until her fingers trembled and her knees threatened to buckle. Her eyes darted around, searching for escape, but found only wood at her back and Gorgon's immovable presence.

A small, involuntary gasp escaped her lips as the creature inside her pushed against the boundaries of her being. The sensation was unlike anything she'd felt before—not pain, exactly, but a pressure that threatened to split her open from within, as though the Dalanite might tear through her skin to reach Gorgon.

"It recognizes me," he said, closing the distance between them with measured steps. The portal remained open behind him, a tear in reality that revealed glimpses of another world. "The Dalanite knows its master."

She swallowed hard, forcing her voice past the knot of fear in her throat. "You're not its master and you're not mine."

Her defiance sounded hollow even to her own ears, undermined by the visible tremors running through her body and the way her eyes kept drifting to the portal. The Dalanite pressed harder, and she felt a curious doubling of her senses. She was still herself, still Olivia, but she was also something ancient and hungry, something that yearned for the darkness Gorgon offered.

"No?" His lips curved into a smile. "Then why does it pull you toward me? Why does your body betray your words? You seek souls to feed it," he said, his voice dropping to a murmur. "A few morsels stolen from Johara's chambers, scraps that barely sustain the hunger. I can offer you a feast."

He gestured toward the portal, and as if responding to his movement, the swirling energies parted further, revealing more of what lay beyond. She saw a vast hall where translucent figures drifted like smoke, their faces contorted in silent screams.

"Let me take you to the Underworld, where the souls await," he continued. "There, the Dalanite can gorge itself on the suffering of thousands. There, you will find relief from its constant demands."

Her body tensed as the Dalanite pushed against her consciousness, drawn to the promise of sustenance. It was like fighting against a riptide. The more she resisted, the more exhausted she became, and the stronger the pull seemed to grow. She swayed forward, her body betraying her will.

"Why?" she managed, forcing herself to meet his gaze. "Why help the Dalanite feed? What do you gain?"

He stepped close enough that she felt the unnatural warmth radiating from him. His fingers reached out to brush a strand of hair from her face. The touch sent a shock of ice through her veins, and the Dalanite responded with a surge of hungry pleasure.

"Because what's inside you is mine by right," he said softly. "A fragment of power I lost long ago."

His ownership and connection to the Dalanite sent a wave of revulsion through her, momentarily overpowering the creature's pull.

"You're lying," she said, pressing harder against the judgment chamber doors. "This is some trick to lure me into the Underworld."

"Am I?" His smile widened fractionally. "Ask it yourself. Feel how it yearns to return to me. He's my demon."

She could feel it. The Dalanite's response to his words was immediate and visceral, a surge of recognition and longing she couldn't deny was real. The Dalanite knew him. It wanted him. Dizziness swept through her as the Dalanite's yearning intensified. Her vision blurred at the edges, the corridor becoming a tunnel with Gorgon at its center. The sensation was like being pulled underwater, her consciousness sinking beneath the creature's desires.

"Come," he said, extending his hand. "The souls await."

With a final push, the Dalanite wrenched control from her. She felt her arm rise, fingers reaching for his outstretched hand, even as her mind screamed in protest. Their fingertips touched, and a jolt of dark energy coursed through her, familiar and foreign all at once.

He gripped her hand firmly, pulling her away from the judgment chamber doors. "You can feel it," he murmured, his voice like velvet wrapped around a blade. "The connection. The belonging."

The Dalanite purred its agreement inside her mind, a sound like distant thunder. She struggled against its control, trying to reclaim her body.

"I can help you understand what you've become," he continued. "What you were always meant to be."

She felt herself being led away from the judgment chamber, toward the portal. Her feet moved of their own accord, the Dalanite's will overriding her own. She tried to scream, to call for help, but her voice remained trapped in her mind while her body obeyed Gorgon's gentle guidance.

She fought desperately against the Dalanite's control. She clawed at the edges of her consciousness, searching for a foothold, any weakness in the creature's hold that she could exploit. The Dalanite was too strong, too eager for what Gorgon promised. The creature's hunger was overwhelming now, a desperate, primal need that threatened to consume her entirely.

"No," she whispered, trying to pull her hand back.

They had reached the portal now. The Dalanite surged forward eagerly, pulling her body with it. Her foot hovered over the threshold, the tips of her toes already tingling with the strange energy of the portal.

"Olivia!"

The voice cut through the corridor like a blade, sharp and desperate. The sound of her name, spoken with such raw emotion, created a momentary fracture in the Dalanite's control. She managed to turn her head, fighting against the creature's will.

Jitatma stood at the bottom of the grand staircase, his face a mask of horror and determination. He took the steps two at a time, his cloak billowing behind him like wings. "Stop! Don't go with him!"

The sound of his voice sent a shock through her system, giving her the strength to fight back against the Dalanite's control. She dug her heels into the stone floor, halting her forward momentum toward the portal.

"Jitatma," she gasped, his name a plea and a prayer. "Help me."

Gorgon's grip tightened around her wrist, hard enough to bruise. His expression remained unchanged, but power radiated from him in waves that made the air itself seem to compress around them.

"We have no time for interruptions," he hissed, pulling her with sudden force.

Behind them, Jitatma's footsteps thundered up the staircase. "Olivia!" he called again, his voice closer now. "Fight him!"

Gorgon's face hardened. With supernatural speed, he yanked her against his chest, one arm snaking around her waist while the other hand remained tightly around her wrist. The pull of the Dalanite and Gorgon's iron grip dragged her forward despite her resistance. She felt herself tilting toward the portal, the heat of the Underworld licking at her skin. Inside her, two forces warred—her own desperate need to stay, and the Dalanite's ravenous desire to go.

"He cannot save you," Gorgon said, his voice a silken caress despite the iron grip on her wrist. "No one can. You belong with me. You carry my creation, my power."

The word "creation" reverberated through her mind, triggering a flash of recognition from the Dalanite—not fear or hunger, but something closer to pride. The creature preened under his recognition, and the sensation nearly made her knees buckle.

Jitatma reached the top of the stairs, his breathing ragged, eyes wild with fear. "Let her go!" he demanded, his voice echoing off the stone walls.

Gorgon didn't even turn to look at him. With a casual flick of his wrist, he sent a pulse of fire that struck Jitatma square in the chest. The impact lifted him off his feet and slammed him against the far wall. He crumpled to the ground, dazed but conscious, struggling to rise again.

"Jitatma!" she screamed, her voice finally breaking through the Dalanite's control.

With a sharp tug, Gorgon pulled her backward into the portal. The last thing she saw was Jitatma lunging forward, his fingers reaching for her, his face contorted in anguish.

Then the world dissolved around her.

Falling through the portal felt like being unmade—her body stretched and compressed simultaneously, her lungs unable to draw breath as reality itself twisted around her. The journey lasted both an instant and an eternity.

Then, abruptly, solid ground materialized beneath her feet. She stumbled, her knees buckling as she fell forward onto a surface that felt like polished obsidian—smooth, cold, and unyielding. The impact forced the air from her lungs in a painful gasp.

"Welcome," he said, his voice resonating with satisfaction, finally releasing her, "to my kingdom."

She stumbled away from him, rubbing the bruised skin where his fingers had dug in. The Dalanite's control had slackened somewhat, allowing her to reclaim her body, but she could feel it stirring inside her.

Her eyes finally adjusted to the dim light, revealing the scene before her. She found herself standing at the threshold of a dark, foreboding castle, its towering spires reaching up toward the sky like jagged claws. The stone walls were ancient and weathered, adorned with intricate carvings that seemed to writhe and twist in the shifting shadows cast by torches that flickered ominously along the castle's ramparts.

Guarding the entrance were creatures unlike any she had ever seen before. They stood tall and imposing, half-Niberian in appearance, with features that inspired both fear and fascination. From the waist down, their bodies seamlessly transitioned into the segmented form of Centipedes, their many legs skittering restlessly over the dark stone floor.

"Lord, you didn't tell me we were having a guest," a woman's voice said.

Olivia turned toward the source of the voice, her curiosity piqued. Her eyes widened as she discovered the speaker. The woman possessed the elegant features of a Niberian, with shimmering skin and eyes that glowed softly like distant stars. Her lower half, however, was a striking contrast, a cascade of segmented limbs that moved with a fluid, mesmerizing grace, each segment adorned with delicate, shimmering patterns that caught the light like a kaleidoscope.

"Yes, this guest was unexpected." He nodded. "I apologize, Centra, for the short notice, but we are going to need food prepared for Olivia and a few tortured souls."

Centra bowed her head in acknowledgment, the movement fluid and elegant despite her unusual form. "Of course, my lord. I'll have everything prepared. The souls in the eastern chambers are particularly anguished today. They should provide adequate sustenance."

"I don't want this," she said, forcing the words through gritted teeth as she backed away from both him and his servant. "I won't feed on souls."

He regarded her with something akin to pity. "You will," he said simply. "The hunger will only grow until you have no choice. Better to do it willingly, with dignity."

Centra's eyes widened, her slender fingers coming to rest against her lips in a gesture of surprise. "The Dalanite? The one you've been searching for?" Her gaze settled on Olivia with newfound intensity, assessing her with the clinical precision of someone examining a rare specimen. "This little thing has the creature in her?"

"The very same," he confirmed, his voice resonating with satisfaction. "After all this time, it has returned to us."

"Centra, post extra guards at the entrance in case we have more guests," he barked. "Let me know if my wife or son pay me a visit."

Centra's many legs clicked across the obsidian ground as she bowed. "As you wish, my lord." She cast a curious glance at Olivia before scurrying away.

She fought to control her breathing as she took in her surroundings. The Underworld was nothing like she had imagined. Instead of fire and brimstone, the air here was unnaturally cold, carrying the scent of decay and something metallic, like old blood.

"What are they?" she whispered, unable to contain her curiosity despite her fear.

"The Exopedes?" His voice held a note of pride. "My first creations. Loyal servants fashioned from the souls of the damned and the essence of creatures that once crawled beneath Niberia's surface." He placed a hand on the small of her back, guiding her toward the castle.

She glanced around the entrance hall, taking in the vastness of his domain. The ceiling arched impossibly high above them, disappearing into shadows where strange, winged creatures flitted like living darkness. The walls seemed to pulse with an inner light, as though the very stone was alive and breathing.

The Dalanite stirred inside her, responding to the strange energies of the Underworld. It stretched within her, as if testing the boundaries of her body, drawn to the suffering that permeated the very air.

"You feel it, don't you?" he said, watching her reaction closely. "The souls. Their pain calls to the Dalanite."

She wrapped her arms around herself, trying to contain the creature's growing excitement. "Why did you bring me here? What do you really want?"

He gestured toward a grand staircase that spiraled downward. "Come. There are things you need to understand."

CHAPTER TWENTY-NINE

ANASAZI

"Watch your step," Anasazi cautioned Talia.

The narrow passageway breathed cold air against Anasazi's skin as they descended into the bowels of the ancient structure. Stone walls, worn smooth by centuries of passage, guided them deeper, where the light grew thinner and the air hung heavy with forgotten memories. Water dripped somewhere ahead, each droplet striking the stone with the precision of time itself passing. Behind them, a torch sputtered, casting their elongated shadows against the uneven walls.

"He's waiting for us," Anasazi said as they approached the cell. Her voice betrayed nothing—no anxiety, no anticipation—just a steady certainty that had weathered the ages. "Tell me, Talia, when did you last see Hunter?"

"The last time Jitatma threw him in prison. I try not to think about him."

At the end, Hunter stood in the center of his cell. His presence exuded an aura of power tinged with resignation, his eyes locking onto Talia's with an intensity that seemed to pierce through the darkness surrounding them.

"You came," he said, his voice a low rumble that seemed to vibrate through the stones beneath their feet. "I wasn't sure you would."

"Lady Anasazi was persuasive," Talia replied.

"You look more like Circe every day," he said.

Her jaw tightened. "So I've been told."

"Not just in appearance. There's something in your manner, in the way you hold yourself. It's as if you're becoming her from the outside in, but you're not her."

"I never claimed to be," Talia said, a defensive edge creeping into her voice.

He tilted his head to the side and smiled. "If you came, that means the situation is getting worse."

"Don't look so pleased. Gorgon has Olivia," Anasazi said, her voice steady. "We need to know how to stop it."

His eyes darkened. "And you think I can help? I'm not exactly in a position of power." He gestured to the bars that contained him. "I can't help you from here." He moved closer to the bars, his face half-illuminated by the torches' flicker. "The only one who can stop Gorgon and the Dalanite is the real Circe. Not her look-alike."

Talia stepped forward, the light catching the determination in her eyes. "We wouldn't be here if we had other options. You know Gorgon better than anyone."

"The Dalanite," he said finally, his voice hollow with memory. "That creature started this whole mess. It feeds on darkness, on the shadows within us all. But Gorgon..." He paused, something like regret flickering across his face. "Gorgon's darkness was particularly appetizing."

Anasazi's posture stiffened. "Tell her everything, Hunter. She needs to understand what we're facing."

He nodded, his eyes distant, as if seeing through time itself. "When I first discovered the Dalanite, it was Circe who had the power it truly wanted. It needed a vessel with strong magic." His gaze returned to Talia. "When it started taking over Circe, it forced her to have an affair with Gorgon."

"I could have forgiven them for giving in to the power," Anasazi said, her voice cold as the air around them. "The Dalanite's influence is manipulating. It fed off their desires, twisting them into something corrupted." Her fists clenched at her sides and her voice was brittle with ancient pain. "The affair continued after she trapped the Dalanite in the amulet. That's what I couldn't forgive. When the influence was gone, they still chose each other."

The air in the dungeon seemed to grow even colder, the chill seeping into her bones. Anasazi still felt the suffocating weight of betrayal pressing down on her. It was this very betrayal that turned her heart to ice, freezing her emotions in a relentless grip that refused to thaw.

With each heartbeat, she felt the icy tendrils of betrayal coil tighter around her heart, locking away any hint of vulnerability behind a mask of stoic resolve. Memories of past deceptions and broken promises clawed at her insides, threatening to consume her. The echoes of betrayal reverberated through the stone chamber, a constant reminder of wounds that had never fully healed.

Hunter's eyes met Anasazi's. Something unspoken passed between them, a current of shared history too complex for others to fully comprehend.

"That creature forced Circe to break our bond so she could trap him in the amulet. She was never the same after that," Hunter said, looking away.

"The Dalanite just reveals what already exists," Anasazi said, her voice barely above a whisper, yet cutting through the silence like a blade. "That creature didn't force Circe or Gorgon to have an affair. They wanted it to happen. It cannot create darkness where there is none. It can only nurture what lies dormant."

Talia's eyes widened as understanding dawned across her features. "This is all about Circe," she breathed. "The affair, the betrayal, the amulet—everything centers on her."

"Of course it does," Anasazi said bitterly. "Even in death, it's still about her."

"If Gorgon has Olivia, I can only think of one reason he would need her." He stepped closer, but his chains prevented him from coming up to the bar. "There's nothing you can do to stop him."

Anasazi took a step toward him. "Tell us what my husband is planning."

"You're not going to like it." Hunter smiled wickedly. "We're all fucked."

"Well, it's a good thing I don't care much for my husband. I would rather burn our world to the ground than have him succeed in his plan," Anasazi said, with all the coldness in her heart.

"He wants to unleash the Dalanite so the Dark Haunting can spread to consume our world. The living world will be forced into darkness and ruled by things like hate and anger, making him the most powerful god. Gorgon wants to rule our world with fear and intimidation as the god of all gods. We'll have to bow to him."

"I'll never serve that asshole."

"How is he going to release the Dalanite? It needs a host," Talia asked.

"Yes, it does." He nodded. "Gorgon is looking for another vessel. One where the Dalanite can thrive instead of being controlled." Hunter laughed, the sound echoing off the damp stone walls, hollow and without mirth. "You see, Talia, I was never the god you should have worried about. It was Gorgon manipulating all of us to gain absolute control. I don't seem so crazy now."

"No, you're still crazy."

CHAPTER THIRTY

OLIVIA

"**W**ow. You really play into this whole Lord of Darkness title. Your castle is exactly what it should be." Olivia stood facing Gorgon, her shoulders squared despite the chill that crept along her spine. "Shady and questionable, like your personality."

"I'm hurt that you don't trust me," he said sardonically.

"On my list of trust, you do rank higher than Hunter, considering you haven't tried to send me to the empty void yet."

"Our visit just got started. There's still time for that."

"I would hardly call this a visit."

He smiled, revealing the sharp edge of his teeth. "You wound me, Olivia. I thought we were developing a rapport."

He gestured toward a winding staircase that spiraled down into darkness. The mustiness of ancient air rose from below, mingled with something acrid that made her nostrils burn.

"How appropriate you're taking me down into the dungeon of your castle. Is this where you plan to keep me?"

"Not exactly," he replied, a hint of a smile playing at the corners of his lips. "This is where my throne room is."

He opened a heavy wooden door at the bottom of the stairs. The room itself was a grand expanse, with high vaulted ceilings adorned with intricate carvings that seemed to tell stories of old. Rich tapestries hung on the walls, their vibrant colors and patterns adding warmth to the otherwise cool stone surroundings. In the center stood a magnificent throne, crafted from dark mahogany and inlaid with gold, its presence commanding respect and awe.

"This is not what I was expecting."

"Did you think I sat on a pile of skulls and bones in a pit of flames? I save that for my private chambers."

"Sounds lovely," she said dryly. "Why were you in the empty void?"

"Were you asking, or was it the Dalanite?"

The entity that shared her consciousness stirred, a whisper of movement like silk against her thoughts. She felt the Dalanite's curiosity blend with her own, two minds seeking the same answer through different lenses.

"Both," she replied.

He nodded, as if her answer confirmed something he'd long suspected. He took a step closer, and the space between them became charged with a different kind of tension—not just the wariness of adversaries, but the peculiar intimacy of conspirators.

"I visited the empty void to check on the gate," he said, his voice lower now, even though they were alone. "Hunter's dark magic compromised it. I needed to know how weak it was." He moved to his throne and sat with casual grace.

Olivia's skin prickled with alarm. "Why?"

"That's a private conversation with the Dalanite." Gorgon leaned forward. "Your little passenger could be instrumental in helping me achieve this."

"You're as delusional as Hunter," she scoffed.

"Yes." His eyes glittered with appreciation. "You understand more than you pretend to. You're not as innocent as you look."

"No," she said simply. No elaborate refusal, no impassioned argument. Just refusal, solid as the stone beneath their feet.

He rose from his throne with a fluid grace that belied his imposing stature. Before Olivia could react, his hand was on her shoulder, his touch surprisingly warm against her skin. Something shifted in the atmosphere between them.

His consciousness pressed against hers, not invading like the Dalanite's symbiotic presence, but mirroring her own abilities. She felt the intrusion—a strange sensation, like looking into a mirror that suddenly looked back. She'd read countless minds but never had someone turn her own ability against her. The walls she'd built around her thoughts crumbled as his consciousness flowed through the breach.

"Interesting," he said. "I see you've been keeping secrets, even from yourself. Now I can see why my son is attracted to you. You're as guarded as he is."

Olivia tried to pull away, but his grip tightened. "Get out of my head."

The entity within her stirred, no longer content to observe. A sudden pressure built behind her eyes, a sensation like drowning while still breathing. The Dalanite was responding directly to Gorgon, bypassing her consciousness entirely.

"Stop it," she gasped, trying to regain control. "This isn't a negotiation."

"Oh, but it is," he replied. "Just not one that requires your input." He released her shoulder, but the connection remained, a psychic tether she couldn't sever. "The Dalanite understands what's at stake. It knows the balance of power is shifting."

"You can't do this."

"I already have," he replied. "Now, shall we proceed with decorum, or must I resort to less pleasant methods of ensuring your cooperation?"

The air before him began to twist, darkness gathering and condensing until it formed a portal. The Dalanite's presence grew heavier in her mind, a pressure that pushed her forward even as her body resisted.

I have to go to the empty void.

No, don't listen to him.

"Well, you can forget it," she said, crossing her arms. "I won't be part of any shit you're planning."

"Consider it a privilege. Few have seen the gate to the empty void and returned to speak of it." Gorgon gestured toward the portal. "After you," he said. "The void awaits, and we have a gate to inspect."

Her legs moved against her will, the Dalanite guiding her body while her mind still reeled from the double betrayal. As she approached the portal's edge, she felt the cold radiating from it—not the ambient chill of the Underworld, but the absolute absence of heat, of life, of meaning. The silence beyond the portal was endless.

She paused at the threshold, summoning what defiance she could. "This won't end how you think," she told Gorgon, her voice steadier than she felt.

The Dalanite's presence throbbed inside her mind like a second heartbeat, heavy and insistent. She could feel it monitoring her thoughts, analyzing her intentions. But there was one connection it couldn't fully block—the twin bond she shared with Talia.

Olivia kept her face neutral as she stood at the threshold of the void portal, the cold emanating from it, raising goosebumps along her arms. She needed to warn someone, anyone, about what Gorgon was planning. The Dalanite would intercept any attempt to reach Jitatma directly; she'd felt its jealous grip tighten whenever his name crossed her mind.

She closed her eyes, pretending to steel herself for the journey into the void. Instead, she reached for that familiar connection to her sister, feeling for the warm pulse that was uniquely Talia. The Dalanite shifted uncomfortably within her, sensing something but unable to identify the exact nature of what she was doing.

She pushed harder, fighting through the Dalanite's influence. The entity inside her clawed at her consciousness, trying to maintain control, but she had spent a lifetime sharing her mind with her twin. This connection was deeper than the Dalanite's invasion.

Pirate's contract.

The entity writhed inside her mind, sensing the transmission but unable to decode its significance. Olivia felt a sharp pain behind her eyes as the Dalanite reasserted control, but she'd done it. She had sent the message, brief and cryptic, but hopefully enough.

"What was that?" Gorgon asked sharply, his eyes narrowing.

"Nothing," she said, forcing a smile that felt brittle on her face. "Just gathering my courage. The void isn't exactly a vacation destination."

She felt the Dalanite push her forward, her legs moving against her will. The cold intensified as she approached the threshold, numbing her fingertips and sending a shiver down her spine. She could only hope that somewhere Talia had felt her desperation and understood.

As the void's darkness began to envelop her, Olivia clung to that small act of rebellion. The Dalanite might control her body, Gorgon might command her presence, but they hadn't claimed everything. Not yet.

His smile was the last thing she saw before the void swallowed her, his words following her into the nothingness, "It never does. That's what makes it interesting."

CHAPTER THIRTY-ONE

ANASAZI

Anasazi's heart hammered against her ribs as she swept into Johara's judgment chambers, Talia a half-step behind her. The conversation with Hunter echoed relentlessly in her mind, each word cutting deeper than the last. The journey down memory lane felt like prying open an old, festering wound, leaving a bitter taste that lingered in the back of her throat.

Now, she had to step foot in the very room where all those memories still cut deep. The chamber was larger than it appeared from the outside, a trick of architecture, or perhaps magic. Johara had done little to change the appearance. Rough-hewn stone arched overhead, meeting at a central point that seemed impossibly distant.

Majestic marble columns framed the expansive chambers, each a testament to the grandeur of the space. However, it was the solitary column tucked into the shadowy corner that drew her gaze. Despite the meticulous repairs that had smoothed over its surface, that column remained an indelible reminder of the furious jealousy that had once consumed her, leading to the tragic demise of Circe. The faint scars of the past lingered beneath the polished veneer, whispering tales of passion and regret.

Jitatma stood at the center of the chamber, his tall figure some-how both solid and ethereal near the pool of blood. Beside him, Storm's muscular frame seemed almost brutish by comparison, and she could see the family resemblance. Scooter fidgeted nearby, unable to keep still, even in this solemn place. Malta and Johara stood together, their heads bent in whispered conversation that stopped abruptly as Anasazi entered. Sully lingered near a far wall, half in shadow, her presence easy to miss until one noticed the gleam of her watchful eyes.

"This is all your fault!" Jitatma snarled, advancing on Anasazi, fists clenched and fury blazing in his eyes. The temperature in the room seemed to drop several degrees. "You said Olivia would not be at risk!"

Anasazi drew herself up to her full height, unfazed by his ap-proach. "Lower your voice when speaking to me," she said, her tone glacial. Despite her commanding exterior, guilt clawed at her insides. She had indeed promised Olivia's safety, a promise now broken.

"You and I have a long, ugly history, but this is low, even for you," Jitatma pressed, his voice dropping to a dangerous whisper. "If anything happens to Olivia, I'll make sure you'll be sharing a cell with Gorgon."

Anasazi flinched at his threat, her composure momentarily shat-tered. She had built her own icy castle on the hill in the Un-derworld. It was her fortress of solitude designed so she would never have to share space with her husband again. The castle's frosty walls glittered with an unyielding coldness, reflecting her determination to keep him at bay.

"That's the last thing I want to do for an eternity."

"Pirate's contract? What is she talking about?" Talia said, her voice distant. She looked up at Storm, her eyes wide. "Pirate, Olivia was talking about you. Gorgon took Olivia to the empty void."

The effect was instantaneous. Jitatma froze mid-step, his anger temporarily displaced by something that looked suspiciously like fear. Storm inhaled sharply, the sound amplified in the sudden silence. Malta murmured something that might have been a prayer.

"The empty void?" Johara repeated, her voice barely above a whisper. "Are you certain? Why?"

"Hunter said Gorgon wants to release the Dalanite so it doesn't need to tether to a soul. He wants it to thrive endlessly. There's only one way he can do that."

Scooter let out a low whistle. "Well, that sounds problematic."

"We can't have a Dalanite with that much freedom," Sully said, pushing herself away from the wall.

"The Dalanite thrives on its host, but it has its limits," Malta explained, his voice taking on the measured cadence of a scholar. "If Gorgon succeeds in freeing it from its tethering requirements, every soul in existence would be at risk."

"It would be free to consume many souls at once to feed the Dark Haunting," Johara said. "We won't be able to stop it."

Jitatma turned slowly, deliberately away from Anasazi and fixed his gaze on his brother. His anger remained—visible in his tight jaw and trembling hands—but he seemed to channel and focus it. "Storm, do you remember what the empty void looks like?"

Storm met Jitatma's gaze without flinching, his expression grave. "That's a place that's hard to forget," he said, his voice surprisingly soft for a man of his size.

Something passed between them then, some unspoken communication Anasazi couldn't decipher but recognized as significant. Jitatma nodded, a barely perceptible movement.

"I need you to hold that vision clearly in your mind," Jitatma said. "Every detail. The feel of it, the sound, the smell. Everything."

Understanding dawned on Anasazi. "You're going to open a portal to the empty void," she said.

Jitatma didn't bother to confirm or deny. He placed a hand on Storm's broad shoulder, his other hand raised palm-up at chest height. His fingers began to trace patterns in the air, leaving faint luminous trails that lingered for seconds before fading.

"Hold the vision, Storm," he murmured. "Let me see through your memory."

Storm closed his eyes, his face a study in concentration. The muscles in his neck strained, as if the memory itself had physical weight. "It's cold," he said through gritted teeth. "Not the kind of cold that numbs. The kind that burns. The air—if you can call it air—feels thin, like trying to breathe at impossible heights. The silence was absolute. It swallows all sound."

As Storm spoke, the chamber began to change. The shadows deepened. The stone beneath their feet vibrated with a low hum that Anasazi felt in her bones rather than heard with her ears.

Jitatma's raised hand began to glow, softly at first, then with increasing intensity. The light was not the gentle blue of the chamber's illumination, but a fierce, almost painful white that cast his face in harsh relief, emphasizing the angles and hollows until he looked less like a man and more like a carving of one.

"What do you see?" Jitatma pressed, his voice strained with effort.

Storm's eyelids fluttered but remained closed. "Nothing. Everything. Empty isn't the right word. It's absence. The absence of all things. But sometimes, if you look too long in one direction, you start to see shapes. Movements. Things that cannot be but somehow are. It was bleak with a stark gray landscape. When I first opened my eyes, I was lying on a cold, rocky plain. There was an immense iron gate, and the hinges appeared to be rusted and several bars were missing."

Jitatma's glowing hand clenched suddenly into a fist, then opened with fingers splayed wide. A sound like tearing cloth filled the chamber, and the air before him split open. It wasn't a neat or tidy opening—the edges frayed and writhed, as if the very fabric of reality objected to being breached. Through the opening, Anasazi caught glimpses of nothing. Not darkness, not light, but the absence of both.

That horrible place was where she sent her sister so long ago. The memory haunted her, casting a shadow over her already icy demeanor. Her stoic facade began to crack, revealing a well of conflicting emotion she struggled to contain. The room felt heavy with unspoken apologies. Anasazi's hands trembled as she remembered the moment she made that fateful decision, a decision that forever altered the course of Circe's existence.

CHAPTER THIRTY-TWO

OLIVIA

The iron gate hung askew from a single rusted hinge, its twin lying twisted on the ground. The creaking of rusted metal filled the air as the gate swayed precariously on its remaining hinge. The dragging of metal against stone echoed through the empty void beyond, creating an eerie symphony of sorts.

Beyond it, the empty void stretched—not truly empty but scattered with countless pinpricks of light that hung suspended in darkness. The air was musty and metallic, tinged with the scent of rust and decay. Something burning faintly lingered in the air, as if something smoldered in the empty void beyond.

"They say no one returns from the void," Gorgon said, his deep voice eerily flat against the soundless expanse before them. "A prison without bars, a sentence without end."

She stepped closer to the broken gate, careful not to touch the jagged metal edges that jutted out like warning fingers. The wind whispered past her ears, carrying with it something so faint she wondered if she was imagining it—a sound like a distant plea.

"Do you hear that?" she whispered, tilting her head.

Gorgon's eyes, dark and bottomless as the void itself, narrowed. "Hear what?"

"That sound," Olivia insisted, straining to catch it again. "Like someone calling."

This time, it came clearer—a woman's voice, high and distant, the words indistinguishable but the desperation unmistakable. The Dalanite inside her seemed to pulse in response, a warm pressure beneath her sternum that spread outward through her limbs. She pressed her hand to her chest, trying to calm the energy that coursed through her veins.

"The void plays tricks," he said. She heard something in his tone, suggesting he doubted his own words. He stepped forward to stand beside her, close enough that she could feel the unnatural heat that always radiated from his skin. "It lures with false promises, with memories and desires. That's why it's the perfect prison. You chase echoes until you forget who you are."

"This isn't an echo," she said. The voice rose again, more distinct this time, a single note that hung in the air like frost. "Someone's in there."

The Dalanite was reacting more strongly now, its energy pooling in her fingertips until they tingled with familiar power. She reached out instinctively, not toward the broken gate but the space just above it, where the air seemed to shimmer with possibility.

The voice called again, and this time, a melody took shape—three notes falling and rising again, a pattern that tugged at something deep in Olivia's memory. The Dalanite recognized it too; she felt its response, a kind of answering song humming through her body.

"There's someone there," she insisted, her voice stronger now. "Someone important."

Gorgon studied her face, his expression unreadable. "You feel it, don't you? The queen's essence is inside you, responding to something beyond the gate."

Olivia nodded, unable to find the words to describe the sensation. It wasn't just the Dalanite anymore—it was something deeper, something that belonged to her soul rather than merely living within her body. Something that knew the owner of that distant voice.

The wind picked up, sending loose debris skittering across the barren ground around them. The empty void beyond the gate seemed to shift and pulse, its scattered lights swirling in patterns that made her eyes water if she tried to follow them. Against this dizzying backdrop, the voice grew stronger, more insistent.

"Help me," it seemed to say now, though she couldn't be sure if she was hearing actual words or simply interpreting the melodic plea. "Find me."

She took another step forward, close enough now that her toes nearly touched the fallen segment of the gate. The metal was cold—unnaturally so—and scattered sparks of void-light danced across its surface, leaving trails like dying stars. The distant cry came again, and this time, she was certain she recognized something in it, not a specific voice, perhaps, but a quality, a cadence that stirred memories she couldn't quite grasp.

The wind died suddenly, leaving an eerie stillness that made the voice from the void even more distinct. It was singing now—a haunting, ancient melody she had never heard before yet knew intimately. The Dalanite throbbed in time with the notes, each rise and fall of the song matched by pulses of energy that made her skin flush hot, then cold.

"I haven't heard that song in a long time," Gorgon muttered, and she realized he was hearing it too—truly hearing it, not just acknowledging her claim.

"You recognize it?" she asked, turning to face him.

Something shifted in his expression—a flash of what might have been pain, quickly masked. "It's very old," he said carefully. "I know only one person who would sing that tune."

The song grew louder, and with it came a pressure in her mind, as if something were trying to push through a barrier. She reached out, allowing her fingers to brush against the cold metal of the broken gate. Images flickered through her consciousness—a woman with hair like midnight and eyes that burned with inner fire. The Dalanite writhed within her, no longer content to observe but demanding action.

"Circe," she whispered, the name falling from her lips before she fully registered its significance. "That's Circe's voice." She tore her gaze from the swirling void, the melody of Circe's voice still echoing in her mind. She turned to Gorgon. "Why did the Dalanite want to come here?" The question escaped her lips like a challenge, direct and unavoidable.

A smile played at the corners of his mouth, but it didn't reach his eyes. They remained dark and fathomless, betraying nothing of the thoughts behind them. "Are you jealous that the Dalanite is keeping secrets?" His tone was light, teasing, a deliberate undercutting of the moment's gravity.

She crossed her arms, unappreciative of his deflection. The broken gate creaked behind her as another gust of wind swept through, carrying with it the haunting notes of Circe's call. "This isn't a game," she said.

His expression shifted, the mockery fading into something more solemn. He moved to stand beside her again, his gaze fixed on the void beyond the broken gate. "Listen to it," he said, his voice dropping to a near whisper. "That's the voice of your queen."

"How is that possible?" she asked, her own voice barely audible over the soft song that continued to drift from the void. "Circe is..." She trailed off, uncertain how to finish the sentence. Dead? Gone? Those words seemed insufficient, especially here at the threshold of a place that existed beyond normal rules of existence.

"Imprisoned," he supplied, his tone flat. "Cast into the void where neither life nor death can claim her."

The void-song grew louder, as if Circe herself were responding to his words. The melody turned sharp, almost angry, before softening again into the plaintive call that had first drawn her attention. The Dalanite pulsed in time with the changes, its energy a physical presence inside her with a will of its own.

My Circe, help her.

"It wants to help her," she murmured, pressing her palm against her chest where the Dalanite's presence felt strongest. "It wants to pull her out."

He turned to face her fully, his massive form blocking part of her view of the void. "With our combined power, we could pull her from the void. You could save her."

She stared pasted him into the swirling darkness beyond the gate. The pinpricks of light seemed to arrange themselves, forming patterns that resembled a woman's face before dissolving back into chaos.

"Why would I do that?" she asked, though the question felt hollow even as she spoke it. The Dalanite's response was immediate—a surge of energy so powerful it nearly brought her to her knees. "Why would the Dalanite want this?"

His eyes gleamed with something that might have been anticipation, or perhaps something darker. "I created the Dalanite and it chose Circe. It's fulfilling its purpose." He took a step closer to Olivia, his voice dropping to a conspiratorial whisper. "Don't you feel it? The connection between you, the Dalanite, and her?"

She did feel it—a tether that stretched from deep within her out into the void, invisible but as real as the ground beneath her feet. The melody continued, weaving through her consciousness like a thread through fabric, binding her to the presence beyond the gate.

"If I truly carry Circe's soul," she said, struggling to keep her voice steady as the Dalanite pulsed with increasing urgency, "and Talia has her spirit, then what exactly is trapped in there?" She gestured toward the swirling darkness.

"Essence," he said. "Her divine essence. Neither soul nor spirit, but the raw power that made her a goddess. The part of her that Anasazi couldn't destroy or disperse."

"There's more to this than you're telling me," she said, forcing herself to step back from both him and the gate. The pull was almost physical now, and she had to resist the urge to simply walk forward into the swirling darkness.

"There's always more to everything, Olivia. That's the nature of existence." He extended his hand, palm up, an invitation rather than a demand. "Circe is trapped. You have the means to free her. The question is whether you will."

The Dalanite surged again, and she gasped at the intensity of its response. It wasn't just energy now but emotion—longing, grief, determination—emotions so powerful they threatened to overwhelm her. The melody from the void rose in harmony with the Dalanite's pulse, creating a resonance that vibrated through her very bones.

"Focus on the voice," he instructed, his hand now hovering just above the broken edge of the gate. "Let the Dalanite guide you. I'll provide the pathway, but you must be the beacon that calls her home."

She closed her eyes, concentrating on the distant melody that seemed to call directly to something deep within her. The Dalanite's energy gathered, focused, its usual chaotic power suddenly harnessed and directed. She felt rather than saw Gorgon's power unfurling beside her—darker, colder, but no less potent.

She extended her hand toward the void, allowing the Dalanite's energy to flow through her fingertips into the emptiness beyond. At the same moment, his power surged outward, intertwining with hers in a spiral of light and shadow that cut through the swirling darkness.

The void seemed to shudder, its scattered lights flaring and dimming in rapid succession. Circe's song faltered, then returned stronger than ever, a triumphant melody that matched the pulse of the energy bridge stretching into the emptiness.

She felt his powers flowing steadily alongside her own. The two energies were distinct but harmonizing, creating something neither could have managed alone. The song grew louder, closer, and with it came a pressure that made the air around them seem to thicken. She felt the void resisting the pull, trying to cling to what it had claimed.

"Almost," she murmured, the Dalanite's excitement bleeding into her own consciousness. "She's almost here."

As the words left her lips, the void convulsed, its darkness contracting before exploding outward in a silent wave that nearly knocked them both off their feet. The energy bridge shivered but held, and through it, traveling like light through a prism, came a figure—indistinct at first, then sharpening into the unmistakable form of a woman.

Circe was returning from the empty void.

CHAPTER THIRTY-THREE

OLIVIA

Olivia's muscles burned with the effort of maintaining the connection. Her shoulders ached, fingers quivering as she reached deeper into the emptiness. The Dalanite's power was both exhilarating and exhausting, filling her with a strength that felt simultaneously foreign and deeply familiar.

The Dalanite had full control, using her body as a conduit with single-minded purpose. Her consciousness floated somewhere behind her own eyes, watching as her hands moved of their own accord, fingers splayed wide to channel the growing torrent of energy.

From the void, Circe's melody shifted into something triumphant, rising in pitch and intensity until it seemed to vibrate through the very air around them. The figure at the end of their energy bridge solidified further, shadows giving way to form—the curve of a shoulder, the sweep of long hair, the outline of a face.

"Olivia!"

The voice cut through her concentration like a blade. Not Circe's song, but something else—something real and immediate. Jitatma's voice.

The Dalanite's rage flooded through her instantly, a scalding wave that momentarily blinded her. In that split second of distraction, the energy bridge wavered, and Circe's form flickered dangerously, threatening to dissolve back into the void.

"Don't stop now!" Gorgon's command cracked through the air. "She's almost here!"

The Dalanite reasserted control with brutal efficiency, pushing Olivia's consciousness further into the background. Through eyes that no longer felt like her own, she saw him—Jitatma—standing at the edge of the void with Talia beside him, their faces twisted in identical expressions of horror. Storm and Sully materialized beside Talia, while Johara, Scooter and Malta positioned themselves next to Jitatma.

Olivia felt herself being used, her energy siphoned away to fuel this forbidden ritual. She wanted to scream, to fight back against the invasion, but the Dalanite's grip was absolute.

"Release my sister! I've had enough of this shit. I fought one obsessed, crazy god," Talia said, drawing her Chakram from her belt. "I've got room to add another asshole to that list. I'm not about to let another one use her. Get your own fucking puppet."

The Dalanite snarled using Olivia's mouth, the sound guttural. Through the haze of her own suppressed consciousness, she felt a flicker of hope at the sight of her sister and friends. She tried to reach for that feeling, to use it as an anchor against the Dalanite's overwhelming control, but it slipped away like water through cupped hands.

"Too late," Gorgon called back, his deep voice resonating with dark satisfaction.

The energy bridge pulsed brighter, and the figure of Circe grew more substantial with each passing second. What had been a shadow now had definition—a woman of impossible beauty, her midnight hair streaming behind her like liquid darkness, her eyes pools of purple fire. Her song had changed again, no longer a plea but a

declaration of triumph that made the very air vibrate with anticipation.

Through the diminishing window of her awareness, she saw
Jitatma take a cautious step forward, his hazel eyes locked on hers
with an intensity that pierced through the Dalanite's control for
the briefest moment.

"Olivia," Jitatma called again, his voice gentler now, reaching for
her through the maelstrom of power. "Fight it. You know this is
wrong."

"Silence!" the Dalanite hissed through Olivia's lips, her voice
distorted and layered with otherworldly resonance.

"She can't hear you," Gorgon taunted, his power surging alongside the Dalanite's. "Her mind belongs to a higher purpose now."

"You can't have her."

Jitatma lunged forward, his movements a blur as he crossed the
distance between them. His fingers closed around Olivia's wrist
with fierce tenderness, a grip that was both a restraint and a lifeline.
Through the haze of the Dalanite's control, she felt his touch
like a shock of cold water—painful in its clarity but desperately
needed. The energy flowing through her arms flickered, the bridge
connecting to Circe wavering for a precious moment as two wills
battled for dominance over her body.

"She is mine," Jitatma growled, his voice carrying a command
that transcended mere words. He wasn't speaking to Gorgon, or
even to Olivia—but directly to the Dalanite itself. "You reside
within her by my grace alone. Return her consciousness now."

The Dalanite's fury surged through her veins, molten and vi-
cious. Her body convulsed, back arching as the parasite fought
against Jitatma's claim. His grip remained steady, his eyes locked
on hers with an intensity that cut through the haze. Somewhere
deep inside her fragmented consciousness, she felt a thread of
connection to him—thin, but unbreakable.

"Fight it, Olivia," he urged, his voice softening to a whisper meant only for her. "Remember who you are. Remember what we've survived together."

For a heartbeat, she found herself reflected in his eyes—not the vessel of ancient power she had become, but the woman beneath. Fractured memories flashed through her mind. The castle in the Far Viscera, the bath, the moments of defiance and strange tenderness. The slow rebuilding of her soul under his watchful care.

With a scream that tore at her throat, she pushed against the Dalanite's control. The energy stuttered, dimming just enough for her true self to break through. "I can't—hold it—back," she gasped, each word a battle won against the presence trying to submerge her again.

"You don't need to hold it alone anymore," Jitatma said, his grip tightening on her wrist.

From somewhere beyond the haze of her struggle, she heard Gorgon's roar of frustration. "No! We're too close! The queen is nearly here!"

The energy bridge trembled, Circe's form flickering like a candle in a draft. She felt the Dalanite's desperation, its frantic attempts to reassert control and complete the ritual. Jitatma's touch had created a fracture in its dominance, and she clawed her way through that crack toward freedom.

His voice rang out, sharp and commanding: "Now! Attack!"

The world around them erupted into chaos. Storm stepped forward, his body already changing—bones cracking and reforming, muscles swelling beneath his skin. Where Storm had stood now loomed a Minotaur, massive and primal, with huge, curling horns and eyes that burned with fury. His massive chest heaved with a bestial roar that shook the ground beneath their feet.

Beside him, Sully's form blurred and contracted, her Sumerian shape folding inward before exploding outward in a flurry of red feathers. As a Saqqara bird, Sully spread her wings and curved her talons.

"Not so fast," Gorgon snarled, his attention wrenched from the ritual. The connection between his power and the Dalanite's fractured, the bridge of energy sputtering. Circe's form wavered at the edge of the void, her song becoming desperate once more. "You have no idea what you're interfering with!"

Johara stepped forward, her sapphire crown catching the glow of the fading energy bridge. With one fluid motion, she drew a wand from the folds of her wings, its crystal tip already pulsing with power.

Malta unsheathed his sword in a single smooth movement, the blade catching the strange light of the void. He moved to flank Gorgon, his footsteps silent despite the urgency of his advance. Behind him, Scooter raised his crossbow, the laser bolt already humming with charged energy as he took aim.

The Dalanite's grip on her weakened further when Gorgon's attention diverted to the imminent attack. She felt her consciousness expanding, reclaiming spaces in her mind the Dalanite had overtaken. Her body still thrummed with the Dalanite's power, but increasingly, that power answered to her will rather than its own.

Jitatma released her wrist to turn and face Gorgon directly. "All of you, keep him from the gate!"

Talia's arm moved in a blur, her Chakram spinning from her fingertips with deadly precision. Lightning crackled along its edges, filling the air with the sharp scent of ozone as it cut through the space between them and Gorgon. "This is for my sister, you manipulative bastard!"

Gorgon's hand shot up, a wall of shimmering violet energy materializing just in time to deflect the lightning-charged weapon. The Chakram ricocheted off the barrier, its path altered, but its momentum undiminished as it arced back toward Talia's waiting hand.

"Children playing with power they don't understand," Gorgon sneered, his hands already weaving another spell. Globes of flame formed between his palms, pulsing with contained fury before launching toward them in a barrage of heat and light. "This isn't a battle you can win!"

The fireballs streaked across the plain, their heat distorting the air around them. Storm charged forward, the flames dissipating harmlessly against his double-edged axe. Above Olivia, Sully struggled to gain altitude, her wings beating frantically against the strange pull of the void. Johara raised her wand, its tip glowing brightly as she traced intricate patterns in the air. The current caught Sully's wings, lifting her higher. Sully tucked her wings and dove, talons extended toward Gorgon's unprotected back.

Gorgon spun at the last moment, one hand shooting up to block Sully's attack while the other continued to hurl fireballs at the advancing group. He formed a defense shield from the onslaught of Scooter's laser bolts. The clash of powers sent shockwaves through the air, rippling outward in concentric circles of distorted light.

Malta maneuvered through the chaos of battle with remarkable precision, his sword held high, gleaming under the harsh light of the battlefield. Out of the corner of her eye, Olivia saw him flicker from one spot to another, as if he were a specter slipping through the fabric of reality. One moment he was a blur of motion, and the next, he was charging toward Gorgon with relentless determination.

Through it all, the Dalanite's grip on her consciousness continued to slip. Each moment of clarity was longer than the last, each breath more fully her own. She turned toward the gate, where Circe's form still struggled to fully materialize, caught between the void and freedom.

For a moment, their eyes met across the diminishing bridge of energy, Circe's gaze locking with Olivia's. In that instant, Olivia understood what the Dalanite had recognized from the beginning. There was a connection between them, deeper than mere possession or shared essence. Exactly what that connection meant—and what it would demand of her—remained frustratingly out of reach.

Despite the chaos of battle surrounding her, Olivia felt the energy around the broken gate shift and intensify. The air crackled with invisible currents that raised the fine hairs on her arms and sent static dancing across her skin. The void wasn't empty, its darkness giving way to pinpricks of swirling light. Circe was coming through, and nothing—not Jitatma's intervention, not her friends' desperate battle—could stop the ancient momentum now set in motion.

Behind her, the sounds of battle receded—Storm's bestial roars, the crackle of Talia's lightning, the whistle of Scooter's arrows, the whoosh of Sully's powerful wings all fading to a distant hum. The Dalanite, sensing the proximity of its true mistress, surged within her with renewed vigor. The momentary control she had gained slipped away as golden energy coursed through her veins once more, hot and demanding.

"No—" she gasped, but the protest died in her throat as the Dalanite seized her voice. Her arms lifted of their own accord, reaching toward the half-formed figure suspended in the threshold between void and reality. Power poured from her fingertips in blinding streams, no longer just supporting the bridge but actively pulling Circe's essence across.

The strain was immediate and crushing. Olivia felt as if her bones were hollowing, her muscles tearing fiber by fiber as the Dalanite channeled more energy than her body contained. Something warm trickled down her upper lip—blood from her nose, dripping unheeded onto her collar. Her skin took on an unnatural luminescence.

"Olivia!" Jitatma's voice cut through the haze of pain. She couldn't turn to look at him, couldn't move at all under the Dalanite's rigid control, but she felt him drawing closer despite the danger. "This will kill you—it's too much power!" He turned and called to the others, "We have to stop this."

"You can't stop this now, son," Gorgon boomed, triumphant even as he deflected another attack from Storm's massive fists.

Gorgon's laughter rose above the din of battle, his face transformed by an expression of such naked triumph that it bordered on madness. With a final, brutal display of power, he hurled a wall of flame that pushed his attackers back, buying himself the moments he needed to turn fully toward the gate.

"My queen," he breathed, the words reverent as he extended his hand toward the materializing goddess.

The Dalanite responded to his words, forcing even more power through Olivia's trembling frame. Her vision blurred, dark spots dancing at the edges as consciousness threatened to slip away. The parasite wouldn't allow her the mercy of oblivion.

Jitatma's voice cracked with emotion. "Olivia, if you can hear me—fight it."

The fighting was beyond her now. The Dalanite's control was absolute, its purpose clear and unshakable. Olivia could only watch through fading consciousness as Circe stepped fully across the threshold, her divine form now completely materialized.

The goddess's eyes focused first on Gorgon, a look passing between them that contained volumes of shared history and secret knowledge. Then, slowly, her gaze shifted to Olivia, who stood with arms still outstretched, body trembling from the strain of channeling such immense power.

Her voice like music given form—rich, melodic, and layered with undertones that resonated in the deepest parts of Olivia's being. "You have done well."

With those words, the last of the energy bridge collapsed. The Dalanite, having completed its task, released its iron grip on her consciousness but remained a pulsing presence within her, now somehow linked to the goddess standing before them. She swayed on her feet, strength deserting her all at once. She would have collapsed if not for Jitatma suddenly at her side, his brawny arms catching her as her knees buckled.

"What have you done?" He whispered the question, but not to Olivia. He fixed his horrified gaze on Circe, who stood fully formed at the threshold of the void, power radiating from her in palpable waves. "Do you know what forces you've disturbed by returning?"

Circe's smile was both beautiful and terrible—the expression of a being who had gazed into the abyss and returned transformed. "I know exactly what I've done," she said, her voice carrying easily despite its softness. "The question is whether you are prepared for what comes next."

Jitatma pulled Olivia closer, one arm supporting her while the other reached for his sword. Around them, the battle had stilled, all eyes drawn to the impossible figure of the goddess. She felt the Dalanite stir within her once more—not to take control, but in anticipation.

"Attack!" Jitatma commanded.

CHAPTER THIRTY-FOUR

OLIVIA

The lightning bolt sliced through the air like a silver blade, illuminating Talia's determined face in stark relief. It struck Gorgon's hastily formed shield, splitting into a dozen crackling tendrils that dissipated harmlessly around him. The air filled with the sharp scent of ozone and singed stone.

"Is that the best you can manage?" Gorgon laughed, his voice deep and resonant, seemingly unaffected by the assault. His eyes flashed with malicious amusement as he casually brushed a speck of dust from his immaculate sleeve.

Storm charged forward, his massive Minotaur form a blur of muscle and fury. He swung his double-edged axe in a wide arc, the blade whistling through the air as it sought Gorgon's flesh.

From above, Sully dove, her red feathers catching the light as she plummeted toward the god. His hand shot up, a ball of fire materializing in his palm. With a casual flick of his wrist, he hurled it at Sully, forcing her to veer sharply to avoid being incinerated. The heat from the fireball singed the tips of her wing feathers, sending the acrid smell of burning plumage into the already charged air.

"Too slow, Little Dragon," he taunted, his attention divided between his attackers.

The fireball that had missed Sully continued its trajectory, heading straight for Storm. The Minotaur brought his axe up defensively, splitting the flames around him. Heat scorched his fur, but he pressed forward. The distraction cost Storm his advantage. His axe cleaved empty air as Gorgon sidestepped. The god's laughter echoed. The miss left Storm momentarily overbalanced, his massive form struggling to recover.

"Hey, Gorgon, how would you like a limp just like my buddy, Malta?" Scooter said as he took aim and shot a bolt.

A sudden gust of wind—unnatural in its precision—caught Gorgon from behind, knocking him off-balance. Johara stood with her arms extended as she manipulated what little air existed. She held her wand in her hand, waiting for him to strike.

"You've always been too arrogant for your own good," Johara called, her voice carrying on the wind she commanded.

Gorgon recovered quickly, his feet finding purchase on the stone floor. His eyes narrowed at the unexpected attack from the queen. "You've always interfered where you don't belong," he snarled, dark blood trickling from the corner of his mouth.

He slammed his fist into the ground, sending a shockwave of violet energy radiating outward that knocked everyone back several feet. Olivia watched in horror as her friends were thrown like rag dolls across the battlefield. The Dalanite inside her stirred, responding to Gorgon's display of power with eager recognition. She pressed her hand against her chest, trying to quiet its excited pulsing.

Jitatma was already moving away from her, his sword singing as it cleared its sheath. The blade caught the strange light of the void, reflecting it in sharp silver flashes as he advanced on Circe. In three powerful strides, he closed the distance between them, his hand shooting out to grasp her wrist.

"I've had enough," he snarled, dragging her to him and pressing the blade against her throat. "You will free Olivia from the Dalanite's influence. Now."

"Jitatma, no, that's exactly what Gorgon wants," Talia warned.

"I don't care. The Dalanite is killing her."

Circe's eyes met Jitatma's with unsettling calm, as if the blade at her throat was nothing more than a minor inconvenience. "You would threaten a goddess to save one mortal?" Her voice carried that same musical quality that had called from the void, but now it held an edge of amusement. "How quaint."

"She's not just any mortal," he growled, pressing the sword closer. "She is mine to command and mine alone. Not Gorgon's. Not yours. Mine." His voice carried the weight of absolute conviction, each word delivered with the force like a royal decree. "I am her master, and I demand you remove that parasite from her body."

Circe tilted her head, studying him with those violet eyes that seemed to hold the wisdom of ages. "You truly love her," she observed, her tone shifting from amusement to something almost like wonder. "How unexpected."

"Remove it from her or I will send you back to the void piece by piece."

"You forget that I'm still your queen."

"You are not my queen. You've never been my queen. Johara was always meant to rule the Far Viscera, and I'll be damned if I'm going to allow you back into that realm."

Circe's laughter was cold. "You misunderstand the nature of power." Her eyes flashed with violet fire. "I am not merely a queen to be crowned or dethroned. I am magic itself, given form and will."

"I don't care what you think you've become," he said, his blade steady against her throat despite the energy crackling around them. "Say the spell!"

"You want the Dalanite removed?" Circe's voice dropped to a whisper that somehow carried across the plain. "Very well, but just know that what you ask will have consequences. I hope this love is worth it."

Olivia felt the Dalanite surge within her, and she doubled over as pain lanced through her abdomen. Blood dripped steadily from her nose now, splattering the stone in bright crimson drops.

"If it means saving her, do your worst."

"From darkness to light, I command the Dalanite to make what is wrong now right. I confine the parasite in this amulet so bright to break the bond with this mortal of second sight."

The spell hit Olivia like a physical blow, knocking the breath from her lungs. Dark light erupted from her skin, pouring out in streams that twisted and writhed like living things. The Dalanite's presence inside her convulsed, its grip on her essence loosening with each word of Circe's incantation.

"No!" The parasite's voice tore from Olivia's throat, distorted. "I will not be contained again!"

Circe's magic was absolute. The black tendrils of darkness began to coalesce, forming a writhing mass above Olivia's chest. She felt the Dalanite being torn away from her, piece by piece, its essence unraveling from where it had woven itself into her very soul.

The pain was excruciating. It felt as though part of herself was being ripped away, leaving raw wounds in her consciousness. She screamed, the sound echoing off the stone and mixing with the Dalanite's own anguished wails as it was forcibly extracted.

With a final, wrenching pull, the Dalanite tore free from Olivia's body. The obsidian entity hovered above her, its form shifting between liquid and smoke, pulsing with rage and desperation. For a moment, it seemed to hesitate, as though considering whether to fight against Circe's command or flee back into the void.

Jitatma moved with lightning speed, releasing Circe to snatch the amulet hanging from Olivia's neck. He thrust it toward the writhing mass of dark energy.

"Into the amulet!" he commanded, his voice carrying the same power that had once controlled armies.

The Dalanite shrieked—a sound that vibrated through bone rather than air—as it was pulled inexorably toward the amulet.

With a final, furious surge, the parasite compressed itself into a tight ball of pulsing light and shot into the amulet where it flared brilliantly, momentarily blinding everyone.

The sudden absence of the Dalanite left her feeling hollow, as if something essential had been scooped from her core. The parasite had been a constant presence—unwelcome but familiar—and now the silence in her mind was deafening.

Warmth spread through her body as her natural coloring returned. She watched in fascination as her skin shifted from the unnatural golden hue back to her natural tone, her hair lightening, curls springing free as the blonde tendrils fell around her face. She reached up to the back of her neck and felt her Nibmarks return to their original state.

She touched her face, studying the familiar contours of her own features. The pointed ears remained, a lingering mark of her transformation, but the overwhelming presence that had dominated her thoughts was gone. She could still feel her telekinetic abilities hovering at the edges of her consciousness, but they were hers now—not the Dalanite's.

"Olivia?" Jitatma's voice was cautious.

She looked up at him, seeing him clearly for the first time in what felt like ages. The concern etched across his features, the wariness in his hazel eyes—all of it directed at her, not the parasite that had been using her body.

"I'm me," she whispered, her voice raspy from screaming. "It's gone."

Relief washed over Jitatma's face, softening the hard lines of his jaw. He reached for her, but before his fingers could touch her, a violent burst of telekinetic energy ripped the amulet from his grasp.

"No!" Olivia cried, watching in horror as the vessel containing the Dalanite flew across the plain directly into Gorgon's waiting hand. His fingers closed around the amulet, his eyes blazing with triumph as it pulsed with blue light against his palm.

"Did you truly think it would be so easy?" Gorgon's laughter boomed across the plain, rich with dark satisfaction. "The Dalanite answers to me, not your pathetic attempts at containment."

Olivia struggled to her feet, Jitatma's steadying hand on her elbow. Without the parasite's constant presence, she felt strangely light, as if she might float away if not anchored by his touch. Her telekinetic abilities flickered uncertainly—still there but diminished.

"Give it back!" Talia snarled, lightning crackling along her Chakram as she prepared to throw again.

"I think not." Gorgon's free hand shot out, a telekinetic force slamming into Talia and sending her skidding across the floor. Her weapon clattered away, sparks of electricity dying as it slid to a stop near the broken gate. "The Dalanite belongs to me. I'll be taking my prize."

Storm charged again, his hooves thundering against the stone as he closed the distance. His massive axe swept in a devastating arc toward Gorgon's midsection, but the god was already moving. A portal of swirling darkness materialized behind him, its edges crackling with violet energy. His hand closed around Circe's wrist with possessive certainty. "My queen, I believe it's time we departed."

"No!" Olivia launched herself forward, her telekinetic abilities flaring despite their weakened state. She reached out, trying to grab the amulet with her powers, but Gorgon's grip was absolute. It pulsed mockingly in his palm as he stepped backward toward the portal.

Circe turned her gaze toward Olivia, and for a moment, something flickered across her perfect features—regret, perhaps, or recognition. "You carry more of me than you know, child," she said, her musical voice carrying clearly despite the chaos. "Remember that when the time comes."

"What does that mean?" Olivia called, but Gorgon was already pulling Circe through the portal.

Storm's axe whistled through the empty air where the gods had stood moments before. The Minotaur bellowed in frustration, his massive form wheeling around to face the rapidly shrinking portal.

"You cannot run forever!" Jitatma shouted, his sword still gleaming in his hand. "I will find you!"

Gorgon's laughter echoed from within the portal, growing fainter as the darkness consumed him and Circe. "I'll be waiting." Gorgon's voice lingered in the air like a poisonous mist long after the portal had sealed itself.

CHAPTER THIRTY-FIVE

OLIVIA

The sudden silence felt oppressive. Olivia stared at the empty space where Gorgon and Circe had vanished, a hollow ache spreading through her chest. Without the Dalanite's constant presence, she felt strangely bereft—like losing a limb she hadn't known she could live without. The emptiness inside her mind was deafening after sharing her consciousness.

"We have to go after them," she said, her voice sounding foreign to her own ears—higher, clearer, without the Dalanite's influence layered beneath it. She took a shaky step forward and nearly collapsed, her legs suddenly unable to support her weight.

Jitatma caught her before she hit the ground, his strong arms wrapping around her waist. The warmth of his body against hers felt different now—more immediate, more real without the parasite's interference.

"You're in no condition to go anywhere," he said, his voice gentle but firm. "I watched your life force drain away with every second that parasite remained inside you."

Olivia pulled back from his embrace, frustration flaring in her chest. "I can't just stand here while he has that thing." She gestured toward where the portal had been, her hand trembling with exhaustion. "The Dalanite—it's dangerous in his hands. You don't understand what it can do."

"I understand better than anyone," Jitatma said, his hazel eyes dark with concern. "I've watched what it did to you."

Talia approached, retrieving her Chakram from where it had fallen. The weapon hummed softly as she clipped it back onto her belt. "He's right, Olivia. You need rest before you can even think about chasing after Gorgon."

Storm approached, his massive Minotaur form already shifting back to Sumerian. Bones cracked and realigned as he shrank, his bestial features softening into his familiar face. He rolled his shoulders as the transformation completed, wincing slightly.

"We barely made a dent in his defenses," Storm said, flexing his fingers as the last of the transformation faded. "And that was with all of us attacking at once. Going after him now would be suicide."

Sully circled overhead before landing gracefully, her red feathers dissolving into mist as she resumed Sumerian form. She touched down with practiced ease, though Olivia could see singed patches on her jacket where Gorgon's flames had nearly caught her.

"The bastard was toying with us," Sully said, brushing ash from her sleeves. "He could have killed any of us if he'd wanted to."

"Then why didn't he?" Scooter asked, lowering his crossbow. His face was pale, green eyes wide behind his glasses. "What's he really after?"

Johara stepped forward, her wings settling around her shoulders as the unnatural winds she'd summoned finally stilled. Her expression was grim, the weight of ancient knowledge heavy in her eyes.

"Power," she said simply. "With Circe and the Dalanite, he has access to magic that hasn't been seen in this realm in a long time."

"I should have seen this coming. I was wrong. Hunter was never the true threat. He only wanted to create a copy of Circe." Malta's gaze dropped to the ground as he sheathed his sword with a slow, deliberate motion, the metallic sound echoing in the tense air. "Gorgon was able to bring the real Circe back."

"Yeah, that took some real balls on that bitch," Scooter muttered, his normally gentle voice hardened with anger. His fingers tightened around his crossbow until his knuckles whitened.

"Scooter!" Olivia's head snapped toward him, her eyes widening. "I've never heard you swear before."

A flush crept up his neck, spreading across his freckled cheeks. He adjusted his glasses with one finger as he looked down. "Sorry. I get mad when someone messes with my friends."

"I don't know about you guys, but do you mind if we leave this place? I'm really not a fan of being here," Storm suggested.

"We need to get back to the Far Viscera," Johara said. "We're going to need a strategy and enforcements to fight the Dark Haunting."

"With Circe free and the Dalanite in Gorgon's possession, the barriers between realms have been weakened. The Dark Haunting feeds on that kind of instability," Malta said grimly, his weathered face etched with lines of worry.

Jitatma raised his hand, and with a fluid motion, conjured a shimmering portal that crackled with energy. He gently scooped Olivia into his arms, cradling her as if she were a precious treasure. The portal's glow cast a soft, ethereal light on their faces as he stepped through, carrying her back to the Far Viscera. Behind them, the others followed.

The transition through the portal felt different without the Dalanite—sharper, colder against Olivia's skin. She shivered in Jitatma's arms, burying her face against his chest to shield herself from the biting chill of inter-realm travel. His heartbeat was steady beneath her ear, a reassuring rhythm that anchored her as they passed through the swirling vortex.

They emerged into Johara's chambers, the familiar opulence a stark contrast to the desolate plain they'd left behind. Anu and Ki were waiting for them. Jitatma set Olivia down on the edge of the pool of blood, his hand lingering on her shoulder as if he were reluctant to break contact.

"How do you feel?" he asked, his voice low and intimate.

Olivia closed her eyes, taking inventory of her body. The constant burn of the Dalanite's presence was gone, leaving her hollowed out. Her limbs were leaden with exhaustion, and her head throbbed dully. But beneath the physical discomfort was something else—a strange sense of nakedness, of vulnerability she hadn't experienced since before the parasite had taken hold.

"Empty," she admitted, opening her eyes to meet his concerned gaze. "Like someone scooped out part of me and left a hole."

"Sweet child, what's wrong?" Ki asked.

"The Dalanite has been removed from Olivia's body," Jitatma explained, his hand still resting protectively on her shoulder. "But the extraction has left her weakened."

"It's like losing a piece of your soul, even when that piece was never truly yours to begin with." Ki's expression softened with maternal concern as she approached, her golden robes rustling softly against the marble floor. "May I?" she asked, extending her hands toward Olivia.

Olivia nodded, and Ki's warm palms pressed against her cheeks. The goddess's touch was like sunlight after a long winter—gentle heat that seeped into her bones and chased away some of the hollow ache.

"The last of the souls have been evacuated," Anu announced, his deep voice filling the chamber. "The Afterlife stands empty for the first time since its creation."

"Good," Johara nodded. "We need to begin the protection spell."

Jitatma stood in front of Olivia. His eyes searched her face with an intensity that made her feel exposed, as if he were cataloguing every change the Dalanite's absence had wrought.

Can you hear me, Minx?

His voice resonated in her mind, like a soothing melody that wrapped around her thoughts. She had missed its harmonious presence dearly.

Yes, Renegade, I can.

We have to close down the Far Viscera. I don't know when I will be able to see you again, but I will keep you close in my mind. The important thing is that you are safe and the Dalanite is no longer in you.

"Storm," he called his brother over, "I have to protect the Far Viscera. I can open one more portal for you guys to get home, but after that, we need to limit travel between the realms."

Storm nodded. "I understand."

"Please, take care of Olivia and protect her for me."

"Yes, brother. I will ensure her safety." Storm extended his hand, and Jitatma grasped his forearm with a firm grip. Their tattoos met and aligned perfectly, a powerful symbol of their solemn commitment to protection. The inked designs seemed to shimmer slightly in the light, as if acknowledging the gravity of the promise exchanged between them.

"Thank you, brother. I trust you with her life."

Jitatma raised his hand with a graceful sweep, conjuring a portal that shimmered and whirled with iridescent light. Olivia's eyes were drawn into the mesmerizing vortex. She glanced back at Jitatma, her heart heavy with the thought of leaving him once more. Memories of her quiet apartment flooded her mind. He had become her sanctuary, her place of belonging.

Gently, Jitatma lifted her from the edge of the pool of blood, his touch firm yet tender. His eyes locked onto hers with an intensity that conveyed unspoken promises, a deep connection that transcended words. Slowly, he leaned in, their surroundings fading away as he pressed his lips to hers one final time. It was a silent promise that no matter the distance or the obstacles, he would always find his way back to her.

He gently let go of her, and Storm stepped in, guiding her to the shimmering portal. Just before she entered, she paused to cast one last, lingering glance back. Jitatma stood there, his expression as stoic as ever, yet the silent evidence of his emotions betrayed him—a solitary tear tracing a glistening path down his cheek.

CHAPTER THIRTY-SIX

ANASAZI

Torches lined the walls of Gorgon's throne room, their flames unnaturally still in the stagnant air of the Underworld. The rhythmic clicking of the Exopede guards' many legs against the stone floor heralded Lady Anasazi's arrival. The sound echoed through the cavernous space, announcing her presence long before she appeared in the massive doorway. Her back was rigid, her chin tilted up in defiance of the summons that had brought her there. The guards flanked her. As they approached the throne, Gorgon lounged with casual arrogance, one leg draped over the armrest.

"Leave us," he commanded, his deep voice reverberating through the chamber. The Exopedes hesitated, their compound eyes darting between the two deities before they bowed and scuttled backward, disappearing into the shadows beyond the doorway.

Anasazi stood before him, her hands clasped tightly at her waist, knuckles white with tension. The temperature in the room dropped noticeably, and the edges of the torches' flames took on a blue tinge.

"You used me," she said, her voice so brittle it might have shattered if spoken any louder.

Gorgon's mouth curved into a smile. "My dear wife, always so quick to accuse." He straightened on his throne, both feet now planted firmly on the dais. "Perhaps you'd care to elaborate?"

"Don't play coy with me, Gorgon." Frost patterns began to spread from beneath her feet, delicate crystalline structures creeping across the stone floor. "The amulet. My gift to Olivia." Her breath was visible now, little clouds of vapor that hung in the increasingly chilled air. "You knew exactly what would happen."

He watched the ice spreading with mild interest, as if observing an amusing but ultimately inconsequential natural phenomenon. "And if I did?"

"You manipulated me!" The words burst from her like shards of ice, sharp and dangerous. The frost patterns accelerated their expansion, climbing the first few steps of the dais. "You were counting on me to panic and give her the amulet."

Gorgon's laughter was low and rich, filling the chamber with its dark resonance. "You played right into my hands," he said. "I cursed that amulet just for Olivia. Your jealousy, your spite—so predictable, so useful."

A translucent pillar of ice erupted from the floor beside Anasazi, startling even her. It twisted upward like a frozen serpent, its surface reflecting their distorted images in fractured patterns. The torches nearest to her sputtered, their flames shrinking as the cold intensified.

"You know nothing of my motivations," she hissed, frost forming at the corners of her mouth. "Nothing of what drives me."

"Don't I?" He leaned forward, elbows resting on his knees, suddenly intense. "Your insecurities are written in every frozen tear you've shed since that day. Your jealousy of Circe—of her beauty, her power, but most of all, of the child she bore while you couldn't."

The ice pillar cracked with a sound like distant thunder. Anasazi's face, usually so controlled, contorted with rage and pain. "You have no right." Tiny ice crystals formed in the air around her, suspended like frozen tears. "You never said a word," she whispered, her voice hollow. "All these centuries, you never once acknowledged—"

"What good would it have done?" His tone was dismissive, cruelly casual. "Your grief, your rage, your envy—those were useful tools." He stood, descending the steps in front of the throne, and moved through the spreading frost as if it were nothing more than an inconvenience. "Tools I've wielded with precision."

"To what end?" She refused to step back as he approached, though every instinct screamed at her to retreat from his oppressive heat. "What could be worth such manipulation?"

Gorgon stopped before her, close enough that the contrast between his heat and her cold created a haze of mist between them. "Power, my dear wife. The kind that rewrites the very fabric of existence." His eyes gleamed with something far beyond mere ambition—a hunger that bordered on madness.

Glittering frost fell from her fingertips. "Now you have both—the Dalanite and Circe."

"Thanks in no small part to your unwitting assistance." Gorgon reached out, his fingertip tracing the line of her jaw with mock tenderness. His touch left a red mark across her jaw. "You should be proud. Your jealousy has accomplished what centuries of direct effort could not."

She jerked away from his touch, her eyes flashing with renewed fury. "What happens when I turn that same jealousy against you? When I decide I won't be used as a mere steppingstone in your climb to power?"

Gorgon's expression hardened. "You are welcome to try, my dear." He gestured around them at the frozen throne room, at the evidence of her unchecked emotions. "But ask yourself—has your rage ever served you well? Or has it always, inevitably, served me?"

The truth of his words struck her like a physical blow. Ice cracked beneath her feet as she took an involuntary step backward. The realization that every burst of jealousy, every act of spite, had been anticipated and redirected to serve his purposes was a cold weight in her stomach, heavier than any ice she could conjure.

Gorgon turned his back on her, ascending the steps to his throne with unhurried confidence. "Feel free to stay and watch what unfolds," he said, settling back into his seat with the air of a man who knows his victory is assured. "Or retreat to your ice palace to lick your wounds. Either way, the game continues—with or without your conscious participation."

Anasazi stood frozen, literally and figuratively, as frost continued to spread around her in diminishing circles. The cold fury that had driven her here now felt hollow, impotent in the face of his calculated manipulation. Her power, her divine rage—all of it had been weaponized against her, turned to serve his inscrutable ends.

The worst part was the dawning suspicion that even this confrontation, this moment of revelation, was exactly what he had wanted all along.

Anasazi paced, each step leaving behind a fleeting imprint of frost that evaporated. "You're a fool," she said at last, her voice low and dangerous. "A blind, ambitious fool who sees only the prize and not the price." She stopped abruptly, turning to face him.

"Your concern is touching," he said, returning to his throne. "If somewhat belated."

"She is not the same Circe you once knew," Anasazi continued, her voice trembling with restrained fury. She moved closer to the throne, frost spreading beneath her feet in intricate patterns that resembled skeletal fingers reaching for him. "The void corrupts everything it touches. It remakes, it twists, it hollows out, and fills the empty spaces with itself. The void is a prison for a reason. What emerges is never what entered."

"Circe was—is—a goddess. Her essence is immutable."

"Nothing is immutable in the void."

"It liberates," came a new voice—musical and layered, like multiple voices speaking in perfect harmony. The sound seemed to come from everywhere at once, reverberating off the walls.

Anasazi stiffened, her eyes widening as she turned toward the shadows behind Gorgon's throne. Frost crept up her arms, a subconscious defensive reaction to the presence she sensed emerging from the darkness.

Circe glided forward, her movements too smooth, too continuous—as if she were floating inches above the ground rather than walking upon it. Her form, once radiant with the warm glow of life and magic, now carried a subtle dark aura that seemed to bend the torchlight around her rather than reflect it.

It was her eyes that revealed the true extent of her transformation. Once warm pools of vibrant purple that had sparkled with life and wisdom, they now appeared hollow and distant—not empty, but filled with something that existed beyond normal perception. Looking into them was like gazing into the void itself, a vertiginous sensation of falling into endless darkness punctuated by distant, cold stars.

"Circe," Anasazi whispered, the name catching in her throat.

Gorgon rose from his throne. He moved eagerly to Circe, reaching for her hand with uncharacteristic gentleness. "My queen," he murmured, raising her fingers to his lips.

He released her hand and reached into his leather jacket, removing something from an inner pocket. The amulet dangled from his fingers. It was the same one that contained the Dalanite, the same one Anasazi had unwittingly prepared as a vessel through her gift to Olivia. The amulet pulsed with dark energy, shadows swirling within its depths like ink in water.

"No," Anasazi breathed, understanding crashing over her like a wave of ice water. "Gorgon, you cannot—"

"I can and I will." His voice was steel, unyielding. With deliberate slowness, he stepped behind Circe, lifting the amulet to place it around her neck. The chain slithered like something alive, settling against her pale skin as if it belonged there. "The final piece."

"What have you done?" Anasazi's voice was barely audible, horror strangling her words. The ice beneath her feet had stopped spreading, as if her power itself recoiled from what it witnessed.

"I have united the Dalanite's power with its true mistress." He placed his hands on Circe's shoulders, possessive and proud. "The parasite was never meant for that mortal girl—she was merely the incubator, the vessel to prime it with life essence and emotion."

Anasazi took an involuntary step backward, ice cracking beneath her feet. The full scope of Gorgon's manipulation unfolded before her—how he had used her panic to deliver the amulet to Olivia, how he had planned for the Dalanite to grow within the girl, feeding on her emotions and life force until it was ready to be extracted and reunited with Circe.

Anasazi's mind raced as she tried to formulate a plan to stop Gorgon before his malevolent purpose could come to fruition. With a steely resolve, she locked eyes with him and spoke, her voice steady despite the fear gnawing at her heart.

"I won't let you unleash this darkness upon the world," Anasazi declared, before turning to leave his throne room.

Ice crystals formed in her wake, a trail of frozen fury marking her path toward the doors. Her hand had barely touched the door when she felt it—a presence that made the air itself seem to thicken. The temperature plummeted so drastically that her breath formed clouds, and for the first time in centuries, she felt cold in a way that had nothing to do with her own powers.

It was the Dark Haunting.

She slammed the massive door behind her, the sound reverberating through the corridor. Her hand trembled, and her breath came in ragged gasps as the weight of her unwilling part in what was to come pressed down on her.

"What have I done?" she whispered, her voice breaking on the last word.

When she left her husband's castle, she turned to see a magical dome forming. The shield crackled with power, distorting the view of what lay behind it. The implications were clear. Whatever his plan, whatever horror he intended to release upon the worlds, it was already too late to stop its creation. She could only hope to warn the others before Gorgon's endgame began.

COMMANDER JITATMA

BOOK FOUR OF THE SUPERHUMAN SERIES PREVIEW

The melody had been haunting Lord Gorgon for days now, threading through his thoughts like a maddeningly persistent hum. It was Queen Circe's voice, unmistakably hers, though he couldn't place when or where he'd heard those particular notes. The song seemed to rise from somewhere deep within his memory, or perhaps from somewhere else entirely.

He paced the hallway just outside Hunter's judgment chambers, his boots striking against the marble floor with each agitated step. The sound echoed off the walls, but it couldn't drown out that ethereal melody that seemed to emanate from the very air around him. Her voice curled around each note calling for him to come to her.

The song had no words he could discern, yet it spoke to him. It whispered of power and passion, of magic that danced just beyond his reach.

"Damn her," he muttered, raking a hand through his dark hair. But even as the curse left his lips, he knew it held no real venom. How could it, when the sound of her voice made his chest tighten with something that felt dangerously close to longing?

He had created the Dalanite, a creature that fed off of dark desires that required a host to manifest its full potential. It chose Circe. He closed his eyes, remembering the way her eyes had changed when the Dalanite possessed her, deepening from their usual clear purple to something fathomless and dark. The way her magic had intertwined with his creation, amplifying it beyond even his expectations.

"I never meant to fall for her," he whispered to the empty corridor, the words scraping his throat raw. "It was supposed to be about power. Just power."

It had become so much more. The Queen of Magic, enhanced by his creation, had been irresistible. Her every gesture had captivated him, her every word had entranced him. He had found himself seeking her company not for the power she represented, but for the quickening of his pulse when she entered a room.

The betrayal, when it came, had cut deeper than he'd anticipated. Circe, in a moment of lucidity or perhaps ultimate treachery, had trapped his precious Dalanite in an amulet, severing the connection between them. The memory of her standing before him, the amulet gleaming in her palm, her eyes clear again and filled with triumph, sent a surge of anger through him that momentarily drowned out her song.

She took what was his. With the Dalanite locked away, his fascination with Circe should have faded. His creation was gone, and without it, she was just another goddess, powerful but no longer uniquely compelling. That's what he told himself, at least. That's what he needed to believe.

Yet there he was, haunted by her melody, his thoughts circling back to her, despite his determination to remain indifferent. Despite the fact he had convinced himself, and everyone else, that he had lost all interest in the queen once his creation was taken from him.

ABOUT THE AUTHOR

My whole life has been spent in Minnesota, never straying far from my childhood home. I'm the middle child and have always had a flair for storytelling and crafting imaginative worlds. Even as a child, instead of having my mom read me bedtime stories, I would tell my own. In middle school, I discovered my love for writing short stories and poems. Thanks to the encouragement of my high school English teacher, Mrs. Colby, I was able to take her creative writing class.

Aside from writing, I also enjoy winning at cards and darts against my best friends. In the summers, you can find me on a boat and in the winters, I love snowmobiling - that's just how we do things in the "Land of 10,000 Lakes." My dogs are like my children and they never fail to entertain me.

Writing has been a passion of mine since I can remember. After a successful 25-year career in accounting, I decided to take a leap of faith and pursue writing. For years, I kept this story inside, only sharing it with my loyal puppies.

But now, I want to share this world that I've created with everyone.

ABOUT THE AUTHOR

Follow me on social media:

Tik Tok: @author.beebe.evans

Facebook: Facebook.com/Beebe.evans.author

Instagram: beebe.evans.author

Website: beebeevans.com

Sign up to become a Super Fan on my website and get access to exclusive content including complete character profiles, the prophecy, a free download for Word for the divine language, the events that I'll be attending, and first look announcements. It's free to join.

You'll also find a complete list of content warnings and a glossary of terms and places.

ACKNOWLEDGEMENTS

There are so many people in my life that I need to thank that made this book possible.

Jenna Jahns – My bestie author assistant and sister by choice, who has been around since this story was just a dream in high school and is my biggest cheerleader. Without her, this book would still be a notebook full of mindless scribbles.

Lori Whitwam – My editor, who allows me to use all the flowery words and cuts them out for readability.

Toni Rakestraw – My proofreader, who thinks that I throw a bag of punctuation at my manuscript and then fixes it for me.

Amanda Smith– My artist, who puts up with my pickiness on the cover designs and character art and always seems to amaze me with her talent.

Thank you to all my readers and sisters by choice that love this story as much I do.

Lastly, I would like to thank my dad, who always wants to be a character in my books, but he'll never read them. "Sorry, dad, I don't write historical nonfiction." He has always believed that I would be on the New York Times Best Seller list. Well, I hope he's right.